WELCOME TO FAE Cafe

COFFEE BEAN
1
HIGH COURT

WELCOME TO FAE *Cafe*

JENNIFER KROPF

ISBN EBOOK: 978-1-990555-29-9
ISBN PAPERBACK: 978-1-990555-30-5
ISBN HARDCOVER: 978-1-990555-31-2

DEDICATION

First,

I'd like to dedicate this book to Booktok, a group of book nerds I love who created a community of book lovers, for book lovers. You cheered me on when I pitched the idea of a book about fae running a café among humans, you tossed me ideas for this book, and you made me laugh so hard I literally fell out of my chair and broke things.

Second…

To every teacher I ever had.
I made it.

In your face.

There are ten golden rules you must follow if you want to survive an encounter with a fae:

1. Don't ask for its name.
2. If it asks you what your name is, lie.
3. Avoid looking directly into its eyes.
4. Don't invite it to your book club.
5. Don't engage in a snowball fight.
6. Never let it burn its mouth on coffee.
7. Don't ask it where it's from.
8. Don't tell it where you live.
9. Never mention its Queene.
10. Don't try to kill it with an ordinary human gun.

If you fail to do any of these things, enslave it immediately.

CHAPTER

1

Kate Kole and a Morning Cup of Murder

The thing about Kate Kole, was that Kate Kole's name did not exist. And though false names may not matter in some situations—such as the introduction of acquaintances, social media personalities, pen names for novels, and the like—in this story, it mattered a great deal.

As summer escaped into the cracks of the world and autumn brushed over Toronto with chilly kisses and a mosaic of red and orange leaves, a human girl with burgundy hair was tucked into the corner of a coffee shop with her nose in a book. The collar of her favourite yellow sweater kept her warm and hid the mountain tattoo on her neck. But despite what it may have looked like, Kate Kole wasn't there for the coffee.

The air smelled of freshly baked croissants and ground coffee beans, complete with the warm fragrance of a small neighbourhood atmosphere even though the coffee shop rested in the middle of the city. Seniors and young adults moved about in pairs or groups, laughing and sipping, pulling out textbooks and poking at their phone screens. The sounds were music to Kate's ears as she laid her thick novel flat, pressing down to crack the spine, and pulled out a pen to jot notes in the margin. After she crossed out her notes twice and rewrote them until they were perfect, she slid her pen away and lifted her book again. She read the words out loud, quietly of course, but with just enough volume that people passing by might assume she was crazy and weird and wouldn't try to take the open seat across from her at her table.

Her phone buzzed. She ignored it and flipped a page.

The bell by the door rattled and cool air rushed into the warm space. Kate glanced up from her novel.

A guy entered and headed to the counter.

Kate couldn't look away. The guy's tight black suit looked like armour from a fantasy movie, and he wore a scowl like he'd stepped in something gross. For a moment, Kate couldn't decide if he was the arrogant, self-indulged, fraternity-type or a total fanfiction-obsessed nerd. On one hand, he was gorgeous—his eyes sparkled a light brown-gold—but on the other hand, his *outfit*...

She wondered if it would be inappropriate or illegal to snap a picture while he wasn't looking. This was the sort of hilarious thing that might have the power to lift her spirits later if she ever had a bad day.

"Get me a beverage," the guy said to the young girl behind the counter. He snapped his fingers in her face, then folded his arms and released a growly huff. Kate lowered her book, watching.

So, arrogant and self-indulged it was then.

"What do you want?" the cashier girl asked in a voice that was nicer than what the guy deserved.

The guy's huff was so loud, Kate was sure he created a bigger windstorm than what currently swept over Toronto. "What do I want? What do I *want*? I want a beverage!" He slapped his hand on the counter and knocked over a cup of straws. He didn't pick them up.

Kate dropped her eyes back to the pages of her novel. She dragged her pen out and clicked it a dozen times over.

"It's not my problem," she mumbled to herself, transforming back into the crazy, weird girl who no one wanted to sit with. "Let it go. Let it go," she chanted. She almost turned it into a song.

The girl behind the counter tapped buttons on the cash register and said to the guy, "You need to pick something from the menu." She pointed to the chalk board listing two dozen caffeinated drinks that ranged from dark roasted beans to milk-based to whipped-cream-topped.

The guy's golden gaze twitched over the options. "Caramel... frappe... mocha... *tall*..." He muttered through the list like he'd never spoken the words "*caramel*" or "*mocha*" in his nerdy life. "Macc-ee-ya-to?" he tried, and Kate stifled a snort-laugh.

The guy closed his mouth, settled his glower back on the cashier, and growled, "Are you deaf, you foolish female? I said I'd like a beverage. Or are you just daft?"

Kate slapped the book shut.

She rose and folded her arms, tucking her cozy *Bella Stone* mystery novel under her elbow. She sauntered over to where the golden-eyed guy glared at the pink-cheeked cashier who fumbled through an apology. Kate casually poked a metal napkin dispenser on the counter, turning it so the morning sun reflected into the guy's pretty eyes. The guy winced against the glaring light.

"You could be nicer. She's only human, you know," Kate said.

His watery golden eyes snapped toward Kate. "Exactly," he muttered in disgust. He shoved the napkin dispenser off the counter, sending a loud tin-like clatter through the coffee shop.

Kate blinked at him slowly.

The cashier slid a coffee over the counter with shaking hands, and the guy released another windy huff. "*Finally*. What a dull-witted serv-ant," he mumbled, and Kate grabbed the coffee first.

"You should leave," she said to him.

The guy's glare sharpened. He reached for the coffee anyway, but Kate's fingers tightened around it when he tried to take it.

"If you want this, then pay her." Kate nodded toward the cashier. "And tip her well for ruining her morning. Then you can have it."

A strange heat filled the space around the counter. For a second, Kate wondered why in the world she came over here. She stole a glance at the red-faced cashier who didn't look like she had it in her to ask the guy to pay.

When Kate showed no signs of lifting her hand, the guy's nostrils flared. "I don't have coins," he said through a snarl, and Kate huffed a raspy laugh.

"You mean to tell me that you waltzed in here with that sanctimonious attitude and expected to get this for free? Are you just discourteous or do you have a forbearance disorder? Is your brain a miniscule raisin?" She chose big words on purpose, though she wasn't sure if it made her sound smart. Or if she'd used any of them correctly.

The guy tore the coffee away, and Kate shrieked. Hot liquid branded her fingers and left a flower-shaped puddle on the counter.

"I'll be off, then," the guy announced.

He turned to leave, and heat flushed Kate's neck. Her fingers tightened around her book. The next thing she knew, she was throwing *Bella Stone* at the back of his head. The *thwack* of a cozy manuscript hitting a complete arse had a nice tune to it.

The guy's coffee splattered to the floor along with Kate's novel. The coffee shop went dead quiet, the only sounds left being the muffled car engines outside and Kate's heavy breathing. If the coffee drinkers didn't already assume Kate was weird and crazy by her morning of mumbling out loud, they would now. Her table would be hers forever.

"You're not leaving until you apologize," Kate said from a dry throat, shrinking beneath three dozen alarmed stares. She jutted her thumb toward the pale-faced cashier. "You can't just treat people like that—"

The guy whirled, and Kate jumped at the look in his eyes. She couldn't pull her stare away from the poisonous lustre of hungry death glowering back at her. Her mouth moved, but the words she wanted were frozen on her tongue. She managed to squeak out, "I—"

4

He charged.

Kate stumbled back into the counter as the guy's splayed fingers rushed toward her throat. Her body jerked into the only martial arts move she remembered, and she kicked him.

Her strike landed harder than she meant it to. She watched in dismay as the guy wheeled backward, his arms spinning as he slipped on the spilled coffee and flew into the nearest table.

When his head struck the tabletop, the *thud* was loud enough to drown out the bustling city noise. His limbs went slack, and he rolled onto the floor, his golden eyes staring up at nothing.

Time slowed. A tense silence rang through the café like an icy breath of winter wind.

A woman shrieked in the corner.

The cashier behind the counter gasped.

The sudden urge to barf up the croissant daily special onto the floor trickled into Kate's abdomen as it became apparent to the early morning coffee drinkers that Kate Kole had just killed someone.

CHAPTER

2

Prince Cressica and How It All Began
Two Faeborn Days Ago
(In A Very Different Setting)

The Hall of Silver was a gaudy place, tossed with tinsel and wreaths for the two months of Yule ceremonies. The air was frost-kissed from the natural North Corner chill, only warmed by the enchanted fireplaces crackling with glowing red logs and the whispers of fairies who'd left tricks inside them. Spiked citrus drinks were carried in by lesser fairies in burlap gowns and rope shoes, and small-self fairies buzzed in the heights of the vaulted crystal ceilings, lighting the room like a scatter of stars.

Harpists and flutists performed ancient melodies of merriment for the visiting nobles from each of the Four Corners of Ever. The representatives congregated around a banquet table piled high with spiced meat and colourful fruit for the first Yule feast.

Cress stepped in, and a hush came over the Hall. Only the bravest High Lords of the Ever Corners stole glances at the fairy Prince. The rest dipped their heads and avoided eye contact while the stares of lonely females prickled his back like warm elfshots. He strode into the quiet banquet, his nose twitching at the scent of cinders polluting the room.

From the banquet table, High Lord Bonswick flashed Cress his crooked smile. The Lord of the East had his leg propped up on the chair beside him. Cress knew no faeborn fool would dare try to claim the seat. "Welcome back. Watch out for poison, Prince," Bonswick said, then leaned forward to whisper, "No one likes you here."

Cress's cold turquoise gaze settled on the High Lord. The other fairy males cowered and shifted in their seats as Cress approached the table, but Bonswick winked.

"They're too afraid of me to like me," Cress said.

"Right." Bonswick dragged his leg back to himself and sat up. "What's worse, everyone?" he called down the row. "To be disliked, or to be feared?"

Noble representatives looked at each other in question, some hiding smirks as they no doubt guessed the High Lord of the East was up to no good.

"Or both?" Bonswick's glassy silver eyes darted back to Cress, his mouth twisting into a smile. "I suppose both is worst of all."

"Shall I get your chair, Prince?" A calm, male voice cut into the cold tension, and the sound of a chair sliding out echoed over the banquet. Cress glanced over to find Mor casting him a knowing look. Mor's black assassins' gloves tightened on the backrest of Cress's chair when Cress didn't sit right away. Cress took his seat without another word.

"Aren't the two of you cute?" Bonswick fluttered his black lashes. "Would you like to get my chair, too, Mor? Or do you only pull out chairs for North faeborn monsters?"

7

Murmurs rippled down the table.

"I cannot decide which of you is worse," Bonswick went on. "The monster-Prince hated by his own court, or the Shadow Fairy leech we've allowed to be in our presence."

Though Cress's fingers twitched to stone with the thought of smashing Bonswick's banquet plate, he stole a glance at Mor.

Mor kept his brown and silver eyes on the floor. Cress expected the assassin's tattooed skin to tighten, but Mor's shoulders remained relaxed. The fairy folded his gloved hands.

"After all, it was your people who nearly destroyed the Four Corners. Right, Shadow Fairy? Would you still call them *your* people?" Bonswick's finger tapped the tabletop as he waited for a response. After a moment, he laughed and turned back to Cress. "You won't speak up for that slave?" he asked with forced blinking.

Cress took a long drink from the goblet of spiked ice and citrus before him. "Mor can speak for himself, you fool. He has a mouth."

Bonswick's smile grew. He nodded to the golden emblem with the wings of the North pinned to Mor's chest. "Gold doesn't belong on slaves. Especially enemy leeches. Give that to me."

Cress's cold stare narrowed on the High Lord across the table. The Prince opened his mouth to intervene, but beside him, Mor said, "What's worse than being feared and disliked, Lord Bonswick?"

Bonswick worked his jaw, his smile fading as Mor unclipped the emblem and tossed it over. Mor answered before Bonswick could offer a reply. "Being naïve."

Bonswick caught the emblem and sizzling sounds erupted. The fairy shrieked and hurled the gold clip to his plate where it rolled over once and landed flat, no longer an emblem of gold, but a heavy coin of cold iron.

Males snickered down the table and heads with gold-braided crowns turned away to pretend they didn't see. Mor's curly, dark hair shifted as he performed a shallow bow and took his leave.

Cress's face threatened a smile. He took another sip of his citrus.

Bonswick didn't blink as he rubbed the fresh burns on his fingertips. For once, the High Lord of the East kept quiet as the banquet food was served, but his stare followed Mor around the room until Mor left with the rest of the High Queene's assassins through the silver arch. His gaze remained fixed there throughout dessert.

Cress finished his sweetened shellfish appetizer and sipped his citrus. He set his goblet on the tablecloth with a loud thud, rattling the candlesticks and making Bonswick jump. When their gazes locked again—turquoise and glass—a ripple of heat and power ruffled the table's napkins and flickered the candles' flames.

"If you touch him—" Cress's voice was a low, horrid growl, "—I will slice your fingers off."

"He's a peasant," Bonswick bit out.

"He's an assassin."

"He's worth nothing."

"He could kill you with a spoon."

Bonswick broke his frown to laugh. "He wouldn't dare."

"He would if I told him to."

A fresh hush befell the table as three dozen sets of fairy eyes went wide.

Bonswick slowly rose from his seat and leaned toward Cress. "Did you just threaten a High Lord of the East, Prince Cressica?" he articulated. "All for the sake of that Shadow Fairy leech? What if I cut out his tongue for calling me naïve? No one would stop me. What if I take his eyes for looking at me the way he did?" Bonswick bit his lower lip. "You might think yourself powerful here in the North, but I'm the most powerful fae in the East. Perhaps we should test our powers, you and I."

Cress shoved his empty plate away and stood with a sigh. "Do you know why my assassin called you naïve, Bonswick?"

Chimes sounded from the silver arch announcing Queene Levress, High Queene of the Ever Corners, and commanding every soul into utter silence. Cress spoke anyway, turning heads and drawing gasps. "Because unlike everyone else in this room, you do not know better than to poke at monsters."

"Silence!" The Queene's command was a whip. Fairies down the banquet table lowered their eyes and bowed their heads. All but Cress and Bonswick.

The rustling of the Queene's robes filled the hall as she rounded the table, bringing an icy wind that made skirts shiver, rattled antlers, and dislodged hair feathers. It brushed the back of Cress's neck and fluttered his long hair.

"Drop your eyes, you foolish, faeborn males." The Queene's ice crawled up Cress's feet and forearms like burns. "I will not hesitate to take your eyes from you, Cressica. It will not bother me to have a son-in-law with no eyes," she said, and Cress's rebellious gaze darted to Queene Levress in surprise.

Across the table, Bonswick bit his mouth shut and fought a smile. The High Lord obediently lowered his eyes like everyone else.

But Cress stared at the Queene with parted lips.

"I'll forgive you for not bowing your head to me this once, Prince, because I imagine this news has startled you," the Queene said. She turned to face the nobles from the Ever Corners filling the banquet hall. "The rumours are true. I have decided that Prince Cressica, my ward and First Assassin of the North, will wed my daughter," she said in her high voice. "Now, eat. Eat until you're sick, all of you. I demand it."

A frigid silence hung in the Hall of Silver; even the harpists held their breath. But as the Queene moved for her throne at the head of the table, fairies dropped to sit and began shovelling hot soup, sweet blossoms, and spiced meat into their mouths too quickly for enjoyment.

Only Cress was left standing.

CHAPTER

3

*Kate Kole and The Absence of Warm Croissants
and Warm Bodies*

The cool morning melted to a sweet warmth in the city. Kate watched a butterfly sail past the police station window and land on a rustic maple branch. The bug stretched its silk wings as though it hadn't a care in the world, as though it was showing off to the watching human girl with a stink face and a stomach full of croissant. Kate snorted at it. She tried flicking the window to scare it off, but it just fluttered its wings, rubbing it in even more that it was free and awesome, and Kate was in trouble and screwed. Finally, the gloating bug lifted from its branch and took off out of sight.

If Kate had wings like that, she'd fly away, too. She imagined the breeze beneath her dinosaur-sized bug wings, and the soothing sun on her back, and every mistake she'd ever made unable to find her. How different life would be if she had wings.

She'd probably also be all over the news as the most absurd abnormality in Ontarian history.

It would make a good novel. She could call it, *The Bolting Butterfly*. A Young Adult Modern Fantasy about a girl who floated into the heavens to run from her problems. And one day she would face a problem she couldn't escape from, and every mistake she'd ever made in her past would all catch up with her at once with back-to-back consequences. The protagonist would probably end up in jail.

Kate moaned at herself. She wound up and flicked her own face, right on the cheek. "Dummy, don't think that way," she said. A second later she mumbled, "Ow," when she realized she'd flicked herself too hard. She rubbed her cheek, wondering if burgundy hair would compliment an orange jumpsuit.

The inner-city police station buzzed with dutiful cops and loud Toronto citizens claiming they didn't do anything wrong. Kate pulled her gaze from the window as Officer Westbow took her in from head to toe, blinking a dozen times over. Probably wondering why she was talking to herself. She usually dropped the weird/crazy act once she no longer needed it, but it seemed to have stuck this time.

"Did you just say you *killed* someone?" he asked.

Kate already forgot how she'd run into the station shouting it for all of Toronto to hear.

"I rushed here as soon as it happened. I can take you to him. I mean… *it*. The body." Kate swallowed. "I just—I should make a phone call." Her hand slid into her pocket. Her fingers banged around in the fabric for a moment, and confusion washed over her. "Where's my…" She patted over her jeans, lifting her coat to check it. She moaned when she realized her phone was still at the coffee shop. "Um… Is Officer Baker here, by chance?" She stole a look toward the break room.

Doubt flashed over Officer Westbow's face. "She's out on duty. Do you know Officer Baker personally?"

Kate chewed on her lip.

"No." She folded her hands on her lap and pulled her eyes off the break room. "Not at all."

Officer Westbow tapped his chin. "Do you have your ID?" he asked.

Kate opened her wallet, slid out her university student card, and passed it over. The officer's brows furrowed when he took it.

"Can I see some *other* ID?" he asked, giving the card back. "I need a driver's license, a birth certificate, or a passport."

Kate shook her head. "That's the only ID I have."

Her wallet burned in her hands where the rest of her cards were stuffed.

The officer clicked his pen over a lined notebook. "What was the name of the person you killed, Miss Kole?" he asked.

"I don't know."

He nodded, poorly concealing an odd expression. "Is anyone else injured? Should I call an ambulance?" He slid his notebook and pen over the desk. "And I'll need you to write down exactly where I should send my partner to go lock down the crime scene. Immediately, please."

"No one else needs an ambulance," was all Kate said. She stared at the pen, the notebook. Her hands didn't move to take them.

A pair of cops hauled a howling middle-aged woman through the station. The woman swatted at their faces, shouting obscene things. She missed the first time, but on her second swing, she flipped one of the cop's hats off his head. It landed at Kate's feet.

Kate blinked down at the hat for a moment before she picked it up. Dust clung to the rim, so she brushed her sweater over to clean it. When the cop came back for his hat, Kate lifted it toward him. She had a brief moment where she considered tossing over Officer Westbow's desk in front of both cops, shouting like the howling woman, and sticking with her crazy person act. Maybe she'd be let off the hook for kicking that coffee shop guy into the table if the cops thought she was crazy for real.

"Thanks," the cop mumbled as he took the hat. He disappeared down the hall where the rowdy woman was taken. Kate watched them, counting down the seconds until her opportunity to tear up the police station passed.

"Miss Kole?" Officer Westbow tapped his pen on the desk, bringing her attention back. "You have yet to write down the address. I need to know where the crime took place, and then we'll talk about what happened and why you attacked the victim. Obviously, you're entitled to a lawyer, since whatever you say to me can be used against you in court."

"Right." Kate swallowed. She picked up the pen and scribbled the street name where the coffee shop was, wondering how many customers had already called the police and reported her by now. "I don't know what to tell you about why I did it," she admitted. "I saw something in the guy's eyes. I knew he was going to kill me. I don't know how I knew; I just did. That's why I kicked him."

Officer Westbow studied Kate for a while before speaking again. "I'll have to keep you in a holding cell until we can investigate. Sit tight, Miss Kole."

Promises of a breezy afternoon whispered in the wind off the harbour two hours later as Kate dragged her arms out of her knit sweater. She, Officer Westbow, and Westbow's partner—Officer Jackson—approached the coffee shop. The nausea that had plagued Kate all morning swelled when her hand found the door handle. She imagined that butterfly again. She imagined growing dragon wings and taking off to live in the sky.

"My life will never be the same now, will it?" she asked the officers, glancing at the irritated skin on her wrist where handcuffs had been up until ten minutes ago.

Officer Westbow sighed. "Let's just go inside and you can explain to me what's going on."

Kate nodded and tugged the door open.

The warm smells of freshly brewed coffee, pastries, and pumpkin spice washed over her when she stepped in, along with the sound of laughter. The fresh bread scent of the croissants didn't have the same allure as before.

Kate stopped inside the doorway.

There was *laughter.*

Her eyes fell on the cashier girl wearing a sweet customer service smile as she took a man's order. Late morning light streamed over the tabletops where muffins and hot sandwiches lay half eaten before chatty university students and elderly couples. People milled back and forth around the counter for refills.

There was no puddle of coffee on the floor.

There was no tense silence or shrieking women in the corners.

There was no body.

Kate took another step in, brows pinching together. Where spilled coffee had been, squeaky-clean tiles looked back at her along with the sickening memory of the golden-eyed guy's blank stare from where he lay. The faint scent of cleaning supplies mixed into the smells of toasted bread and brewing coffee.

"We questioned everyone while you were in holding, and no one seems to think someone died here. In fact, no one even remembers you being here this morning. Are you sure this is where you think you killed someone?" Officer Westbow raised a brow.

"I don't think I did; I *know* I did," Kate said, pointing. "He was right here when I left."

The officer looked from the floor, to Kate, to Officer Jackson, then to the customers around the café. His mouth tipped down. "Are you on any medications, Miss Kole?" he asked.

"What? I'm telling you, there was a body here this morning!" she yelled. "Ask the girl behind the counter! She saw everything."

Officer Westbow folded his arms. "You wait here. We'll ask again." The two officers brushed by and approached the counter where the cashier gave them a smile Kate couldn't believe.

Kate took in the cheery coffee shop. She stared at *the spot* on the floor. She looked out the windows at the pedestrians passing by.

She hadn't taken any medications this morning. She didn't take any medications, *ever*. And despite her weird act to claim her morning table, she wasn't crazy.

Her hand shook as she brushed it through her hair. For the first time since this morning, she had the brief, terrifying thought that maybe she'd made it all up in her head: The guy. The rudeness. The kick.

Sunlight reflected off a shiny surface behind the leg of a nearby table. Kate's pulse quickened when she recognized the glossy green book cover. She darted over and dragged out her copy of *Bella Stone*. A new brown coffee stain muddied the page corners. She flipped it over. *KATE KOLE* was written across the back cover with a sharpie, and she breathed a sigh of relief.

"So, you're saying everything has been normal here today?" Officer Westbow's voice trickled past the conversations in the shop. He murmured something too quiet for Kate to hear and he and the cashier chuckled as Kate turned, holding up her book for them to see.

"I guess we better get her tested for drugs. We should hold her overnight until we get the results." Officer Jackson's words to Officer Westbow weren't quiet enough.

A lump formed in Kate's throat as she lowered her book. She stood, her wrists burning like the handcuffs were already back on. She stepped toward the officers, but her feet came together when a cool breeze tickled her warm neck from someone leaving the coffee shop. Her gaze darted to the door and fell on the table in the corner by the exit.

There sat her phone.

Kate huffed in disbelief and shoved her book into her coat pocket. She grabbed her phone off the table and abandoned the coffee shop before Officer Westbow and Officer Jackson turned back around.

Thelma Lewis's small kitchen was fragrant with the warmth of freshly baked cookies and grandmotherly love. Her buffet hosted collections of crystal vases and old photos that should have been put away long ago. Along the windowsills were well-watered ivies and balls of yarn with gray needles sticking out. It was with those needles Grandma Lewis had made Kate's favourite yellow sweater—the one Kate had worn this morning when she'd killed someone.

Kate gripped a mug of tea, her thumbnail scraping against a chip in the handle. She imagined a rude, deep voice trying to order coffee. A black and navy leather outfit made for a high fantasy theatre performance. Golden eyes that turned wild when provoked. Her fingers still burned from where the coffee had splattered over the to-go cup when she'd tried to keep the guy from taking it. She lifted her hand to see the red marks on her knuckles again.

"Are you even listening?"

Kate's gaze sprang up. "Hmm?"

Her brother Greyson grunted and leaned back in his chair with folded arms. "Grandma!" he called to Thelma at the sink, "Kate doesn't care that I might get eaten by an alligator in Florida."

"You're going to Florida?" Kate blinked.

"Seriously? I *just* told you I'm going to Florida with Lincoln and Tegan until Christmas."

"Oh."

"Oh?" Greyson arched an eyebrow. "Aren't you going to try and talk me out of it?"

"You're out of high school, you have no job, and you're mooching housing off Grandma. You're practically an intermittent vagrant. Why would I try to talk you out of it? Besides…" Kate swallowed the lump in her throat, waiting for loud knocks to echo through the house and Officer Westbow's voice calling for her to come outside. "Maybe it would be good for you to get away from here for a while." She sipped her tea, glancing out the bay window at the windy afternoon and the dark clouds bringing more shadow to this day.

17

"That's not how the word *intermittent* is supposed to be used in a sentence. And did you really just ask, *'Why would I try to talk you out of it?'* Hmm, I don't know Kate," Greyson's sarcasm filled the kitchen, "because you always try to talk me out of anything fun?"

"Oh, cut it out, Greyson. Can't you see something is troubling your sister?" Grandma Lewis carried over a fresh plate of cookies and set it between them on the table.

"I'm fine." Kate forced herself to sip her tea again. She was almost too distracted to notice her grandmother try to lift the heavy slow cooker dish. Kate jumped to take it from the old woman's hands, and she carried it to the cupboards. She nudged the door open and hauled the dish up onto the shelf.

Grandma Lewis sat back at the table. Kate followed, returning her tight grip to her mug. Her grandmother shoved the plate of cookies in her direction, but Kate looked away.

"Heavens, Katherine, your hands are shaking worse than mine." Grandma Lewis eyed Kate's mug. She sighed. "There's only one thing you could have come to my home for in this condition."

Kate pulled her hands below the table. "What's that?"

"Comfort." Grandma Lewis leaned back with her arms folded, mirroring Greyson. Suddenly Kate felt like she was being interrogated. "I see far more than you think, Katherine," she added.

"Can you see I was with the police today?"

"Do you know what I did?"

"Are these cookies a bribe to start talking?"

Ten more responses flooded Kate's mind, none of them right to say aloud. Grandma Lewis was a shrewd woman. She'd hear the truth in anything Kate said about her day, even if Kate tried to tell her about what she had for breakfast that morning.

Kate chewed on her bottom lip. "You know what? Lily and I actually have a lot of work to do for our café." She stood, taking one last longing look at the tea she was abandoning.

"Well, I'll be offended if you don't eat one of these before they get

18

cold." Grandma Lewis picked up a cookie and tossed it to her. Kate fumbled for a second before she caught it. Crumbs decorated her chest, and she scowled.

"How is Lily, by the way?" Greyson leaned forward a little.

"Why don't you find a girl your own age to give you advice?" Kate grunted at him. "It's weird to try and have a best friend who's also your sister's best friend."

Greyson scowled. "All the girls my age are annoying. And Tegan and Lincoln are my best friends. Lily's just... my *older* best friend."

"Well stay away from Lily," Kate said, stuffing the whole cookie into her mouth at once like a monster. "She's mine." Chocolate coated her teeth. Greyson made a repulsed face, but Grandma Lewis chuckled.

"I'm going to steal her from you," Greyson announced.

Kate ignored him. "Thanks, Grandma. Bye, Greyson," she said through sugary chunks as she headed for the door. Apparently, her crazy and weird act was back on.

"Wait." Grandma Lewis's chair scraped over the floor, and Kate held in a sigh. She didn't have the heart to ignore the old woman, so she turned back to see her grandmother shuffling cookies into a paper bag.

"Take these. Lily will be hungry after her shift." Grandma Lewis brought the bag around the table and held it toward Kate.

Kate stared at it, warmth pressing in at the corners of her eyes. Her mouth was too full of cookie chunks to say anything without spewing chocolate and crust.

They were just cookies. It's not like they meant anything. It's not like they were a warm, sweet hug, or a word of comfort, or an entire lifetime's worth of guidance and love like the sort Grandma Lewis always gave away for free.

Except that her grandmother's cookies were exactly all of those things.

"And I wish you'd tell me what's bothering you. It's not healthy to hold it all in," the old woman added, pouring salt on the wound with her gentle voice which she only brought out for special occasions.

Kate looked at the floor and swallowed the wads trapped in her mouth. "It's nothing for you to worry about, Grandma," she said when she could speak.

Grandma Lewis put the bag in Kate's hands. The kitchen grew quiet, and Grandma Lewis glanced over at the framed photos resting on the buffet where a full family covered in snow smiled back.

"Well, when you're ready to talk, my door is always open, my cookies are always warm, and my tea kettle is always hot." Grandma Lewis folded her wrinkled hands, soft and shaking with age. Even when she was doing nothing, Grandma Lewis smelled of soft powder, herbal tea, and pleasant conversations.

"I know." Kate turned away from the photos and opened the door.

"Give Lily my love." Her grandmother flashed a smile that could light up a room.

From the back of the kitchen, Greyson yelled, "Give Lily my love, too!" and Kate shot him a look that promised she wouldn't.

CHAPTER

4

Prince Cressica and The Thing that Happened
One Faeborn Day Ago

The doors to Cress's chambers burst open, and there stood Mor, his tanned, tattooed arms glistening with sweat in the early sunlight from the hall windows. The fairy's nostrils were flared, his curly hair a mess.

"What happened?" Cress imagined the courtyards in chaos with Shadow Fairy arrows speckling the grass, and the bodies of his brothers around them. He grabbed his fairsaber, but Mor stopped him.

"It's not what you think." Mor's dark brown-silver eyes hardened. "But I suppose in a way, it's worse."

Cress dropped his hands. "It's not Shadow Fairies?"

Mor shook his head and stepped back into the hall. "It's Bonswick."

Cress's jaw hardened. He strapped his fairsaber harness to his back, the blade a light weight between his shoulders. He followed Mor out. "Bring me to that faeborn fool."

Their footsteps echoed through the crystal hallways of the Silver Castle. Sunlight prismed in all directions, reflecting off the walls in tangled streams of emerald and gold.

Mor brushed a lock of hair from his eyes. His lashes fluttered.

"You seem nervous." Cress flicked the latch of the side door and kicked it open with a *bang*.

"You'll see why in a minute, Your Highness." Mor followed him out, digging a hand into his pocket and drawing out a black ribbon. He handed it to Cress.

"What's that for?" Cress asked as they rounded the starbud bushes. The blossoms unfolded as Cress passed, showing off velvet midnight blue petals that bowed at his ankles with respect.

"Your hair," was all Mor said as they emerged from the garden.

Cress stopped at the top of the hill. His cold turquoise eyes narrowed on the two dozen assassins in black and navy lining the training square's edge. They stood at attention, their gazes forward. One was missing.

"Where's Whyp?" Cress asked.

"I'm not sure. The Queene sent him on a special assignment yesterday. He hasn't returned," Mor whispered.

Bonswick prowled back and forth in the middle of the training square. It looked like at least four of Cress's brothers had been punched. At the far side, Cress spotted one of his assassins—Dranian—with a wet collar from blood dripping down his chin. He saw Dranian dare a glance over to where Cress and Mor were on the hill.

"If looks could kill," Mor muttered.

"What has Bonswick done to them?" the Prince asked.

"He came here for me. Unfortunately, a few members of the Brotherhood tried to stand in his way. It turns out he's more powerful than he looks," the fairy warned.

Cress snatched the black ribbon from Mor's hand and tied back his long hair. "His nobility doesn't give him the right to attack the North Brotherhood of Assassins. *My* assassins."

"Unfortunately," Mor cut him a look, "it allows him to do what he likes. Our brothers were forced to stand there and take his hits. And he demanded that I fight him in a deathmatch. I was going to do it, but—"

"Absolutely not."

Mor nodded. "I figured you'd say that."

The grass rippled at Cress's ankles as he descended the hill. The star-bud blossoms released a wind-like gasp and closed back into buds, ducking behind thorny branches as his power spread.

"Cress..." Mor called in a loud whisper. "Be careful with him. He's inherited more power than any other male in the East. He might have beaten me if we'd really fought."

Cress's flesh tightened. "That's precisely why I will not allow it."

The Prince marched to the clearing, and Bonswick's feral grin widened.

"Prince Cressica!" he greeted. "I see I finally have your attention." Bonswick tossed his sword aside and Cress watched it roll through the grass.

"It seems your favourite slave has run off scared." Bonswick's gaze flickered past Cress to where Mor approached the square's edge and folded his gloved hands to wait with the other assassins. "I suppose I don't blame him. I've mastered the touch of death, you know, and I'm itching to use it on someone."

"Stop running your mouth, you fool," Cress said. "How dare you harass the High Queene's assassins?"

"They disrespected a noble of the East. Surely you would do the same if *my* assassins had disrespected *you*, Prince." Bonswick's glassy eyes glittered. He finally tore his gaze off Mor and placed it back on the Prince. "You know, I only suffered through the dreadful trek to the North in the first place because I knew you'd be here. Why else would I have bothered to visit such a cold, boring place?"

"Your feud with me is one-sided," Cress assured. "You can hate me because the High Queene chose me as her ward, but make no mistake," he stepped in until he towered over the black-haired fairy of the East, "touch one of my brothers again, and I will chop off more than just your

23

fingers in your sleep."

Bonswick's laughter roared over the square—he threw his head back, showing his wide smile to the heavens and his teeth to the Brotherhood.

"Step aside, *illegitimate* Prince!" The air changed directions and Bonswick's dark lashes fluttered in disgust. "I have a deathmatch to win with that leech!" He pointed over Cress's shoulder to Mor, and Cress's hand flashed up to grab Bonswick's. He squeezed, crushing Bonswick's fingers. He didn't stop until the High Lord's glassy eyes flickered, and a split second of fear crossed his face.

"Release me!" Bonswick ground out through his teeth.

"You will fight me instead this morning," Cress said, tilting his head in a crossbeast-like way. "And I will enjoy sending you back to your precious East as ashes in a jar. I'll tie it with a bow like a gift for the nobles who will be glad to finally be rid of you."

Cress released Bonswick's hand, and the fairy tore himself back.

From the side of the square, Dranian's solemn face cracked the slightest smile over his blood-soaked chin.

A metallic ring echoed over the training space when Cress drew his winged fairsaber. His blade formed from the magic and metal in the air into a sharp, long point. "You should have kept your weapon in your hand. Fool." Cress's fairsaber punched forward.

Bonswick spun out of the way. He came back glaring, and Cress smiled wickedly.

"It seems your betrothed is watching." A slow, cruel smile returned to Bonswick's face as he nodded up the hill. "Shall we put on a show for her?"

Cress glanced over his shoulder.

He had not seen Princess Haven in three months. The Queene's daughter looked far too much like the Queene herself with her white hair fluttering in the morning breeze and her savage lips tipped down at the corners. Cress turned away and mumbled an ancient curse. Haven must have noticed he'd been avoiding her all this time.

Cress knew the exact moment when her cold gaze settled on his back.

It felt as sharp and deadly as the Queene's.

His sword was ripped from his grip.

Bonswick hurtled Cress's blade over the training square, over the castle grounds, and far into the belly of the Corner of the North. The High Lord spun back around, chest pumping. "No weapons," he declared.

Cress's hands balled into fists.

Shadow encompassed the yard. Without lifting a faeborn finger, Cress summoned ink-black clouds overhead; they rolled in like black waves off the Jade Ocean, blotting out the sun and turning the day to dusk. The grass at the Prince's feet curled in, crisping to ash, and the breeze laced with frost.

Bonswick's lips turned blue as he shivered. The fairy's hair fluttered while he prowled around Cress.

"You don't impress me, Prince." Bonswick flicked his fingers and disappeared from sight.

Cress spun, scanning the air, sniffing the wind. He glanced at Mor in surprise as if to ask, *"He has the powers of a Shadow Fairy?"*

"Did no one ever tell you my mother was from the Dark Corner?" Bonswick's whisper appeared at Cress's ear. "You faeborn fool."

Bonswick vanished again as Cress turned. He felt Bonswick's glassy eyes roaming up his back and over his throat.

Cress snatched Bonswick from the air by his neck, and Bonswick growled, reappearing. The fairy's limbs thrashed, his black hair falling out of place. Cress squeezed, pulling him in to whisper, "You should have stayed out of the North."

He lifted Bonswick's whole body with one arm, ready to finish the fight, but a voice ripped over the square. Every assassin dropped to one knee with their gazes on the ground.

"Cressica Albastian!"

Cress released Bonswick like a compulsion, and the fairy of the East fell to the grass, sputtering and red-cheeked.

Assassins around the square began to shiver, their fingers gripping the grass. Cress did not move a muscle. A terrible cold deeper than the mountaintop snow chilled his bones as Queene Levress descended to the training space.

"Assassins of the High Court," the Queene called over them. "You shall each carry one thousand rocks from the quarry into the dungeon before sunset tonight. Then you will carry them back to the quarry in the morning. Whoever fails to complete this task will die by my own hand."

Cress turned to face her. "Your Majesty—"

"Silence!" Queene Levress grabbed Cress's shoulder, her long nails digging into his flesh. "You shall also be punished with the Brotherhood, Prince. You will carry two thousand rocks."

Cress closed his mouth, stifling a reaction as she pierced his skin.

"We will not fail you, Queene!" the assassins shouted in unison, but Queene Levress's silver eyes remained on Cress, waiting.

"I will not fail you, Queene," Cress promised through his teeth.

Finally, the Queene unearthed her nails from Cress's shoulder and drew them back to look at his faeborn blood blotting her fingers.

"I thought losing your memories changed you for the better, Cressica," she said below the sounds of the assassins marching toward the quarry. "But perhaps I was wrong."

Cress stayed silent as the High Queene of the Ever Corners drifted back up the hill to join her daughter. The air remained cold.

A moment later, Queene Levress returned to the castle with slow, careful steps, flanked by a tetrad of fairy guards. But Haven stayed put. She pinned Cress with her stare.

The Princess continued to watch Cress in cold silence as he headed for the quarry. As he lifted his first great rock. As he carried it toward the castle, and as he came back out for another.

He thought she would leave after that, but she watched him for the rest of the morning, during the orange and yellow afternoon, and into the purple evening. She watched until the sky sank to gray and red.

Cress felt every single prickling, icy second of her gaze on his back.

The sky was angry. Cress glared at it from the study of the Crimson Glass Tower as he held a block of ice to his aching shoulders. His faint reflection looked back at him in the window: his piercing turquoise eyes and his long, smooth, brunet hair.

Dark clouds roared outside, spitting flashes of white light across the heavens and unleashing tears upon the villages of Ever North. The rain pounded against the ruby glass as though it wished to break through and drown Cress with a flood.

There were days the Prince would have welcomed such a death. But today he stared back at the rain with a deadly glower. Today, if the rain tried such a thing, he would burn the sky and turn the clouds to cinders. He would steal the sun and curse the stars and make the cruel deities of the heavens pay.

A headache blossomed behind his eyes, and Cress squinted them shut.

"Are your thoughts troubling you again?"

Thessalie wandered in with an armful of books. The old scholar set them atop the desk, briefly glancing down at the half-written letter of apology Cress was working on to send to the Low King of the East Corner of Ever. A moment later, the scholar joined the Prince at the window.

"It's just a headache." Cress folded his arms and faced the storm.

"Hmm." Thessalie took a hairbrush from the shelf and began stroking it through his long, golden locks. The scholar's hair wasn't quite as long as Cress's, but it almost reached his waist now. "How are you feeling about the marriage arrangement?"

Cress released a grunt. "I'm relieved. After all these months, I'll finally be able to hunt down whoever stole my memories."

Thessalie's brushing slowed. "Ah. So that's what you plan to do once you ascend."

"I've thought of nothing else. Once I'm bound to a mighty mate and receive the Queene's inheritance gift, I'll be too powerful to stop. Fairies like Bonswick will cower in my presence."

"You're already powerful enough without the help of a faeborn mate." Thessalie set his brush back where it belonged and folded his wrinkled hands. "Bonswick is out of his faeborn mind. We all know it. Perhaps you should have a different goal for after you ascend to the highest throne in the Corners of Ever."

"Second highest," Cress corrected. "And I *will* find out who tricked me, Thessalie. I'll make the memory thief pay terribly."

Thessalie sighed. "Queensbane," he cursed. "When I agreed to be your mentor, Cressica, it was to put your birth mother at ease after she sold you to the Queene. I figured I'd be teaching you the languages of the South, not conspiring with you to fight against nobles," he muttered. "And never in a million years did I think the Queene would force you to marry her daughter—"

"Force me?" Cress laughed. "I'll gladly do it. I'll smile through the ceremony and bow during the Elder's blessings. And then I'll own the North, and I will crush those who are trying to destroy me. If my real mother could see all that I've…"

Thessalie glanced over at the Prince when the sentence remained unfinished. "Could see, what?"

The silence carried on, pierced only by the rain.

Thessalie turned back toward the window. "If only she could see how dangerous you've become? If only she could see how the citizens of the North fear you? If only she could see how even the nobles shudder when you brush by them in the Silver Castle?"

Cress's mouth closed.

"There are dark minds here, Prince," Thessalie warned. "You were blessed by the deities of the sky when the Queene recognized the power in your blood and saw the weapon you could become. It's a true miracle she made you a prince and gave you a new *real* name. But don't become like those with dark minds. I promised your mother I would keep you safe from all that."

Cress's gaze dropped to the golden floor tiles. "I must ensure that neither the South Corner nor the Dark Corner would dare come to war against me. You know I will do whatever is necessary to protect the Brotherhood. Even marry *that woman's* daughter."

"Perhaps it won't be so dreadful being wedded to the Princess. At least Princess Haven can sing. You've always had a weakness for music."

"I have no weaknesses," Cress stated. "And I will not be swayed by her songs, no matter how lovely they are. I'll never be ruled over by that scheming witch."

Thessalie turned toward his pupil and opened his mouth to speak, but the door to the study burst open and three males in assassins' black marched in. The fairies stepped into the foggy light of the paper lanterns, and Cress recognized Mor's dark, curly hair.

When the trio parted, Queene Levress emerged from behind them. She drifted across the study. Cress's mother-in-law to be.

The Queene's hair was as white as snow blossoms in the dim light, giving off a sheen of innocence. But her smile undid all that was pretty about her. The High Queen of the Ever Corners carried such cruelty and savagery in her curled lips that it left only shivers in her wake.

The assassins bowed on one knee and waited for orders.

Levress stopped before Cress.

The Prince felt his heartbeat slow, his blood cool, and his shoulders tighten as though she reached her cold, pale hand right into his chest and squeezed his heart. Though Cress offered her a smile, he fought a scowl. She would cut his tongue out if he scowled.

Queene Levress's sharp eyes cut to Thessalie like she wondered why the old scholar was there. "Prince," she said to Cress, "I've come to deliver the tragic news myself." Her white lashes glittered in the lanterns' glow.

"Tell me your news, my Queene," Cress said.

"A human assassin attacked us from across the gate. She killed a fairy of the North this morning. She must pay for it with her life, but I plan to wait until the new faeborn year to deal with it."

"What?" Thessalie blanched at Cress's side. "A *human* killed a fairy? That hasn't happened in a hundred faeborn years—"

"Why have you come to tell me this yourself?" Cress cut off the scholar to ask the Queene.

Queene Levress looked at him for a long while, tapping her long nails together. "Because the murdered fairy was part of your Brotherhood," the Queene said. "He was the second son of High Lord Gwess of our North Court."

The life drained from Cress's chest. "Whyp...?" he whispered.

"He crossed the gate against our laws. He would have likely been killed when he came back anyway." The Queene glanced at her silver nails. "Thankfully, I had a spy following him who cleaned up the mess."

The sky seemed to fall around the Crimson Glass Tower. Red pooled into Cress's vision.

"Let me avenge him," he begged through his teeth.

"No."

"*Please* give me your blessing, Queene."

"You don't have it. You are my future son-in-law now, Prince. I forbid you from breaking the law and crossing the gate. *That* is why I came to tell you myself." The Queene's cruel lips tipped down. "Lord Gwess's second son was hardly worth having around to begin with. He had measly half-power and an obnoxious laugh."

Something snapped in Cress's chest. "The High Court will demand that Whyp be avenged!" he shouted. "How can I come into power over the North before that human is killed and justice has been restored in our court?"

The Queene looked back and forth between his eyes. "That sounded dangerously close to defiance," she said.

"You'll send *them* to hunt the human, then?" Cress nodded toward the triad of kneeling males waiting beneath the lantern light. "I have been the North Court's greatest assassin for over a decade," he objected. "Can I not be granted this one request?"

"You attacked a lord of the East yesterday!" Her voice blasted through the room with the volume of a horn, and frost crawled up the walls. Cress and Thessalie slammed their hands over their ears; the kneeling assassins by the lanterns went rigid.

The Queene's eyes narrowed. "The High Court will conspire against you if you disobey me. And no, I will not be sending your brother assassins after the human, either. There are more important things approaching in the new faeborn year—like the wedding. As I said, we will send an assassin to kill the human for breaking a fairy law in due time."

Cress shook his head in disbelief. "Don't do this to me—"

"Don't you *dare* take a step toward that gate," the Queene cautioned. "I will only give you one warning." The Queene turned to leave, and the triad of assassins stood and bowed at their midsections. "Also… my crafters will be cutting your hair today, Cressica," the Queene called back. "You cannot marry my daughter with hair that's longer than hers."

A muscle feathered in Cress's jaw. "Do you know how long it took me to grow this hair?" he growled.

Groomers entered through the open study door carrying embellished scissors. The Queene cast him one last terrible smile before she left, leaving the assassins behind without giving them permission to stand. Her footsteps faded down the hall, and Cress fought the impulse to shout something horrific after her.

After a moment, the trio of assassins stood. Mor wandered over with a sigh. "Don't mourn your hair, Cress," he said. "With your pretty face and soft skin, it makes you look like a female anyway."

Cress's wide, deadly gaze slid over. "I'll take your tongue—"

But Mor's tongue was already stuck out, waiting.

Cress released a low growl and marched out of the study, shoving one of the crafters into the wall as he passed.

"Don't do anything foolish, Cress!" Mor called after him.

"Killing a human can't be that hard!" Cress shouted back. "I just need to speak her real name and command her to die!"

His boots thundered down the hall until he reached the crystal spiral staircase. He travelled down three levels into the dark pits of the Silver

31

Castle where the cold morgue prepared faeborn bodies for candlelight ceremonies.

When Cress burst into the room, he found it empty of servants. But he saw Whyp. He saw the body of the golden-eyed fairy. His brother assassin.

Mor jogged in behind him. "*Cress—*"

"Steal his memories for me," Cress said. "Just this once, Mor. Do this for me."

"You know I can't do that."

Moisture filled the Prince's turquoise eyes when he looked at his friend. "Have you ever done it before?" he asked, and Mor looked like he'd turned to faestone.

"Yes. Once," he said.

Cress nodded and marched over to Whyp. "Good," he said. "Do it, Mor. Please. I'll never tell a soul that you used your Shadow Fairy gift. I want to see Whyp's last moments. I want to feel what he felt as his faeborn heart stopped."

"You can't do anything about it, Cress," Mor said quietly. "Promise me."

Cress laid his hands along Whyp's temples. "I can't even take a breath anymore without the whole North High Court watching me. How could I do something about this?"

Mor hesitated, but after a moment, he drew over and placed his hands lightly over Cress's on Whyp's temples.

Immediately, Cress's mind filled with a bright picture of a human female with brown-green eyes, dark burgundy hair, and a tattoo peeking from her yellow collar. A book was tucked beneath her arm. A name was scribbled on the back in shiny black ink.

5

Kate Kole and the Present

Kate stared at the calculator blankly, not caring for the first time in a while that only negative numbers stared back after she added up every penny to her name. She sighed and dug her fingers into her hair as she leaned against the café counter. A bowl of chocolate-covered strawberries gave off the aroma of sweet fruit and cocoa beside her face. She inhaled it, trying to muster its potent powers of relaxation. She'd thought maybe stopping at the *Pasty Fruit Shack* and getting a dozen of her favourite treats on her walk home would soothe her racing mind, but it seemed even the whimsical store with candy apples and nutty fudge in the windows didn't have any magic left for Kate tonight.

The only good thing about being completely alone was that you could burp, sneeze, cough, sing, or talk to yourself when you wanted, where you wanted, with no consequences. Kate began to hum an indie band song she knew at a pitch high enough to make dogs cry. After a painful minute of it, she cleared her throat and got serious.

The café was empty of life, light, and answers. Only the dirty wall sconces gave the storefront any illumination. Kate had meant to restore the fireplace in the corner before the café's opening day, along with a handful of other tasks still waiting to be done. As it was, this place was still quieter, dirtier, and more run down than an abandoned building.

Her knuckles drummed a slow beat on the counter's surface. "You'd better save us," she said to the empty storefront. "Or I'll seriously be in trouble."

She wasn't above begging. She would beg the unpainted walls, the rusty coffee maker in the corner, and the cabinets with crooked doors. She would beg the bugs on the walls if she thought they would listen.

Not that it mattered. Even if the café did well in its first year and paid off Kate's debts, she wouldn't be able to bask in the glory of being debt-free if she was in jail for murder.

What if the police found the body? What if they showed up for her tonight and dragged her off to spend the rest of her life behind bars? What would happen to Grandma Lewis if Kate was taken away after everything else the old woman had already been through?

Kate stopped doodling on the budget clipboard when she realized she'd scribbled in deep, cutting strokes: *WHY DOESN'T ANYONE RE-MEMBER?*

She stared at it for a few moments. Then she tore off the corner of the paper and crumpled it.

The café bell rattled, and Lily marched in, panting. Spirals of her hair stuck out from her blonde bun. She stopped inside the door and leaned forward with her palms on her knees to catch her breath.

"Did you run here?" Kate asked.

"Are you crazy, Kate?! You can't trust other cops!" Lily sprang back up and yelled. She left footprints in the dust on the floor as she marched over. "Why didn't you call me? I had to find out from *Officer Westbow* that some crazy girl named *Kate Kole* came into the station shouting that she killed someone!"

Kate grabbed the sandpaper and started scrubbing at the dried putty on the cabinets. "I forgot my phone. That's why I didn't call you," she said. "And we *can* trust cops. Don't let your pretentious partner make you think otherwise. He's one of a kind."

"You're lucky Westbow didn't recognize you from the annual fundraiser last year! Why didn't you ask for me at the station?"

"I did. You weren't there."

Lily's exasperated breath filled the dusty air. She untangled her arms from her police vest and ripped at the buttons of her shirt until she was in only her under-tank. She tossed her uniform on the counter and squatted beside the cupboard Kate was working on until Kate met her eyes. "Unreal, *Kate*," she said.

"What was I supposed to do? It was an emergency!" As she said it, Kate stole a glance toward the windows to search for red and blue flashing lights outside.

"Why did Westbow say some medicated university student thought she killed someone today?"

"Because I did." Kate dropped the sandpaper and stood. "I totally killed someone," she rasped in a loud whisper. "But I'm pretty sure no one believes me."

Lily folded her arms, showing the collage of tattoos inked up her muscled forearms. "I believe you. Which is why we need to get moving, because if there's a body out there somewhere, Kate, we need to find it before anyone else does—"

"There's not." Kate drew a glass from the cupboard. She filled it up at the sink and drank, thinking of a tossed book and spilled coffee, thinking of vanished bodies and smiling cashiers. Of Lily's whole career getting ruined over this.

Lily scratched her jaw. "I'm no detective, but if you really killed someone, there should be a body—"

"It's gone!" Kate slammed the glass down on the counter so hard, it cracked. She bit her lips together. "Sorry, I know you're just trying to help. It's been a weird day and I'm super hangry."

35

"No kidding." Lily took the drill off the counter and dragged over the case of screws like she needed to find something for her hands to do. She paused and chewed on the inside of her cheek. "Are you okay?"

Kate's eye twitched. She swept the cracked glass into the garbage. "I'm fine. Right now, I just need to eat a thousand pounds of burgers and get some sleep so I can think straight." She glanced back out the windows at the dark street. The alley looked empty, and the lights were off at the breakfast diner across the road. It didn't mean a SWAT team wasn't hiding out there, preparing to storm the storefront.

"I know you'll be mad if I bring it up, but," Lily crouched and took a screw from the case, then pressed it against a cabinet door, "are you sure you're not mixing up real life with one of those novels you're writing? If you're starting to get confused, I know a good therapi—"

Kate sighed. "Really, Lily? A therapist?"

Lily bit her lips shut. A moment later, she mumbled, "There's nothing wrong with going to see a therapist. I saw one for years after—"

"Here's what happened." Kate cleared her throat loudly. "I went to the coffee shop down the street this morning to check out our competition, and some guy walked in and was a total jerk, and I *accidentally* kicked him into a table, and—"

"Accidentally kicked him into a table? How do you *accidentally* do that?" Lily rested the drill on her knee.

"—but the body was gone when I came back to the café with *Officer Westbow*, and everyone was acting like nothing happened and saying they didn't remember me being there." Kate went to the chair where her coat was flung over the backrest and pulled her *Bella Stone* book from her coat pocket. "But this proves that I was there and that it *did* happen." She flipped the pages so Lily could see.

Lily took the book and brushed over the coffee-stained corner with her thumb.

Kate reached for the novel and tugged it back, thinking better of it. Suddenly, she wondered why in the world she'd been so quick to drag Lily into the story. No story that started with murder had a happy ending.

"I mean, maybe you're right. Maybe I'm just getting mixed up because of the novel I'm writing. My story has major constituent vibes." She glanced off. The chocolate on her strawberries was starting to melt.

Lily rubbed her temples. "First, I don't think you realize what *constituent* means." Her pale blue eyes settled on Kate. "And second, I already told you I believe you," she said and folded her arms again. "Let's go find the body."

Kate clasped her hands around the book. "I've got my literature class in the morning. Maybe tomorrow afternoon."

"Someone could find the body by then, Kate."

Kate swallowed. "Unfortunately, Lily," she went over and shoved the book back into her coat pocket, "I think someone already did."

When she turned back around, Lily was massaging her eyes with her palms.

"I'll go to the coffee shop and take a look around," Lily said. "But I'm doing a double shift since we're so low staffed. I have to go back to the station after or the chief is going to wonder where I am."

"Be careful," Kate said, moving for the rusted coffee machine on the counter and pouring a fresh cup for Lily to take. "Something weird is going on at that coffee shop. I'm sure of it."

Lily dragged her uniform off the counter and took the coffee with her other hand. "I'll call you in the morning," she promised. "Just stay here until then and keep out of trouble, okay?"

Kate nodded, and Lily headed for the door while threading her arms back into her uniform with her one usable hand. The bell echoed through the empty storefront when she left. Kate watched her friend head down the sidewalk until she disappeared from the windows.

The moon turned the roads silver, and gray leaves tumbled by in the wind. The soft patter of rain filled the café as it began pelting the windows. Kate didn't realize how long she was standing there staring out at the spot where Lily had disappeared until the café door squeaked open again. She hadn't even seen anyone walk up.

Ben—the loan shark—walked in with his shirt untucked. The bottom of his large stomach hung out, and his shoulders were speckled with fresh raindrops. His scowl was deep and volatile enough to start an earthquake on his face.

Kate swallowed her moan. "I don't have it," she told him before he could ask. "I'll make both months' payments next month."

Ben's chin doubled when he tilted his head and grunted. "You're the one who talked me into giving you and your cop friend my money. I gave you that loan three months ago and you haven't even opened your store yet!"

"It's a café," Kate corrected.

"Whatever. I want my money back! Don't make me send someone after you," he threatened, and Kate raised a brow. She realized Lily left her vest on the counter, so she went over to pick it up and turned it so Ben could see.

"I'll be sure to pass that message along to my *cop friend*," Kate said, tapping the police logo. "Or did you forget the law doesn't look kindly on men who act like thugs?"

Ben's thick finger came out. "Give me my money back, Kate! You don't want to find out what I'm capable of!"

Kate cast him a doubtful look, but she sighed and nodded. "Give us a chance to open this place. My cop friend and I will give your loan back with interest like I promised."

Ben looked around at the unfinished cabinets, the unpainted walls, and the cold fireplace in the corner. His only answer was a snort as he spun and left, letting the door smack shut with a thud. His voice drifted in from outside as he yelled at someone, "Are you her cop friend? Tell her to pay me back!"

Kate picked up her clipboard with a sigh and walked around the counter as the café door opened again. "Did you forget your vest—"

Two hands grabbed Kate by her waist. She was pushed backward and pinned against the wall—the clatter of her clipboard filled the empty café as it hit the floor. Her gaze fired up to find a pair of menacing turquoise eyes looking back, and the air slipped from her lungs. The stranger held her against the wall, his lips pinched, his jaw set. He said nothing. He just stared with a hatred colder than Kate had ever felt before.

"Who...?" The word got stuck in her throat as her stare dropped to take in the rest of him.

He wore a police uniform. Rain drenched his clothes and hair, running down his face in streams. His lashes were glued together in sections from the water.

"I..." Her throat swelled; tears warmed her eyes. "If you're here to arrest me, at least let me call my grandma." His hands were cold, and she shivered as his fingers tightened on her hips.

"You should know why I'm here, Human." The guy's voice was low, hoarse, and dark. But it wasn't his striking tone that brought Kate's racing mind to a halt.

Human?

Her stomach dropped as that word burrowed holes into the memory she'd already torn apart since morning.

A predatory, turquoise-eyed monster looked at Kate. This guy before her was the same as the golden-eyed guy from the coffee shop.

Kate's gaze flickered toward the café door that felt too far away. "What do you want?" She could hardly hear her own quiet voice.

"Kate Kole," the guy said in an icy tone. "I want you to die."

"W... what?" she rasped. "What did you just say?"

His penetrating stare narrowed like he was waiting for something. He didn't blink, even when beads of rainwater rolled into his open eyes. After a few seconds, his lips thinned in an impatient way.

Kate's hands balled into fists. "What's the matter with you?" she whispered.

The guy's face changed. The death-look dissolved into surprise. He looked her over, his gaze snagging on her throat. That's where it stayed as he reached behind him for something that drove an uneasy feeling into Kate's chest.

She swung her fist toward his face. He dodged her punch, and her knuckles struck his shoulder. It barely moved him. She shoved his arm out of her way and ran toward the café door, but the guy grabbed a fistful of her sweater and yanked her backward into his chest. His arm wrapped around her waist, sealing her against his damp police uniform, and he said into in her ear, "I'll learn your *real* name, Kate Kole, and I'll give you the painful death you deserve. If you tell any other humans about me, that human officer outside will die beside you."

He released her, and Kate staggered forward as the bell of the café door sounded.

In marched Lily with her soaked shirt unbuttoned at her throat.

"I totally forgot my—" Lily skidded to a halt. "Officer Riley," she said in surprise, glancing to the guy in the police uniform. "What are you doing here?" She stood a little taller and idly brushed her fingers over her messy collar.

"Following up on the murder confession." The guy's response came out clean and cool, nothing like the icy tone he'd just used to threaten Kate.

Kate blinked at Lily as the guy brushed by them both. An earthy, floral scent passed with him. He opened the door to leave but glanced back at Kate one last time, his turquoise eyes making extra vows his next comment didn't:

"I'll see you again soon," he promised.

He stepped out into the rain, pulling on a police hat, and he let the door slam shut behind him.

Kate stared at the empty doorway. Prickles were left all over her skin.

"Unreal," Lily said as she sighed and rolled her eyes. "I literally *just* told Westbow I would take this case. But it seems like he already sent out the new guy."

"How do you know that officer?" Kate asked from a dry throat. Her back was still wet from his uniform.

"Officer Riley? He's a transfer from Ottawa. He just started today. He actually showed up super late, if you can believe that. On his first day."

A chill ran up Kate's damp spine as she thought of the real Officer

Riley lying in a ditch somewhere.

"If you tell any other humans about me, that human officer outside will die beside you."

Kate turned toward the counter so Lily couldn't see her face. On an ordinary day, Kate wouldn't believe such a bizarre threat. But there was nothing ordinary about today.

"Hey, you okay?" Lily's voice travelled across the café as she grabbed her vest off the counter. "Don't worry about the investigation, Kate. I'll take care of it. Officer Riley won't be coming back here with any more questions."

Kate reached for her coat and book bag, trying to suppress the tremor in her movements. "I'll go see that therapist," she said. She bit her lips hard enough to leave a mark. "Be careful on your walk back to the station, Lil. You have your gun, right?"

"Of course I have my gun. Why would you ask me that?"

Kate took another look out the window. "Just making sure."

Lily brushed a hand down her rain-covered face, smearing her makeup. "Go get some sleep, Kate. We'll figure this out tomorrow after your class," she promised.

Kate waited in the staircase to her apartment until she heard the soft ring of the café bell. She raced back to the windows to watch Lily walk to the end of the road and turn left toward the station.

Kate's skin tingled with a strange sensation, as though ants were crawling over her arms and legs. It was like a cool wind had slipped beneath her clothes. Like ice and heat and air and steam all breathing over her at once. It felt like...

It felt like she was being watched.

When she ascended the stairs to her second-floor apartment, she imagined turquoise eyes in the stairwell.

When she brushed her teeth, they looked back at her in the mirror.

When she climbed into bed, they were all over her sheets.

At midnight, she finally gave up on sleeping and climbed out of bed. She went to the window and peeked out at the quiet city. It wasn't raining anymore, but the roads glistened with moisture beneath the streetlights.

Kate saw a head of orange-red hair slip into the alley across the street. She pushed her curtains aside and cracked open the window, letting in the sounds of yelling. There were two voices—one high and one low. And crying.

An anguished huff escaped Kate; her fingers tightened around the windowsill. "She'll be fine," she told herself. "It's not my problem. This is *totally not my problem*."

She moved to close the window and drown out the noises outside, but her hand hesitated on the lever. Her gaze slowly dragged to the shadowed alley beside the breakfast diner. It was too difficult to see what was going on from her vantage point.

"She'll call the cops if she needs them. Probably." Kate nodded to herself. "She has hands. Fingers to dial." She bit her lip too hard and sealed her window shut. "She probably has a phone…"

She turned toward her bed, stealing a wary glance at her own phone glowing with a clock that told her it was too late for her to do anything about anything, and anything she could do wouldn't do anything to help anyway, and… anything, anything, anything.

Her clock changed, telling her another minute had passed.

"Argh. Unreal," she scolded herself as she grabbed her phone and fled her bedroom. Her apartment floor was cold, but she kicked aside her shoes as she pushed through the front door into the stairwell.

"Yeah?" Lily answered on the first ring as Kate jogged down to the café.

"Good, you're up," Kate said, pushing out the café door and embracing the cold night.

"I'm still on duty."

"She's in trouble, Lil."

"Who's in trouble?"

"The redhead across the street!"

Lily moaned. "Aw, Kate! Go back to bed!"

"That lowlife guy is back, and it sounds like they're having a big fight..." The phone slipped from Kate's shoulder and clattered to the sidewalk, but she left it and raced in bare feet across the road into the alley.

6

Prince Cressica and All the Human Foolishness

Cress felt the whispering magic of the Ever Corners calling him back to the Silver Castle. He felt the Queene's icy gaze across the gate. But more than anything, he felt the loss of Whyp deep in his faeborn soul; a hollow, crushing pain worse than hunger.

Things could have gone terribly wrong when Cress had uttered Kate Kole's false name. Had he not sniffed his human target's affection for the light-featured human officer outside, he might have been overtaken by the fairy-killer himself as Whyp had. An assassin of fairies, it seemed Kate Kole was. That meant it was assassin against assassin, and only one of them would survive in the end.

The balcony outside Kate Kole's dwelling was covered in dirt from dry, abandoned plant pots. Cress remained there through the night, glaring at his short hair in the reflection of the glass doors and listening to the human's restless breathing through the walls. Hoping someone might show up and say the human's *real* name.

Cress watched her roll out of bed and teeter on her feet as she stumbled toward the window. The streets were dark this late at night, apart from a few tall metal lanterns at the roadsides. The curtain only hung open a slit—Kate Kole didn't spot Cress there.

The human nudged her curtain aside while rubbing her eyes. She opened the window, and Cress held his breath. But human bickering lifted from the alley across the street, and Kate Kole seemed far more interested in that.

His human target sputtered some nonsense to herself. She shut the window, and a moment later, she darted across her apartment. Cress listened to her distant thudding down the stairs. She reappeared below, pushing out of the building with a glowing rectangular device pinched between her ear and shoulder. She aimed for the alley where Cress sensed the two additional human heart rhythms.

Cress released a bored huff. He hopped the rail of the balcony, landing lightly in a shadow, and walked around the building to watch from the darkness.

"Let's go inside! I'm freezing!" a grumpy male human said. He took hold of a red-haired female's shoulder.

"Hey!" Kate Kole shouted, swooping in to stand between the male and female.

"Who are you?" the red-haired female asked Kate Kole, and Cress grunted.

He would also like to know.

"Get out of the way," the male said.

Cress sighed, checking his nails for human realm dirt. His fairsaber handle pressed lightly against his back in his belt. He wondered if he ought to just race into the alley and slay them all. He'd done more reckless things than attack an assassin he knew little about.

"Go find someone else to bother," Kate Kole said to the male.

The male's fist lashed out toward the wall and *not* toward either of the human females. Yet, Kate Kole leaped into his knuckles, and Cress's deep laugh rolled out, filling the darkness. When the male's fist slammed against Kate Kole's shoulder, the hit was hard enough to send her into a full spin.

But it seemed she got what she wanted. Cress listened to the elevated heart rhythm of his human target, and to her raspy breath. He waited for her to slice the human male open in retaliation like any cruel female assassin would.

But Kale Kole turned back to the white-faced male human and didn't draw her weapons. She didn't unhinge him with trickery. She didn't even make a threat.

"What's the matter with you? Are there really still idiots who smack girls around in this day and age?" was all she said.

Cress dropped his hand, interested now.

The male human blinked in surprise. "I…" He staggered back a step. "I wasn't really trying to… I mean you jumped right into that! I was going to miss and just scare you. You made me hit you on purpose!"

Wailing trumpets erupted down the road, and the male's face paled further. He turned to run, but Kate Kole snatched his plaid shirt. The male nearly dragged her down the alley with him, and Cress snorted another dull laugh.

The male shoved Kate Kole away—she tripped over her own feet and tumbled into the brick wall, barely catching herself on clumsy-looking hands, and her forehead smacked a brick. Her lashes fluttered for a moment as she blinked, and Cress chewed on the inside of his cheek.

What in the faeborn-cursed Corners was she doing?

"Stop! Police!" It was the voice of Officer Lily Baker that boomed down the alley. Her partner Officer Connor Backs was beside her.

The male in plaid came racing around the building where Cress leaned against the wall in the dark. The fairy Prince sighed. With an easy shove of his heel against the male's fleshy stomach, Cress sent the human spinning back into the alley.

Officer Connor Backs snatched the human in plaid and dragged him to the ground from there.

In the darkness, Cress watched as Kate Kole touched her forehead with a delicate hand.

"Are you all right?" Officer Lily asked her.

Cress folded his arms, his brows tipping in as Kate Kole nodded and dropped her hand from her head.

"You need to come to the station with us," Officer Lily said, and Kate Kole released a breath.

"I can't do that after I already showed up there yesterday," she said. She nodded toward the redhead human whose wide doe eyes took everything in. "She's a witness though. She saw everything."

Officer Lily folded her arms and glanced to where Officer Connor hauled the male in plaid toward the four-wheeled chariot with flashing lights. "Then get out of here before my backup shows up," she said.

Just like that, Kate Kole scampered back across the road and disappeared into her building.

The fairy Prince tapped a forefinger against the handle of his fairsaber as he realized how difficult this would be. His human target was the finest actress he had crossed in his twenty-two faeborn years of life. Even those she cared for were being fooled into thinking she was some delicate, weak thing who needed help, instead of a lethal assassin who killed fairies.

Cress moved deeper into the darkness, deciding he wouldn't get answers by waiting around on Kate Kole's balcony if not even Officer Lily Baker knew her secrets.

His stomach growled. "Hush," he commanded it as he walked.

The feasts of the North Corner called him home. It seemed like an eternity had passed since he'd tasted blossom syrups, sweet bell corns, and rose dough. Perhaps he wasn't built for peasant life, or human life. He'd been out of the Four Corners of Ever for less than a day.

The night frost in the human realm smelled different than the frost in the North. It was clear, empty, and carried only the memories of the branches it coated. Cress followed the air's fragrances until he smelled one that was familiar. His feet came together.

"Queensbane," he cursed.

He turned.

The silhouettes of three faeborn males filled the shadows across the street. Shayne's crossbow glimmered silver in the moonlight, but the rest of the males were concealed by the dark.

They must have guessed they'd been discovered because the triad emerged from the shadows and met the Prince in the empty road.

Mor's brown-silver eyes were hard, his lips thin. Dranian looked angry, but that was nothing new. Shayne looked like a fieldpup ready for an adventure. His bare faeborn feet were blueing from human frost.

"What," Cress began through his teeth, "in the name of the sky deities are you three doing here?"

"We're saving your faeborn life, Cress," Shayne said, swinging his crossbow up and resting it on his shoulder. "Why else would we have broken a sacred fairy law?"

Cress looked to Mor, who said nothing.

"How did you get across the gate?" he asked anyway.

"We bound our fate to the success of this quest, Your Highness," Shayne told him, and Cress's blood turned cold. "You can't fail now, or we're dead. That was our agreement with the North High Court when they allowed us to cross and aid you."

Mor had not blinked for several minutes. His gaze hadn't moved from Cress in that time, either.

"Lucky for you, a few of the High Court members wanted justice for Whyp." Shayne shrugged, and his crossbow slid off his shoulder. It nearly toppled to the road before the fairy caught it again.

Cress ran his hands through his horrendous, terribly short hair that barely covered his pointed ears. "I failed to learn the human's real name."

"Great. Well, we need to find it, or we'll all suffer the death of traitors," Mor said, speaking for the first time.

A tall lantern flickered down the road as a few tense faeborn heartbeats passed in silence.

"We will follow all the rules while we are here," Cress finally said, pointing at his brother assassins. "No witnesses to fairy acts. No mentioning our realm or our Queene. No unnecessary tricks on the humans—"

"Do you think we don't know the rules?" Mor said through his tight lips.

"—and absolutely no lying. We don't need to fight extra curses for trying to fool humans with falsehoods."

"Careful, Your Highness," Shayne warned as he ran his thumb over the sharp edge of his bow. "You're getting a bit bossy."

Cress's jaw slid to the side. "Am I?" Sarcasm.

Shayne sighed. "How about a kiss?" he suggested, flicking his white hair from his eyes. "You said you don't have her real name. So, take her will instead. Maybe she will *want* to die for you if you ask her to."

Dranian made a repulsed face. "You cannot ask the Prince of the North to kiss a human!" he growled.

But Cress folded his arms and tapped a finger against his bicep. "Shayne, you were the only one of us who spent your childling years at an academy. Did they teach you the six dangers of the human realm in your lectures?"

Shayne nodded. "Of course. Humans conspire differently than us. They will try to trick us into eating bread," he promised.

Cress quieted to think. "We should learn who the human assassin answers to if we can," he said. "I want to know if she was told to kill a member of the Brotherhood by a higher master, and how she was able to outsmart a fairy. I want answers."

"Maybe if you return with answers, the Queene won't destroy you for leaving the Ever Corners before her daughter's wedding," Mor said. The comment was loaded with the wrathful reminder of the promises Cress had broken.

CHAPTER

7

Kate Kole and the Class that Changed Everything

Kate stared at her reflection in the bathroom mirror. A girl with dark, wine-red hair in a messy bun, tired hazel eyes, and a ridiculous, bruising scratch on her forehead stared back. The face was one she barely recognized in this state. She ripped her elastic out and her wild hair billowed free over her shoulders. Frankly, she looked like a cross between a clown that hadn't slept in seventeen days and a Barbie that had been melted in the microwave.

Kate hadn't been watching the girl across the street this week. The redhead wasn't home much, but when she was, Kate spent too many hours spying like a lunatic and trying to muster up the courage to go over and say hi. Kate had moved into this apartment six months ago, and her tongue still felt fat when she thought about going over to tell the girl who she was.

Now, after the forehead-bashing alley incident, Kate probably just seemed like an idiot who flung herself into a bad situation for no reason. She slapped a hand over her eyes as she thought about how in the world she was going to introduce herself after that gong show.

Also, she killed someone yesterday morning. So, there was that life-altering event to take into consideration, too.

"Hi, I'm Kate. I meddle in other people's business because I can't stop myself from getting involved. Oh, also, I kill people sometimes. I probably won't kill you, though. Hopefully."

"Was that really only yesterday?" she mumbled to herself as she ran a cloth under cold water.

She winced as she dabbed it against her throbbing forehead.

When she was finished, she leaned with her palms against the counter, staring into the mirror where she saw monstrous turquoise eyes instead of tired hazel ones. Even after the long, exciting night, she couldn't shake the blue-eyed guy from her head. He would have been pretty if he wasn't so frightening.

"What's wrong with you?" she whispered to the girl in the mirror, wondering how she could think such a thought after he'd stormed into her café and pushed her against the wall. She couldn't stand pushy guys. Though, it was him telling her flat out that he *wanted her to die* that was the real dealbreaker.

Even after Kate had smoked her forehead on the wall in the alley, her first thought had been of *him*. It was like she wondered if he'd seen it. Though she couldn't imagine why she wondered about him at all. If her life was a horror novel, this was the part where she'd run screaming into the forest, and he'd stalk her through the trees to her gritty, gruesome end.

She grabbed her brush off the counter and began yanking it through her hair. There was no point in bothering with makeup today when her forehead looked like a glowing red beacon.

Thirty minutes later, Kate pushed out the café door. She half-jogged down the street, balancing a piping hot latte as she took the long way around the block to avoid Ben's convenience store. She flicked through red-tag flights on her phone as she moved. She'd never been on a plane before, but Greece was starting to sound like a good option for a trip. Or forever.

Her heart began to feel less heavy as she made a plan. She could sit by the sea and eat Greek salads while sipping on cool, fresh fruit drinks. Maybe they had cafés in Greece. Maybe she could open a café there instead with French pastries and English tea and goodies from all over Europe like a cozy Travel Romance novel.

Her phone buzzed, and she stifled a yawn as she answered it. "Mm?" It was more of a moan than a *hello*. If she thought she was capable of sleeping, she would have gone back to bed this morning. But she didn't want to be in the café building alone.

"We had to let him go, Kate."

Kate stopped walking. "What?"

"Not to sound judgey, but the guy was pretty adamant about his story. Are you sure you didn't step into that punch?" Lily asked.

Kate chewed on her lip. "Maybe a little."

"Kate, I know how worried you get about the girl across the street, but she's an adult. She can handle her own problems. This guy doesn't really fit the profile of someone who randomly punches people."

"He was yelling at her while she was crying!"

"Well, that girl doesn't have a single mark on her body to show us. I don't have any evidence an assault happened because you didn't come in with them, and the girl is agreeing that you basically forced him to strike your shoulder."

Kate released an exasperated sigh and set her latte on a bench. She dragged a hand through her hair. "Maybe he's learned his lesson already just from getting taken in."

"Kate," Lily said.

"Yeah?"

"Stop trying to play God. Let me chase the *real* bad guys."

"Fine," Kate said through a mixed mumble and grunt. She rigidly adjusted the fit of her yellow sweater.

"There's another solution, you know." Lily's phone cut out for a moment, and Kate turned toward the distant cell tower like that might give her a better signal. "You can join the force like I've always said you should. Then you can catch all the bad guys you want."

"No way," Kate said. "I shouldn't go anywhere near the station ever again."

A long silence was all that came through the phone before Lily finally spoke again. "There's supposed to be a thunderstorm tonight. Do you want me to stay over?"

Kate swallowed. "No."

"They're calling for stormy weather all week."

"I know."

Another pass of silence. A pair of birds fluttered by and landed in a tree by the path. They started singing.

"Well, you know where to find me if you need me. Have a good class," Lily said.

The *click* of Lily hanging up came through the speaker. Kate slid the phone into her book bag and grabbed her latte from the bench to finish her walk-jog to the university. She stole a wary glance at the morning sky on the way. The clouds still looked white.

Crisp leaves drifted from the trees, sparkling the morning air with twirling browns and spinning yellows, crafting a blanket of windblown maple confetti over the campus walkway. Kate sipped her latte, rolling cinnamon and nutmeg over her tongue and soothing her spinning, aching mind with the comforts of milk and espresso as she marched up the stairs. The great stone building of historic architecture swallowed her in.

Professor Palmer's voice trickled through the student crowd. Kate passed him and Professor Eres deep in conversation.

"...and I'm talking about the strange happenings at this university. You know the *library incident*, and the *growling in the floor*..."

"You're blaming it on mythical creatures again? Come on, Palmer. No one believes that nonsense. You've been teaching mythology for too long."

Kate slowed her walk. She'd heard the rumours about the school library like everybody else. They'd circulated like wildfire over the summer when a pack of students trashed the place and ripped up half the books. No one had been arrested yet.

Kate swallowed, thinking about how the turquoise-eyed "Officer Riley" had called her *Human*.

"Mr. Palmer," she said, cutting into the professors' conversation. "Can I meet with you after my literature class this morning?"

Professor Palmer raised an eyebrow. "I suppose, Miss…?"

"I'm Kate Kole. And I have some questions about… some of the things you teach."

She felt her cheeks warm when Professor Eres gave her a doubtful look, as though he wondered why any student would want an audience with the school's "crazy professor." She ignored him and waited for Professor Palmer's answer. "I'm a writer," Kate clarified. "I'm writing a mythology-based high fantasy novel."

Professor Palmer seemed to grow irritated the moment she said, "*fantasy novel*", but he nodded. "I'll be in my office all morning," he mumbled.

"Thank you." Kate mustered a smile and turned for her classroom. As she did, her gaze snagged on someone who didn't belong with the young adults and book bags, and she sighed.

Five-year-old Gracelynn Morris spun in circles in the middle of the hall where students twice her height pushed by. The little girl's eyes were brimmed with tears. One of her shoelaces was untied and her nose was running. She wiped it with the back of her sleeve.

"Are you lost?" Kate asked as she approached the girl and squatted to a knee. She hadn't seen Gracelynn since her summer job at the daycare facility. Mrs. Morris had been teaching summer classes at the university.

Gracelynn burst into tears at the sight of her. "Miss Kate! I can't find my mommy!"

Kate checked her watch. "I'll take you to the teacher's lounge to find her. Let's go."

Gracelynn sniffed as Kate took her hand and began leading her down the hall. "Are you coming back to daycare again next summer?" the little girl asked through a wail as they walked.

"No, I'm going to be a barista," Kate said, reaching over to smear a fat tear off Gracelynn's cheek.

"A ba-rees-tah?"

Kate laughed. "Don't worry about it."

"Miss Kate," Gracelynn said again. "I'll only feel better if you sing the daffodils song for me."

"Wait, what? You want me to sing? Here?" Kate chuckled again and shook her head as she headed for the busiest hallway intersection in the building. "I can't do that right in the middle of the hall. Let's find your mom before I'm late or I'm going to be totally implausible."

Gracelynn walked for a few seconds before she asked, "Miss Kate?"

"Yeah?"

"What does *implausible* mean?"

Kate opened her mouth to answer, but she paused. She twisted her lips to the side as she thought about it. "Honestly," she cleared her throat and lowered her voice, "I'm not actually sure."

Kate rushed into her classroom ten minutes later and sat at her usual desk, relieved she still made it before the lecture started. She slid on her glasses and pulled out her phone, her attention catching on the background photo of a woman with dark, wavy hair beneath a knit toque, a man with light, hazel eyes like hers, and two tweens tossing snow at them. The picture was taken the same day as the ones on Grandma Lewis's end table. It had been a sunny day, even though the air was cold. The snow had been slightly damp—perfect for packing into snowballs.

Kate stared at the photo until Professor Stanner launched into a lecture about popular books and their character-driven plotlines. He went on for the better part of an hour, repeating himself at least a dozen times as though him saying things over and over would magically transform any students within earshot into geniuses.

Kate rubbed her temples, thinking of everything except for the topic of literature class. She had no idea what Professor Stanner was talking about anyway; she skipped her last two classes to help Lily get the café ready. They were still a month away from opening, at least. Stacks of delivery boxes rested in the café's entryway. After Kate had failed miserably to lift them, they'd sat there for over a week.

Her fingers flicked the corner pages of *Bella Stone*, feeling the brittle, liquid-stained paper. She repeated the motion as she eavesdropped on the whispering girls behind her.

"Did you see that guy who just came in? I'm positive he's never been in this class before." The girl had a distinct nasally sounding voice. It would have been good for the narration of a villain in an audiobook.

"How do you know that? Maybe he's always sat at the back," another girl said.

"No, I would have remembered if he was ever in this room with us. Do you think he just joined our class? Do you think he has a girlfriend?"

"I'm asking him to Sophie's party on Saturday. I call dibs."

Grunts and snickers erupted from the girls, but they suddenly went quiet.

The chair beside Kate moved. Someone sat down.

"What did I miss?" a voice whispered. It took Kate a moment to realize the guy was talking to her.

"A really boring chat about character-driven plots," she answered without looking up.

"Ah. My favourite."

Kate pulled off her glasses and shoved the book away from herself. She was sure the guy was smiling, but she ignored him. His deep, husky voice said enough. She wondered if he used it for something nice like singing, or if he used it to get girls to pay attention to him.

Based on how sociable he was being, there was a 376% chance it was the latter.

The guy reached over and tapped the stained novel. "You must drink coffee—"

"I'm not really in the mood for chit-chat," Kate admitted. She kept her gaze on Professor Stanner to prove it. A second passed when he didn't respond, and she wondered if she'd been too harsh. She bit the end of her tongue as she contemplated a nice, yet *"this isn't an invitation to talk"* type of thing to say. But a low, dark chuckle escaped the guy, stopping her from saying anything at all.

"As you wish. Human," he said first.

Kate jumped at the shrill screaming of the class bell. Students stood from their chairs with screeches and clatters, but Kate stayed put, her ears ringing as Professor Stanner quickly scrambled through the last few seconds of his speech.

The guy didn't leave.

Kate grabbed her novel and shoved it into her bag. She braced to stand, but the guy reached toward her, and she slowed her movements, refusing to look at him.

He took a gentle hold of her chin. His other hand was fastened tightly around the strap of her book bag still attached to her shoulder.

She contemplated leaving her bag behind, but before she could, he turned her face toward his. Kate met a pair of cold turquoise irises, and heat sailed through her abdomen.

"Officer Riley…" she rasped.

A mean smile formed over his mouth. "Not even close."

He grabbed her chair between her legs, turned it, and yanked her toward him. The chair screeched through the classroom. He leaned in, coming so close she could feel his breath on her cheeks. Kate stopped breathing.

"What do you want from me?" she asked, not daring to move her lips too much this close.

"Just this, Human."

Earthy and floral fragrances swept in as he placed his sneering mouth against hers. The kiss was soft, almost delicate. Warmth sailed down Kate's chest and into her abdomen like hot tea.

"Get a room," someone behind them mumbled.

Not-Officer-Riley kept his lips pressed firmly against hers for another second of unbearable temperature. His long lashes brushed her cheek. His flowery scent enveloped her senses.

Kate's eyes were wide when he pulled away, taking the smells of petals and sweet pollen with him.

He looked calm. Pleased with himself. Proud, even.

She slapped him.

The person behind them who grunted before stifled a laugh, and a few of the remaining students whispered. Some of them stood and shuffled out of the classroom, and new students made their way in for the next lecture. The room filled with chatter again as the next class found their seats.

The guy stared in silence. He looked more stunned than he had in the café.

"Don't touch me," Kate said.

At the front, Professor Stanner put his hands on his hips. "What's all the fuss about?" he asked their section.

Neither the guy nor Kate answered.

Kate's chair squeaked when she stood. The guy didn't stop her this time as she grabbed her bookbag and bounded down the aisle, out of the classroom, across the hall, and into the stairwell. Her mind raced. Her heart raced faster.

She looked over her shoulder as she descended the stairs. She almost made it to the bottom before two strong hands appeared over the rail. Kate shrieked as she was lifted off her feet and pulled into the shadow of the stairs. Her back came against a cold wall.

The guy's ash-brown hair was dishevelled, his turquoise eyes glittered in the dimness, and he emitted a terrible and bone-shuddering presence.

"Kiss me again, Human," he demanded. "Immediately."

"Let me go," she whispered, but her words were too quiet to be a real threat.

The guy looked back and forth between her eyes, a pinch of frustration pulling at his face. But his mouth recovered its mean smile a second later. "Queensbane, you must have known I'd come for you," he said instead. "No one kills a fairy and lives."

Kate tried to tug his hands off. It only made him smile wider.

Laughter filled the stairwell above, and the guy's smile fell. His hands tightened slightly on Kate's sides as a group of students scampered down. The second the students appeared around the landing, his hands slid off Kate.

He waited, his dark-lashed gaze roaming over the mountain tattoo on the side of her neck, then travelling up to the swelling gash on her forehead. There his attention stayed as the students clamoured by.

"I'm surprised you let him hit you," he murmured with bland curiosity.

It took Kate a moment to realize what he was talking about. Her hand flew to her tender forehead. "How did you know..." He sneered again, and she paled. "Stay away from me," she whispered.

The humour in his face melted away, replaced by a chilling glare. "Absolutely not."

When the last student reached the floor, Kate sprang out from between the guy and the wall and fell into step behind the group. She kept in pace with them until she reached the doors, wringing her trembling fingers together.

A low, menacing chuckle filled the stairwell behind her. She was almost too far away to hear what he said next:

"Yes, run from me little human. I'll only play games with you. But my assassins will find you soon enough, and they don't have the patience for games like I do."

His words rang in her ears the whole way through the main hall. All she wanted to do was throw her shoes at him and shout, "Creep!" but she didn't stop moving. She didn't even look back over her shoulder.

She took a right turn when the path split and sped through the adjacent hall to the opposite side of the building, scanning the nameplates on the office doors as she moved. When she didn't see the door she wanted, she headed for the stairs and went back up to the second level.

Kate practically sprinted into Professor Palmer's office when she found his name, and she slammed the door shut behind her. When she turned around, she found the professor wide-eyed, sitting at his desk with a hand over his heart.

"Sorry," Kate said, panting. She opened her mouth to come up with a story about why she came in like that, but instead she blurted. "I'm in trouble! I'm being followed by someone... or some*thing*..."

Professor Palmer blinked behind his glasses. A half eaten peanut butter sandwich lay on his desk with no plate beneath. Crumbs were everywhere.

Kate waited, shifting her footing. She expected the professor to call security, but instead, he checked his watch, stood, collected his briefcase and coat, and said, "*Finally*. Follow me." With one dramatic swipe, he flung his whole peanut butter sandwich into the garbage beside his desk.

He marched past her to the door and swung it open, peering both ways down the hall over his glasses. Kate swore he was suppressing a tiny, eager smile.

Without warning, Professor Palmer took off down the hall like a speed walker. Kate scrambled after him, trying to balance her bookbag strap on her shoulder. Even crammed between other moving students, Kate's skin felt warm, and she felt exposed, too out in the open. Professor Palmer didn't say a word as he hurried through the fire doors, down the stairs, and came out into the cold fall air while stuffing his arms into his coat.

They moved past the university buildings, into the city, and came to a street of magnificent, glassy skyscrapers. The air smelled of exhaust and damp earth this far into the city, laced with just a little bit of this professor's rumoured madness.

"How long have you been outrunning this *mythological* creature?" Professor Palmer finally spoke as he squinted up at the buildings.

"Um, about two days. I…" Kate bit her tongue. "I killed one of them. It was a total accident."

Palmer stopped walking and turned toward her. He didn't look surprised or horrified. He looked impressed.

"How?"

She blushed. "I kicked him into a table."

"Hmm." Palmer nodded, thinking that through. "Why? Did it attack you? Did you provoke it?" He looked her over, eyeing her forehead in particular. "You seem the sort to provoke an innocent creature," he said, more to himself.

Kate's face changed and she stood taller. "He was *not* innocent."

Palmer grunted and stuffed his free hand into his coat pocket. "Your parents must have a hard time with you," he thought aloud.

"I don't have parents." Kate wasn't sure why she told him. She hadn't told anyone since high school. She'd kept that part of her past far away from her new name, her new hair, her new tattoo, and her new life.

But Professor Palmer's face lit up. "You don't? Excellent!" he said with a big smile.

In an instant, he turned and half-ran to a building with large glass doors. Kate watched with an odd face as he approached a keypad, ignoring the doorman, and jammed his thumb into a yellow button while the doorman eyed him. Kate had the strangest impulse to take notes so that the next time she needed to act crazy, she would hit the nail on the head.

"I'm here for Freida Nightingale," Professor Palmer leaned in and said into a tiny microphone.

The words barely left his mouth before a side door swung open, and an old woman with long silver hair, lush red lips, and deep black lashes appeared. She wore a navy business suit and expensive looking heels.

"I told you never to come here," she said coldly to Palmer.

"We need to attend the meeting," the professor told her.

"No males allowed. You know that." The woman folded her arms. "And no humans, either." She stole a glance at Kate standing there.

"Yes, well, she's being chased. And…" Palmer leaned in with a satisfied smile. "She's an *orphan*," he articulated, "who needs a fairy godmother."

The woman's gaze darted back to Kate. Her red lips bunched at the side. After a moment, she said, "If you come here again, I'll make you forget who you are, and everything you know."

She slammed the door shut.

Professor Palmer turned back to Kate, scratching his chin.

"Well, I can't say I'm surprised, but that didn't go as well as I'd hoped. There is a chance I've made things worse," he admitted. "Now I suppose you wait."

"Wait for what?" Kate looked back the way they came, expecting to see a pretty-eyed, handsy guy in a police uniform heading their way.

"Unfortunately, I can't tell you that. They'll cut out my tongue if I do," Professor Palmer mumbled, more to himself. Without warning, he brushed past her toward the bus stop.

Panic swelled in Kate's throat. "Wait… that's it? You're just going to leave me here?" she called after him, sure all the students who whispered about this man being a lunatic were spot on. "Wait!"

"You should keep moving!" Palmer called back. "Waiting in one place will let them catch up with you!"

A bus swept to a stop and Kate watched the professor step on. He walked past the bus aisle windows and found a seat at the back. The bus snorted out a puff of exhaust and took off again a second later. Palmer didn't even look back at Kate from his window seat.

Kate slowly lifted a hand to her chest, feeling the wild thudding of her heart as the bus reached the end of the road, turned left, and disappeared around the buildings.

Everything that happened in the last half hour felt like a dream. Even the last moments of Professor Palmer bringing her here.

Where was here?

Kate looked around, realizing she hadn't paid attention to the turns they took, and she had no idea how to get back to her apartment.

It was early afternoon by the time Kate found the right police patrol car parked on the curb in front of the *Street Meat* food truck. Lily and Connor were cleaning up their lunchtime garbage. Both of them had exhaustion rings around their eyes and looked like they'd give their whole life savings to be able to crawl into bed and sleep for days.

Kate fiddled with a loose string on her coat sleeve as she waited for the crosswalk light to turn. She sprinted across the road the second it changed, and she reached the officers out of breath.

"Lil."

Both Lily and Connor turned at the sound of her voice.

"We need to talk." Kate cleared her throat and smoothed down her wild hair that looked more purple than normal in the direct sunlight.

Lily looked her over. "No kidding." She grabbed Connor's garbage, too, and carried it over to the trash can. "Give us a minute, Connor," she said when she came back.

"No." Connor flashed a gloating smile. "You two don't have secrets from me."

Lily glared at her partner.

"Forget it. Our shift ends in thirty minutes. Longest shift of my *life*," she said to Kate. "Can you wait until then to talk? We can meet back at the café."

Kate scratched her head. "Uh… yeah."

Lily mumbled something about going to use the bathroom and turned for the nearest storefront. Connor stood a little taller after she left, his chest puffing out. He reached to flick a loose hair away from Kate's face.

Kate pushed his hand off.

"Keep your paws to yourself, Connor," she said. "I'm seriously not in the mood."

Connor snorted. "You're in no position to make demands. I know your secret, Kate," he reminded her. "You've always kind of liked me anyway."

Suddenly Kate wondered why she was still standing there with the one person she hated most in the world.

"Tell Lily I'll see her later." She turned toward the street again, but Connor chuckled.

"Don't boss me around. Wait here and tell her yourself."

Kate pretended not to hear and crossed back to her side of the street. Connor must have given up because he didn't shout anything else as she left.

She walked for twenty minutes through the busy downtown crowd, fiddling with the loose string on her coat cuff until she ripped it off. When she rounded the block toward the café, her back warmed. It was like a light finger was tracing up her spine and over her shoulder—

Kate spun around.

People shifted to walk around her. Car engines and chatter washed the air, and Kate pressed her fingers against her chest to feel the fresh thuds. She inhaled and exhaled, pulling her cell phone from her pocket as she walked.

"Yes, run from me little human. I'll only play games with you."

She spun around again.

Where was he?

"Watch where you're going," a shaggy haired boy mumbled and swerved before they could collide.

Kate swallowed and waved in apology. Her thumb hovered over the call button on her phone.

"...my assassins will find you soon enough..."

What kind of messed up prank was this? Kate was sure she'd never seen that turquoise-eyed fake cop before he showed up in her café. But in the university stairwell, he'd looked at her like he *knew* her.

Kate glanced down at her phone and realized the name on the screen was her grandmother's. She'd been about to dial Grandma Lewis, of all people.

Kate dragged her feet forward, guessing it would take Lily another twenty minutes to show up at the café even after Kate got there. She took her thumb off the call button and slid her phone back into her pocket, scolding herself for nearly calling the one person in the world she was certain she should *not* call.

Mitten-covered hands pushed her shoulders. Kate spun just as she was shoved off the sidewalk.

She tried to hit him as she was forced into the alley—her hands balled into fists and came up in front of her—but she didn't see wicked blue eyes, a mean smile, or a stolen police uniform.

A mid-twenties girl with big, curly hair blinked at Kate through large, bug-eyed glasses. A knit scarf wrapped her neck, and a high-collared knit sweater peeked out from a knit coat over top of that. Kate might have laughed at the sight another time, but with her pulse pounding in her ears, she could only stare.

"What are you running from?" the girl asked in a bored voice.

Kate blinked. "I think I was running from you," she admitted.

The girl nodded like that made sense. "We're going to be late for the meeting." She pointed her mitt in a random direction and began heading through the alley. Her boots sloshed through dry leaves every other step, and she walked with a slight limp.

Kate didn't follow.

The girl paused and turned back. "Oh, I forgot. I'm supposed to give you this." The girl's mitted hand disappeared into her coat pocket and brought out a postcard. She came back and handed it to Kate, then she left again, kicking the leaves.

Kate turned the card over. Pink yarn wove around the edges like an embellishment. Written on the page were a few simple words:

TO: THE HUMAN
YOU'RE INVITED
TO WHAT: THE KNITTING CLUB
WHERE: THE YARN & STITCH
WHEN: NOW

Kate looked back up at the girl covered in knitted attire, and her mouth parted in disbelief. If this really was a messed-up prank, someone had gone to great lengths to make it detailed and believable.

A finger jabbed Kate's back, and she shrieked and whirled. The alley behind her was empty.

"Keep up or I'll poke you again!" the girl called back as she disappeared around the building.

These had to be the people Professor Palmer had been trying to get her to before. Kate sprang after the girl, gripping the card in her fist.

The girl's wild, curly hair bobbed above the crowd—the only map Kate had to follow. Kate wove through couples and moms pushing strollers, trying not to lose sight. The girl didn't stop to wait even once; she kept moving, kept her attention forward, her back to Kate.

After ten minutes of battling the city hustle, they reached a narrow storefront tucked between two quaint shops. A chipped sign hung over a tinted window that said: *Yarn & Stitch*. The curly-haired girl pushed through the door. It slammed shut behind her.

Kate stood outside, looking both ways down the street. The girl didn't come back out again.

Chimes filled the space as Kate opened the door and poked her head in. Fragrances of cinnamon, herbal tea, and warm vanilla flooded her senses, too. She closed the door behind her, eyeing a steaming, old-fashioned teapot on a table in the corner with trays of cracker-coated sandwiches and macaroons. In the middle of the store, three Victorian style couches made a "U" shape. They were filled with women—a few youthful, some middle aged, some old—hunched over, knitting.

"It seems you're still alive." An elderly woman with a bun atop her head rose from her seat, and strands of pink yarn spilled off her legs. Kate realized it was the same woman from the skyscraper, only she looked different now. Now she wore no makeup and was covered head to toe in yarn outfit pieces.

She waved Kate forward. "You can call me Freida. That's my unhidden name."

Kate spotted the curly-haired girl among them who'd found her in the street. A half-scribbled name tag was on her sweater now that said: HAZEL. The girl was focussed on knitting a scarf and paid Kate no more attention.

"Um… I don't know how to knit," Kate said, wondering why in the world she bothered to tell them that. A few chuckles rose from the older ladies.

"You're not here to knit." Freida rolled her eyes and shook her head. "Just pretend for a while."

Kate hesitated.

"My assassins will find you soon enough."

She slid her book bag off her shoulder and wandered in with slow steps. When she sank into the last seat on the edge of a couch, Freida grabbed a ball of mint yarn and stuffed it into her hands with two long gray needles. A woman across the couches slid a small dish with a light blue macaroon toward Kate.

"I'm supposed to pretend to do this?" Kate made a face, and a woman with a large red braid pointed with her needle toward a video camera in the shop's corner.

"They can see us, but they can't hear us in here," Freida said as she sat back down and picked up her yarn. "You've been black marked, Kate Kole," she added. "The fae Prince has come to kill you. And he'll succeed."

The yarn tumbled from Kate's fingers, but she caught it before it hit the floor. "What did you just say?" She gripped the ball.

"We don't allow humans into our knitting club. But we took a vote, and I suppose we want to ask you a few questions before you're dead. Most of all, we wish to know why you killed that fae the other morning? Did someone pay you in gold to do it? You can't trust the gold, you know. It's rarely real."

Kate stammered, "Did you say... *fae*?"

"No one kills a fairy and lives."

Freida sighed. "Is she deaf, Gretchen? I did say fae, right?" she asked the woman with the red braid beside her.

The woman—*Gretchen*—nodded but didn't look up from her knitting.

"Fae," Freida said it loudly and articulate this time, like Kate was stupid. "Otherwise known as fair folk, elves, pixies, dokkaebi, yojeong, or any number of other names depending on which culture in this world your folklore derives from, but most commonly, *fairies*. Haven't you seen the fae Prince, yet? Haven't you noticed his ears?" Freida shoved her hair aside to reveal a pointed ear with a heavy, opal clip-on earring hanging from the lobe.

"I met him," Kate said, trying not to react to Freida's pointed ear. She couldn't look away from it. It was like Freida was a character from every children's fairy tale she'd ever read. "He's pretending to be a police officer and he totally kissed me out of the blue," she said, and her cheeks warmed.

A few moans lifted from the group, and Freida grimaced. "Well, that's unfortunate." But she paused. "Wait, he kissed you and you're not longing to race to him, or having dreams of him, or wanting to move heaven and earth to see him?" she asked, and Kate made a repulsed face.

"No way!"

A few shrill giggles lifted from the group.

"It must have reversed," Hazel muttered from her seat. "Joke's on him," she then said with a grin that showed a row of wide, twisted teeth.

Kate set her yarn and needles down on the table in the middle. "Is this a joke?" she asked. "Or are you really talking about a *fae*, like something from a fantasy book?"

"Ah. I see you're well read." Freida smiled.

"Yeah, well... I read a lot when I was younger."

A few needles slowed their knitting. One of the women grew teary-eyed and took in a shaky inhale, and the atmosphere in the room became glum in a heartbeat. A girl sucked in a nose-full of snot, wiped her sleeve over her face, then tossed down her knitting on the table with a clatter and stomped off to a room in the back where Kate couldn't see.

"What did I say?" Kate asked, and Freida set down her knitting with a sigh.

"It's your tone, Kate Kole. We all know that tone. We've all suffered and lost ones we love. Like you have."

"How do you know... I mean..." Kate dropped her gaze to the carpet as the air in the room turned heavy. "I never said I lost someone."

"You can learn a person's whole life story from a tone," the teary-eyed old woman across from her said.

Freida pursed her lips. She snatched her knitting back up and began working twice as fast. "I suppose Palmer was right, though I haven't been a fairy godmother in nearly ten faeborn years," she mumbled. "But first, I think you could use a good sweater."

Kate stood. "I don't need any of that," she said. "Listen, some guy is saying he wants me to die, and you're telling me he's a *fae prince*?! I'm dead serious that I will walk out of here and call the police if this is a joke. I only came here because I thought you could help—"

"Why do you think I'm making you a sweater?" Freida interrupted. "And if I'm going to come out of retirement for this nonsense, you're best off to not ask questions and just listen. We have only five more minutes until knitting club is over, and then we can't speak of anything of the faeborn-related until next week. Do you understand, Human?"

Kate shut her mouth.

"Perfect. And don't ever threaten to call the police on us again," Freida scolded. "We have kindly invited you into our knitting club, Kate Kole, even though you will be dead in a matter of days, maybe even hours. But perhaps, if you're smart, and with some help from your very skilled fairy godmother, you can figure out the answers you need to live. Unfortunately, almost *all* fairies are tricky, manipulative, cruel, and would jump at the opportunity to torment a human. You cannot trust a fairy. Not even us, really. Not even me."

Kate searched the faces around the circle for traces of suppressed laughter, but every woman was looking down at their knitting. Hazel was stuffing her face with cracker sandwiches.

"How can you tell me to trust you and then warn me *not* to trust you in the same sentence—"

"I didn't tell you to trust me. And don't ask me to intervene and save you from the Prince, Human. I can't." Freida glanced up from her work to shoot Kate a look. "I can only nudge you toward the answers since fairies can rarely give straight answers. The fairy-kind cannot speak the name of the place we are from, nor can we speak to direct any human on how to find it. It's the same for the ancient *Book of Rules and Masteries*. It's just not possible—our mouths won't move to do it. However, you seem well read and intelligent. If you want our help, you'll have to follow the signs."

The small door on a cuckoo clock sprang open in the corner, and a bird popped out with a chime. All the ladies tossed down their knitting at once. Gretchen reached over for one last macaroon and shoved the whole thing into her mouth. Crumbs tumbled down her chin into her braid.

"It seems we're out of time. Have a lovely day, Kate Kole, and don't be afraid of using a *real* name."

Kate stood, her ball of yarn rolling off her knees and hitting the floor after all. "Wait—"

"No more questions." Gretchen pointed to the cuckoo clock with her needle again and a lob of macaroon fell onto the coffee table from her mouth. "Knitting club is over."

"Until next week." Freida slid her bag onto her shoulder. "I do hope you survive until then, Kate. But it's unlikely. I suppose we won't get to hear your story after all."

The women stuffed their balls of yarn into their bags and left one by one. Kate quickly grabbed her book bag and followed them out.

"Wait," she said again as she reached the street, but every woman had gone in a different direction. They moved so fast; she couldn't have followed them even if she'd sprinted.

CHAPTER

8

Kate Kole and The Games of Fairies

Wind howled through the night, and thunder boomed over the city.

Kate awoke with a start. Lingering traces of bad memories mixed with the present sounds of pounding rain.

Her clock showed ten past midnight. The apartment was frigid, and she realized the window had unclasped during the night. It hung open an inch, squeaking on its hinges. Rainwater soaked her dresser below the sill.

She rubbed her eyes and placed a hand over her thudding heart, climbing out of bed to seal the window shut. She grabbed two novels from her nightstand, pulled a thick blanket off the shelf, and headed to the drawer in the kitchen for her flashlight.

The kettle whistled as loud as the thunder minutes later. Kate poured boiling water into her favourite mug, twisting the string of the tea bag as the windows lit up with a flash of lightning.

She braced for the thunder that would follow.

Her bones became clattering instruments, her blood rushing through her veins as the sound cracked over her apartment, rumbling the floor below her. She couldn't bring her feet to move until the thunder died away.

When the noise became an echo in the distance, she crept to collect her blanket, flashlight, and tea, and she went to the coat closet beside the pantry. She crawled inside and sat on the pillow she left there, closing the door quietly behind her. When the flashes of light were blocked and the noise was muted, she felt like she could take in a full breath again.

It was on nights like tonight that Kate felt she was a child. She was still that little girl hiding in the backseat of a car. She was still laying in that hospital bed, confused about where everybody was. She still liked popsicles and ice cream and wanted to read picture books about dragons past her bedtime.

It was on nights like tonight that Kate wondered if she was still stuck in that day, and if everything in her life since that point had only been a dream.

Kate organized her blanket over her legs, clicked on her flashlight, flipped open her book, and got lost in the novel about a boy who could speak with dragons. He became the Dragon King. He led dragon armies, and he spared the dragons from disaster.

During the long hours of the night, Kate read by flashlight beneath the blanket, whispering the words of the story out loud and scribbling notes in the margins of the pages. She made it through the entire book from cover to cover before dawn. She moved on to the next one just as the wind went quiet and hazy white sunlight peeked below the closet door.

Kate cracked the door open and peered out with tired eyes. Glittering morning light rolled over her apartment floor like a carpet inviting her out. She tossed the blanket and books ahead of her and crawled into the kitchen, moaning at the ache in her legs. She went to the window first. All traces of the storm had vanished from the sky, leaving a milky blue horizon speckled with cottony clouds.

The redhead girl was nowhere to be seen across the street. A young man with tanned skin and a bun of dark curly hair ate breakfast at the diner. A hoodie peeked from beneath his jean jacket. Kate watched the eggs on his plate disappear until someone sat down across from him and cut off her view.

The morning was quiet as Kate headed downstairs and filled the café with the aroma of freshly brewed coffee. Tales of dragons lingered in her mind, but they faded away as reality set back in, leaving her with holes in her own story and unanswered questions.

She finished sanding the counter and dragged over a can of deep green paint. She swept and mopped the floors until they sparkled, then hung the artwork she and Lily had picked out from the thrift store last week. Last, she dusted off the old fireplace in the corner now that it had passed inspection.

Heavy boxes rested by the front door in a pyramid. The two largest paintings leaned against the wall, waiting for Lily to find time to help Kate lift them. The rest of the mugs had to be unpacked, and the windows still needed to be washed.

Kate kept herself from thinking about mean smiles and old women knitting for as long as she could. But when noon arrived, and the floors were clean, and the counter was painted, and the coffee was gone, Kate folded her arms and shouted, "What do you mean, *'the fae Prince has come to kill you'*?!"

Lily burst through the café door in jeans and a hoodie, and Kate jumped. "Are you crazy?!" Lily accused, waving her phone in the air. "What's *wrong* with you?"

For the first time since before knitting club, Kate realized she was supposed to meet Lily here yesterday.

"Why have you been sending me all these crazy texts?!" Lily shouted again, and Kate's brows furrowed as she took Lily's phone.

A conversation filled the screen:

1:30pm: **Lily**: Where are you? I've been waiting here for like thirty minutes.

1:45pm: **Kate**: Kate is unfortunately occupied and cannot make your very important appointment. Apologies, impatient human.

1:47pm: **Lily**: Are you trying to be funny?

1:50pm: **Kate**: Very.

1:55pm: **Lily**: Get over here so we can talk. I want to go to bed.

2:15pm: **Kate**: A human sleeping in the middle of the day? How odd. And how unproductive.

2:17pm: **Lily**: Seriously, Kate, I was on shift all night and this morning. Can you just get here?

2:45pm: **Kate**: Kate Kole doesn't know how to knit. Perhaps you should teach her before you go to bed.

2:48pm: **Lily**: Seriously, Kate?

3:35pm: **Kate**: I'm quite serious. Perhaps if she followed the ways of the yarn, she might understand a few things.

3:38pm: **Lily**: I'm going to bed. I'll talk to you tomorrow.

4:50pm: **Kate**: Kate Kole might not live until tomorrow.

4:51pm: **Lily**: Where are you?

6:59pm: **Kate**: Tell Kate to remember what Freida said.

7:01pm: **Lily**: Who is this?

9:03pm: **Kate**: Only fools give real names.

Kate dragged a hand through her hair, making it stand on end. She wanted to march back to the *Yarn & Stitch* and toss a brick through the window. "Crazy old ladies," she muttered.

"Does some weirdo have your phone?" Lily demanded.

Kate handed the phone back with a nod. "Looks like it."

"This isn't funny. You told me you had something to talk about and then this person said you might not live until tomorrow. That's not a joke to me, Kate." Lily put her hands on her hips. "I've seen a lot of bad things happen in my line of work. I didn't sleep all afternoon yesterday over this, and your apartment was still empty when I came back and checked!"

"I was busy," Kate said, remembering the hours she spent searching the streets for the knitting club after they dispersed. She'd walked to Grandma Lewis's house after. It had been late when Kate finally came back to her apartment.

When a heavy pause took up too much space, Kate shifted her footing and nodded to the wall art. "What do you think?"

Lily glared for a moment—assuring Kate the conversation wasn't over. But her eyes darted around the café for the first time. "You did all this today?" She did a full turn, taking in the green counter. "I like it. How long until we can open and get your buddy Ben off our backs?" Her face was still hard. "We need to hire some help," she added.

"We have no money left to hire help."

"If we want this place to stay alive during its first month, we don't have a choice. And no carefree high school students—we need hard working people who have time to be here, you know?"

Kate nodded. "I'll take care of finding some workers. I'll add it to my to-do list," she promised. She drummed her fingers along the counter, waiting for Lily to bring up Kate's flaky day yesterday again.

Lily folded her arms. "Don't you have another class this morning?" she asked.

"I want to quit university," Kate said.

"What?"

Kate pointed to the shelf behind the counter. "I'll publish my novels instead. I'll fill those shelves with one-of-a-kind books that people can only read while they're here. It'll be a great draw in for business."

"You want to live off your books?" It was a monotone question. "I've always been in support of you publishing your stories someday, Kate. But don't you think you've become a little too attached to your pen name? It's like you've forgotten it's not your real name. And now you want to quit university?"

Kate glanced off as her mind filled with an old woman's voice, *"Don't be afraid of using a real name."* She shook the thought from her mind.

"I'm not going back to being Katherine Lewis. People are finally treating me normally," she said.

Lily ran a hand over her neat bun. "I'm working hard to get my hours in so I can take some time off when we open this place. I'm going in to do paperwork this afternoon now that I know you're fine, so we'll talk later. But you're freaking me out." She reached for the door. Cool air rushed into the café when she held it open. "I'm only working a half-shift today. I'll come back later after I'm done. Show up this time."

Kate nodded.

"And you're still planning to come to the department fundraiser with me next week, right?" Lily added. "I know you've got some things going on right now, but please, for the love of all that's good in this world, don't make me go there alone with Connor."

It was all she said before letting the café door fall shut behind her. Kate watched Lily cross the sidewalk to where Connor waited in the patrol car.

After the car rolled away, Kate released a heavy breath and began to pace.

The *Yarn & Stitch* store was closed that afternoon. Kate glared at it for the better part of an hour before she finally pulled out her invitation and scribbled on the back with a pen:

To whoever stole my phone:
Please return it to the storefront on Hanes Street with the purple awning.
Kate Kole

She stuffed it into the narrow crack beneath the door.

Downtown was busy and loud, filled with the scents of crisp air and car pollution. Kate passed the university buildings, retracing Professor

Palmer's steps. After only two wrong turns, she found the same sky-scraper with the double glass doors. The doorman was different, but he cast her the same scowl as the first one had as she walked up to the key-pad with the yellow button.

It buzzed when she pushed it.

A click sounded on the other side like someone answered, but only the sound of breathing came through.

"Hi, um… I'm looking for Freida Nightingale." Kate scratched her head and looked both ways. She gave the glaring doorman an awkward nod.

A long pause followed from the speaker. Kate questioned whether the person was still there. She was a breath away from saying, "Hello?" when a voice came back.

"There's no one by that name who works in this building."

Click.

Unreal.

Kate's jaw tightened. She walked over and smacked her palm against the side door. "Give me back my phone, Freida!" she shouted. But she reeled back when the doorman took a threatening step in her direction.

Kate raised her hands in apology and turned for the sidewalk.

The entire walk back to the café, her hands tightened into fists as she tried to decide what to do next. No one would believe a band of old fae women had stolen her phone. No one believed she killed a fae, either.

No one but Lily.

"If you tell any other humans about me, that human officer outside will die beside you."

Kate moaned, knowing full well that despite any threat, it was time to bring Lily into this madness.

Lily came to the café in the evening. Over a steaming mug of freshly brewed coffee, Kate told Lily everything from the murder of the golden-eyed boy to the knitting club that stole her phone. She didn't tell Lily about the fae Prince, or that he was impersonating Officer Riley.

Lily listened in silence. After a while, she said, "I believe you." But Kate's shoulders dropped.

The look on Lily's face told Kate that she didn't.

The next morning, a pamphlet was waiting on the café counter when Kate came down. It listed options for reputable adult therapy. Kate sighed and stuffed it in the garbage on her way to the counter. She made a set of lattes with rigid movements and spilled a puddle of hot milk on the floor. After sliding the lattes into a tray, she grabbed a new cozy mystery novel from the bookshelf she was saving for a rainy day and tucked it under her arm.

Before heading to the university to find Professor Palmer, she set a hot caramel latte outside the rusted apartment door across the street where she knew the redhead would come out in exactly two minutes. She didn't knock or leave a note.

CHAPTER

9

Prince Cressica and How it All Started Wrong

Twenty-Four Faeborn Hours Ago

The fae Prince leaned against a brick wall, running his hands through his short hair and tilting his pointed ears to listen to his human target. She spoke into a glowing rectangular device that she held up to her ear. The distinct voice of Officer Lily Baker came back through it.

"We had to let him go, Kate," Officer Lily's voice said.

Kate Kole stopped walking. His human target appeared far too flustered. Cress watched her set a paper goblet on a bench as her rhythms pattered. He might have forced one of his own assassins to eat rocks for being so emotional and losing composure during a negotiation.

His gaze traced down the human's yellow yarn sweater and the leather bag hanging on her arm. Her legs were quite slender in comparison to how a warrior's ought to be. Her eyes seemed curious, too, as opposed to the hard, lethal darkness that haunted a killer's, like his.

Truly, the mask she wove for herself was perfection. Anyone would be fooled, especially by how she sipped her paper-cupped beverage. She looked down instead of keeping her eyes up and alert, like she hadn't a clue she was in danger. Even her burgundy hair was loose instead of tied back, fluttering in the cool breeze with the red leaves.

In every way, she did not appear ready for a fight.

Slipping from the building's shade, Cress walked several paces behind, keeping her in view as she ascended the stairs into a large building of gray and black stones. If Kate Kole knew she was being followed, she showed no signs of it.

Humans filled the tight halls with their ugly, scrawny bodies and sweaty scent. Cress adjusted his hair to hide his lovely ears, keeping his sights on his target as he strode into the congested crowds. He came to a halt when he spotted her crouched before a chubby-cheeked childling. The child wiped snotty fluids from its weak human nose.

Truly, Cress had wondered since he arrived here why humans even had noses. They could hardly smell the truth or lies in the air, or the complex history interwoven into their own fragrances.

The childling began to cry in the hall. Cress rolled his eyes.

The rectangular device buzzed in his pocket, and he nearly sprang out of his faeborn flesh. He scrambled to draw out the glowing magical device—which Shayne sometimes called a magic mirror and sometimes called a *phone*. The sticky-fingered fairy had wasted no time pickpocketing to supply the assassins with magic mirrors so they might blend in.

A very close-up painting of Shayne's face filled the rectangular mirror as it buzzed in Cress's hand.

Cress cleared his throat and squinted at the screen. There were two circles to choose from: green and red. He chose red.

"Queensbane," he cursed when the picture of Shayne disappeared. He turned the thing over. "Where did he go?" He put the device against his mouth anyway. "Shayne?" he called into it. He waited, but nothing happ—He released a shriek and nearly dropped the phone when it buzzed again.

The Prince glanced right and left, worried someone had heard his weak squeal. The humans all seemed preoccupied with their own human-y things.

When his faeborn heart settled, Cress chose the green button this time.

The screen changed, showing Shayne's unmistakeable chin.

"Where are you?" Cress asked, turning the mirror this way and that to try and see the rest of the white-haired assassin through it. "I can see only your mouth."

"I can only see your forehead," Shayne's voice came from the mirror. "You're showing me the ceiling, Cress."

"You're showing me your stubble, you fool."

Shayne's close-up mouth spread into a grin.

"Where are you?" Mor's voice came through the device next, but Cress couldn't see him past Shayne's chin.

"I'm watching the human," Cress said, his gaze flickering back to the hallway where Kate Kole took the childling's hand. "See?" He turned the phone.

"You're showing us the ceiling again."

Cress aimed the phone lower.

"Now we can only see the floor."

A growl lifted from Cress's throat, and he turned the mirror back toward himself. "I'm ending this preposterous meeting," he decided.

"Wait! When can we leave this tavern and come help you?"

Cress could see just Shayne's neck now.

"Not yet. We'll speak again once I've enchanted the human," Cress said. He slid the phone into his pocket and turned back to spy as Kate Kole led the childling through the crowd.

Cress shoved off the doorframe, slipping into the bustle of humans to follow. He thought about red velvet cream cake, and hot pepper-roasted forestboar meat, tapping his fingers along his stomach. "Queensbane, hush, hush, *hush*!" he muttered at it when it growled again. He was thankful humans had shamefully terrible hearing.

His target and the childling stopped in between halls where every ounce of human flesh seemed to collide. The humans pushed past each other, talking so loudly that Cress couldn't choose a conversation to eavesdrop upon. His gaze snapped over the throng when he lost sight of the yellow knit sweater.

Shoving his way past a weakling, Cress entered the middle of the junction, squeaking to a halt on his damp boots and nearly toppling over the pair; the human girl—his target—kneeling on one knee right in the cursed middle of the crowd, and the childling who had begun wailing like a dying hogbeast. He didn't have time to redirect and disappear among the bodies before his human target began to...

Sing.

She was singing.

His target sounded raspy for a female, but her song voice was sweet in the centre. On a calm day in the North Corner, Cress might have followed such a sound to discover the female responsible. He had never heard a song voice quite like this—clean and pure.

"Can you keep singing for me, Miss Kate? I'm still scared!" the childling whined.

Kate Kole's soft lips curled into a smile, and Cress tilted his head as he studied it. For a human insect, her smile was pleasantly striking. Possibly even slightly attractive to an untrained eye.

Cress pulled back and slammed his palms over his ears.

"Queensbane," he muttered. What if his human had the gift of sirensong?

Cress turned to leave before he might be lured in and trapped by a songspell, stifling a growl as humans pushed in and trapped him there. But when his target's raspy singing lifted to his ears again, he turned back, skin tightening as rolls of music rippled along his flesh.

"Daffodils sway and the golden sun sings, la, la, la, la. Rivers rush and the silver stars sing, la, la, la, la..."

His target hugged the childling and rubbed its shoulders.

Cress blinked a few times. He waited for the song's magic to rapid his heartbeat, or a trick to follow and fuzzy his mind. But the air remained sweet and clean. The childling stood an inch taller, and his human target smiled again like a sprouting blushflower in the morning. It all appeared annoyingly innocent.

He turned to face them fully, no longer caring if he was seen. How in the faeborn-cursed Corners did she hide her cruelty so well?

Cress didn't realize how close he came to the pair until his human target nudged him back with her elbow to make way for the childling to walk again. His hand flexed and he fought the impulse to grab her—How dare she shove a *prince?*—but the stone in his blood melted as he watched the two head down the hallway. His target ditched her paper goblet in a barrel on her way. The pair disappeared around the bend, and Cress inched toward the barrel. He glanced inside to find atrocious food scraps and crumpled parchment all mushed together. Kate Kole's paper cup rested on top of it all. A word was scribed across: *Coffee.*

"Coffee," he said to test the word.

He marched in the direction the pair of humans went, muttering, "Coffee, coffee, coffee," all the while so he would not forget.

"Are you drinking coffee? You shouldn't do that, Your Highness. It's how the bravest humans poison themselves." Shayne's voice appeared, and Cress stopped marching. He turned once, then twice.

"Where are you?" Cress demanded because he hadn't smelled Shayne approach.

"You didn't end our conversation," Shayne said. "I'm still in your mirror."

Cress glanced down at his pocket. He drew the thing back out, and lo and behold, there was Shayne's chin again.

"You need to touch the red circle if you want to be free of the mirror," Shayne explained. "Otherwise, we're trapped in this conversation forever."

Cress turned the mirror over to study it. "What a terrible, binding spell," he said.

"Only if you don't poke the red circle."

"Well, since you're stuck in my mirror, you should know the human target may have the gift of siren-song," Cress said first. "You three are forbidden from approaching the female now until she is absolutely, mind-sputteringly in love with me. We all know that a female who sings *cannot* be trusted."

A long pause followed. Shayne was still there.

"Are we finished speaking now?" Shayne asked.

"Yes."

Cress squinted at the mirror again. He lifted a finger, and he stabbed the red button with it.

Shayne vanished.

He got lost.

By the time Cress had searched every hall and sorted through the old meat scents of un-showered humans to locate his target, she was already sitting in her class, halfway to the front. He watched her flick the corner of her book as he pushed into the classroom and headed down the outer aisle toward her.

Several whispered conversations came to a halt. Human females turned in their seats to look at him, but not Kate Kole. *She* paid him no attention as he chose the seat at her side and plastered on his most beautiful smile.

"What did I miss?" he asked in a melodic, low voice.

"A really boring chat about character-driven plots," she answered after a moment without looking up. Her speaking voice was filled with the same sweet rasp as her singing voice, and Cress's mind flooded with that song: *"Daffodils sway and the golden sun sings, la, la, la, la..."* It was a voice filled with curves and cracks and likely tasted of the human beverage of fresh coffee.

But what was insufferably irritating about it was that her speaking voice sounded just as innocent as her song one.

Cress's smile faded.

What a clever, deceitful thing she was. When underneath that pretty mask of innocence, she was a cold-blooded killer.

He slid his jaw back and forth and mumbled, "Ah. My favourite." He watched her slide off a pair of silver-rimmed spectacles and set them on the table, revealing her human-y green-brown eyes. His gaze travelled down to the brown stain on the corner of the book below her hand. It was the very book he'd seen in Whyp's memories. The book that had made him believe her real name was Kate Kole. He reached to tap it. "You must drink *coffee*—"

"I'm not really in the mood for chit-chat," his human target stated with a tone as icy as the Queene's.

Ah. There it was.

So, she was cruel after all.

Cress's smile returned, and he released a chuckle. "As you wish. Human."

A shrill sound exploded over the classroom, and around the room, humans stood from their seats. Cress eyed his target who stayed in place, his smile broadening as he concluded she must have figured out who he was.

She tried to pack away her book, but Cress reached for her delicate little human chin, and redirected that pretty face of hers toward his.

"Officer Riley…" she rasped with that adorably innocent sounding, pathetic human voice.

Cress smiled. "Not even close."

He didn't give her time to sort out her feelings before he yanked her chair toward his and stole a kiss, light and feathery and lush and infectious. And completely enchanted.

The human's eyes were big when he pulled away, gazing at him with all the love and adoration of a silver-winged castle puppy.

Yes, she would see it all now.

He was the feared Prince of the North, dangerous assassin of—

She smacked him.

Cress's face recoiled to the side; his lips parted in disbelief. He dragged his gaze back to her, unable to blink.

Never...

Never in his faeborn life...

"Don't touch me," the human said.

Deadly words rushed to the end of his tongue, but they never escaped. Cress found that he couldn't blink. It was her face—Cress was sure that her face was gilded by the sun and beloved by the moon, molded together by the deities of the sky with soft, clay skin and an entire forest in her eyes.

Oh no...

The human's chair squeaked. She was running out of the classroom before Cress could snatch her. He blinked away the fog spreading through his mind. He stifled a growl and stood, marching out and following her to the stairwell. She was too frantic to see him hop the rail and land silently at the bottom. He waited until Kate Kole flung herself down the last steps before he grabbed her and dragged her to the dark cranny below the rail.

His target's hazel eyes were wild when she took him in. In them, Cress saw approximately twenty years' worth of history and triumphs and failures and joys and pains. Though, for the life of him, he *could not spot her cruelty*.

"Kiss me again, Human," he demanded, eyeing her lush, violet-tinted lips that had not seemed so *violet* or *lush* ten minutes ago. "Immediately."

"Let me go." Her whisper sailed through the dimness. Cress smiled at the defeat in her tone—like that of a thornrabbit who fell from its nest and found itself before a powerful crossbeast. The surprise on her face was nearly delicious.

"Queensbane, you must have known I'd come for you," Cress said. "No one kills a fairy and lives."

The human tried to pull his hands off her hips.

Human chuckles echoed down from the tallest stair, and Cress's mind scrambled through rules of the fairy law—including being spotted doing fairy works. Perhaps trapping a human was considered such a thing.

He reluctantly dropped his hands from his target's sides, studying her wild red-purple hair, her oval-shaped mouth, and the black brand on her neck that told him she must belong to someone powerful. Only the strongest assassin houses branded their slaves.

There was also that fresh gash on her forehead from her scuttle in the alley. Cress's brows tipped inward as he studied it, feeling an altogether different feeling when he looked at it now versus when he saw it in the street. A strange heat moved through him, and he fought the impulse to clench his fists.

"I'm surprised you let him hit you."

Kate Kole's face went white. "How did you…"

Cress smiled. Yes, he had been watching her. She was doomed.

"Stay away from me," she said.

His target leapt from beneath his stare and joined the pack of humans heading away. Cress raised a hand to stop her, but he left it there, a weightless thing in the air. And he laughed, letting her get away after all.

"Yes, run from me little human," he invited, more relieved than he could admit. "I'll only play games with you. But my assassins will find you soon enough, and they don't have the patience for games like I do."

The human didn't reply. When she swept around the corner on the heels of the others like her, Cress's smile faded. He slumped back against the wall and slammed his palm against his thudding heart.

No. This could not be possible. No.

What wicked curse against his fairy blood was this?

CHAPTER

10

Prince Cressica and His Merry Band of Breakfast Assassins

A red brick burst into pieces and three fae assassins jumped in surprise. Cress inhaled as he gathered his bearings. He pressed a hand over his chest to check the wild temper of his heart, looking around at his brothers as if to ask them what happened.

Brick chunks littered the tavern table between them. One sank to the bottom of Dranian's cup of warm beast milk, and the fairy scowled.

"You fell asleep." Shayne folded his arms and leaned back in the booth.

Human families around the morning tavern leaned to see what the commotion was. Mor sighed and swiped the arm of his denim jacket over the table to clean it.

"Hey!" Shayne slammed a hand down to protect the shallow pile of trinkets he stole—one for each new place he went: coins, rocks, and other useless human items he couldn't seem to keep his hands off of.

"There's a hunk of human brick in my cooked bird eggs," Dranian complained in a low, monotone voice.

"That's what you get for sitting across from the Prince of Nightmares," Mor said, wrestling a human-mouth-cloth from the metal box contraption and extending it to the perturbed auburn-haired fairy. Dranian took the human-mouth-cloth. He stared at his eggs for a moment. Then he began dabbing them with the cloth to get the bits of brick out.

"Don't call me that." Cress rubbed his temples as a headache blossomed there.

"Why ever not?" Mor asked. "You woke us all up *every hour* through the whole faeborn-cursed night."

"Because I can't stop dreaming about *her*. This is torture!" Cress slammed his fist on the table and the whole thing rattled. "This is your fault, Shayne! You said the kiss would enchant *her*."

Shayne only grinned.

"He said it would enchant her *if she already had slight feelings for you*. None of us expected the reverse to happen—"

"That is absolutely *outrageous*!" Cress barked, and a young human mother at the table beside them grabbed her childlings and rushed out of the tavern. Cress's shoulders relaxed. He sighed. "We need to kill the human target to end my suffering, and we need to get back to the Ever Corners before my future mother-in-law loses her faeborn mind and covers the whole North Corner in a sheet of ice." He paused, glancing at the ruined bricks where his head had been resting. "When did I fall asleep here, anyway?"

"About thirty minutes ago. I was going to wake you, but Mor said you needed rest," Shayne said as he lifted his own glass of warm beast milk to check it for red brick chunks. He deemed it safe and began to guzzle.

"We didn't expect you to have a bad dream and punch out half the wall," Dranian muttered.

"Well, you shouldn't allow me to fall asleep in a random human cookhouse that smells of hog meat." Cress glared toward the kitchens where the loud sizzling of food came from.

"We're only keeping you here until the enchantment begins to wear off. We'll attack the human target as a *group* the moment the magic weakens. You're not leaving this tavern, Cress, even if we have to let Dranian sit on you," Mor told him. "We'd be fools to let a powerful royal assassin wander the human streets while maddeningly in love with a human. And besides, we can watch her just fine from right here." He nodded toward the window.

Cress couldn't help but look out and try to spot Kate Kole across the road. Even a glimpse of her burgundy hair would have satisfied him. But she hadn't come out of hiding in several days.

"And the hog meat is good here," Shayne added, holding up a strip and dunking it into a heap of thick fruit juice the humans called *ketchup*.

Cress made a repulsed face as he watched Shayne shove three more pieces into his mouth at once, followed by a scoop of cooked bird eggs. "Human food is repulsive," the Prince muttered. He pulled his warm milk over and took a long drink.

A second later, he choked on a piece of brick and spat it across the table into Dranian's eggs.

CHAPTER

11

Kate Kole and The Problem of Sweaters

Kate turned her apartment into a fortress. It got more out of control as the week went by. Tools, brooms, and umbrellas were tucked into every nook and cranny in case she needed a makeshift weapon. The only time she stepped out of the café was to see Greyson off at the airport, and even then, she tugged a hood over her face and slipped right into an Uber waiting at the sidewalk.

She kept everything locked, including her bedroom window. She only opened the café door when Lily showed up to help in the evenings as they scrambled to get the place ready to be a real business. There was still way too much to do, and Kate didn't find any decent baristas to hire. Neither of them mentioned anything Kate had said about the fae.

But Wednesday carried something different in the air. The city warmed from the threat of frost, and the sun was alive and fresh instead of hiding behind clouds. Kate sat at a bistro table by the café window in her sweater with her laptop open, thinking too hard about what to write.

She had an idea for a story, but every time she typed a line, she deleted it. Nothing sounded right. Not: *Once upon a time a mean guy walked into a coffee shop, and I killed him...* Or: *On a cold autumn day, a golden-eyed demon strutted into a café and couldn't figure out what a frappe was...*

The next voice she heard in her head was Lily's: *Maybe if you actually went to your literature classes, you'd know how to write a good story.*

"I resent that my conscience's voice is the same as yours, Lily Baker," she mumbled to the empty café, stealing a glance at the large clock on the wall that told her she only had forty-five minutes until the class began if she wanted to go. She'd skipped her classes all week.

Kate dropped her gaze to her laptop as her lips suddenly felt light. It was embarrassing to admit she'd never been kissed in her life before last week. She didn't even tell Lily about that.

When her cheeks grew warm, Kate snuggled deeper into the chair and started her story over.

A horn sounded outside. Kate looked out the window to find an old woman gripping a large paper grocery bag in the middle of the busy road. Oranges spilled out and rolled across the asphalt as the woman teetered. Kate sprang from her seat and pushed out of the café, catching the grocery bag a second before everything could dump onto the street. Held-up cars honked their horns, and Kate cast them a look to say they could wait a little longer as she balanced the grocery bag on her hip and reached for the old woman with her free hand.

"Thank you." The woman's voice shook. Sweat pooled at her temples as Kate guided her the rest of the way across the road.

"Don't mention it. And ignore the horns. You didn't do anything wrong."

When they reached the sidewalk, Kate glanced back at the young driver whose engine revved as he took off. "Can I carry this home for you?" she asked the old woman.

The woman breathed a shaky sigh of relief and wiped the sweat at her brows. "Are you sure you don't have anywhere else to be?"

Kate stole a glance back at her café-fortress. She forced a smile. "Lead the way."

The woman hobbled away from downtown. A cold wind rushed through the buildings, threatening the first snow of the season, and Kate eyed the bumps forming on the woman's brittle, bare arms as she followed. "Don't you have a coat?" she asked.

The woman chuckled and shook her head.

A loud gust of wind tunnelled through the street, lifting dust, leaves, and paper litter into shallow whirlwinds. Kate's thumb ran along her knit sleeve.

Not her problem. This woman's cold, weak, bare arms were *not* Kate's problem. Kate had already helped by carrying the groceries.

She stifled an agonized noise as she set the grocery bag down, pulled off her sweater, and held it out to the woman. "Here." There was no point in trying to fight it. Kate knew she would give in eventually and whether she handed over her sweater now or in five minutes, she would be going home without it.

The woman blinked. "Oh, I couldn't take that!" She hugged her shivering arms to herself.

"I have a dozen more sweaters at home just like this one," Kate insisted. "Please take it. I'll feel better if you do."

The woman stared at it. "What did you say your name was, young lady?" she asked, and Kate smiled.

"You can call me Kate." She turned the sweater over to find the hole and put it over the woman's head for her. The woman slid her arms into the sleeves.

"This is the warmest sweater I've ever worn!" the old woman said, and Kate laughed.

"I know." She picked up the woman's groceries. "My grandma made it."

Twenty minutes later Kate waved goodbye, holding a large orange the woman had given her as a thank you. Early morning sun pounded on the roads, reflecting off moving cars like blinding mirrors. Suddenly the street felt large and empty, even with the early students and office workers dotting the sidewalks. Brittle leaves detached from nearby maples and brushed over the path ahead.

Kate hugged her cold arms to herself and began the walk home, running her thumb along the orange's rough skin. She didn't get gifts often. A small smile found her mouth as she pulled the orange out to look at it again. It was bright and crisp, perfect for eating.

The florist pushed a cart of fresh gourds out the front door of her shop. She nodded good morning to Kate, and Kate stifled a shiver as she nodded back. When Kate rounded the corner, the sweet scents of freshly baked bread and muffins flooded the street from the *Bread Bakehouse*, and she inhaled.

Peace and friendliness ruled the city this morning. For a moment, Kate wondered why she'd hid away all week. Nothing odd had happened in days.

She thought of the therapy brochures Lily left behind last week. Kate chewed on her lip as she considered that maybe she didn't actually meet a real fae and the mythological knitting club didn't really exist.

What a terrifying thought that was. More terrifying, maybe, than the thought of it all being real.

A guy leaned against the wall of the breakfast diner across the street from her apartment. He lifted his head as she came closer. He looked right at her, and Kate slowed her steps. His dark, curly hair was pulled back into a bun like before. He wore the same hoodie and jean jacket as when she'd spied on him eating eggs through the window.

His deep, beautiful eyes were piercing. He didn't look away.

Kate turned around and headed in the other direction, clutching the orange tightly to herself. Her fingers flitted over the pocket of her jeans even though she knew her phone wasn't there.

Something moved on the roof of the flower shop. A guy stood at the roof's rail, basking in the sun, his white hair glittering. He released a deep breath and glanced down—right at where Kate stood. When he smiled at her, it was mean. It was inhuman.

It was fae.

Kate broke into a jog, pushing between couples and apologizing when she nearly shoved a girl off her feet. She swerved around moving cars to cross the road. The knitting club had abandoned her, including her supposed fairy godmother, so the only other person she could think to get to was Professor Palmer. But her feet skidded to a halt when a guy in a black coat and a high collared sweater walked down the stairs of the courthouse like he'd been waiting there. Slightly pointed ears peeked from his auburn hair.

He looked at her, too.

Kate turned and raced for the university. When she reached the block, she trampled the bed of leaves on the walkway toward the teachers' offices, trotted up the stairs, and slipped into the crowded halls. She bounded into Professor Palmer's office and moaned.

The light was off, and his desk was empty.

"Seriously?!"

She hid there for several seconds to catch her breath.

The hall was crowded when she went back out. Students moved between classes, carrying conversations at full volume. Someone with curly hair, a jean jacket, and pointed ears emerged from the stairwell, and Kate nearly fell backward as she tried to scramble in the other direction.

She took turns she didn't mean to take and ducked into a narrow hall she knew. She raced to her literature class, sneaking in with only seconds to spare before the bell went off and Professor Stanner launched into a lecture. Kate tried to quiet her panting. Her heart thudded in her ears as she travelled down the aisle and took a seat at the end of a row. It took several seconds of heavy breathing and her hands clasped tightly together before she could think straight. Her orange rested before her, filling the tense air with the smell of citrus.

The fae wouldn't try anything in front of a whole class of students, would they? Kate swallowed.

"What is with everyone coming in late these days? Hurry and find your seats!" Professor Stanner said.

Kate's gaze slid to the back of the class, and her face blanched.

Four broad-shouldered fae strolled into the classroom. They split up—one heading to a desk in each corner of the room, except for the fourth.

The fourth came down the aisle and took the seat beside Kate. His lips curled into a smile as the weight of his turquoise eyes settled on her—right on her neck, as though he was pressing down upon her mountain tattoo with gentle fingers. His deep voice filled her head:

"Yes, run from me little human."

"You must have known I'd come for you."

"No one kills a fairy and lives."

A lump formed in her throat. She should have never left the café. She thought about punching a hole into the orange with her finger and squeezing acidic juice into the fae Prince's eyes so she could run. Her hands slowly drifted over the desk toward the fruit, and she wrapped them tightly around it.

All the sounds in the room turned to mud in Kate's ears. She was aimed toward the front, but she couldn't hear a word Professor Stanner said.

"You've been black marked, Kate Kole. The fae Prince has come to kill you. And he'll succeed."

The fae Prince's turquoise eyes didn't leave her once during the lecture. He seemed relaxed, patiently waiting for class to end. As though he knew she was trapped. As though he couldn't wait to end her life.

Kate abandoned the shooting orange juice idea and sat on her shaking hands. She didn't even have her phone to call Lily. But she wasn't entirely out of options. She could beat the snot out of the fae with the orange until it was mush, at least.

When Professor Stanner paused his lecture, the quiet that came over the room was painful. Kate stole glances at the guys blocking every corner of the classroom. They were fast; the turquoise-eyed guy had beaten her to the bottom of the stairwell last week. She yanked her hands out from beneath her legs and put her palms flat on the desk's surface.

Kate looked to the faculty door at the front of the room. It was the only other exit apart from the wide double doors at the back where she came in. The fae might expect her to try and run for the back doors. The large glass window in the faculty-only door didn't reveal what lay beyond. The hall was dim, likely empty.

The fae Prince whispered, "Did you know," he stole her orange and set it aside. Kate stifled a gasp as his hand slid over hers on the desk. He laced their fingers and flipped her hand over, exposing her wrist to the ceiling, "that a fae's touch can be lethal?" His gaze felt like an anvil when he met her eyes.

Her pulse beat inside her wrist. She tried to tug her hand away, but his fingers morphed solid gray and heavy like rock, trapping her fingers beneath his. Kate's mouth parted in horror.

At the front, Professor Stanner turned to his whiteboard, uncapping a marker lid with a *pop*.

Kate considered raising her hand and asking to go to the bathroom. Having the attention of the class might shake the Prince—he'd removed his hold on her in the stairwell when the other students had shown up.

She glanced at the faculty door again, and her eyes snagged on a pink string dangling from the doorknob. She went perfectly still, eyes widening as she realized what it was.

Yarn. Tied in a delicate pink bow.

"Fairies can rarely give straight answers… you'll have to follow the signs."

Kate slammed her eyelids shut. She kept herself still for the rest of the lecture. She felt the fae Prince's gaze drifting over her. She felt his hand turn back into warm flesh like he was getting ready now that class was ending.

Her blood cooled as she inhaled, exhaled.

Professor Stanner stopped talking.

The bell rang.

Kate's eyes flew open.

She tore her hand away and jumped onto the desk, grabbing her orange and drawing a startled cry from the girl in the next row as she hopped from desk to desk until she reached the front. Kate grabbed the handle of the door and flung it open, pulling it closed with her on the other side. She twisted the lock just as a hand slapped against the glass.

A set of piercing turquoise eyes absorbed Kate through the window as she took a step back. The handle shook, but the lock held. The Prince's lips thinned, all his smiles were gone.

They stared at each other for a moment. His blue eyes were like a magnet forcing her to look back at him. She couldn't blink. She could hardly breathe. Time seemed to stand still until she became aware of a ticking clock somewhere down the hall.

She turned and ran.

Kate's shoes echoed over the tiles of the empty hall. She came into another dark walkway with construction tape sectioning it off. The glass doors were sealed at both ends, and students passed by them on the other side.

A bang sounded down the hall, and she shrieked.

Three doors down, a pink bow of yarn wrapped a set of door handles. As soon as Kate saw it, she moved for it. She came face-to-face with a paper sign on the glass window that read: LIBRARY IS CLOSED FOR CONSTRUCTION. NO TRESSPASSING. Kate yanked the library doors open and darted inside, wincing at the loud latch clicking shut at her back.

The library was a quiet medley of dust, shredded paper, and splayed books covering the floor. Kate inhaled damp air sweeping in from an open window. Her shoes left footprints in the dust as she ventured into the bookshelf-filled space, peering into the dark corners.

Low voices emerged from the hall. Kate ducked around a shelf and peeked through a gap between books.

The fae with white hair stood outside the library doors. He looked both ways.

Kate nearly tripped as she stepped back. She grabbed the shelf for balance, but the noise echoed through the vast space, and her eyes widened.

The white-haired fae turned his head toward the library.

Kate ditched her orange on a shelf and scrambled deeper into the books, lifting her feet to step over a strand of yarn stretched between the shelves. She paused when she realized.

The tight pink yarn wove around the corner. Kate hurried to follow it as the library entrance doors squeaked open. The yarn twisted around a post and led to a secluded shelf at the back. Kate ducked around it as the quiet sounds of footsteps drifted into the library.

They didn't speak.

The fae were a cold presence like a nightmare Kate couldn't wake from.

Kate's vision went in and out of focus as she followed the yarn up the shelf to where it wrapped around a thick book at the top.

"The fairy-kind cannot speak the name of the place they are from, nor can they speak to direct any human on how to find it. It's the same for the ancient Book of Rules and Masteries. It's just not possible—our mouths won't move to do it."

"Rules and Masteries..." Kate whispered. How could a *book* be the help Freida was talking about?

She jumped for it, yanking the heavy tome from the shelf. Its thick cover read: THE FAIRY BOOK OF RULES AND MASTERIES.

Kate's heart pounded as the footsteps grew nearer. She flipped the book open and slapped a finger to the page to read. The first few lines made her blink—she was sure she was seeing incorrectly. The stress was blurring her eyesight.

She took in all the eloquent text, then she flipped to the next page that said:

...But beware: This act is entirely forbidden.

Enslaving a fairy comes with consequences.
Fairies are cunning, and they almost always find a way out of it. And
when they come to seek revenge, it is better to already be dead.

Kate flipped another page:

The real names of North Corner royals cannot be recorded, as it is the
eternal decree of the Four Ever Corners in section III of the Ancient
Fairy Law.
But the names of all others, including peasant, noble, servant, slave,
and master, must be one of the following, as per section III, so that the
High Queene of the Ever Corners may command them as she sees fit.

The ten real names of the fae of the North are as follows:

A book tumbled from two shelves away, and Kate leapt back, her
shoulders hitting the wall. It was too late. There was no more time. She
had no choice.

Kate's heart hammered as she stepped out from the shelf into the
aisle.

Four muscular fae turned in her direction.

"Obsideous Hamma Greystone," Kate read aloud.

The auburn-haired fae pulled a leather handle from his coat, and
metal burst out at both ends to form a sharp spear.

"Snatch her up," the Prince commanded in a low voice.

Three fae moved for her, the white-haired one knocking over a stack
of books in his way.

Kate's voice cracked as she rushed, "Foxen Bristen Tripol, Ammilee
Sel Jeong, Leviden Christa Shomwan—"

The fae with the auburn hair stopped walking. His spear hung lifeless
at his side.

"Elene Sidius Willow, Mariie Emlenton Corra, Lane Esthpen Nor-
quill, Muji Noh Pentipar, Hur Issicar Ashteen—" The guy with the dark,

curly hair stopped where he was. Kate's eyes flashed up. She said the last name, "Nam Baek-Hyeon."

The white-haired guy froze in place. His face was ashen.

A dead silence filled the library.

The fae Prince stepped forward with a dark glare. "Human," he growled.

"Protect me from him!" Kate shouted, pointing at the Prince.

The Prince staggered to a halt. He blinked and glanced over to the guy with curly, dark hair.

A long, terrible pause followed, and Kate took a step back, afraid it hadn't worked. But then...

Slowly, three muscled, sharp-eyed fae turned away from Kate and toward the Prince.

Kate slapped the book shut and held it tight against her chest as what she read on the first page of the book rang in her mind:

The first rule of enslaving a fairy is to learn its real name. Once you speak the real name of a fairy with the intent to enslave, you become its master. Once you become its master, you can command it to do any-thing.

This trick works both ways. So never tell your name to a fairy, no mat-ter what it offers.

"...don't be afraid of using a real name."

Freida hadn't been talking about *Kate's* name at all.

"If he so much as touches me, beat him up," Kate added, her raspy voice filling the library. She slowly inched past the group toward the library doors.

The fae Prince looked as white as a ghost. His heavy gaze was glued to Kate, and in his hard expression, Kate saw that she just did a very bad thing, very well.

Kate Kole had just enslaved the fae Prince's three deadly assassins.

CHAPTER

12

Prince Cressica and All His Enemies

Cress could only watch as his human target backed away from the shelves. A lock of her dark, purplish hair spilled over her shoulder, brushing the ancient book humans were never meant to touch.

Kate Kole's big, hazel eyes didn't leave him as she inched far around the tables. Her back came against the library doors. She stared brazenly without bowing her head, and Cress's hands balled into fists. Did she wish to lose her eyes?

"How..." Cress whispered through his teeth to the others, "in the name of the *sky deities* did she know about that book?"

Shayne stood rigidly at Cress's side, his own glare pinning the human. But his hand lifted slightly toward the Prince, like he was prepared to stop Cress if he tried to lunge.

"You have caused me riling trouble, Human," Cress told Kate Kole in his darkest voice. "The pain that awaits you... the lengths I will go to cause you to suffer... And this"—he nodded toward his brothers—"is nothing. I have many ways to get to you."

The girl blinked. And then…

She smiled.

Smiled.

Cress's legs twitched; he stepped toward her, but Mor's and Shayne's hands came against his shoulders. He could have tossed one of them aside, but not both. And perhaps he didn't want to watch his faeborn assassins fly across the room at his own hand because of a human.

"You know I cannot let you touch her," Mor whispered, apology and frustration creasing his face.

Cress glared at his human target. "I will crush your heart in my fist," he promised.

The girl bit her lower lip over a terrible laugh. "I don't think you can," she said.

Heat drove into Cress's chest.

The human tossed the ancient book at them—Shayne caught it before it touched the ground. She escaped through the doors, her burgundy hair vanishing into the dark hallway. The doors clicked shut, echoing through the library where the assassins stood. Silence returned to the shelves.

Mor was the first one to move; he inched over the floor, studying the splayed books more than anything else. Shayne and Dranian looked to Cress like he would have answers.

"Did she…" Cress's chest tightened as the heat began to spread, "*laugh* at me?"

Dranian tore off his black coat and tossed it to the dusty floor.

"I am the greatest, most terrible assassin in the North. How…" Cress worked his jaw. He shook his head. Curled and uncurled his fists. "*How* does she keep escaping me?"

"She must have help." Shayne scuffed his white hair and eyed the ancient book in his hands. His bare foot nudged a paper on the floor when he turned. He took in the mess of tomes and torn spines littering every surface. "What happened here, anyway? Don't the humans know how to keep a study clean?"

"You fool. Don't you know what this place is?" Dranian mumbled, and from down the centre aisle, Mor's gaze flickered up. "This is where the Queene's crossbeast was slain."

"What?" Shayne's light blue eyes widened. "Here?"

Cress could feel Mor's stare on him. He wanted to ask what in the faeborn Corners Mor's problem was, but try as he might, Cress could not pull his eyes off the spot by the door where his human target had just been standing.

Her laugh.

He had never heard a laugh like that, one without traces of malice and the threat of power that turned plants to ash and poisoned the air and forced the heavens to growl. Why did it ring in his ears? Why did it sound like a rusted flute or a cracked harp or the crisp crunch of dry leaves or a broken, delicate wind embracing the heights of the trees?

He hated this day.

He hated her laugh.

Cress flipped the pages so harshly, he tore one. After glaring at the flimsy paper that had refused to hold together beneath his frustration, he tossed it aside, grabbed the next page, and accidentally tore that one, too.

"Queensbane," Mor scolded from across the table in the human academy library. "You're going to lose more than your hair if the High Court discovers you ripped up a sacred book."

Cress slumped into a chair. "I kissed her right on her human mouth," he said. "She didn't even bat an eye."

Mor reached for the *Fairy Book of Rules and Masteries* and dragged the book over to himself. He flipped the pages slower and with much more care.

"It was a good kiss, too. It should have painted the heavens with gold and made the air smell of gingerberries," Cress added with a mutter. He crumpled forward and rested his forehead against the cold tabletop. Perhaps a nap was in order.

"Here it is. This is the trick Shayne was talking about when he suggested the faeborn-cursed idea in the first place." Mor turned the open book and pointed to a paragraph, and Cress peeked up from his position. The lines of dark text seemed to go on forever.

"Read it to me," Cress commanded and closed his eyes, thinking of his fur-coated bedspread at the Silver Castle. Wishing for deep dreams that were clean and did not involve the object of his failed enchantment. Though, he hadn't dreamt of his human target for several days. Perhaps he was starting to become free of her.

Mor's deep voice filled the dark library like the old storytellers of the North. After a few stale paragraphs telling of things Cress already knew, Mor got to the part that said, "The key is to ensure that the human you wish to enchant has a spark of romantic feelings for the fairy bestowing the kiss *before* the enchanted kiss is performed. Even just a shallow feeling will be enough…"

Cress looked up to find Mor biting his lips together. A grin was dangerously close to showing.

"You think I did it wrong?" It was more of an accusation. "Should I have forced our lips together for longer?"

Mor ignored the question and kept reading, "But as with many rules of the fairies, the opposite can take place too, and a fairy ought to be careful not to kiss a human if there are any romantic feelings—"

"How did she not have *any* romantic feelings for me?" Cress stood— his chair screeched over the library floor.

Mor slapped the book shut and set it back on the table. "I can't imagine how." He was too composed to reveal if it was sarcasm.

"Females have been proposing to me for ten faeborn years. That measly human cannot possibly be an exception to my appeal."

Mor placed a fist over his grinning mouth. "I apologize, Your Highness," he said through his fingers. "This is the funniest thing that I have seen all year."

"It's not funny!" Cress kicked his chair, then folded his arms and paced. "She hid her real name, and it seems she cannot be swayed by an enchanted kiss. And now she's enslaved my brothers! I've never been this furious in my entire faeborn life!"

"Yes. I know." Mor nodded and turned the book back to himself. He bit his lips together tightly as he flipped through more pages. The corners of his mouth almost lifted again.

Cress stared long and hard at the curly-haired fairy. "We need to end this, Mor. We need to get back to the Ever Corners. Every day we're here, it'll be worse for you when we go back." His shoulders dropped. "I'm worried about what the Court will do to you for my disobedience in coming here. I'm worried I won't be able to stop them this time."

Mor sighed and closed the book. "Don't worry about me, Cress. The human just got lucky. We've watched her long enough for me to believe she's not that good at this. Shayne is right—someone is helping her. We just need to figure out who it is and do what we do best; hunt him to his terrible death," he said. "And in the meantime, you need to stay away from Shayne, Dranian, and me so we don't learn your plans. We'll be compelled to try and stop you from harming the human target if we know them."

Cress's chest filled as he ventured to the window. He watched the humans out in the cold as deep, rumbling clouds stole the heavens, toiling and darkening with his mood. He was going to wipe out the human realm with a storm soon if he didn't calm himself. "You must swear to silence about all this once we return to the Ever Corners. None of our brothers will hear about how this human outsmarted us, and especially not the nobles of the North High Court. Do you understand?" he said over his shoulder. "I will be the talk of the North if they find out. Which is why I will hunt down every human Kate Kole loves most. I will return the suffering she's caused me." He breathed in that promise. He let it soak into his faeborn bones. He let it turn his will to flame.

After a moment, Cress sniffed. "Queensbane, why does this library smell like old fairy blood?"

Mor stood from the table, picked up the book, and tucked it beneath his arm. "The human didn't specifically say *we* couldn't harm her, did she? She only specified that we couldn't let *you* harm her," he thought aloud. "And the Queene only forbade me from using my Shadow Fairy gifts in *'any of the Four Corners'* when I became her slave to join the North Brotherhood, correct?"

Cress's jaw slid back and forth. "That's correct." He glanced back at Mor. "When was the last time you shadow-slipped?"

Mor looked off. "It's been a while," he admitted. He carried the ancient book to the back of the library and returned a moment later holding a large orange fruit. "Look!" he said, tossing the fruit to Cress. Cress caught it and held it up to study it. "It's a human grape," Mor said. "You have to peel it."

Cress turned it over. A second later, he jutted his nail into the peel and began tearing off the skin. "It smells like a citrus drink." He bit into it and sweetness bled into his mouth. He nodded, pleased with the taste, until something crunched between his molars. He stopped.

He spat the whole thing onto the floor and flung the remainder of the grape out the library window. "It has seeds," he complained to Mor.

Mor was busy brushing dust off his sleeves. "Let's go find Shayne and Dranian. I sent them ahead to gather supplies," he said.

Cress shook his head. "No. Let's split up now."

Mor didn't answer right away. "Are you certain?"

"Yes. You spy on the human and learn who's helping her. I'm going to learn her real name, and soon I will tear apart her home with her inside it."

Mor's quiet moan filled the library. "*Cress.* Why did you tell me that?!"

CHAPTER

13

Kate Kole and Hot Mochas with Hotter Tempers

Kate could feel the Prince's burning rage rippling over her skin on the walk back to the café. But every time she looked behind her, only regular Toronto citizens were going about their business. She took the longest route possible coming home, worried about what might be waiting there.

Lightning burned over the sky, and the air smelled of dampness and chill when she reached her road. Wind ripped down the street, turning the late morning dark and roaring like wailing monsters through the alleys. Normally Kate would have cowered and curled into a ball in such weather, but all she could think about was getting home and locking everything.

The café bell jingled when she entered. She shut the door, imagining a hand smacking the glass on the other side and enraged turquoise eyes glaring through the window.

She took in a deep breath and let it out as she turned the lock.

"Why did I say that to him?" she whispered to herself into the silence. "And why did I laugh?"

"I don't think you can."

She moaned and fell into the seat of the closest bistro table. She might as well have invited the Prince to chase her into a dark corner of the city and get his revenge.

Kate hated her impulse to giggle when she was nervous—it made her feel like a child. It was a thing she'd spent years trying to overcome to no avail. Katherine Lewis laughed at inappropriate times—that was the gossip that had followed her all through her early teen years. She'd been told she was rude more times than she could count. She'd been told she was heartless, too. All because she couldn't keep it together in those terrible moments when she was the most nervous of all.

The scent of old coffee came from where her laptop still sat open with the half-filled mug beside it. She never had a chance to put her things away. She hadn't even locked the café door—it was a miracle no one had wandered in off the street and stolen her computer.

She left her laptop behind and headed for the stairs, brushing her fingers over her chilly arms.

The lights in her apartment were out and her drapes were drawn, leaving the space in shadow. She headed to her bedroom first. The bony silhouette of the tree outside her window filled the backside of her curtains when lightning flashed over the street.

Kate realized her hands were shaking when she yanked open her dresser drawer. Only one folded sweater rested inside—an oversized hoodie that used to be Greyson's. She usually only wore it on Saturdays when no one was around to see it.

She sighed, thinking about the yellow knit she'd never see again, and dragged the hoodie out. Her head was still inside it when a loud knock echoed from downstairs, and she froze.

The knock sounded again. Kate fought with the sleeves to get her arms through, and she crept back down to the café, grabbing the broom on her way. She held it above her head and peered around the staircase wall.

No one was at the door. The windows were being splattered with the icy tears of the sky, sending a clapping sound through the hollow café. Kate inched toward them and looked both ways down the sidewalk. She turned the lock and cracked the door open an inch, letting a breath of the storm's rage rush inside.

Only the violent wind was out there making a ruckus. Not a single pedestrian was in the street, and even the storefronts seemed to be shutting down because of the weather. The lights flickered at the breakfast diner across the road. A second later they went out, along with the streetlamps lining the road, and the buildings in both directions were encompassed in blackness.

Kate flicked the switch for the outside lights, but they remained unlit. She released a heavy breath and started closing the door, wondering where she'd stored the candles. Storms were a thousand times worse when the power was out.

As she turned, someone materialized out of thin air, filling the darkness with a body that wasn't there a second ago.

Kate stifled a scream as a bronze hand flashed past her and shoved the door the rest of the way shut. She swung the broom, but he smacked it out of her grip, and it tumbled to the floor. The fae grabbed a fistful of Kate's shirt and nudged her away from the windows and against the wall.

Dark eyes laced with silver took her in. The fae's skin was as smooth as an acorn shell, his eyes as rich as cocoa and stars. He was as strikingly beautiful as the Prince. Only this close did Kate realize his jean jacket was too snug for his broad muscles and tattoos covered his neck.

"Don't hurt me," Kate whispered, and his mouth twitched. "Don't hurt me, and tell your friends not to hurt me, too. That's a command."

The fae's jaw tightened. "I'll admit, you think rather fast for a human," he said darkly. "But this enslavement trick will not save you from *him*. Prince Cressica has never failed to kill his target. Not once. And the longer his target evades him, Human, the worse their death becomes when he finds them."

Kate swallowed the lump in her throat, her lips shaking over her words. "He sounds like a monster."

A vicious smile brushed over the fae's mouth. "That's precisely what he is. The most terrifying beast of the North."

Thunder boomed outside, and Kate's skin tightened.

She shook her head to clear it. "I didn't mean to kill that golden-eyed guy. You're all after me for something that was an accident." She pushed against his arms as she spoke, but he was a solid mountain of muscle.

"Perhaps I believe that, Human." The fae leaned in, dark eyes swimming. "But that doesn't matter. A fairy law is a fairy law. A broken one is always broken. A killed fairy is a dead fairy any way you look at it," he said, his fist tightening on Kate's shirt.

A click filled the café.

From around the large fae body, Lily emerged with her gun pointed at the back of his head. "Get your hands off her," she said to him. "Now!"

The fae didn't move.

"Do as she says," Kate instructed.

A muscle feathered in the fae's jaw. "Just for this instance?" he asked through tight lips. "Or forever?"

"*Get back!*" Lily screamed again.

The fae slowly drew his fingers off Kate's shirt. He stepped backward, and Lily nudged her way between them. "Go upstairs, Kate," she said through heavy breaths. "I'll take him down to the station."

"No." Kate put her hand on Lily's shoulder. "Just let him go."

"What?" Lily looked back at her with round eyes that said, *"Are you serious?"*

The fae vanished and reappeared before Lily, slapping the gun away while her head was turned, and Lily jolted as she tried to hold onto her weapon. The fae snatched her wrist and twisted until the gun dropped from her hand into his.

In a heartbeat, he was pointing the gun at Lily against the wall.

"You can't... *shoot* a cop," Lily said, raising her hands.

"Is that a command?" The fae scowled, positioning the gun.

He pulled the trigger before either of them could move—Lily's shriek rang through the café, Kate's heart faltered. But there was no blast.

The fae glanced down at the gun, his mouth twisting to the side. He shook it a little. He tried pulling the trigger again, and still—nothing. A low growl rumbled from his throat as he turned it over in his hands. "Queensbane," he muttered to himself.

Kate stifled an untimely grin. An anxious laugh squeaked out. She slapped a hand over her mouth to stifle it, but it wasn't enough. She snorted through her fingers.

Lily's glossed-over eyes dragged to Kate. Her hands were still frozen in the air.

A lock of the fae's curly hair fell from its bun as he shook the gun up and down. He tried tapping it against the counter. Lily watched, and even though it looked like she might cry, a slow smile spread across her face, too.

"Are you crazy, Kate?" she whispered.

"I hope not." Kate's raspy laughter sailed through the café, too loud to stifle now.

"Then why are you laughing?"

"B…" Kate dropped to a knee and flattened her hand against the floor to support herself as she lost control. "Because he's an idiot."

The fae's brown-silver eyes lifted from the gun at that.

"He can't shoot a gun," Kate said, and Lily's gaze snapped back to the fae. She seemed to realize Kate was right. She slowly reached for her pepper spray.

Not even the pounding rain could drown out Kate's laughter. The fae's chest rose and fell. He lowered the gun and held it at his side as he looked between the girls.

"Get out," Kate said when she could speak again.

When he didn't move, Kate picked up the broom off the floor. "Get out!" she shouted, and Lily began shouting, too, raising her pepper spray as a threat.

"Get out!"

113

"Get *out!*"

Kate swung the broom, missing the fae as he staggered backward. "Out!" she called again, chasing after him with it. Lily followed behind with her finger on the spray button.

"Get out! Get out, get out, get *out!*" Kate swung the broom again, and the fae barely ducked it. With one last glare at the two girls swinging cleaning utensils and pepper spray, he vanished into thin air and Lily's gun clattered to the floor where he'd been standing.

Kate leaned forward with her palms on her knees. "Un. Real." Her whisper was dry.

Lily staggered back and fell against the wall, her pepper spray clutched in her bone-white fingers. "Is..." she stammered, "Is that the guy who's been messing with you, Kate?"

"One of them."

"He just... disappeared..." Lily pulled her radio from her belt with slow movements and held it to her mouth. Her lips parted to speak, and she pushed the button, but no words came out.

"Don't say anything," Kate said. "You can't call this in."

Lily's thumb came off the button. She was still staring at the spot on the floor where the fae had vanished. "Why not? Didn't you see what just happened?!"

Kate's fingers curled tighter around the broomstick. "Because no one will believe your story. These guys have ways of making evidence disappear and making people forget what they saw." She stood to her full height as she caught her breath. "Don't call it in. You'll lose your job. Officer Riley, whom you've met, is one of them, too."

Lily lowered the radio.

Heavy wind whistled outside, and leaves brushed across the windows. There was no sign of the fae with curly hair and pretty eyes.

After several moments where neither of them spoke, Lily said, "You can stay at my place tonight."

14

Prince Cressica and The Haunted Library

Cress waited until nighttime to return to the human academy library when he knew his brothers would be long gone. He inched over the filthy floor, inhaling the scent of old books, new knowledge, and something else he couldn't quite put his finger on. He didn't bother to light a candle since he hadn't come to read. Cold air swept in from an open window at the back.

He stood as still as if he'd turned his whole self to stone. Torn pages ruffled along the floor as power moved through the space. The collar of his human officer uniform fluttered along with his hideous short hair.

Traces of mischief were left out everywhere like it had been dumped over the academy floor, and the faint scent of old fairy blood laced the air. There were exactly two scents of fairy blood—one old and one new. The old smelled familiar in a way that reminded Cress of a dream he once had. The new blood was fresh—maybe only days old. It was unfamiliar. It left bumps over his faeborn skin and a quickening in his veins.

Cress tilted his ear toward the library's past, reaching for the old blood to learn its story first. He listened.

Phantom howls rose in the wake of his power drifting through the shelves. For a moment, he thought he saw someone from the past tucked around the corner of those shelves, panting and gripping a long fairsaber sword. Monstrous wails rumbled below his boots, whispering along the walls, and tucking themselves between the tight pages of unopened books.

But the glimpse of the past vanished as human footsteps echoed from the hall just outside the library. Cress unflexed his arms, and the rustling of the pages ceased.

The Prince tucked himself behind a shelf and waited in the spot his senses told him a fairy had once hidden days, months, or years ago. Two humans entered through the double doors in bright orange vests and yellow war helmets, carrying short, oddly shaped metal weapons. Cress tilted his pointed ears toward them.

"The police finally closed the investigation," the first one said. "They decided it was just a bunch of teenagers who trashed the place. The dean gave us the green light to start doing repairs. I'm estimating about four weeks of construction until we can get the students back in here again."

"So, you don't believe the rumours?" the second human asked as he scanned the heaps of litter and damaged books.

The first one laughed. "About that whack job professor who thinks he heard growling in the floor? No way! Do you?"

The first human released a strained laugh. His eyes nervously darted up to the cobwebs in the corners. "No."

Cress crept to the back shelf where the ancient *Fairy Book of Rules and Masteries* hid. Once he ensured it had not been tampered with again, he turned for the open window and noticed a piece of yarn on the floor. He shrank to pick it up, rolling it between his fingers. He sniffed it and held back a faeborn curse.

Fairy yarn.

He stuffed it into his pocket and hopped out the window.

Cold bit his bare arms as he marched beneath the stars, pulling a slip of parchment from his pocket. He read an address in his own elegant script, and he headed to a building with seven identical human chariots on wheels outside marked by the human brotherhood of officers.

"You're here." Officer Westbow leaned back in his office chair as Cress entered the police building. "We thought maybe you changed your mind about the transfer."

"I've been ill. Can you tell me the name of whoever lives here?" Cress handed over the parchment. He hadn't time to waste on humouring these charmless fools like he did on his first day in the realm. And this officer in particular was chatty.

Officer Westbow frowned as he read the address. "Sure. But you should really call the boss the next time you're sick. He was pretty mad when you didn't show up all week." The human officer's chair squeaked as he turned toward his large, glowing rectangular device and began tapping buttons.

Cress stole a glance at the dark, storming skies as he waited.

"Thelma Lewis." Officer Westbow squinted at the glowing rectangle. "Oh, I remember her," he said. "Sad story. Are you re-opening the car accident case? That was handed over to the detectives."

"That's her *real* name?" Cress asked, just to be sure.

Officer Westbow handed the parchment back. "Of course. You want a sandwich?" The officer pulled two poisonous bread-coated snacks out of a brown paper sack, and Cress suppressed a snarl. "Hey, did you hear about the deal the Chief is negotiating with Desmount Tech Industries for our new gear..."

But Cress was already out the station door, trotting down the stairs, and pulling off his police hat. He unbuttoned the uniform as he followed streets and crossed roads, breathing in cold air and the dull human stories lacing the wind. He didn't stop moving until he reached the edge of the city.

It took him half an hour of twists and turns and hopping rails before the Prince found a small house in an assembly of trees. An old human woman walked from room to room inside, turning out the lights. Plants and a collection of photos in frames filled the windowsills, and the smell of fresh baking leaked from the dwelling. Cress breathed it in, reminded briefly of a time many faeborn years ago when he smelled a similar sweetness and ate cocoa crisps in the grass.

But this was not the time for childling memories.

It was the time to hit Kate Kole in the place that would hurt her the most.

Cress stepped to the front door of the old woman's house and knocked. Shuffling sounded on the other side. He slid the balled-up police garments behind his back as the human came to the door. Scents of syrup and herbal tea flooded over him the moment she opened it—just a crack. The old woman peeked out.

"Good evening," Cress said, stuffing down the cruelty from his gaze and replacing it with a look that could melt ice and sweeten bitter beans.

"Evening? It's well past evening, son. And you're not wearing a coat," the old woman said.

"I don't get cold easily. May I—" he looked her over—her cottony slippers, her knit sweater with large wooden buttons, her thick glasses. None of it looked threatening—"come in?"

"I don't trust strangers," she stated. "And I should warn you that I'm armed. I've learned the hard way to take precautions. I hope you understand."

Cress's smile dropped at her tone. There was a clatter behind the door where he couldn't see. He didn't leave.

After a moment, the old woman sighed. "Fine. Get inside if you have something to say. But I *did* warn you." The old woman swept aside, pulling the door open with her.

Cress stepped into the dwelling and was encompassed with the aroma of baking. There was something else though... His gaze darted to the living room to where he detected traces of ill intent and human fear lingering there from many years ago. It seemed the old woman wasn't lying when she said she had to learn the hard way not to trust strangers. Cress shifted his footing, but kept his face composed and forced a smile when he turned back to face the human.

"I've only come to—"

He nearly bit off his tongue. She was, in fact, armed—the same sort of human weapon the officers carried was pointed at Cress's chest, only this woman's was much larger with a long snout. Shayne claimed that human weapons were the equivalent of crossbows that shot lead rather than arrows.

Cress sorted through several words, but nothing proper came to mind. Finally, he pointed to the weapon. "Can that thing kill me?" he asked with legitimate curiosity.

The old woman's laugh was raspy, and his abdomen tightened. It sounded far too much like Kate Kole's wretched, spellbinding laugh.

"It can. But I won't shoot you, son, unless you try any nonsense. I'll just listen to what you have to say at this inconsiderately late hour, then I'll let you be off so I can go to bed. All is well."

Cress worked his jaw as he considered that. He was sure he could snatch the weapon and take it from this frail old woman. But if she was anything as clever as his human target, she would probably see it coming.

"You're not smiling anymore," the old woman added. "It seems I've flustered you."

"I'm not easily flustered," Cress shot back. "Nothing frightens me."

When she laughed again, Cress accidentally took a small step back.

"I can see through you, son. I'm not sure why; maybe it's my age. I can tell you're afraid of a lot of things." She dropped the snout of the weapon to the floor. "But I don't think you have any real interest in robbing me. This gun's not loaded anyway." Her grayish gaze swept down his clean attire and healthy body as she came to her own conclusions. "Though you're the most unusual looking salesman I've ever seen."

For the first time, Cress noticed the old woman had a simple, easy smile amidst her wrinkles—a smile that had held up better than his.

The old woman sighed and set the human weapon against the wall by the coats. "You're practically shivering." She brushed past him into the next room where the scent of baking came from. "Hurry on in. I'll make you tea and give you some fresh cookies before I send you away. You can try to sell me whatever it is you came here to sell while we eat."

Cress hid his police shirt inside one of the coats by the door and followed the woman to a feasting table. The chairs looked ready to snap beneath someone of his stature. But she nodded to the closest one and he slid into it obediently. He watched the old woman hobble to a metallic jug and fill it with water. A moment later, she slid a platter of thin round cakes off the counter and lifted the corner of a clear blanket to pull one out. Cress nearly choked on the whiff of sugar that rushed toward him— he slammed a fist over his mouth so he would not lunge for the entire plate and gobble it down right in front of her.

"What is this?" he asked when she set a thin round cake before him on a paper cloth.

"It's a freshly baked chocolate chip cookie." The old woman pulled a tin box from the cupboard and walked over to the metal jug.

Cress poked the thin cake. Dark brown chunks speckled the surface. It didn't look like bread.

He had never smelled something so beautifully intoxicating in his entire faeborn life.

"Is this poisoned? Are there any tricks hiding in this *freshly baked chocolate chip cookie*?" he challenged.

The old woman shot him a scowl for even suggesting such a thing, and for some reason Cress slammed his mouth shut and sat up a little straighter.

"Why in the world would you ask me that?" Thelma Lewis tilted the metal jug to fill a goblet with steaming water, and Cress eyed the *freshly baked chocolate chip cookie*. His insides ached to try it. His mind warned him not to.

"Where I come from, tricks are hidden in everything. If you're not careful, you'll have your memories stolen, your back stabbed, and your whole life taken away." Still, he lifted the cookie and turned it over, studying the flat underside.

A goblet of tea was set before him, giving off the warmth of peppermint that reminded Cress of spearflower petal soup back home. The old woman's chair creaked when she sat down across from him.

"I'm sorry to hear that. It sounds like you come from a terrible place. I'm sure your life hasn't been easy," she said, and Cress's turquoise gaze darted up to her.

He watched her sip her own goblet of tea.

He watched her lift a paper cloth to dab her mouth afterward.

He watched her arms shake as she lifted herself and fetched a cup of honey from the cupboard.

Cress's hand tightened around his *freshly baked chocolate chip cookie*.

He rarely got stuck on questions, but he could think of nothing else now: Why didn't these humans appear cruel? Was this old human woman only pretending to have a kind smile and weak arms? Was she the one who trained Kate Kole to act innocent and to kill? Cress's gaze slid to where the woman had stashed the weapon by the front door.

Mor thought Kate Kole was only clever by accident, and that she had help. Cress eyed the old woman's back, wondering if she'd been that *help* the whole time.

"Why don't we play a game?" Cress suggested as the woman returned and set the honey before him. He tried not to notice that it smelled the same as Kate Kole in this house—warm honey and powdery hair soaps. "How about we ask each other three questions. They can be any questions at all, but we *must* answer honestly."

"Sure. How about we start by telling each other our names?" the old woman suggested, and Cress lost his smile again.

"What?" he growled. "Our *real* names?"

"Yes. I'm Thelma Lewis. But most people just call me *Grandma Lewis*."

Cress felt his veins thicken with power as he opened his mouth to speak this human's name, to command her to tell him everything about Kate Kole and her accomplices, but the old woman spoke again first.

"Let me ask you the first question. Who raised you to believe that everything in the world is a trick and everyone is trying to hurt you?" she asked.

The hairs on Cress's arms lifted as he realized how dangerously close he was to breaking a fairy law. Queene Levress would cut out his tongue if he mentioned her to the humans—especially human assassins.

"That I cannot say," he admitted.

"Well, so much for answering our questions honestly. You have *'a hard upbringing'* written all over you, son. It doesn't take an old, experienced woman to see that. You have scars on the back of your hands and coldness in your eyes. I can only imagine the things you've seen."

Cress looked away and took a sip of his tea.

"I have two granddaughters, you know," she went on. "My oldest, Katherine, would scold me for inviting you in. She's not even the cop in our family, yet she's the most protective of me." Thelma Lewis glanced over at the photos of a human family resting atop the windowsill. "She's been through a lot, like you have."

A strange silence dragged through the room, and Cress took a large gulp from his goblet this time. He winced. Human tea was repulsive—it tasted of old leaves and dirt. He took the bottle of honey and squeezed a long amber stream into the tea.

"You assume too much. I have not had a difficult upbringing. I have been given riches and glory my whole life," Cress finally said.

"But you were raised to believe that everyone is trying to hurt you," the woman said. "It seems like your mother didn't show you the kindness of the world."

Cress opened his mouth, then closed it again. He took a tight-jawed sip of his honey-filled tea. Then he said, "I was taken from my real mother when I was a childling. The woman who raised me is the one you're referring to. The one who made me wary of tricks."

"Ah. So, you lost your mom like Katherine did."

It was Cress who glanced over at the photos this time. He glared at them. He had done research on his human target, but he hadn't learned until now that Kate Kole had lost her mother.

Without warning, Cress stood from his chair. "I'll be leaving now. It's late." He turned for the door and slipped his uniform out of the coat where he'd hidden it. He paused by the front door. A second later, he reached back and grabbed the *freshly baked chocolate chip cookie* off the table. He headed out into the cold.

CHAPTER

15

Kate Kole and the Fairy Intruders

Kate thwacked her head on the wall when she awoke. She moaned, realizing she wasn't in her own bed, and where her open bedroom air should have been was Lily's apartment wall.

Lily stirred on the pullout couch in the corner but didn't wake up.

Kate rolled to the other side, tangling up the sheets. Her bare feet landed on the cold floor, and she shivered as she crept past Lily to the kitchen, thinking of coffee.

Lazy morning sun soaked the kitchen counters and the overloaded bookshelf beside the fridge, flickering as trees outside rustled in the wind. It seemed the storm didn't die down entirely overnight. Kate checked the pantry and grimaced at the pathetic excuse for breakfast supplies. She'd be fine if all she wanted for breakfast was curry spice and nutmeg.

The fridge was no better. The coffee tin was empty, the milk was old, and even the orange juice sounded like thick syrup when she shook the jug.

Kate went to the window to watch the early morning travellers instead. She imagined curly hair and tattoos, or a set of deadly turquoise eyes waiting around every building corner. They would starve her to death soon at this rate.

Kate took her hoodie from the back of the living room couch and grabbed her wallet from the basket by the door. If she could at least get coffee, it might help ward off the shock Lily would experience when she woke up and remembered how a person had vaporized in front of her last night. Kate sniffed the collar of her sweater and sighed, deciding she would steal a clean shirt from Lily's closet after she got back.

The wind froze her fingertips as Kate trotted down the sidewalk. She hugged her arms to herself and pulled on her hood, stuffing her wild red hair inside as she scanned the building tops for white-haired assassins and eyed the alleys for jean jackets.

She spied on Hanes Street on her way, peering around a building and realizing she left the outside lights on at the café. Cars puttered by, and customers went in and out of the breakfast diner across the road. Overall, things felt quiet. Toronto seemed to still be half asleep.

A mail truck rolled up to the café curb. Kate chewed on the inside of her cheek, contemplating whether she cared if a parcel sat outside for a while. Locals had sticky fingers when it came to unattended parcels on doorsteps.

But death wasn't worth the trouble.

Kate almost turned away, pausing as the post woman slid out of the truck.

A package was beneath the woman's arm, and her shiny opal earrings could be seen all the way down the street. She pulled around a clipboard and brushed a hand over her silver hair, revealing the slight tips of pointed ears.

Freida.

Kate bolted across the road as Freida leaned the package against the café door. "Wait!" she shouted. She panted as she reached the door.

Freida folded her arms to wait while Kate caught her breath. The fae woman wore lush, red makeup again and expensive heels... and a mail vest.

"Summer job?" Kate said sarcastically when she could speak.

Freida smiled. "Congratulations, Human," she said. "I'm pleased you're still alive. When you missed knitting club yesterday, we assumed you were dead."

"Where's my phone?"

"Ah. That thing." Freida dug into her vest pocket and drew it out. She tossed it, and Kate scrambled to catch it before it smashed on the pavement.

"Don't you think I would have needed this if you wanted me to survive?" Kate asked, sticking the phone in her own pocket for safe keeping. "I've been followed for days, threatened, and attacked. You stole my one way of communicating with my friend who could help me."

"You're wrong, Human. That thing wouldn't have saved you if the Prince had gotten his hands on you." Freida nodded to Kate's pocket. "So, tell me, how did you do it? How did you live through the week?"

"Well, I found that book," she started, "and I—"

"You enslaved them," Freida interrupted with a weird grin. "Didn't you?!"

"All but the Prince."

Freida burst out laughing so loud, Kate was sure everyone down the street could hear.

"Hazel owes me fifty human dollars," Freida said, wiping a tear from her eye. "The Prince of the North will tear the whole city apart now, I imagine. I heard he has a temper." She sighed through her smile. "You better prepare your house, Human goddaughter. You'll need ingredients to bake bread, fresh honey from a hive, cold iron butterknives, and... hmm..."

Freida lifted the package from the door and shoved it against Kate's chest. "This."

Kate turned the package over in her hands. "I thought we weren't supposed to talk about anything fairy related until knitting club?" she said as she tore it open.

"Oh, we're not. I should cut your tongue out for bringing it up," Freida admitted.

Kate made an odd laughing sound.

Freida didn't seem like she was kidding.

A pink sweater tumbled out of the package when Kate tipped it upside down. She held it up, her thumb brushing over the snuggly yarn. A smile broke out across her mouth.

"Is this for me?"

Freida pulled her mail bag onto her shoulder. "It should do the trick," she said.

Kate lowered the gift. "A sweater isn't going to save me. I've successfully ticked off four fae assassins." At the thought of those assassins, she stole a look both ways down the street.

"Yes, you certainly did. You'll be the talk of the knitting club now."

Kate's face fell. "Can't you please just tell me everything I don't know about the fae?"

The woman rolled her eyes. "Or we could cut an apple in half and watch it turn brown. It would take less time."

"Please? If you hadn't told me about that book, I'd be dead already," Kate said.

Freida raised a hand. "I didn't tell you anything about that book. *You* found it and read it yourself. And ask your questions at knitting club," she said. "I imagine you'll live until then. Keep your sweater on."

Freida chuckled to herself as she climbed into the post truck. She revved the engine and drove away without saying goodbye. At the end of the street, she turned left, and the post truck was swallowed into the city buildings.

Kate drew her gaze back to the café. It looked dark inside. Nothing moved, so she dug into her wallet for the key. She flinched when she pushed the door open and it struck the bell, as though it would alert all of Toronto that she was back in the café, ripe for a fae prince kidnapping.

All was still, all was calm. All the lights were still out. Kate relaxed.

Her sigh filled the storefront as she tossed her wallet on the nearest table and jogged up the stairs to her apartment to find a change of clothes. She raked her fingers through her messy hair.

When she reached the top, she pushed the door open and a startled, strangled sound escaped her throat.

A cold hand slapped over her mouth, and a set of mean green eyes appeared. The fae's high-collared sweater smelled of freshly brewed coffee—no, Kate's *apartment* smelled of fresh coffee.

"Do you want to alert the Prince to where you are, Human?" The white-haired fae asked from the kitchenette as he sauntered over. He looked to the fae with the high collar and said, "Take it easy, Dranian. You're going to scare her." But *Dranian* didn't move his hand from Kate's mouth. So, the white-haired fae smacked Dranian's hand off.

Kate gaped at the three fae assassins in her apartment. The curly-haired one with brown and silver eyes sat at the island, sipping from a chipped mug Kate had bought at a yard sale last year. He grimaced after he took a drink.

"What are you doing here...?" Her gaze took in the spilled coffee grounds covering the counter, the puddle of coffee water on the floor, and the heap of wet coffee filters that all seemed used. Tiny piles of random things were strewn between it all: coins, straws, jewelry, etc.

The white-haired guy shrugged when he saw Kate looking at the piles. "I steal things," he said.

"What do you mean, what are we doing here?" Dranian took a threatening step toward Kate. "*You* commanded us to protect you from the Prince of the North!" he growled.

"Seriously, settle *down*, Dranian." The white-haired fae folded his arms. "It's not like she had a choice. You were going to snap each of her bones in half, one at a time."

"I would have let Cress do it," Dranian mumbled to the white-haired fae, who grinned.

Kate looked between them, hyper aware that her door was only a short sprint away. But the auburn-haired fae's words cut through the tension in her brain and sank in.

"Wait… you're here to protect me?" she asked in disbelief.

"Prince Cressica is planning to come here for you. Mor heard him say it." The white-haired fae nodded to the curly-haired fae at the island. "Do you think we're here by choice, pesky little Human? We were compelled to come. And we waited all night for you, but you never returned home."

"Honestly, I thought the faeborn Prince finally got you," the curly-haired fae—*Mor*—spoke for the first time. "I'd hoped he had." He glanced at his nails.

"You can call me Shayne, Human." The white-haired fae shoved Dranian out of the way like he wanted to get a look at Kate himself. Kate felt like an ant in the shadow of his strong, folded arms. He looked as stunningly appealing as the others, possibly more so. He seemed to have some Asian heritage, but his hair was pure white, and his irises were wildly blue. They studied Kate's small frame, catching on the mountain tattoo on the side of her neck.

"What does this mean?" He tapped the tattoo with a finger and Kate moved out from between him and the wall, slapping a hand over the side of her neck to hide it.

"It's none of your business," she rasped.

All three fae looked at her doubtfully.

Mor stood from his island seat and carried the mug to the sink. He dumped out the liquid with a big splash, getting it all over the counter. There was hardly a speck of clean space left on the countertops.

Kate swallowed. "How many times did you guys try to make coffee?" she asked them, eyeing the half empty bag of sugar.

"*Coffee* is repulsive," Mor muttered. "All human food is repulsive." He cast Kate a look like it was her fault. His gaze stopped on the pink sweater in her grip, and his brown eyes narrowed. "Where did you get that?" he demanded.

Kate's fingers tightened around it. "I made it," she lied.

Mor's glare promised he didn't believe her.

Kate turned for the coffee maker and dragged the heavy machine toward herself, nudging a pile of trinkets out of the way. "Let me show you how to make coffee *properly*."

But Mor's mug slammed onto the countertop. "You will poison it," he accused.

Kate blinked. "Poison it? Are you kidding me?"

Minutes later, fresh coffee chugged out into the pot, filling the apartment with the scent all over again. Kate stayed facing the coffee maker as long as she could, even when there was nothing left for her to do.

The fae all scowled at her like one terrible monster with six eyes.

Finally, she couldn't take it anymore. Kate turned and faced them, forcing herself to keep her chin up. "Now that I've shown you how to not trash the kitchen with coffee filters, tell me who you are and what you're really doing here," she said to Mor especially.

Mor bit his lips together in a way that looked painful. He looked off and flicked one of the tentacles of Kate's aloe vera plant. His neck flexed, and a vein became prominent.

"Don't fight it, Mor." Shayne sighed. "You know you'll blurt it out eventually."

"I'm not trying to command you like some heartless master or whatever. But I need answers," Kate said. "You're here to kill me after all, right? It's not cool to leave me guessing."

An exasperated breath left Mor. "My unhidden name is *Mor*," he finally said with a deep voice. "My real name is"—his throat bobbed—"one of the ones you uttered in the library of the human academy. I'm an assassin of the North Corner Brotherhood of Assassins. Yes, I'm here to kill you."

Kate's fingers traced over the dull thuds in her chest. "Right. And why did you choose to become someone who... *kills* people? Tell me the story."

Mor cracked his knuckles, seeming to fight a snarl. "I was born in the Dark Corner of Ever among the Shadow Fairies. I abandoned the Shadow army during the war for their immoral choices. I met Prince Cressica on the battlefield when we were both sixteen faeborn years old, fighting against the Dark Corner. He and I got separated from those we fought alongside, and so we fought together, and we survived the war that way. He brought me back to the North and petitioned the High Court for me to join him in the North Brotherhood." He paused and glanced off. "I did not know he was a prince of the North, nor did I know whose ward he was when I met him. The luck of the sky deities was on my side that day."

Kate fiddled with a dirty mug on the counter. "How old were you when you decided to leave your family?"

"I was fifteen faeborn years old when I left. But I do not pity my past self."

"Do you miss them?" Kate dared to ask. She couldn't meet his eyes. She slid the mug over and dropped it in the sink as quiet came over the apartment.

Dranian looked like he might split Kate's counter in half. He inhaled and exhaled loudly, and he began to pace. His footsteps weren't light.

"Yes."

Kate noticed Dranian and Shayne both glance at Mor in surprise.

Mor went to the window and turned his back to the room. His dark eyes flickered over the streets. It seemed like the conversation was over. Kate chewed on her lip as she thought about his story. She turned to Dranian and Shayne.

"What about you two?" she asked them and hugged her arms to herself. There was no normal way to have a conversation with people who wanted her dead, but the first rule of negotiation in every spy novel was to make your captor reveal things about themselves, and in turn reveal things about yourself to try and build up sympathy. Though, Kate hadn't expected Mor's story to be like that.

"It is cruel of you to ask," Dranian said. "We do not speak of where we come from once we join the Brotherhood and serve the Queene—"

"I grew up rich," Shayne cut in. "I'm a Lord by birthright. But my brother took the family title after I kept getting into trouble. Dranian was hired by my parents as my fairyguard when I was twelve faeborn years old, but he couldn't keep me out of messes, hard as he tried." Shayne dragged a huge crossbow from beneath the counter, and Kate's eyes widened. "So, my parents disowned me and sent me off to the High Court who hired me to kill Cress. The Prince."

Kate raised an eyebrow in surprise. "Looks like you never managed to do that," she remarked. "Too bad for me."

Mor released a quiet grunt from the window.

"Oh, I tried. I hid behind one of the seven thrones and attacked the revered *Prince Cressica* during a High Court meeting. We fought until we bled, right before the High Court of the North. The Prince put me at sword point, and the Court instructed him to kill me for failing my task. But Cress refused and scolded them for wasting my talents." Shayne rubbed his thumb over the loaded arrow in the crossbow as he smiled to himself. "I've been supplied with the most excellent weapons and training since I was a childling. It's why I'm the best assassin in this room." He glanced at Dranian like he dared him to challenge it, and Dranian snorted.

"Right. Well, I guess that tells me Dranian's story too then," Kate said.

Shayne and Dranian exchanged a look, but neither of them objected.

"I only have one more question." Kate clutched her sweater tighter, picking at a loose piece of yarn. "What happens if you *don't* kill me?"

Shayne laughed like that wasn't a plausible outcome. He set his crossbow on the counter with a loud thud.

"We can't return home with an incomplete task. If we fail, we'll be executed," Mor said from the window with a low voice.

The sweater slid from Kate's fingers and fell to the floor. "E… executed?" All the hope drained from her body. Her knees weakened and she grabbed the edge of the counter so she wouldn't crumple.

"We won't fail," Shayne promised, his grin turning wicked. "There's no assassin in any Corner more deadly than Cress. And there's no creature more cunning than a fairy. We love to manipulate and crush small human minds."

Kate glanced over at the mess of coffee filters doubtfully. She cleared her throat. "Anyway"—she picked up the trash can and swiped everything off the counter into it—"there are some human rules of common courtesy when you're in someone else's home. For example: if you make a mess," she turned to face the fae, "then clean it up—"

Before the last word left her mouth, three muscular assassins were moving through her kitchen, grabbing cloths and brooms, and scrubbing the floor and countertops. Kate watched in amazement, even when Dranian snarled at her for getting in his way. She shouldn't have let it go on as long as she did, but she was too surprised to intervene as the apartment began to shine in a matter of minutes.

Kate's phone rang, cutting off her fascination. She answered it without taking her eyes off Mor picking grinds of coffee off the counter with his bare fingers. Shayne soaked a cloth at the sink and began scrubbing the window where Kate hadn't even noticed coffee had splashed.

"Yeah?"

"Where'd you go? I thought we were going to talk about where to list our barista job posting this morning." The urgency in Lily's tone told Kate that the reason she called had nothing to do with the job posting.

"Right..." Kate watched Mor give up and use his jean jacket sleeve to wipe up the coffee grinds.

"Come back to my place *right now*, Kate." Lily's voice sounded dry.

Dranian began washing the mugs, drizzling dish soap over them like honey on bread. The suds overwhelmed the cups.

Kate watched, mind spinning.

"You know what, Lil," Kate said. "I have a really bad idea."

The air smelled of flaky pastries and freshly crushed coffee beans. Mor got the fireplace going in the corner and singlehandedly unpacked and put together all the bistro tables that were left. He scowled about it at first, but after a while, he got into a routine and had the place set up in less than an hour. Shayne arranged stir spoons into spare mugs along the counter, and Dranian practiced brewing on the coffee machine in the corner.

Mist hovered in the streets outside, making the café feel warmer and the hot coffee scent more alluring. But a beam of light broke through the clouds, glowing against the sparkling café windows and showcasing Lily's tight expression as she marched to the front door. It swung open with a clang and her hair fluttered in the wild wind.

"Un-real, Kate!" she shouted. "Are you out of your mind?!"

Dranian stopped scooping ground coffee from the tins. Shayne continued smoothing down his barista apron as he studied his reflection in a spoon.

Kate rushed to Lily. "I can't decide if this is brilliant or terrifying," she admitted with an unusual, horrified grin as she jutted her thumb toward the fae.

"It's terrifying!" Lily assured, folding her tattooed arms. "Can I have a word in private?" Her gaze darted back to Mor lifting a heavy box to the counter. He glared right back.

"We'll probably be able to hear you even if you go outside," Shayne said as he rubbed a smudge off the spoon. "We have very sharp hearing—"

Dranian smacked Shayne. "Why would you tell them that?" he whispered. Mor seemed to fight an unusual smile. He turned his back to them and began unloading mugs from the box.

Kate followed Lily out to the street. Lily's hair was down for the first time in ages and unbrushed. Likely unwashed, too. She fashioned an oversized concert t-shirt from an indie band she and Kate saw two years ago.

"That guy attacked you last night!" Lily said, and through the window, Kate noticed Mor look up from the glass display as though he could hear them like Shayne said.

"Yes, but now I've told them *not* to attack me," Kate explained all over again. "And besides, it's just for a week so we can open on schedule. We'll still hire, you know, a *human* or whatever."

Lily shook her head and pointed at the café. "This is insane. You need to get far away from these people. Let me arrest that guy who attacked you! What he did is no joke!"

"I can't, Lil. Let me just do this my way, okay? We could really use the help right now," Kate tried again.

"No!" Lily's cheeks flushed. "I don't trust them, Kate. And you shouldn't, either! You can't just command someone not to hurt you and expect them to obey!"

"Actually, I can—"

"Send them away!" Lily shouted. "Send them away, right now, or I'm officially done with this café. I won't come here while they're here!"

Kate gaped. "What? Seriously? You're really doing the whole, 'choose me or them' thing?"

"Yes." There was no joking in Lily's face. "Send them away."

The wind grew cold. Kate slid her hands into her pockets and released a heavy breath. "I'm not sending them away yet. We have no one else to help us, and you don't realize the opportunity this is. Can't you just trust me?"

Lily was quiet for too long. When Kate looked up, she saw a strange mix of anger and hurt on Lily's face. "I always knew you'd go crazy one day, Katherine Lewis, but this takes the cake!" Lily finally blurted.

"Gah-p-shhhh!" Kate slapped her hand over Lily's mouth. "Don't say that name *ever* again!" Kate's wide eyes drifted to the counter where the three fae had gone perfectly still inside.

Kate cursed and burst into the café with her finger up. "Don't ever repeat that name!" she shouted. "Do you hear me? Don't say it, don't write it down, don't even think it! Don't help that fae Prince learn my name!"

Shayne moaned and went back to admiring himself. Dranian shoved his cappuccino away and stared back at her with death in his eyes, and Mor snatched the dish soap to scrub the new mugs.

Lily *grabbed* Kate and dragged her back outside.

"Kate! Get it together!" she shouted. "You don't really expect me to believe that you enslaved a bunch of mythical beings, do you?"

"What? You said you believed me." Kate looked back and forth between Lily's eyes. "You were there, Lil. You saw him evaporate into thin air—"

"I lied, Kate. I don't believe you. How could anyone believe those things you said? And I don't know what I saw." She glanced toward the fae assassins setting up the café. "Who are those guys? Please, for the love of all that's good in this world, give me *names* so I can do background checks."

"I can't do that," Kate said. She cleared her throat that suddenly felt tight and dry. "I wish you really believed me."

A beat of silence moved between them, filled only with the rumble of car engines and the distant chatter of early-morning pedestrians. A horn sounded in the distance. A storefront door slammed down the road. A child began crying by the flower shop.

Lily's chest rose and fell. "I can't associate with criminals. So, if you're really choosing them, Kate, then I'm gone." A strange flash of fear crossed her face, like she was realizing for the first time Kate might not pick her. But she still didn't take her words back. She didn't apologize or try to assure Kate that she was still on her side. "Send. Them. Away."

Kate looked down at her hands, thinking about the money she owed Ben. About the bills waiting to be paid. About how she'd have nothing left if this café failed. "This might be a bit unconventional, but these are going to be the best workers you've ever seen. You just watch."

Without another word, Kate went back into the café. She didn't turn around. She waited there, hoping to hear the café bell. Finally, when minutes passed, Kate turned and looked back at the street.

A family crossed the road to get to the breakfast diner. A bird soared past the window.

There was no sign of Lily Baker.

CHAPTER

16

Prince Cressica and the Way of the Pen

Cress was waiting outside the front door the next morning when Thelma Lewis came hobbling out, leaning her weight on a cane. The old woman raised an eyebrow at him standing in the early chill. Cress lifted two cups of coffee—purchased with human currency he traded some young fool for with a pile of pebbles.

The Prince's mind shouted in frustration when he thought about how he'd spent his evening at this old woman's house, and he hadn't even gotten what he came for.

For that, he forced another non-cruel smile to try again.

The old woman, however, went back inside, and Cress lowered the coffees. But she came back out with a thick plaid coat in her wrinkled fingers. She extended it toward him.

"Heavens, son. How are you not sick yet?"

Cress stared at the ugly human overcoat. He hid his scowl as he set the coffees down on the porch stairs to take it and put it on.

As hideous as human garments were, he had to admit, the coat was exceptionally warm.

"I'm heading out for my morning walk. Why don't you join me since it seems you still have something to try and sell to me, hmm?" Without waiting for him to pass it to her, Thelma Lewis took one of the coffees for herself and began heading toward a path in the bush.

"I'm not trying to sell you anything," Cress said as he grabbed his own coffee and jogged to catch up, struggling to clasp the coat's buttons with only one hand. "Perhaps I was simply curious. I smelled your baking from the road last night."

"Ah." Thelma nodded. "That is a terrible lie. Try harder," she advised, but Cress looked up from the buttons.

"It wasn't a lie," he said.

Thelma only laughed as a response. A moment later, she set her coffee on a rock and swatted Cress's hands away to button up his coat for him.

Mor would have told Cress to just say the old woman's name and be done with it.

Four hours later, Cress waited for Thelma at the kitchen table. The old woman came down the stairs with a soft navy sweater in one hand, and a box half her size balancing high on her opposite shoulder.

Cress leapt to take the box before she might tip right over. He set it on the table, eyeing the sweater that Thelma held up for him to see.

"I bought this for my grandson, Greyson. But he's gone to a warmer place for the winter, so you can have it." She extended it toward him, and he took it with hesitation. "It's a name brand, and it was expensive. So, take care of it," she added as she dragged the box over to herself.

Cress's thumb ran over the fabric. This was nothing in comparison to the luxurious fabrics in the North Corner, but it was better than wearing a garment with no sleeves as he had been doing. He pulled the sweater on to see if it fit.

"Look at these muscles," Thelma said, knocking a knuckle off his arm. "Big muscles won't do you any good if you freeze to death, you know."

Cress stretched back and forth. The sweater was too tight.

"Now, onto the next thing. My hands shake too much to write proper letters these days. You need a place to sleep from what I can tell since you still aren't trying to sell me anything. And I need someone to help me do a few simple tasks."

Cress raised a brow. He did *not* do tasks for humans. "What sort of tasks?" he asked anyway, leaning to try and see inside the mysterious box.

Thelma handed him an ink pen with a blue lid. "Well, the firewood out back needs chopping. My granddaughter Lily usually does it, but she's been too busy. But before I make use of your muscles, I need you to write some letters."

Cress glanced down as Thelma stuffed papers into his hands. "How many letters?" he asked.

"Well, we'll start with one to the neighbours. We've been at war for three years now over them hauling their leaves into *my* yard and dumping them there. Last year I had to hire someone to get all the leaf piles removed," Thelma said with a grunt. "I'm too old to stuff them into bags and haul them away myself. I think they're trying to take advantage of me. I'd like to let them know that I see exactly what they're doing."

Cress nodded and sat at the table, spreading the first page flat. "I shall tell them they are insubordinate fools who will suffer the wrath of the sky deities—"

"Don't be ridiculous. Tell them I have a granddaughter who's a cop. And that she'll be paying them a visit soon if they try tossing their leaves onto my property again."

Cress made a doubtful face. "You think threatening to send one measly human after them will frighten them into obedience?"

"I think that's just where I'm going to start. *Plan A* is this letter. *Plan B*—" the old woman smiled. Cress knew the look of a plotter when he saw one. "—*Plan B* comes later if they don't smarten up."

"All right," Cress sighed. "I'll write your preposterous letter. Who else must I write to after this?"

"Katherine, Lily, and Greyson."

Cress's fingers tightened on the pen. He smoothed out the paper again when he realized he'd crumpled the corner.

"I think a letter will be easier. I'll leave them on the kitchen table on my last day here." A water bead glistened in Thelma's eyes before she brushed it away. "I have good grandchildren and they've suffered enough losses. This is one loss I can take care of on my own."

Cress set the pen down and turned in his seat to face her. He felt the North's cruelest cold frost over his eyes, and he was sure he was startling the old woman even though she didn't react. "You want me to write your farewell letters?"

Thelma nodded and raised her ever-shaking hands to show him. "I can't do it myself." She drifted to the counter and filled the kettle. Then she pulled her tea tin from the cupboard.

Cress took in a deep breath and huffed it out. "One should always write their *own* farewell letters," he mumbled. But he turned and snatched the pen back up. "Dearest neighbours," he read aloud as the pen soared over the paper in beautiful, elegant strokes. "I'll have you know that my granddaughter is a deadly, powerful, menacing—"

Thelma's deep laugh roared through the kitchen.

Cress smacked the pen down on the table. "Do you insist on letting your neighbours harass you, then? I am excellent at writing letters, Thelma. Allow me to take care of this for you." But Thelma's laughter didn't cease, and he bristled.

"Just call me *Grandma Lewis*," she said when she finally collected herself. "And only write what I tell you, all right? I can't really send Lily after them anyway. If I tell her what was going on, she'll lose it."

Cress dragged a hand through his short hair and rolled his eyes. "Fine."

"Dear neighbours," Thelma began. "I'd like to politely inform you that I'm aware you've been dropping your leaf piles into my yard."

"That's terrible," Cress mumbled. "This won't frighten them at all."

"I'd also like to give you a fair chance to come apologize before I send my granddaughter to see you. She is a member of the Police Department. Sincerely, Thelma Lewis."

"I am *not* using the word 'politely'," Cress stated.

Thelma drifted over and read what Cress had written so far. She jabbed the page with her finger. "I didn't say that part. Take it out."

Cress released a quiet growl as he dragged the page aside and started over.

It took Cress an hour. After he ate twelve *freshly baked chocolate chip cookies*, drank himself full of warm beast milk, and scribed a note *exactly* as Thelma told him to, she passed him a fresh page.

"Now for Katherine," she said.

Cress chewed on the inside of his cheek. "Katherine," he said, mulling over her name. "Katherine Lewis?" he guessed.

The old woman set down a fresh plate of muffins like she didn't hear him. "You sure have an appetite," she remarked. Then she added, "And don't get any ideas. My granddaughter is off limits. She's way too good for you."

Cress's thoughts spat objections. If only this old human knew who Cress was, his title, his power. He cast his attention on the blank page instead of pointing it all out. "Just tell me whatever nonsense you wish for me to write to her."

"Katherine," Thelma began. The old woman hobbled around the kitchen as she thought aloud. "You are the best kind of human there is—"

Cress sighed loudly.

"—You're kind and caring. You're always helping those weaker than you, even when it doesn't make a lick of sense."

Cress stopped writing. Thelma continued to speak, but his fingers lifted to trace over a warm spot in his chest. It had been many faeborn years since he felt a spot of warmth.

"You were never the same after the accident," Thelma went on. "That day was terrible for all of us, but it was the worst for you. Something like that would have broken most people, but—"

"What accident?" Cress asked quietly, and Thelma stopped pacing.

Rain began spitting against the window from outside. The sound filled the kitchen as Thelma drifted back to the table.

"The day her parents were killed. She was in the back seat of the car. She survived, and they didn't." The old woman swallowed. "Katherine woke up in the hospital and asked for them, but they were already gone."

Thelma stared out at the rain. "It's why she's afraid of thunderstorms," she added.

Cress folded his hands, and squeezed his eyes shut. He'd gone several full days without feeling the affects of the enchantment. He thought that meant it had worn off. But it knocked at the door now as it dawned on him why he hadn't been able to hear any tricks in his human target's laugh.

Why he hadn't been able to detect any cruelty on her when he first saw her.

Why she'd raced across the street to save the red-haired female in the middle of the night and got smacked for it.

Why she'd stopped to help the childling in the academy hall.

Why she'd sneaked outside her building to help an aged woman and donated her yellow sweater when the woman was cold while the assassins had stalked her.

Queensbane.

Cress dropped the pen onto the table and stood as the windows darkened. Icy rain began pounding against the glass, the sound roaring through the small house now.

There was no more time for Cress to dally around with Thelma

Lewis, to try and lure Kate Kole out, or to try new, clever games. He needed to find her, *now*, even if he had to fight his way through his own brothers to do it.

Cress could hardly breathe.

He could not fall *in love* with a human.

Cress stood across the road, waiting for Shayne to glance up from lazily washing a dish in the lower level of Kate Kole's building. When the white-haired fairy finally looked out the window, he almost didn't spot Cress there, leaning against the tavern wall.

Cress waved.

The fairy's bright blue eyes widened. Shayne scuttled around the counter and slipped out of the building unnoticed. Mor and Dranian were still upstairs with the human target. They would catch Cress's scent soon if he didn't hurry.

"You shouldn't be here," Shayne said as he crossed the road. "All my instincts are telling me to attack you for being this close to the human."

"I needed to speak with you about the enchanted kiss that went wrong," Cress whispered, tugging Shayne around the side of the building. "What are you wearing?" The Prince made a face at Shayne's human cooking apron.

"I'm cleaning," Shayne said. "Well, I'm *sort of* cleaning. Honestly, I just flit around from corner to corner until Mor and Dranian do everything."

Cress rubbed his temples. Though the thought of his immaculately trained, glory-receiving assassins cleaning human dirt placed the hottest shade of blue fire in his faeborn veins, he reminded himself of his larger problem.

"I'm enchanted, you fool. What do I do?" he asked.

Shayne grinned with obnoxious wideness. Cress scowled and looked

144

off, fighting the impulse to tear the apron off the light featured fairy and hurtle it across the human city.

"You just have to reverse it," Shayne said. "I did it with Lady Rosebellow when I was a childling. She enchanted me with a kiss, and so I enchanted her right back. Only one can be enchanted at a time, you know."

Cress's rounded eyes darted back. "Why didn't you tell me this before?!"

Shayne put his hands on his hips. "Queensbane, where were you when the rest of us were studying defense at the Assassins' House? Most of what I know of these things aren't even from my childling days at the academy!"

"I was on assignment more than the rest of you," Cress pointed out, and Shayne rolled his eyes.

"Yes, yes, you were *so much better* than all of us. Please, keep reminding everyone," he said.

Cress snarled and glanced back at the building. "She'll probably smack me if I try to kiss her again."

Another grin spread over Shayne's face. "Yes, she seems absolutely fantastic like that."

"I'll have to think of a way to make sure she endures the kiss and doesn't pull away too soon, now that she knows my play. This must work."

Shayne's irritating smile was full and glowing like the sun. "Careful, Cress. You're going to make her your forever mate at this rate. You're dabbling in things you're not good at."

"I'm good at everything," Cress objected.

"You're dreadful at romance. You're like a crossbeast blazing through a twig forest. You leave a mess."

"That is *not* true."

Shayne snorted a laugh. "Well, hurry it up then before you enter the territorial stage. If you can't shake this, you might start ripping other males apart for standing too close to her, and no one wants to see you go through that embarrassment." Shayne tapped his chin and added, "And remember, if you plan to kiss her, don't tell me. I have to beat you up if I find out you've touched her."

CHAPTER

17

Kate Kole and Lattes with a Side of Thunder

One minute, the sky was blue. The next, gray rolled in, and cold rain fell upon Toronto faster than Kate could blink. Water splashed over the sidewalks as cars plunged through roadside puddles, soaking Kate's jeans. She yanked off her pink sweater and pulled it over her head to shield herself from the freezing water pellets.

The change in her pocket jingled as she jogged for the corner store. "What a bunch of babies," she grumbled, thinking of how long the fae assassins had gone on about not having any warm milk.

Lightning cracked across the clouds, and a deep thunder rumbled through the air. Kate's feet came together. The rain pounded down like glass bullets, seeping through the cracks of the knit and soaking her hair. Suddenly she felt a vast space open around her like a monstrous, hollow throat. She felt like she was falling into it...

The rain stopped pelting her skin. She blinked the water from her eyes as she came back to her senses. When she looked up, she realized an umbrella was above her head.

"*That* is an interesting sweater."

The fae Prince looked almost serene without his mean smile. Still, Kate tried taking a step back. He tilted the umbrella to trap her in, and her back came against the metal spokes.

"If I scream, will your assassins come running?" she asked. It came out hoarse and she cleared her throat.

For a moment, the Prince stared at her—differently than the last times they'd met. After a few heartbeats, the meanness returned to his smile. "Not to worry, Human. My assassins have not let you out of their sight since you left your dwelling. Shayne is currently perched on the rooftop across the street with his crossbow aimed at my heart," he said.

Kate's eyes widened and she turned to look, but the Prince's umbrella was in the way.

"It's the only reason I haven't killed you yet. It's why I haven't so much as touched you since our encounter in the academy library," he added. "But I'll find a way around it."

"Why are you here now then? Do you *want* to get your butt kicked by your friends?" Kate tightened her fingers around her sweater.

"We need to have a discussion, Kate Kole," he said. "Just a few words."

"No thank you. I'm fully aware you want to trick me," she said. She leaned sideways and stole a look at the building tops behind her, but she couldn't spot the fae assassins.

"Of course I do." The Prince smiled, but his turquoise eyes darkened. "However, first I want to know what in the faeborn-cursed world you're doing making my assassins wash dishes."

He was worried about the dishes? Kate could have laughed.

"Honestly, I think they sort of like it," she said, abandoning her hunt for the fae in the street.

"They do *not*. I assure you. And they will get revenge."

"We'll see."

The rain picked up again, pattering the umbrella with shallow thuds. Only Kate was shielded because of how the Prince had the canopy tilted. Rainwater saturated his silky hair, running down his face in clear beads. Kate tried not to stare, but she was sure there wasn't a face in existence as symmetrical as his. With his pretty eyes, he looked like he was in a luxury perfume commercial, and the rain was staged. Kate cleared her throat and dropped her gaze to the sidewalk.

A loud boom of thunder made her jump. Her back slammed the umbrella, nearly toppling them both over, but the umbrella scooped her up before she could fall. The Prince's hand was out, his fingers dangerously close to touching her arm like he'd been about to catch her. He tore it back and shoved it in his pocket.

Kate hid her own trembling hands beneath the damp sweater, and an odd look crossed the Prince's face.

"That's right," he said more to himself. "You're afraid of the sky's anger." His voice seemed bored, but there was a strange edge to it.

"What?"

Even though the Prince was a cold presence, Kate's skin turned warm when his gaze travelled up from her hidden arms to her face. It was a sensation she'd never felt prior to him showing up in a police uniform in the café.

She scratched behind her ear. "Listen, I'll release your assassin friends from their chores if you all promise to leave here and never come back." She quickly raised a hand. "Actually, if I could just keep them for one more week though, that would be great."

The Prince laughed, deep and sweet. Joyous and twisted. It reminded her of the sound of a deep classical bass string being plucked. Kate set her jaw.

"Stop doing that," she said.

"Doing what, Human?"

"I don't know—whatever it is you're trying to do with your soft kisses, and your warm stare, and your deep laugh." She hugged her cold arms tighter to herself, and the Prince blinked in surprise.

149

"Do those things make you feel something?" He stepped under the umbrella with her, escaping the rain. "Anything at all?"

Something doubled over in Kate's chest. "What? No—"

"Kiss me, Human. I'll leave you alone after that," he promised, and Kate made a revolted face.

"Not a chance."

He bit his lips together like he was fighting the impulse to shout. "Can we make a bargain for it?" His hand came out of his pocket with a handful of gold coins. He extended them toward her. "Please. Just one quick, easy kiss. And in return, I'll fill your purse with this treasure."

"Why would I want a bunch of fake coins?"

"Fake? Take one and see for yourself what it is." The Prince rolled a coin from the pile and pinched it between his fingers. When Kate didn't reach for it, he gently pressed it against her chin, keeping the cool metal as a barrier between her skin and his thumb.

"Does it feel real?" he asked.

Kate blinked. She swatted his hand away. "It feels like a trap."

He stepped so close they were nearly against each other, his eyes vivifying. A warm wind ruffled the damp hair at Kate's neck. The back of her shoulders bumped his umbrella again.

"Please," he whispered, lifting the coin and placing it delicately on her shoulder where it balanced. His tone was sugary and tender, and for a moment, Kate thought about doing it.

But *no*. No way, no chance, no.

"Last time you never bothered to ask," she pointed out. "And I hate pushy guys."

"Well *last time* I didn't have a crossbow pointed at my heart ready to shoot if I so much as touched you." Sharpness returned to his irises.

"Ahhh." Kate smiled as she realized. "So, you need *me* to kiss *you*." She laughed, her scratchy voice echoing through the pattering rain. The coin fell off her shoulder and rolled down the sidewalk.

The Prince frowned as she moved to walk around him now that she knew what he wanted, but the umbrella cut her off again. Kate let out an exasperated sigh.

"Why don't you just go home, your royal-pompous-fae-highness? I already told you I'll give you your assassins back if you leave forever. It's not that difficult to just say yes."

A muscle feathered in his jaw. "Do you really think I would bring my brothers home to a cruel death? I kill for a living, Human. But I'm not entirely heartless."

It was Kate who frowned this time. She glanced back toward the café. "Then we should come up with a plan. Obviously, I can't roll over and die for you, so if that means those assassins can't go home, then you should leave them here with me. And you should go home alone."

The Prince's lips thinned. "I would never leave my brothers under the rule of a human."

Kate nodded. "Then we'll keep doing this."

He stared. Stared, stared, stared. His gaze felt like a splash of warm water in the cold. "I have one last question before I let you go," he finally said, and Kate reluctantly gave him the last ounce of her attention she could manage. "Tell me, where in the name of the sky deities did you get that *sweater*?"

A slow smile spread across Kate's face, and she tried to smother it by biting on her lip. It was a terrible time to laugh. "No," she said.

The Prince glared at her smiling mouth.

Kate shoved the umbrella pole to put it back over the Prince. "Now, since you can't touch me, I'll be on my way, your royal fae Prince-ness." She brushed by him toward the corner store, tapping her pocket to make sure her change was still there.

"My unhidden name is Cress," he said without turning around. "I am not *your* Prince. Do not insult me with such ridiculous titles."

Kate chuckled as she headed into the store, dragging in a puddle of water with her. But as soon as the door closed at her back, her smile faded, her pulse pounded, and she let out the breath she was holding.

It took her a few minutes to find milk and pay. When she came out of the store, the fae Prince was gone. A plain flat rock sat on the sidewalk in the exact spot where the gold coin had rolled away. Kate huffed in disbelief.

Thankfully the sky held in its rain as Kate jogged back to the café. She brushed a finger over her chest. Her lungs felt tight, and her hands were shaking again.

She came in to find three rain-sprinkled fae assassins focussed uncharacteristically hard on little tasks, apart from Shayne, who lounged across the entire countertop on his back like he'd been taking a nap there.

"Oh, just stop." Kate rolled her eyes. "I know you were all out there watching me."

She carried the milk over to the fridge. Shayne perked up at the sight of it and scrambled to sit. His legs dangled over the counter's edge, and his bare heels thudded against the cupboards.

"I don't know if my friend is going to be here next week for the café's opening day, but we're going to go ahead with it either way. I owe some people a lot of money," Kate told them. "I'll convince Lily to come back later."

"What's so important about that human friend? Why must you keep her?" Shayne asked as he dragged over his milk mug and eyed the fridge.

Kate thought about answering, but she turned to Mor instead. "Tell me why your Prince keeps trying to kiss me," she demanded.

"He's trying to enchant you," Mor blurted, then chomped his mouth shut and flexed his jaw.

"How many more games is the Prince going to play before he gives up?" she asked. None of the fae spoke, so Kate put her hands on her hips. "Tell me when he'll give up!"

All at once three voices spoke,

"Never."

"Never."

"*Never.*"

Kate tossed her sweater on the hooks to dry and wrestled a hand through her wet, tangled hair. She stared at Freida's intricate knitting pattern on the sweater's sleeve, and a beat of frustration moved through her. She had to wait six more days to meet with the knitting club when she had so many new questions about the Prince. Or... *Cress*, as he'd called himself.

Cress.

For a moment, her mind's eye filled with his turquoise eyes going soft, his lips parting, and his tone changing as he stepped in and asked her to kiss him—

She smacked her warm forehead. Kate couldn't decide if she was flattered or repulsed. Maybe a shameful bit of both.

"Were you telling the truth when you said that if you go home, you're going to get killed?" she asked the assassins puttering about. She rubbed her stinging skin, realizing she smacked herself too hard.

"Yes," Shayne said. "But only if we fail."

She nodded. "I'm sorry that's the fate waiting for you. But I don't plan on offering myself as a sacrifice. In fact, I'm changing my orders. I don't want you to just protect me from the Prince, I want you to protect me from *everything*. If he—or anyone else—is trying to trick me, I want you to give me a heads up. If someone tries to kill me, I want you to stop them. And since that means you can't go back to where you came from"—she glanced at the bookshelf behind the counter and pulled three novels from her collection: all popular fae fantasy books— "you might as well get reading. You should really know how humans perceive a fae if you're going to live among us." She walked around and smacked a book against each of the fae's chests. Dranian lifted his book in disgust.

"Human literature," he grumbled. "How preposterous."

Thirty minutes later, three assassins sat around the café sipping warm pumpkin spice lattes and flipping the pages of their novels quietly.

Kate wandered up to her apartment and closed the door behind her when she was inside.

For a moment she stood in the silence. The rain picked up again, and in the distance, thunder called her name. She wondered when the fall thunderstorms were going to stop. They'd lasted longer than ever this year. Kate craved cool snow, clear skies, and a storefront filled with happy people sipping piping hot drinks.

She sank to the floor and hugged her knees to herself, sorting through the sounds of the storm to hear Shayne's question in her mind,

"What's so important about that human friend? Why must you keep her?"

THE
BACKSTORIES
THE &
FRONTSTORIES

CHAPTER

18

Kate Kole and The Week Lily Baker was (Unofficially) Adopted

When Lily Baker was led into the grade seven classroom of Sir Joseph Elementary, Kate put her gaze on the floor like the rest of the students. And there was only one real reason for it—Lily Baker looked like trouble.

Kate didn't want trouble. Her best friend Holly had just moved to British Columbia, and since then, Kate spent most of her lunch hour reading quietly at her desk or out beneath the maples in the playground. She could have tried to make new friends, but all the girls were mean and loud and demanded that you pick a side in the class that was divided right down the middle between Sophia Cuthbert's friends and Layla Meeb's friends. The two sides hated each other, which was why Kate had never bothered to pick one.

Occasionally, Kate played soccer with the boys, but she couldn't keep up with them. And she didn't like being the only girl on the field.

"I heard she just moved into the youth home down the road," Sophia

Cuthbert whispered a few seats away as she nodded to the new girl at the front. A few snickers bounded through the room from people who were loyal to—or afraid of—Sophia.

Kate dared a glance up at the new addition to their class, taking in the set of messy braids that reached down to Lily Baker's waist, and the daring pale blue eyes that seemed ready to challenge anyone whose stare lingered a little too long. But as Lily Baker strutted down the aisle to the only open seat in the classroom, a book fell out of her bag. She stooped to scoop it up, but not before Kate saw the title: *Folktales on Fridays.*

A smile found Kate's mouth. She put her attention back on the teacher at the front, thinking of her own copy of *Folktales on Fridays* hiding on her bedroom bookshelf with its margins filled with scribbled notes, its folded down page corners, and the three bookmarks she kept to mark the passages she loved most.

It seemed Lily Baker liked to read.

Shouts rang from behind the portables at lunch hour recess. Kate only heard them after chasing a soccer ball that far. She paused when she picked up the ball, listening to the threats of high-pitched girls.

"What did you call me?" Sophia Cuthbert's voice was unmistakeable.

"I said you're *scared* to face me yourself. You really had to bring a whole pack of girls to back you up?"

Kate rounded the corner of the portables in time to see Sophia grab Lily Baker by the braids and start shoving. The rest of Sophia's pack moved; clawing, shrieking, and some too shaken to do anything but watch.

The ball grew heavy in Kate's hands. And when she raised it—aiming right between Sophia Cuthbert's gray eyes—she picked her side after all.

Sophia screamed as blood spurted from her nose. The soccer ball spun off, and all the girls turned toward Kate like a pack of wolves.

Lily Baker blinked at first. Then, she burst out laughing. "Are y..." she interrupted herself with a cackle. "Are you *crazy*?" she shouted to Kate. "I wasn't really going to..." she bent over, holding her stomach as she laughed so hard, she shook. "I wasn't really going to hurt her; I was just talking smack!"

That was the day Kate went home with a bruise on her lip, a smile on her face, and a detention notice for her parents to sign. It was also the day she told her mother she wanted a sister.

CHAPTER

19

Prince Cressica and The Thing That Happened
Seventeen Faeborn Years Ago

Cress wouldn't let go of the sharp emerald-green branches even when his tiny faeborn hands stung. He climbed until the treetop teetered, and he released a giggle at the flutter in his stomach. There he gazed at the crystal skies of the Ever Corner of the North, smiling at the sky deities and the silk birds dancing in the heavens.

"Cressica!" his mother scolded as she emerged from their house of gold-spun straw. She repositioned the large pot balanced on her hip. "Come down from there, now!"

Cress began the descent, thinking of rice pancakes and warm lowbeast milk for breakfast. But he paused on the middle branch when a thundering rhythm brushed in from the trees. The branches shook beneath his fingers, and a gasp lifted from his mother below. Cress shoved a collection of silvery leaves out of the way to see what had arrived.

Standing before his mother's small frame was a crossbeast. Cress's six-year-old chest tightened as he took in twelve faeborn males on glittering reindeer emerging from the woods, too. They wore antler crowns that matched the beasts they rode.

"Peasant," a sweet voice sang. Cress inched over the branch until he saw a woman sitting atop the crossbeast. Her long silver hair became wings in the wind, and her sharp nails looked ready to draw blood.

"Queene Levress." The pot smashed to the ground as Cress's mother dropped to a knee and lowered her eyes.

A smile curled on the Queene's face. "You recognize me? Even all the way out here?"

"Of course, Your Majesty."

"I'm impressed!" The woman on the crossbeast laughed. The sound made the hairs on Cress's arms stand on end. He slid down a few more branches and peered through a crack between the tree's limbs.

"Tell me your name," the Queene demanded, and Cress's mother flinched.

"My unhidden name is Glorya."

"Not that one, you fool. Tell me your *real* name."

His mother's mouth moved, but no sound came out as the Queene's crossbeast stepped closer. Dripping fangs came inches from his mother's face, and Cress scrambled the rest of the way to the lowest branch. He crept to the end, trying not to shake the leaves as he came directly over the silver-haired Queene and her beast.

"Your name!" the Queene screamed, making the woods shudder and the grass turn to black ash in all directions. "I have all ten names memorized. Don't make me recite them all."

Cress's mother released a whimper. "My real name is Elene Sidius Willow. But please, I'm not alone. I have a son—"

"Elene Sidius Willow," the Queene chanted, and Cress watched his mother's back stiffen. "My crossbeast is hungry. Feed it all the food you have." Her wild smile returned. "And if my beast is still hungry when it's finished, perhaps it will eat you, too."

Heat rippled through Cress's legs. He sprang from the branch and landed between his mother and the beast. The animal lurched back with a shriek as Cress raised his fists, feeling the low pulses of power growing in his veins.

"I'll kill your crossbeast," Cress promised the Queene who blinked down at him with large silver eyes. "And you," he added, "if you don't leave this instant. I don't care how important you are."

He brought cold wind up from the ground to prove it. It rippled through Cress's long hair, brushing itself along his frost-coated eyes.

The Queene dismounted her crossbeast, but he didn't bow or lower his gaze as his mother had, not even when she appeared over his childling frame.

The silver-haired woman stared at Cress in silence. Her gray eyes twinkled with the same sheen as the fluttering leaves above. Her stare was potent, and heavy, and hot as flame.

"I want him," she said to the males on reindeer.

"Please!" Cress's mother begged. "He's too young—"

"I will pay you for him fairly." The Queene finally tore her gaze from Cress and put in on Cress's mother. An ounce of respect was in her tone for the first time. "You have a powerful child. I can give him a better life than this; one of faeborn riches and glory. I can be a worthy mother to him. I want him."

Cress's hands tightened to fists, and he glanced back to his mother's tear-stained face. But he took in her quivering lip, the straw house at her back, and the dying garden in the yard. He thought about the cupboards that had grown empty and the well that had dried up.

His mother looked at him, and in her eyes, Cress saw that she was tempted—not because she wanted him to leave, but because she knew she could not give him a good life.

But Cress did not need a good life. Cress just needed his mother.

During quiet, candlelit dinners, his mother had whispered stories. Some of them were about this Queene. Most of them were dreadful. He realized she could not say no.

Cress brought his stare back to the gray-eyed female standing over him. "Mother," he called back, "what do you need to be happy? Gold? A house?"

Cress's mother did not reply.

"Give him to me, or I will let him fight my crossbeast as he wishes," the Queene threatened over his head.

"That's not necessary," Cress said. "Give my mother everything she wants from this day forward. Give her safety, a large house, a fruitful garden, pretty clothes, and true happiness. And I will come with you in exchange for that."

The Queene's wide smile returned. "A fairy bargain. Smart boy," she said, seeming to think it over. "I shall do as you wish on one condition: You must never speak to your faeborn mother again. I shall be your mother from this day forward. Your *only* mother."

Cress heard a sob escape his mother. He thought of all the years she had fed him crushed grains, taught him how to play the old harp with missing strings, and how she had warned him of every fairy trick she knew.

Cress chewed on the inside of his cheek. "This bargain seems fair."

"Get off your deer, Chimestar," the Queene called back at one of the males with her. The male obeyed. "You will walk back. The boy will ride with us."

"Wait," Cress said.

The Queene and her males paused as dark clouds rolled in overhead, shadowing their faces. One or two of the reindeer staggered back toward the woods when ash formed at Cress's feet and clawed its way over the ground toward them.

The Queene lifted a silver brow.

"If you betray my trust in regard to my mother"—Cress's bright eyes narrowed and the wind changed directions, thrusting back the Queene's silver hair—"I will kill your crossbeast and ensure you lose whatever power it gives you."

For a moment, dead silence filled the yard.

Then, the Queene's loud, crazed laughter rang through the forest.

CHAPTER

20

Kate Kole and The Thing that Happened to Grandma Lewis

The ground was muddy from melted snow; it stuck to the soles of Kate's boots. The air was humid, the sky was gray, and the trees were naked. Kate laughed as she tore through the sparse woods behind Grandma Lewis's house. Lily cackled as she tried to keep up, glancing back at Greyson howling threats as he chased them with a stick in his fourteen-year-old fingers.

"I'll get you for that, Lily Baker!" he shrieked, kicking up mud with his rainboots. He tried clawing clumps of dirt out of his hair where Lily had lobbed a handful.

Kate reached Grandma Lewis's porch stairs first. The tea kettle whistled loudly from the kitchen inside as she raced up and flung the door open.

"Grandma, shut off the kettle!" she complained.

It wasn't until Lily slammed into Kate's back that Kate realized she had frozen in place. Somewhere in the vast space, Kate heard echoes of Lily start to shout something. She felt Lily try to grab her, but Kate was gripping the doorframe too hard. Lily took Greyson instead, tearing him away from the house.

"Kate!" Lily's voice sounded like it was under water. "Kate!"

Kate didn't respond. She stared into the living room at the man holding a blade toward Grandma Lewis. A mask covered the lower half of his face, and a ruby necklace peeked from the gloves he wore. It was a necklace Kate's late grandfather gave to Grandma Lewis on their fiftieth anniversary. He'd passed away the following week.

The thief stared back at Kate standing in the doorway.

"Katherine!" Grandma Lewis shouted. "Run!"

The thief bolted first. He shoved through the house, kicking over the rocking chair, and disappearing into the back cellar.

Kate's wobbly legs broke into a sprint. Her mind blanked as her body moved through motions.

The back door squeaked on its hinges as the thief escaped. Kate's shaking hands tore the keys off the hooks and fiddled with the lock of the gun locker in the cellar. Her hands were around the cool barrel of her grandfather's hunting gun before she knew what she was doing, and she sprinted out the back door into the forest.

Her mind spun: She would drag him to the police. She would not let him get away with threatening an old woman. She would—

Kate turned right, then left. She spun all the way around, looked up at the sky, then over at the neighbour's house hardly visible through the woods.

Her boots slowed in the mud.

Empty trees and leafless shrubs greeted Kate coldly. Her heart was pounding, her chest was heaving, her eyes were wet. There was every kind of plant and leaf and tree and dirt and bug within grabbing distance. But there was no masked thief with a ruby necklace in his grip.

"It's just a necklace," Grandma Lewis said later that night after the police left.

"It's not about the necklace!" Kate shouted. "It's about a stranger coming into your house and doing that to you! I'll never be able to look at that living room the same way again!" Kate stomped over and picked up her grandfather's gun. "You're going to keep this by the door from now on, and every time a stranger shows up, you're going to have it in your hand. Do you understand, Grandma?"

Her grandmother only sighed.

Kate and Lily sat at the kitchen table long after Grandma Lewis went to bed that night.

"What are we going to do about this?" Kate laid forward, her hot cheek resting on the cool tabletop and her newly dyed wine-red hair splaying.

"We should become cops," Lily said, glancing out the window in the direction the police car had driven off. She'd been mesmerized by the pair of officers the moment they'd shown up with their lights on. She'd asked them all kinds of questions about the bad guys they stopped. "Maybe we can protect her that way. I think I want to go to police college."

"I can't be a cop. I'd have to go back to using my real name, and everyone I meet would pity me and avoid me like before once they realize I'm the girl from the news. I can't go through that again."

"Then I'll take care of you both," Lily said, leaning back against her chair and folding her arms. "This family has taken care of me all these years. We're graduating in a few months, and I have good grades now thanks to you. I think I can pass the police tests if I study hard."

Rather than answering, Kate slid her hand over the table toward her friend. Lily half-smiled and linked her pinky finger with Kate's. They stayed like that in silence for a long time, listening to the nighttime breeze against the window.

They both fell asleep with their cheeks pressed against the table.

CHAPTER

21

*Kate Kole and the Present Hobbies of Knitting,
Book Club, and Fist Fights*

There was a time long ago when the city of Toronto was called *York*. In the days of York, and since, there were whispers amongst locals claiming to have spotted a giant sea serpent-like creature weaving below the water in Lake Ontario. In one of these sightings, witnesses were sure they spotted a turquoise serpent soaking up the sun on a beach near Fort York before slithering into the water's depths. The witnesses claimed the monster was over forty-five feet in length. Though accounts were many, the existence of York's serpent was never confirmed or denied with substantial evidence.

Every city has its monsters. Every town has its secrets. Every neighbourhood has its history and the unconfirmed dangers that lay sleeping below the ground.

The bookstore smelled of new books, pleasant stories, and clashing egos.

Kate tried not to fall asleep as she sat on the floor listening to the fae argue with her face leaning on her fist. The rest of the book club members gaped from their little half circle on the floor in the bookstore's meeting room. All except for Mor—he sat off to the side, basking in the sun by the window and making ridiculous guesses to solve a crossword puzzle in the newspaper. It was like he didn't even realize his fellow fae were fighting. Every few seconds, he reached for the latte Kate had made for him before they left her apartment that morning, and he took a sip without looking up from the paper.

"That's not at all what it's like!" Dranian shouted. It had been ten minutes since he jumped to his feet. He'd been that way ever since Shayne suggested one of the books Kate made them read depicted a fae's personality adequately.

"What about Lord Swendle? The writer was practically telling his life's story!" Shayne objected, throwing a book at Dranian. It hit Dranian in the chest and tumbled to the floor.

"How dare you?! Lord Swendle is practically a saint of the sky deities!" Dranian growled.

When the fae had first walked into the book club five days ago, the girls in the meeting room had stared, giggled, or blushed. Kate had hoped that bringing the assassins every day might give them some real human exposure, but it seemed like the *Book Nerd Herd* girls were no longer interested in book club at all.

The fae Prince didn't show up once in those five days. Mor kept a close watch at the apartment window each night, Dranian stood guard down at the café door, and Shayne spent most of his evenings on the rooftop with his crossbow loaded. For the first time in ages, Kate was sleeping like a baby.

Kate released a startled sound when she dozed off and fell off balance.

Shayne glanced over at her, taking his attention off Dranian for the first time since the discussion began. "Tell him he's wrong, Kate!" he shouted, pointing at his fellow assassin.

Kate rubbed her eyes, smearing her makeup. "Well, I don't know Lord Swendle, so obviously I can't comment on that."

Mor released a snort-laugh from the side of the room. But his laughter fell away when Dranian swung a real punch and nearly landed it in Shayne's face.

Shayne and Dranian went back at it, Dranian opening his own book to point at a paragraph. He muttered something too low for the rest of the book club to hear.

Iris—*Book Nerd Herd* organizer—slid wide around the fae-fight to reach Kate's side. "Where did you meet these guys?" she asked, beaming. "They're so invested in the story. It's adorable. Why can't all guys be like this?"

"Well, today's your lucky day." Kate lifted a hand toward Shayne and Dranian. "Take your pick. I'll set you up on a date—"

"Human." Mor appeared behind Kate. "We must leave before this situation escalates."

Kate looked up just in time to see Dranian charge Shayne. He grabbed him around the middle and lifted him off the floor. Shayne whacked Dranian's back with his book as he was carried and slammed against the wall. The wall cracked up to the ceiling while Shayne punched Dranian's nose in retaliation, drawing blood. A second later, he kicked Dranian with his bare foot while the fae was hunched.

Blood dripped to the floor.

Fae growled.

Shayne's muscles flexed.

Girls shrieked and scurried away.

Iris clapped.

Kate sprang up and ran over as Dranian's hands wound around

Shayne's throat.

"Stop! Stay still!" she shouted, and both fae froze with their limbs in mid-strike. "It's time to go." She shot a look back to Mor who was scooping up the scattered books. He bowed in farewell to the book club girls who bit back smiles and waved.

"See you next time!" Iris shouted, but to Kate, she mouthed, "Make sure you bring that one back." She jutted her thumb toward Shayne as Mor snatched the fae by his shirt and dragged him toward the exit.

They tumbled out of the bookstore a bloody, heated mess of alpha male pride and sore attitudes. The chilly air didn't cool anyone down fast enough, and Dranian leaned away and eyed Shayne behind Mor's back. Shayne unexpectedly grinned through a bloody lip, and that only seemed to anger Dranian more.

Kate's phone alarm went off. She stopped walking to pull it from her pocket, leaving Mor to hold Shayne's and Dranian's collars. She gasped when she realized. "I'm late! I have to go!"

Mor looked back at her with the widest, most accusing eyes she'd seen on a fae.

"Sorry," she said as she jogged across the parking lot.

"Wait... Human, *wait!*" Mor called after her. "You can't leave me with these two! Command them not to fight at least!" His words drowned out as Kate rounded the bookstore and chased speeding cars down the road.

Minutes later, she stopped outside the *Yarn & Stitch*, panting and breathing a sigh of relief when she saw the lights on inside. Her fingers traced her pocket where she hid the note of questions she planned to ask. She'd spent an hour this morning at a table in the café scribbling down the things she felt were the most important to know.

She rubbed her warm neck as she trotted up the steps and opened the door. She'd just lifted her foot to go inside when a fistful of her knit sweater was grabbed from behind.

Kate was torn back out of the shop, her shoulders hitting a broad chest. She was tossed in the other direction—she barely caught her footing as the person who'd pulled her out marched past and entered the yarn store. An earthy and floral scent swept over her, and she gasped.

The fae Prince stood in the entryway of the *Yarn & Stitch*. He glared at the shelves of yarn, at the snack table with the steaming teapot, and at the group of knitting women on couches.

Freida stood, knocking the teapot to the floor and soaking the carpet with hot liquid. Gretchen and the others dropped their knitting, too, and soon, every fae woman faced the Prince—*Cress*.

"I thought I recognized that dreadful smell of wool and tea." Cress's words were ice-cold. He dared another step in. "So, this is where you've been hiding, Sisterhood. I can't wait to inform my Queene of this treachery."

Kate looked from the Prince to the knitting club as it dawned on her how he must have found this place. She hadn't even felt his gaze on her back as he'd followed her. She never would have brought him here on her own. She never would have sold out the knitting club...

Her attention fell on the handle of a decorative dagger sticking out from Cress's back pocket, and tightness bloomed in her chest. She crept in behind him, her fingers reaching toward his weapon. But Freida's emotionless words filled the shop, and Kate halted.

"Kill him."

Kate staggered back against the wall as Hazel leapt over the couch. The fae girl's knitting needles were out like claws. The Prince caught her whole body and hurled her back into a shelf of yarn just as two older women slid over the floor and stabbed him in his legs.

Cress growled, yanking the dagger handle from his pocket. A long silver blade appeared from the handle, binding together out of thin air. He aimed for both women in one terrible swing, and Kate screamed, grabbing his arm, and making him miss.

Freida appeared out of nowhere and kicked Cress out the front door. He tumbled into Kate and took her down the stairs with him, landing on top of her and forcing the breath from her lungs on the sidewalk. A strange look crossed Cress's face when his eyes settled on Kate wheezing under his weight. He rolled to his feet, bringing her up with him. He spun her around, pulled her back against his chest, and placed his blade at her throat.

The knitting club spilled from the shop with their needles raised. Freida looked unnaturally calm, frightening almost.

"Surrender," Cress commanded them.

Hazel wiped a bead of blood from her lip as she glared at the Prince. A bone in her arm looked broken. She snapped it back into place without breaking eye contact.

Cress's heartbeat punched Kate's back. One of his hands was flat on her stomach, holding her in place, and the other nudged his cold sword closer to her throat.

"W... Where's Mor?" Kate whispered, trying to steal a look at the street without letting her jaw brush his blade.

Cress released a dark chuckle. "Mor will not come for you, Human. He is well distracted with the others you left behind."

Kate's mind filled with Lily's sad blue eyes. A sob slipped from her mouth. She hadn't patched things up with Lily. She meant to—she'd thought about doing it every day—but she was so preoccupied with teaching the fae how to run the café. And maybe she'd been scared Lily wouldn't come back even if she asked.

The pressure of Cress's hand tightened against her stomach. "Don't do that," he mumbled through his teeth. It sounded like begging. "Don't you dare cry, Human—"

"Not to worry, Kate Kole." A savage look entered Freida's eyes, and a strange smile crept over her mouth. "He's come here to die. All your troubles are about to end. Just"—she inched a step toward Kate and the Prince—"hold still."

Freida's needle shot like a dart. Kate felt Cress's body flinch; his sword clattered to the ground. Gretchen vanished, and a set of tiny, glowing wings the size of a walnut took her place.

The knitting club charged. Cress pushed Kate away, and Kate collided with Hazel, eating a lock of the girl's curly hair. Gretchen zipped by like a firefly.

Kate spun and saw chaos. She expected Cress to be overrun, but terror fumbled her heartbeat as she watched him stab and snap bones with inhuman speed. He didn't even need his sword to inflict harm, but after tossing half the club to the ground, he scooped it up with menacing intensity and swung at them. A fast, heavy wind lifted through the street, flapping the women's hair into their eyes. A black patch spread over the road like a burning puddle from Cress's boots, and the scent of ash filled the air. More women stumbled and fell, their boots melting right off their feet.

Kate backed toward the *Yarn & Stitch* store until she was against it. Rain speckled her cheeks as the sky changed its mood, and Toronto citizens halted in their tracks at the sight of the young man destroying a mob of knit-covered women in the street. People who tried to race away were chased by the remaining members of the knitting club who vanished and appeared to cut them off. The fae grabbed people's hands, and afterward it was like the citizens forgot where they were.

Moaning knitting club members lay across the road in Cress's wake. The few remaining women smothered the Prince; biting, clawing, and kicking. The knitting club took hit after hit, and some who were on the ground snapped their arms and legs back into place and got up again. Kate's breath caught in her throat as she watched them persevere by a miracle.

Cress was a monster.

A turquoise-eyed monster.

She led him here.

Kate sank to a sitting position as the women stole the Prince's sword, broke his fingers with a gruesome *snap*, and struck him until he stopped hurtling them. They forced him backward into the alley where Kate couldn't see. Her feet were frozen to the ground—she couldn't follow. She couldn't watch what would happen next.

Gretchen reappeared in her full size. She drew out the longest needle of all and marched into the alley after the others. Her high voice sang from around the corner, "Goodbye, Your Highness."

"Wait!" Kate heard her own scream echo into the alley. She leapt up and scrambled around the store just as Gretchen raised the needle over the Prince's exposed throat. Gretchen hesitated, looking back at Kate with wild, questioning eyes.

From inside the *Yarn & Stitch*, the loud chirp of the cuckoo clock sounded. Freida wiped a smear of blood from her lips and dropped the brick in her hand. It rolled down the alley and landed in a shallow puddle of fresh rain.

Gretchen's fist tightened around her needle. "Ah, *humans*," she growled, climbing off Cress's body where he leaned against crates of trash.

Kate expected them to go back into the *Yarn & Stitch*, but the knitting club dispersed without a word to each other, including the grumbling Gretchen. Some lifted their fellow knitters off the road and carried them away in silence.

Freida stayed behind. The old woman stared at the Prince for a moment as she yanked her one remaining opal earring from her lobe. "Until next week then, Kate Kole." She glanced back at Kate and nodded toward Cress. "Be careful with him. He's got a fairy crush on you," was all she said as she left.

Kate's throat was too thick to reply.

The rain turned heavy, flooding the air and the streets as Kate stood there gaping at Cress's relaxed, punctured face. His eyes were shut, his clothes and hair absorbing the rain. He wasn't moving.

Every second that passed, Kate meant to leave. But all she could see was Mor, Shayne, and Dranian's faces, and how they would look at her if she told them she killed their Prince. It would be fair if Cress died this way—he'd tried to kill Kate first. He deserved to be left here with the garbage.

The alley turned into a shallow stream of rainwater. Kate's shoes squeaked as she walked toward the fae Prince. She crouched down and flicked an old candy wrapper off his shoulder. Some liquid substance from a leaking garbage bag had stained the side of his shirt green. Blood dripped from a pattern of gashes on his face.

"Cress?" she tried.

He didn't move a muscle.

Kate slowly reached to check his pulse. She put her fingers against his throat, searching for a sign of life. His pulse didn't show. She scooted herself forward, pressed her fingers in deeper, and leaned forward to try and feel if he was breathing.

His hand flashed up and grabbed her wrist. She tried to pull back, but his grip tightened, trapping her fingers to the side of his neck. Cress didn't open his eyes fully, but his lashes fluttered, and his mouth pinched just a little.

"Let me go, you monster," Kate said.

She didn't think he'd reply, but he whispered through cracked lips, "Stay. Please."

Kate stopped wriggling. Cress's neck grew warm beneath her hand. She spotted the top of a tattoo peeking from the collar of his shirt, and she carefully tugged the collar down to see the rest. A mountain with a crescent of tiny snowflakes arching over it covered his heart. It was almost pure black, but apart from that, the tattoo wasn't that different from the picture on her own neck.

Kate waited for him to open his eyes, but his fingers slid off her wrist and his arm went limp at his side. His head tilted, his breathing slowed, and Kate was sure he'd passed out.

She stood, flexing her fingers where he'd held them. "I can't stay. You'll kill me if I do."

No response came from the Prince.

Kate used her hand to shield her eyes as she turned and raced back to the café in the rain. The puddles were deep and the air was cold.

Freshly brewed espresso and hot milk were on the countertop when she came in. Mor was adding whipped cream to lattes. The fireplace crackled in the corner where Shayne and Dranian had dragged plush chairs down from Kate's apartment to read.

"Your Prince is hurt, badly," Kate said. Mor slowed the whipped cream spraying, and Shayne and Dranian looked up from their books. "He's in the alley beside the *Yarn & Stitch* store. I can tell you how to get there."

Dranian stood so fast, his chair toppled over.

Kate shoved aside the dozens of stolen buttons, spoons, dimes, and other shiny objects heaped on the countertops in her apartment. She laid her novel flat and tried to get through a chapter. After going over the same paragraph six times, she slapped the book shut and began to pace in the kitchenette.

"Why did I do that?" she asked herself. "Why did I help him?"

The Prince was going to get medical help from his assassins and then come back and kill her. Kate leaned against the counter and dragged her nails through her damp hair. She leaned her weight against her book to crack the spine so it would stay open on its own.

Her apartment door burst open. Mor marched in, drenched.

"Are you sure that's where you left him, Human?" he demanded.

"We looked everywhere. He's not there." Shayne's bare feet slapped over the tiles leaving watery footprints. He tossed his crossbow on the chair by the door in a damp heap.

"He's *gone*?" Kate rushed around the counter. "That's impossible. He was hardly breathing when I left!"

"Our deaths will be disgraceful and public if we let the Prince of the North die!" Mor started pacing. He stopped to yank off his jean jacket and hurtled it into the chair by the door over Shayne's crossbow. "Why hasn't he been in contact with any of us for the past five days?" he asked the other fae.

"Maybe he doesn't want to reveal his plans to us again," Shayne said.

"He must be plotting something."

"He attacked my knitting club," Kate told them, and Shayne made a face.

"Your what?"

"It's a long story. My knitting club saved me from him. That's how he got hurt."

Shayne tilted his head doubtfully. "That doesn't make any sense. What sort of—"

"I'm not telling you any details about my knitting club. I've already caused them enough trouble." Kate fled into the hall and ducked into the bathroom. She closed the door behind her and let out a heavy breath, placing a hand against her chest. She'd barely peeled off her rain-soaked shirt when the door flew open, and she shrieked.

Shayne stood there, eyeing her.

"This is totally inappropriate!" Kate said.

"Tell me about your knitting club." He leaned against the doorframe and folded his arms. His pale wet hair stood on end. "It's the only chance we have to find Cress."

Kate folded her arms to cover her sports bra. "I won't."

"Do it, or I'll let Dranian at you." Shayne flashed a charming smile, but his eyes narrowed. "Trust me, Human, you don't want to know what he'll do to your hair."

"Seriously, *shut the door* and don't ever bother me again when I'm showering!"

Shayne's jaw slid to the side. His nostrils flared, but he obeyed, clicking the door shut. A second later, he yelled through it, "Why did you concern yourself with our Prince, anyway? You ran back here to tell us about him."

Kate sighed. "I don't know."

A pause followed before Shayne spoke again. "His enchanted kiss didn't work on you, Human. You shouldn't be concerned for someone who wants you dead."

"Is that advice?"

Something thumped lightly on the door like Shayne was leaning against it. "Perhaps."

"Are you telling me because I commanded you to keep me safe? Or are you actually worried about me, Assassin?" Kate wandered to the shower but waited for him to respond before turning the water knob. She looked back at the door again when Shayne didn't answer. After a moment, Kate crept over and opened it just a crack to see if he was still there.

Shayne stood directly on the other side with his arms folded like he'd been waiting.

"Do you *want* to be saved by me, Human?" he asked. A tantalizing smile danced over his mouth. "Are you the sort of female who likes to be saved by a strong male?"

Kate grunted, thinking about slamming the door in his face. "No way. I think women are perfectly able to save themselves."

Shayne's smile grew. Finally, the laugh he was bottling tumbled out and he turned to leave. "Tell me that again when the Prince of the North finds you and pins you in a corner with his fairsaber," he mumbled as he left the bedroom.

Kate shut the bathroom door, breathing in the quiet. She twisted on the hot water. It seemed like Shayne's questions were always the ones that ran through her mind long after he asked them.

The noise of the water roared in Kate's ears.

"Why did you concern yourself with our Prince, anyway?"

Only you would save someone who's trying to kill you, Katherine Lewis.

Her conscience took on Lily Baker's voice again.

CHAPTER

22

Prince Cressica and The Last Five Days

It was exactly five days ago that Cress saw them for the first time. Midnight dawned over the human city, bringing forth the monsters Cress had been sniffing out since he picked up their trail in the academy library. He followed the path to a much larger public library on the cusp of the city where traces of fairies were left in the spaces between books and mixed into the dust on the shelves, along with a flirtatious, menacing wickedness that had haunted Cress's dreams for many faeborn years.

The brand of the Shadow Fairies.

He refused to believe it until he saw them for himself.

Cress waited for two hours tucked atop a shelf until they came. Faeborn folk of the haunting sort drifted into the quiet space with no candles, lanterns, or torches. Their ears hosted a sharper point than Cress's, their tattoos were painted on thicker, and their eyes...

Silver and brown, just like Mor's.

A thousand fast memories of battle, narrow victories, and dreadful losses washed through Cress's mind as he pulled himself further into the shadows, watching the band of seventeen fairies congregate in the middle of the room. They wore the darkness of night and held the menace of beasts in their faces.

What in the name of the sky deities were fairies of the Dark Corner of Ever doing here among the humans? Cress's hand drifted toward the winged handle of his blade in his back pocket, but his fingers froze as one more fairy joined the rest; one Cress knew the mad-minded scent of all too well. The very one who had been the reason Cress despised fairy nobles of the East.

Bonswick pulled thin gloves onto his pale hands as he joined the congregation, and it was as though Cress was back in the Silver Castle, guessing at what the glassy-eyed fairy's secrets were.

Cress rolled to his feet in silence and raced on padded toes toward the window before his Northern scent might sweep across the library. He leapt through the opening, his body turning as weightless as feathers as he glided on the wind a good quarter mile. He cooled himself to stone and sank back to the ground, landing with a thud.

He whirled to ensure he had not been followed. Only dark streets and distant sounds met his senses—the air was clear, open, and honest. He grimaced at the long crack he'd made in the street from his landing.

For the next hour, Cress jogged through random streets, slipping into every alley, racing through every park, brushing his scent across every landmark and lamppost.

When he was satisfied with his complex web of traces, the Prince headed for the trees.

"Why does everything of the sinister and magical sort always happen in a library?" he muttered to himself.

His mind was haunted. He saw the Queene smile cruelly as though she was there with him. He felt her phantom presence crawling on his shoulders like a glass moonbug. Levress ruthlessly guarded the gate herself. Cress would be a fool to believe she did not know about the Shadow

Fairies in the human realm.

He tugged at his tight sweater as he marched across the road. The trees swayed in the midnight breeze, doing their best to relax him. But he came to a halt at the edge of Thelma Lewis's yard before a heaping pile of dry leaves.

A low growl rumbled through him. Cress strode to the house ever scented of tea, *freshly baked chocolate chip cookies*, and honey. He came in quietly so he wouldn't wake Thelma, and he crept up the stairs. The large clock on the wall said it was the earliest of morning hours, deep within the night's belly. He nearly sprang all the way back down the stairs when Thelma stepped from her bedroom with her arms folded.

"Cress," she said sternly. "If you're going to live under my roof, you need to follow my rules. Every one of the young people I've raised has had to abide by them. Being strong enough to chop my firewood doesn't make you an exception."

Cress sank to a knee on the stair and nodded.

"No more coming in after dark. Do you understand?"

Cress nodded again, unable to look the old human woman in the eyes.

Thelma's shoulders relaxed. "Get to bed, then."

Cress trotted the rest of the way up and disappeared into his room.

Well, not *his* room, but the one he had chosen of the three spare bedrooms available.

He shut the door with a soft click and let out a heavy breath. A goblet of tea rested on the dresser, oozing the scent of honey. He poked it. It was still warm.

Cress listened until the soft footsteps of Thelma Lewis disappeared. He ventured to the dresser to pull off his sweater, stopping before the framed photos where a dark-haired human girl with hazel eyes and an oval mouth smiled beside a younger Officer Lily Baker.

Queensbane, that faeborn-cursed smile.

Cress grumbled and tossed his sweater, heading for the bed that was absolutely covered in the sweet fragrances of Kate Kole. He picked up the book from the nightstand where he'd left it the evening before and flipped it open to the folded page as he hummed to himself.

"Daffodils sway and the golden sun sings, la, la, la, la. Rivers rush and the silver stars sing, la, la, la, la."

A much raspier voice sang it in his head.

Cress turned the book over. Every paragraph had messily handwritten notes in the margins, a few pages had the corners pressed down, and the cover was scuffed. It seemed Kate Kole had read this book a lot. He wondered why. It was terrible.

The fae Prince sighed and dropped it to his chest, his mind spinning with thoughts of enemy fairies hiding in libraries, human girls he never should have kissed, his brothers he was trying to avoid, and insolent human neighbours who didn't know their place.

"Wait! Wait!" Thelma whispered, and Cress shot her a look for stopping him. "Not yet!" The old woman held the sleeve of Cress's plaid button-up coat. Cress huffed impatiently as Thelma peered around the tree trunk. Her spirally gray hair glowed with morning dew.

The low rumble of a human chariot on four wheels trickled through the air and Cress waited, crouched with his fist smooshed against his lazy cheek. A large black bag was slung over his shoulder.

"Now!" Thelma said, shoving him forward.

Cress caught his feet and glided across the yard as smooth as the Northern winds, peeking through trees and shrubs to ensure no humans were watching. The neighbour's chariot rumbled down the street as Cress came to their spare chariot parked before the house. He flung the vessel door open and began hauling fistfuls of leaves into the backseat from the large bag.

"That's not enough!" Thelma's voice came from beside him. Her floral gardening gloves covered her hands.

"I thought you were going to stay back and keep watch!" Cress whispered in return.

"Heck, no! I came to show these neighbours of mine not to mess with me." Thelma picked up the whole bag and dumped half into the vessel. Cress's eyes widened. He reached to help her until only half the leaves were left.

"We can't fit much more," he said, glancing into the bag.

"Then we'll put them somewhere else." Thelma headed to the house and nudged a loose window open. She glanced back at Cress with a wicked smile and gave him a nod.

Cress looked between the old woman and the window.

"Queensbane," he muttered, hiding a preposterous grin. He hoisted the bag over to the house and held it up, tipping it into the window so the remaining leaves spilled into the quaint living room beyond.

Thelma looked over her shoulder and gasped. "They're coming back!" she said, and Cress tore the bag back out. Leaves spurted across the grass.

He looked both ways for somewhere to hide until Thelma grabbed his arm and began tugging him back toward her own yard. The old woman snickered as they hustled, and Cress smothered a grin.

"What will you do if they come over angry?" he asked.

"I'll just get you to answer the door!" Thelma's roaring laughter rang through the pines as Cress reached around to support her weight. She leaned against him, limping as fast as she could.

"You're an evil human," he said. But the old woman's joy seeped into his bones, leaving a thousand phantom giggles in the air, and after a moment, Cress's smile faded.

Evil was immoral agendas hidden behind cruel smiles and the threat of death in the air.

The truth was, Thelma Lewis was far from being evil. Cress didn't believe there was a drop of evil in her, whether her granddaughter was a fairy killer or not.

When they came into the house, Thelma hobbled into the kitchen. "I'll make tea. We earned it."

"I'll help," Cress said, but he paused as his own words rang clear in his ears. "Actually… I'll be right back, Grandma Lewis." Before Thelma could ask, Cress disappeared up the stairs and into his room. He shut the door.

His hand pressed roughly against his chest. "What are you doing, Cressica?" he growled.

He should not care that the old woman was kind, or that she promised to teach him how to make *freshly baked chocolate chip cookies*, or that she had a contagious laugh. These were his weaknesses, and he had fallen into them with disgraceful ease. If she was a fairy, Thelma would have been excellent at laying traps, not because she wanted to hurt anyone, but because everyone would be drawn in by her warmth and baking.

Cress turned to lean his back against the door. His gaze traced the objects in the room. Objects that reminded him of a human girl he had come to kill. Hair ties, mirrors, and crimson lipstick lay in baskets atop the dresser. Forgotten clothes were tucked into the drawers. A small book collection filled the far shelf, and a tall lamp rested beside the bed, perfect for reading.

Cress closed his eyes with a tight jaw, inviting the cold to return to his gaze.

He moved for the nightstand and tore the drawer open, lifting out the gold-winged handle of his fairsaber. His thumb traced over the button that would draw out the hidden blade. Enough was enough. He had to destroy Kate Kole before it was too late and he lost everything that mattered.

The scent of herbal tea drifted into the room from downstairs and Cress released a heavy breath. There was no point in hurting the old woman. She'd already admitted that her human illness would bring upon her end soon anyway.

But. Kate. Faeborn-cursed. *Kole.*

Cress had to end this today before his constant need to be near her, to learn all about her, and to hear her raspy voice overtook him and drove him mad. Hiding in her quarters was all he could do to keep himself from charging through the city of humans to find her for all the wrong reasons.

He was not ready when he saw her.

It had been several days since Cress laid eyes on his human target, but for whatever absurd reason, he had forgotten the preposterous depths of green in her eyes and the potency of her offensively innocent fragrance.

He also forgot how to breathe when she intervened in Shayne and Dranian's petty male fight at the human bookshop. Cress watched it from the window with fire in his blood. He wanted to smack Shayne and Dranian for being such faeborn-cursed fools.

Cress twisted the yarn in his pocket between his fingers as he observed them all tumble from the bookstore entrance like a pack of messy swamp-loons. Shayne had blood in his teeth.

Kate Kole parted from his brothers and fluttered off in the other direction despite Mor's shouting. Cress stalked after her with several cold words cooling the tip of his tongue. He had warned her. He had been clear. Yet still his brothers were cleaning up after humans, attending human functions, and forgetting their true place among the dignified fairies. Forgetting that they were trained killers created to show little mercy in a hunt.

After a few blocks, a store came into view and Cress stopped walking. Smells of tea and sweets flooded the street from it, but most potently... the itchy scent of cursed fairy yarn tickled his nose. Kate trotted up the front steps.

Cress marched to the front door and grabbed Kate Kole before she could go inside. She released a quiet gasp when he pulled her backward, shoved her aside, and went in himself.

His deadly turquoise gaze fell over the group of females nestled together with magic in the air and yarn on their fingers.

Assassins.

Of course.

No wonder his human target had been able to enslave his brothers. Cress wanted to laugh at the lovely revelation. Kate Kole was not cleverer than him.

Seconds later, Cress took the sisters down two at a time right in the dreaded middle of the human street, but the treacherous members of the Sisterhood of Assassins kept getting back up. They beat him, only by a miracle of the sky deities, with claws and needles and wills of iron. They forced him into an alley, and there Cress laid his head back as the dizzy, endless dark came to steal him. But then *her* voice sailed in against the black waves, plunging into his mind and releasing ripples through his thoughts.

"Wait!" she screamed before the Sisterhood killed him. And that had been enough.

Cress stifled a moan as the heartache rushed in, worse than any puncture in his flesh. For the first time, he was too weak to deny his wants. When she came to him, he begged her to stay like a fool who deserved to lose his tongue.

23

Prince Cressica and the Present Issue of Ouchies

One could learn a lot from watching people. If you watched them long enough, you'd learn their habits, their hearts' desires, their instincts, the little things they do when they think no one is looking. Cress had stalked many foes, hunted them to the darkest corners of the North and beyond. He had slayed giants, disbanded armies of elves, and he had taken down evil fairy Kings. He had killed great serpents, travelled to distant mountains, and swam to the bottom of the Jade Ocean. And there, in all those places, he had watched. It was his greatest skill—to be a silent presence in a shadow, a mere breath on the wind. To be the invisible beast of nightmares, the monster under the bed of his enemy, the evil hiding in the closet at night. Always watching and waiting for his moment to strike. He had trapped many prey after learning about their evils, their ploys, and their attempts to invade or overthrow the High Court of the North. He was an information-gathering assassin.

An assassin whose heart had nearly been cut out by a knitting needle because of a human he'd learned far too much about.

Warm light kissed Cress's eyelids. He grimaced as he tried to remember where he was. When he opened his eyes, he saw peeling white paint on a dull square ceiling, not the muralled artwork of the faeborn artists of the Silver Castle.

Memories of a fight flashed through his mind—flying knitting needles and an old fairy female snapping the bones in his fingers. He dragged himself up to sit, his brows furrowing.

A thick yellow blanket covered him, tucked in around his feet. A cold mug of tea rested on the bedside table.

Cress could hear Thelma hobbling around downstairs. He vaguely recalled knocking on the front door of her home. She'd answered just as he'd collapsed a blood-spattered mess in her entryway.

When Cress pulled the blankets off, he saw that his pants were rolled up and white bandages wrapped his legs. He remembered snapping his fingers back into place and feeling the bones meld back together before he fell asleep. Thelma had gone pale-faced.

Cress turned his leg to see the old woman's work. He imagined Thelma's shaking hands bandaging him up while he slept. He had never been taken care of by anyone apart from castle healers before. If he'd shown up in such a condition before Queene Levress, she would have laughed and sent him off with a promise she'd have him killed if he didn't get better before she needed him next.

Cress didn't want to think about the Queene now though. He took in the quiet room, sniffing the healing ointment in the air. He could also smell…

He inhaled a whiff of his shirt and winced.

A moment later he entered Thelma's kitchen and announced, "I could use a bath."

Thelma whipped around from the sink where she washed berries. "Heavens, you scared the life out of me!" she accused. She lifted her spectacles off the counter and put them on to look him over. "You look pretty good considering the condition you showed up in."

"I'm exceptional at self-healing," he bragged.

Thelma made a doubtful face, but she returned her spectacles to the countertop and went back to her berries. "You've been asleep for two days. You can't be that good at self-healing."

Cress's face fell. "What?" He staggered toward her a step. "Did you say *two days*?"

"I sure did, son. Now go get cleaned up. You can help me with the strawberry pie when you're done since you seem to have your energy back. I don't want to know what happened to you though. Keep your crook friends and crimes out of this house."

Crook friends?

It all hit Cress at once:

The Sisterhood of Assassins were protecting Kate Kole.

The Shadow Fairies were in the human realm.

Bonswick...

Cress's mind felt like a heavy stone. He rubbed his temples over a blossoming headache, thinking of Shadow Fairies finding his brothers while he was asleep.

When he realized Thelma was waiting for him to get clean, Cress marched to the water room, shut the door, and cranked the lever on the bath. Steam filled the small space, blurring his vision to match his clouded mind.

Had the fairies of the Dark Corner come for Cress? What if Levress had grown impatient and made a bargain with Bonswick? For the first time since Cress had squared off with the Lord of the East at the Queene's feast, he regretted his behaviour. Perhaps the Queene no longer wished for Cress to rule the North Corner of Ever. Perhaps she felt only a host of Shadow Fairies would be strong enough to kill off four of the greatest assassins of the North.

Cress scrubbed his forehead and sighed. But a new thought entered his mind. He glanced in the direction of the kitchen, hidden by the closed water room door.

What if the Shadow Fairies weren't here for him at all? What if Levress had sent them to assassinate Kate Kole so that Cress could come home guiltless and marry Princess Haven?

An agonized breath escaped him when he thought of his human target. How could he have begged Kate Kole to stay with him like that in the alley? He could not decide if he was more humiliated or angry that he had sputtered such nonsense.

He reached to wrench the water off when the tub was full and billowing steam. He grabbed the bottle off the counter and dumped in a lob of soap.

"Come then, Fairies of the Dark," he invited as he tore off his foul-smelling shirt. "End Kate Kole and set me free of her. I shall be better off for it."

Cress sank into the hot water and leaned his cheek against his fist. He needed to warn Mor. If the Shadow Fairies were after Kate Kole, then his brothers would be in danger, too.

Thelma would scold him for being out late tonight.

Even though Cress's judgements were heavy and shadowed, an unexpected smile found him at the thought.

CHAPTER

24

Kate Kole and the Fundraiser No One Wanted to Go To

Sun warmed Kate's back, and she stirred. She had a vague recollection of hearing snickers through the night, but when she opened her eyes, her bedroom was empty—though, a few books were missing from her nightstand TBR pile.

Kate squinted in the late morning light and sat up.

Her first thought was about the Prince. It had been two days since she abandoned him in the alley. If the fae assassins had found him and he was all right, they would be in the kitchen making coffee like every other day. But no sound came from the kitchenette. They must have still been out looking.

Kate's phone beeped. When she tapped the screen, a notification from her calendar popped up:

DEPARTMENT FUNDRAISER DANCE
8:00pm

Lily's fundraiser. The one Kate had sworn up and down she would attend.

She still hadn't heard from Lily. She wondered if Lily would even still want her to come.

Kate chewed on her lip as she dragged herself out of the bed and into the bathroom. But when she looked in the vanity mirror, she screamed.

"It's…" Mor fought a smile. He was the only one not buckled over, stifling snickers. "…it's called 'fairy-locks'."

Shayne burst out laughing and buried his face in the couch cushions. He'd become a red-faced mess the moment the trio of assassins had walked into the apartment and seen Kate. Dranian had slapped a fist against his mouth, but it hadn't silenced his snorts.

"Well how do I get them out?!" Kate screamed at them. "I tried brushing, but it's like you knotted my hair and glued it!!"

"You'll have to cut your hair off," Dranian composed himself long enough to say, and Shayne threw his head back and roared.

"Don't lie to her, Dranian," Mor said. "Your trick is cruel enough on its own. And we don't need the extra curses of falsehoods following us around." Mor headed into the kitchenette and pulled over the coffee maker.

"I warned you," Shayne said as he stood from the couch. "You should have just told us about your knitting club."

"I have to go to a formal dance tonight!" Kate shouted at Shayne this time. Shayne ignored her by scooping the coffee for Mor, so Kate smacked his arm. "I can't go looking like this."

"So, don't go." Shayne shrugged.

"I *have* to go. It's the only way to get Lily back," Kate said.

Shayne stopped what he was doing and turned to face her. "You care about that human friend that much?" he challenged.

WELCOME TO FAE CAFE

"Yes. And I'm going to make you pay for putting these knots in my hair!"

A wicked smile spread over Shayne's face. "I don't think I've ever seen you this upset, Kate Kole. You weren't even this mad when we tried to kill you at the academy."

Kate bit her lips together and turned on Dranian.

"Okay. First, you're going to tell me how to get all these horrible knots out of my hair."

Dranian tried to keep his lips pinched, but after a second he blurted, "Rinse it with hot water and the paste will melt." He smacked a cactus plant off the counter as he said it. Then, after dirt and roots scattered over the tiles, he rigidly stomped to the broom closet to clean up his mess.

"Second"—Kate pointed to her hair—"you're going to redeem yourselves from this terrible prank by coming with me tonight, and we're going to collectively make my friend have the best night of her life at this stupid fundraiser. Do you all understand?"

Mor's smirk vanished. "That is a bad idea. One of these fools will cause a scene." He nodded to Shayne and Dranian.

"Not. My. Problem." Kate snatched her brush off the countertop and went to flush her hair with hot water.

Whispers of winter arrived. The air ached with prickles of frost, and Kate's breath became a fountain of pale mist every time she opened her mouth. The last remnants of fall were being swept up by the icy breeze and tucked away to hide until next year. The city was still; Ontarians were nestled into their homes with their fireplaces on, unaware of the creatures that walked the roads of their town as dusk arrived.

"This is a waste of time," Dranian muttered as Kate and three fae assassins walked into the community centre beneath strings of twinkling bulbs and cheap party streamers. "What if Cress is dead?"

Moonlight glistened into the lobby through the unwashed windows, marking a silver path across an otherwise dark hall. Kate brushed a hand down the front of her sleek black dress, asking herself whether she looked okay or completely ridiculous in such a form-fitting outfit. She missed her fluffy slippers and the yellow sweater she'd given away.

Her first step in sent her wobbling on her heels. Dranian's hand flashed to her arm to steady her. As soon as she was balanced, he tore his hand away and rolled his eyes. Kate stifled a smile. Dranian still appeared sore about Kate forcing him to spend the morning delicately untangling her hair with a wet brush.

The other half of the morning Kate had spent trying unsuccessfully to teach Shayne how to drive a car he said he *bought*. The lesson lasted until the fae admitted the car was stolen and Kate had jumped out of it and smacked his shoulder. The shortened lesson was for the best anyway since it turned out Shayne had horrifyingly aggressive road rage. He nearly ripped the steering wheel out of the car when someone cut him off downtown. After they got back to the café, Shayne had gotten abnormally charming, feeding Kate dozens of totally fake compliments which she knew he was only doing so she wouldn't command him to return the stolen car.

But none of them had complained this afternoon when Kate told them all to dress up and do their hair. She'd come out of the bathroom and was caught off guard by how fast, and how *well*, they cleaned up. Their glamourous charm was only the icing on the cake though. It was the comfort of having them walking into this fundraiser beside her that was the biggest relief of all.

The truth was, Kate might not have come if she'd had to walk in alone.

"When are we going to continue looking for Cress?" Dranian muttered in a growl to Mor again as the scent of warm appetizers drifted out from the main hall. The comment sounded like it was meant to be a whisper.

"Listen, if even one of you can make my friend laugh tonight, I'll help you search for your Prince in the morning," Kate decided. "I'll tell you everything I can about what happened, with the exception of details regarding my knitting club." She didn't mention that there weren't many details that didn't include the knitting club.

Dranian and Mor exchanged a glance. They both looked at Shayne.

Shayne sighed. "Fine. I'll do it. Point me in the direction of your human friend with the ugly hair," he said to Kate.

Kate's jaw dropped. "Lily's hair is *not* ugly."

Shayne didn't reply, but his face said it all.

"What if Cress is watching us and wondering what we're doing *here* when we should be searching for him?" Dranian's hands were in fists. They'd been like that since they left the apartment.

"Stop worrying. Your Prince isn't watching us," Kate assured.

Dranian snarled, "How could *you* know that, Human?"

"Because I don't feel his prying gaze all over my back," she said, and Mor's hand found her arm fast enough to jolt her to a stop. Kate blinked up at his sharp brown-silver eyes.

"Did you just say... you can *feel* his gaze?" Mor asked.

Kate tugged her arm back. "You guys are all seriously *so* grabby."

Music started playing from inside, and when a young woman in a red dress with a dozen arm tattoos stepped into the dancefloor lights, Kate bolted for her. Mor's hand slid off her arm.

"Lil!" Kate shouted, drawing Connor to glance up from where he was accepting a drink across the room. His snoopy eyes travelled over Kate's black dress until Kate turned her back to him.

Lily seemed rigid, but she wasn't quick enough to hide her sigh of relief. "I didn't think you were still coming," she admitted.

"I promised I would."

A slight smile found Lily before she shooed it away. She glanced past Kate and slow-blinked at the trio of fae marching into the hall with their slicked hair, their perfect faces, their pretty eyes, and their stylish suits. Shayne was the only one who didn't walk like he was on a runway, and Kate imagined him curling his toes in the shoes she'd forced him to wear.

"Please tell me they're not here for the—"

195

"I brought backup," Kate said.

Lily shook her head. "Seriously, Kate? Why are you still letting those guys near you? I spent the whole week trying the tough love thing and you didn't even budge! Do you know how hard it was not to go barging in there every hour to see if you were okay?"

The question barely left Lily's mouth when Shayne swooped in and took her hand. He made eye contact as he planted a light kiss on her knuckles. "My task this evening is to make you laugh, pretty human—"

"Don't call her that. Her name is Lily," Kate said.

"—and I rarely fail at my tasks."

Lily scowled. "Seriously?" she said to Kate again.

"Yeah, well. They weren't actually supposed to tell you about their task."

Shayne flashed his beautiful grin that left no room for apologies.

When Shayne's allure took up too much space, Kate took Lily's other hand and tugged her away from the assassins. They reached the edge of the dance floor where a table held hot finger foods. Lily grabbed a bun and shoved half of it in her mouth in what was clearly stress eating.

Kate chewed on her lip. "I don't want to fight," she said, and Lily's face softened.

"Me either," Lily said through a wad of bun.

"I'm going to send them away after tonight. I think the power is getting to my head." Kate nodded toward the fae. "I should have just listened to you in the first place."

"What power? Are you talking about that *enslaving them* nonsense again?" Lily whispered back. She made an exasperated face and took another large bite of bread.

"This morning I made one of them brush my hair." Kate grimaced. "I need to send them away, right? I wanted to keep them around to run the café for the first few days, at least. But it feels wrong to make them stay now when..." She looked off, unsure how to finish the sentence.

Lily sighed through her full mouth, tossed the last bite of bun into the nearby trash can, and put her hands on her hips. "Did you go see that therapist I suggested? The one in the pamphlet?"

"Oh, come on, Lil! You saw Mor evaporate into thin air!" Kate waved a hand toward the trio of perfection glowing like a porcelain water fountain depicting the gods.

Lily opened her mouth like she was about to object, but as she studied the fae, her words seemed to get stuck somewhere.

"If I tell one of them to kiss your shoe, they'll do it," Kate promised. "I mean, I wouldn't actually force someone to do something like that, obviously—"

"Do it." Lily's gaze fired back to Kate. "If you want to prove that this isn't all a sham, make one of them kiss my shoe."

Kate swallowed, thinking of the fairy-locks. Her gaze settled on Dranian with his popped collar and smooth auburn hair. As though he was being summoned, the fae marched over, eyeing Kate peculiarly.

"I apologize for this in advance," Kate rasped when he was close enough. "But I need you to do something."

"Your tone worries me, Human," Dranian warned. His ever-present snarl seemed to deepen.

"Well... you should never mess with a girl's hair." Kate shook her finger in the air. "Now... *please*, kiss my friend's shoe."

The assassin's green eyes narrowed.

Lily looked back and forth between them. "Why do you keep calling her that? *Human*?" She imitated his voice when she said it.

"Take off your shoe, Lily," Kate said when Dranian twitched forward.

"What? Why?"

"Because this is going to be way too embarrassing for him if he has to get on the floor."

But Lily wasn't fast enough—Dranian dropped to a knee and Lily jumped back with a shriek when he snatched her foot. He tried to raise it just as his shoulder was grabbed and he was torn back up to his feet by Connor.

Connor inserted himself in front of Lily and Kate, staring Dranian down even though he was shorter.

Kate cringed and slapped a hand to her forehead. "Well, this just got interesting."

"Out of my way." Dranian's tight lips curved around the words, enforced by his wild eyes and rigid jaw. "Or I'll tear you to pieces."

Connor's chin dropped. "Did you just threaten a cop?"

"Take off your shoe, Lily!" Kate pleaded, reaching for it herself.

Lily scrambled to get her heel free, and she threw it at Dranian. The fae caught it in midair and pulled the black slingback heel to his mouth. He pecked it.

Connor made a repulsed face. "What's wrong with you?"

Dranian's shoulders relaxed. He dropped the shoe on the floor with a clatter, but his deadly glower didn't leave Kate. His cheeks were flushed; he looked like he'd been slapped.

"Are you out of your mind, Human?!" Mor's deep voice boomed as he marched over. "Don't you know about his past?! You just made him..." It was like he couldn't even spit out the horrid words. Back by the lobby entrance, Shayne wasn't smiling anymore, either.

Dranian pushed past Connor to get to Kate. He stood over her, a tower of muscle and fury. It was the first time Kate realized how small she was in comparison. How easy it would be for him to snap her in half with one hand.

"Hey," Lily tugged Kate back an inch, "take it easy." But her voice was soft. "I'm sorry about the shoe. It's my fault—I made her tell you to do that."

"You'll pay for it, Human," Dranian promised Lily without taking his loathing eyes off Kate.

"No, Lily is totally off limits," Kate said back. "You know what? Go home, all of you. Bringing you here was a huge mistake." She swallowed the new lump in her throat and put her gaze on the floor. Lily wrung her hands beside her.

Dranian turned his back to them and left without another word. Mor followed.

A second later, Shayne sauntered over to Kate with his hands in his pockets. "Can I have your permission to stay?" he asked. "I have a task to finish." He gazed over at Lily and bit his lip over a taunting smile.

"Forget it," Lily said. "I won't laugh for you."

"You will. I promise."

Kate stared after the other two fae disappearing into the cold night. When the community hall door slammed shut behind them, she felt the rush of wind sail all the way through the lobby, across the dance floor, and over her warm skin.

"Why was Mor so upset that I made Dranian do that?" Kate asked, and Shayne's smile faded.

"Well, you never learned Dranian's story." He glanced at his shoes, tapping the toe against the floor like he wanted to kick them off. "I'd better stay here to make sure Dranian doesn't come back with his fair-spear and stab all these lovely plastic air bubbles in a fit of rage," he said, glancing up at the balloons.

Kate chewed on her lip. "You can stay."

"What? No, Kate, command him to leave! We need to talk about all this!" Lily said.

But Kate nodded toward Shayne. "You didn't want to be here alone, and now you've got us. And I guess this means you believe me now," she pointed out. Lily's mouth parted, but she seemed to have no comeback for that.

A new song came through the static speakers, and Shayne extended a hand to Lily to seal the deal. He wiggled his fingers when she didn't take it. Finally, Lily raised her hand and Shayne snatched it, lacing their fingers together so she couldn't change her mind.

"Make sure Lily has fun," Kate said to Shayne.

"Yes, Human." Shayne escorted a stricken-faced Lily to the dance floor where other couples were swaying. He twirled her into his embrace, and they blended right in, taking up the spotlight in the middle.

Kate glanced warily at Connor, still gaping beside her. She thought about escaping to find a drink. Someone carried out a punch bowl right on cue, and she turned for the refreshments table.

The chandelier of gold balloons swayed when the lobby door opened again, and Kate's gaze darted back to it, hoping to see a pair of well-dressed fae. But only Officer Westbow came in. Kate brushed her bangs down over her face so he wouldn't recognize her, though she doubted he'd miss the unmistakeable colour of her hair. She was a breath away from darting for the washrooms to hide when Connor drifted to her side with his finger tapping his glass.

"I know I didn't just imagine all that," he remarked, staring down the white-haired fae spinning Lily and dazzling the other couples on the dance floor.

"Those guys are just actors I hired, so let them be," Kate said.

Connor released a doubtful grunt and sipped his drink. After a moment, he set it down and grabbed Kate's arm, pulling her to the dance floor. The jerky motion caught Shayne's eye from where he hugged Lily to himself.

Connor tugged Kate until they stood below the balloon chandelier. She thought about coming up with an excuse to not dance—broken ankle, feeling sick, allergic to idiots—but she reluctantly settled in when she caught a sympathetic look from Lily.

"Allow me to tell you a joke, Human," Shayne said loudly to Lily, turning heads. The fae's attention dropped to where Connor's hands locked behind Kate's waist.

"Of all the ugly humans in this room, *that* one"—Shayne nodded toward Connor's back, and Connor craned his neck like he knew he was being talked about—"is the most repulsive one of all. Though, I suppose that's not really a joke, is it?"

Connor stopped dancing.

Kate's lips peeled apart.

After a moment, Lily's laughter erupted across the dance floor.

Shayne could have left after he got what he wanted, but he didn't. He became a marvelous date to Lily for the entire evening. He made people laugh all night, and he became so popular among Lily's coworkers that they tried pressuring her into bringing him to next week's bake sale at the station.

Kate told Shayne to walk Lily home afterward, even though Lily insisted she was fine and reminded her that she carried a gun for a living. Even so, Shayne ripped off his shoes with a dramatic flair and ushered Lily off toward her apartment in his bare feet.

Apart from the night traffic, Toronto was fast asleep. Only the heavy moon and the chugging boats in the distance kept Kate company as she wandered the docks by the lake. She imagined Mor would be brewing decaf lattes back at the café for some late-night reading time to cool Dranian's temper.

She realized she was smiling. Maybe Kate was crazy to try and get them to fit into regular human life. The fae had completely destroyed book club, but they'd also unpacked everything at the café, got the fireplace running, and had put up signs in the windows to announce the opening tomorrow morning. Even moody Dranian spent the last days studying drink combinations in preparation for the big event, and Kate had caught him in the back sneaking tastes of whipped cream and humming to himself as he put together the menu.

"Aren't you cold?" Connor's voice cut into her thoughts.

Kate glanced toward the road that would take her home before she answered. "Yeah." Suddenly the docks felt less peaceful.

The sound of Connor shucking his coat filled the cool night air. Kate sighed and walked down the dock before he could try offering it to her.

"Wait up!" Connor took her arm and whirled her back. "Are you trying to get away from me or something?" He threw his jacket over Kate's shoulders and held the flaps tight together at her front, turning it into a straight jacket. He didn't look like he was in a rush to let go.

"It's weird that we've known each other as long as we have and you still don't seem to catch on when I try to avoid you," Kate said, glaring down at his coat prison.

Connor grunted. "Remember your place, *Kate Kole*. Remember that I know who you really are."

Kate worked her jaw, wishing she'd gone home with Lily and Shayne. Wondering why on earth she'd felt like going for a walk in the middle of the night. "How could I forget when you remind me every time you want something?" She couldn't even look at him right now. She settled her gaze on the distant boats glowing against the dark water.

But Connor shoved her face back toward him with his thumb, and Kate winced at his breath that smelled like chewed appetizers and a compulsive need to assert dominance at inappropriate times.

"You're right, I do want something. I always have, Kate, and maybe I'm feeling brave enough tonight to ask for it." His gaze dropped to her mouth, and he took in a fast, deep breath.

"Oh, for the love of—*please* don't—"

Connor's mouth smashed against her face, and Kate released a shrill sound. His big lips encompassed hers like a wet muzzle. She kicked his foot with her heel.

"Connor!" she shouted as soon as he let her breathe.

He laughed and pulled the flaps of the coat tighter when she wriggled her arms to try and push him off. When that didn't work, she threatened him. "Lily's going to kill you for this!"

"I'm not afraid of Lily Baker," he said, puckering his mouth again.

Connor was torn back so hard, Kate fell forward. Someone's arm caught her as the coat slid off her shoulders, and she found herself grabbing onto a navy sweater for support.

Cool wind sailed against Kate's skin with the jacket gone. She stared at the spot where her fingers curled tightly around the soft fabric at someone's chest. The fragrance of deep, cold earth and sweet flowers washed over her.

"Officer Riley?" Connor half-asked, half-shouted from where he stumbled back on the dock.

Kate looked up and instantly dropped her fistful of Cress's sweater.

The fae Prince's turquoise eyes flickered over to the policeman.

"C... Connor..." Kate wasn't sure if she was accusing Connor or warning him to run for his life. She also didn't know what to do next as Cress strode down the dock and took hold of Connor's collar, squeezing the fabric the same way Connor had trapped Kate.

Kate reached out to do *something* as the policeman gasped. In one sweep, Cress kicked Connor's legs out, lifted him, and tossed him off the dock.

A loud splash sounded below, and Kate released a raspy gasp. "You can't do that!" she shouted, racing to the dock's edge.

Cress said nothing—he reached for her, took her hand, and began leading her back up the dock.

"Wait, we can't just leave him! What if he drowns?" she said.

The fae Prince stopped walking. When he turned and looked back at her, it was clear he wasn't concerned about the outcome. After studying Kate's face for a moment, he released a low growl and marched back. Cress pulled off his sweater and dove into the dark water.

Kate pressed a hand against her chest as she crept along the dock and searched the lake. She didn't even see bubbles. She scooped Cress's sweater off the ground as she waited, fidgeting with the navy material.

Sputtering filled the air as Connor's face appeared above the water. The fae Prince climbed the ladder, dragging Connor by his shirt and lifting him onto the dock with one hand like Connor was a bag of garbage being tossed to the curb.

Connor coughed as he hit the moist wood panels.

Cress marched back. Kate extended the sweater toward him with a shaking hand. He took it, found the hole, and reached to pull it over Kate's head. He freed her hair with quick flicks and adjusted the shoulders as she slowly threaded her arms through the sleeves. He didn't make eye contact. He just took her hand again and began walking back into town.

"Aren't you freezing?" she asked him. She hugged her free arm to herself, trapping in the sweater's heat. It was soft on the inside.

Cress's hand tightened in hers, but he didn't respond.

Kate felt like she was dreaming as they left the harbour path and crossed three roads to reach Hanes Street. The Prince avoided the street-lights and kept to the edges of buildings.

"Where have you been?" Kate tried again in a small voice. "Your assassins have been looking everywhere for you. They think you're dead."

His gaze stayed ahead as the glow of the café windows came into view. All the other shops and apartments down the street were dark. There were no cars left on the road.

Cress walked to the café door, swung it open, and dropped her hand. When she didn't walk in, he said, "Get inside before the cold makes you ill." His voice was low and quiet; not the bossy, demeaning tone he'd used before.

They were the only words he'd said since he appeared at the docks.

Kate shifted her weight on the sidewalk. "You shouldn't have done that to Connor. The police will be looking for you now—"

"Go in, Human, before my brothers find out I've touched you."

Kate still didn't move, so Cress put a hand against her lower back and shoved her inside. He closed the door behind her, and the scents of coffee beans and pastries filled her nose.

She spun around, but the fae Prince had already left.

CHAPTER

25

Prince Cressica and the Baristas He Knew

Only the glowing patches from the human lamps on the road gave the night any life. Cress waited at the streetside until the silhouette of Mor's curly hair appeared in the alley. Shayne's crossbow was in his grip, but the assassins were otherwise unarmed. Though it was dark, Cress saw that they were dressed in decorative, human-like garments, and their silken fairy hair was smoothed back and not loose as it should be.

"Your Highness!" Dranian's shadowy shape dipped into a bow, and Cress bristled at the formality. He opened his mouth to speak but Mor cut him off.

"Cress, where in the cursed human realm have you been?" Mor stepped into a patch of light. "We didn't know if you were alive!"

"It's complicated. I had to keep my distance. I've only come here now to warn you." Cress hugged his damp arms to himself. Mor pulled off his fancy human jacket and handed it over, so Cress took it without objection and stuffed his arms inside.

"What's the warning?" Shayne asked from where he and Dranian remained in the darkness.

Cress scuffed his wet hair as he sorted his words, but he was cut off by Mor's deep voice again.

"Why haven't you contacted us in a *week*? Why did you disappear after you were left in that alley to die?"

"Left to die? It was just a few broken bones, Mor. I melded them back together. What in the faeborn Corners did you think happened to me?"

"Kate said you were nearly dead," Mor said, his brows pulling in.

"*Kate*...?" Cress said, articulating her name spoken so casually from his assassin's mouth. He almost said several things in response. Almost, but he held up a hand instead. "That's not important." Cress took in a deep breath. "The Shadow Fairies are in the human realm."

Silence filled all the cracks and spaces between the four assassins. Cress waited as the heaviness of the news settled in.

"You're not just being funny, right Cress?" Shayne tugged on the drawstring of his crossbow and inched toward the puddle of light.

Cress made a face. "When have I ever done that?" he asked. "I sniffed fresh traces of them in the academy when we were there. Then I smelled them in the park and followed their trail. I saw them for the first time at another human library not far from here."

"That doesn't make any faeborn sense. How did they sneak past our Queene?" Mor asked.

Shayne scratched his head. "Do you suppose they came through the Seoul gate and took a human air vessel to get here?"

"No," Cress said. "They came through *our* gate. The North gate."

"How do you know that?" Shayne asked.

"Because Bonswick is with them."

One of the assassins inhaled sharply—Cress did not see who. Shayne's blue gaze darted to the rooftops, his fingers drifting back to his arrows to loosen one. Mor looked over his shoulder toward the dark alley they came from, then both ways down the street.

Dranian stepped into the light to meet Cress. His dark auburn brows were furrowed, his flesh appeared tight. "Do you think..." He swallowed. "Do you think they're here for us?"

Cress shifted his feet. "Our Queene still can't seem to decide if she wants me as her heir or if she's jealous of my power and wants me dead. That wicked faeborn female." He muttered the last part.

Mor had a strange look on his face. His gaze dropped to the sidewalk.

Shayne loaded his arrow and kept his shooting hand on the bow's trigger. "Do we kill the Shadow Fairies, then? Do we try to negotiate? Do we..." He chewed on his lip. "Do we go back to the Queene and try to beg for forgiveness for whatever we did to bother her?"

"Absolutely not," Cress said. "The Dark cannot be negotiated with, and we cannot go back to the High Court when we have yet to kill that human who's enchanted me."

"Go inside, you two," Mor abruptly said to Shayne and Dranian. His silvery brown eyes hovered on Cress. "There's something I need to speak to our Prince about."

Shayne's hands tightened around his bow. A beat of silence passed, but the two assassins dipped their heads and left. Their silent footsteps carried them back to the dimly lit café. Neither of them turned their heads or ears to the road to eavesdrop.

"What's this about, Mor?" Cress asked when Shayne's white hair disappeared inside.

Mor stared with hard, unblinking eyes. "That enchantment should have worn off a week ago."

Cress's mouth tipped down at the corners. "What are you implying?"

"You like her."

"What—"

"Because she's innocent," Mor said. "And she's kind when she doesn't need to be. I think you realized a while ago that Kate Kole is everything the opposite of what you hate."

Dead quiet stole the air, making it hard to breathe. Cress bit his lips and stepped toward his friend with a warning tone.

"And what do I hate, exactly?" he asked darkly. "Since you seem to know my thoughts so well."

"Levress."

Cress drew back. "Watch your tongue—"

"Haven," Mor went on. "All the women of the faeborn court. I know that's why you refused to form a bond with a mate all these years, Cress. I could see how much you *hate* them. And I know a mate would have just been one more female you had to try and keep from stabbing a dagger into your faeborn back."

At first, Cress only glared. But then he released a strange, dull laugh. "Nonsense. I'm pleased to marry Haven."

"Maybe. But you have a fairy crush on a human."

Cress laughed louder this time. It was dreadful and tacky. "*Please.*" He waved a hand toward Mor. "How repulsive."

"Yes, most would say so. But that's not what I need to talk to you about." Mor's hard eyes drained to shimmering glass, and a moment later, he swallowed. "There's something you don't know, Cress," he added. Mor's lips rounded to form various words, but it took a few tries before he spoke. And when he did, the wind stopped rushing. "You attacked Levress. You tried to take her down," he said.

It was so preposterous that Cress almost didn't register the testimony. Mor could spit a decent jest at times, but the fairy's tone was pure.

Cress's face changed, draining of all laughter, and colour, and life. Suddenly, he was the one who couldn't spit out words. All he managed to utter was, "When?"

"Six months ago." Mor hugged his arms to himself and cast his brown-silver eyes back on the ground. "I stole your memories. It was me."

All the air was sucked out from between them. It was as though the sky deities themselves had gasped and recoiled. It was as though the night heavens had fallen and crashed down and shattered to a thousand pieces upon the human road, marking the great distance between Cress and Mor.

"You?" The Prince's voice cracked. It came out barely a whisper.

No. It could not be true. Mor was playing a game. Cress felt his stomach twist and his heart turn to stone. Mor's face didn't show signs of falsehood.

"Why?"

"Because you attacked Levress from the shadows. She doesn't know it was you. No one does, except for me and Thessalie. Thessalie ordered me to never tell you," Mor said. "We did it to save you from her. She'll kill you and everyone you ever loved if she finds out you broke a fairy law, crossed into this realm, and tried to take her down in the one place it would hurt her the most."

But Cress shook his head. "I've never been to this realm before."

"You have. You tracked the Queene's crossbeast to a secret room below that academy library. You fought it, and you killed it, and you nearly drained the Queene of her power. She was ill for two weeks," Mor promised. "She's never been the same since. She hunted for the killer; for *you*. I made sure she never found out who it was. The High Court demanded that everything about the case stay hidden as they performed their investigation to learn the identity of the traitor. That's why no one ever spoke of it to you until now."

Cress dragged a step back, feeling his stone heart sink deeper into his chest. "Why would I do such a thing?"

"Because Levress killed your birth mother." The streetlights reflected a glint of moisture in Mor's eyes. "I'm sorry, Cress."

Cress staggered away, sure the heavens were falling again, and again, and again. That the ground had turned to an ocean, and he was sinking to the bottom of it.

All the days he'd spent pacing, wondering who was trying to trick him. Wondering who was trying to steal his life. All the suspicions he carried for months, never trusting anyone.

Except Mor. He'd trusted Mor.

"I've wanted to tell you since the day I did it."

Cress's fingers traced over his back pocket where he usually kept his fairsaber handle. He didn't have it with him. "Levress must have found out," he said from a dry throat. "That's why the Dark army is here."

"I don't know for sure. Maybe the sky deities are looking on us with favour and the Dark simply came to dally around and mess with humans for a while." Mor shrugged, but his shoulders dropped heavily. "But yes. Probably they are here for you."

Cress's turquoise eyes took on the cold and rage of the North Corner snow. "I'm not afraid of the Dark. Let them come for me."

Mor raised a finger; his voice wavered. "What are you saying, Cress?"

"You know what I'm saying." Wind ruffled through the streets, and the lamps flickered as a flush of power prowled along the air.

Mor blanched. "Cress—"

"I will get the Shadow Fairies out of the human realm before they come for the rest of you and punish you for my crimes," the Prince said.

Mor's curly hair bounced as he frantically shook his head. "No! You shouldn't be alone right now! It's far too dangerous—"

"Give me one day to think all this through. Alone," Cress commanded, unable to look at his friend for the first time in over five faeborn years.

Mor looked like he wanted to object. But he nodded. "There's another problem, Cress. I'm sure you've picked up on it," he said.

"Go home now, Mor. I have things to do."

Cress turned to leave, and Mor's deep voice followed him. "Why in the faeborn Corners can that human feel your stare? I don't know what's going on in your faeborn heart, Cress, but if you're not careful, this will end badly for her, too. You must see that."

Cress kept walking. His fingers traced over his belt toward his back pocket where his fairsaber was missing.

"She's the least of my problems now," he called back. "Goodbye, Mor."

Mor did not reply.

Though it was a simple farewell, the tone of Cress's voice had said, *"Stay away from me."*

210

CHAPTER

26

Kate Kole and the Decisions that Came After

The apartment seemed darker after the assassins left. They were almost silent in their escape, but Kate heard the soft click of the front door. She'd never been afraid to be alone before, and tonight was no exception.

But tonight, the darkness seemed darker, and the coldness seemed colder, and the emptiness seemed emptier.

She wandered from her bedroom and peered out the window. It was too dark to see much, but the wind had picked up and some of the street-lights teetered slightly. For a moment, she stood there in her quiet kitchenette, listening to the silence. Listening to all the voices that weren't there.

She pulled out a notebook from the kitchen drawer and scribbled across a blank page:

Dranian,

I'm sorry I made you kiss my friend's shoe.

- Kate

After nearly rewriting the note three times, she went to her small desk by the window. She dug through her drawer for her blue-light glasses and flipped open her laptop while shoving them on her nose. The spine of the most recent book she read cracked when she pressed it open. She dragged her finger down a page where notes about things that inspired her for her own novels were scribbled in the margins. Ten minutes went by of her glancing at the door every few seconds. Eventually, she abandoned her novel and made a chamomile tea.

Finally, the door inched open and two fae assassins tiptoed in. Dranian jumped when he saw Kate standing there. He slapped a heavy hand over his broad chest like she'd startled him, like he'd been caught in the act of doing something he wasn't supposed to.

"You're up late," Kate commented, pulling off her glasses and sitting back down in her desk chair. She took a long sip of her tea, waiting for an explanation she worried wasn't coming.

"You're up late, too," was all Shayne said back. He set his crossbow against the wall and stretched with a yawn.

"Well, the café's grand opening is tomorrow. And honestly..." Kate set down her tea and hugged her arms to herself. "I thought you'd left."

"We did leave."

"No, I thought you'd left *forever.*"

Shayne almost smiled. "Would you miss us if we did?" he asked. He looked way too flattered. He even came over, crouched down in front of Kate, and set his chin on his palm while he batted his eyelashes.

When Kate didn't answer, his smile widened, revealing the faint traces of dimples. "Queensbane, Human. You like us, don't you?" He poked her nose. "I think I like you, too."

Kate tossed her blue-light glasses back to her desk and stood. "I'm going to bed."

Warmth bled into the storefront, turning the café into a sauna even though the world outside was getting close to winter temperatures. When Kate followed the scent of fresh coffee down from her apartment in the morning, she nearly fell off the last stair at the sight of two burly fae males racing through the empty café, throwing something clear and squishy against the wall.

"What is *that*?" Kate asked.

"I have no idea," Mor mumbled from where he sat by the fireplace with his feet up, reading. "Shayne stole it when he was out getting paper drinking goblets this morning."

"Look!" Shayne's eyes were wide as he tore the goopy thing off the wall. He hurled it across the room again. It stuck to the window, and the googly-eyed little figurine held onto the glass by its feet. Dranian lunged over a chair to get it, shoving Shayne out of the way.

"Hey! It's still my turn!" Shayne barked after him, but Dranian got there first and tugged the thing off the wall. He turned with a taunting sneer and jiggled it in the air.

Shayne hopped the chair and tried to grab it, but Dranian flung it away. It sailed toward the café door as Lily opened it and walked in. The goopy figurine smacked her forehead and clung there, and both fae jerked to a halt. Shayne's hand was still out, frozen in midair, reaching toward it.

Lily peeled the thing off slowly with a horrified face. "What *is* this?" She threw it into the garbage, and both fae grumbled and moaned. Mor snorted a laugh by the fireplace.

"Wait, who are all those people outside?" Kate pointed toward the window.

"I'd also like to know," Lily said. "They're lined up all the way past the flower shop." The girls pressed against the glass to take in the people

213

on the street. "They aren't here for our opening, are they?"

"Yes, they are," Mor said without looking up from his novel.

"How?" Lily asked.

"It was those two." Mor lifted a foot and pointed at Shayne and Dranian with his toes. "They visited every bookstore, academy, and storefront for miles and flirted shamelessly with all the humans." His gaze finally flickered up with a look. "They made a lot of promises. There will be plenty of disappointed young—and old—females in here by the end of the day."

Kate's face fell. Lily looked repulsed.

"Unreal." Lily muttered, casting Shayne and Dranian a look. She turned to Kate. "Hey, let's talk upstairs for a sec."

"But we're supposed to open in like ten minutes."

Lily took Kate's arm and redirected her toward the staircase. "I'll be fast." She bounded up the stairs first and pushed into Kate's apartment. She started talking as she whirled. "I just got a text from Connor. He says *Officer Riley* attacked him last night."

Kate put a hand on her forehead. "Oh, that. Well, it's not what you think. Connor totally came onto me and—"

"Wait, you know about this?" Lily put her hands on her hips, and then, "*Wait*, did you just say Connor *came onto you*?"

A flood of loud noises filled the café below, and Kate's head snapped toward the stairs. "Did they open the doors already?"

Lily grabbed Kate's shoulder before Kate could race back down. "Kate—what happened? You can't just say that and then run off!"

"I'll tell you about it later. We need to get back down there." Kate jutted her thumb toward the café.

Lily dropped her head and pinched the bridge of her nose. "Actually... I'm so sorry, Kate. I have to cover the extra shift Connor was supposed to work today. He's not coming in now, and I need to leave in like thirty seconds. I'm the worst, I know," she said.

Kate dragged a hand through her hair. "It's okay," she promised, coaching herself mostly. She nodded toward downstairs. "I have them.

We'll be fine. Go do what you need to at work."

Lily nodded, but her face was hard. Kate was sure they weren't finished their conversation about Connor.

They headed down the stairs, slowing to a stop on the bottom stair at the sight of the café *full* of customers, and…

"Oh no—"

"Wow! Look at all the people here for our coffee!" Lily exclaimed, but Kate didn't hear her.

Shayne's bare chest glistened in the morning sunlight like a beacon for every lonely woman in the city to come running. He fastened an apron to himself that didn't hide much, and he winked at a lady coming in.

"What are you doing?" Kate rushed over to ask. "Shayne, get a shirt on *right now*. You're going to get my coffee shop shut down!"

"Shut down? Look at all the coin you're making! I'll make you rich, Human." Shayne opened his arms like he was presenting himself as her greatest asset.

"There's a thing here among the humans that's called, *No Shirt, No Shoes, No Service!*" Kate argued.

Shayne's face fell—he glanced down at his bare feet.

"Just put on a shirt and I won't make you wear shoes," Kate negotiated, shaking her head in disbelief.

"As you wish, Human."

Before Shayne reached for his shirt below the counter, he blew a kiss at Lily as she headed for the door, and Lily's enthusiasm changed to a scowl.

Kate sighed as she pulled the to-go cups from the cupboard and began setting them out for Dranian to fill. It took all of three seconds before she caught Shayne reaching across the counter and encouraging some random customer to feel the muscles in his arm who didn't ask to.

The first hour went by like a breeze. Orders were taken, Dranian whipped up drinks, and Shayne charmed every person who came to the counter. Mor tidied up as people passed through, sweeping the floors, wiping tables, and resetting the chairs.

Kate watched them with a strange amazement. She kept expecting one of them to lose it and throw a table across the room, but none of the fae raised a single protest about their chores. Mor even hummed as he worked. Shayne didn't stop smiling once.

"Feel free to take a break whenever," Kate said to them, but they ignored her and didn't stop moving.

When she headed to the chalk board to come up with a daily special, she found a remarkably detailed drawing of a whipped coffee drink filling up half the board. Beside it were the words: Ca-FAE Mocha.

"I came up with it," Shayne bragged when he noticed her looking. "It's espresso, milk, chocolate syrup, a pinch of whipped cream, and the free handsome smile of a fae serving it on a silver platter."

Kate burst out laughing. Her raspy alto filled the shop and turned heads. "How about next week's special can be a *Fruit and Yogurt Par-FAE*?" she suggested.

"Brilliant." Shayne grinned.

"What about a *Spearmint Ca-Fae Latte*? With a magical touch," Dranian said in a monotone voice from where he sorted milk and cream pods. "We can put a trick inside that'll make human tongues tingle. And the drink can have those little crunchy bits of candy you sprinkle on top of whipped cream. Coffee should always have those in my opinion."

Kate's smile warped. "What do you mean—*that'll make human tongues tingle*?"

"Speaking of names, this establishment doesn't yet have one." Shayne folded his arms and leaned against the counter. "I had all kinds of trouble telling the humans how to find a place with no name. I want to make a sign to hang out front."

Kate sighed. "Lily and I haven't been able to land on the right name yet. I know, it's terrible business to open without one." She tapped her chin in thought as she watched Dranian put away the cream and Mor scrub the drips off the front counter.

"What about *Fae Café*?" Shayne suggested.

What was left of Kate's smile faded and she dropped her arms to her sides. "You're talking like you're going to be here forever," she said.

Shayne's grin disappeared, too. Mor slowed his cleaning, and Dranian muttered something and disappeared through the door to the kitchen.

"I can't enslave you forever. My conscience isn't happy about even doing it up to this point," Kate said, glancing down at the squeaky-clean tile floor. She chewed on her lip as she wandered to the coat hooks and pulled down the navy sweater. Her thumb ran over the soft fabric. She folded it and extended it to Mor.

"Give this back to your Prince when he turns up again."

Mor looked like he wanted to say something. He took the sweater slowly.

"I think I've forced you to do these jobs for long enough. It's not fair for me to ask you to help here, even if I need it. From now on, you don't have to work in this café, or attend social events, or come to book club."

The air turned strange. Kate fidgeted with the hem of her shirt. Then she pulled her coat from the hook, shrugged it on, and headed for the door to give them the space to leave quietly. A cold hollowness filled her chest when she thought about them not being there when she came back. The income they already earned her café in the first hour was more than she could have ever made on her own with her simple coffee recipes, unpublished books, and social media page for marketing.

Kate tugged her coat tighter and shivered as she walked over the fresh snow, scanning the streets for an off-duty patrol car. She guessed Connor would be stopping by at some point to give her an earful.

The trees had lost most of their leaves, but a few still clung to their branches, not ready to let go. Kate eyed them as she stuffed her hands into her pockets, wondering why she never thought to bring a hat and mittens.

She walked for thirty minutes before a speckle of white floated down and landed on the tip of her nose. She went cross-eyed watching the snowflake melt. She lifted her hand to catch another one, cracking a faint smile. Snow was responsible for so much joy in her life. It brought out-door adventures, cozy sweaters, hot drinks, sweet pies, and Christmas. But it was also responsible for deep, numbing pain. Kate's favourite memory was in the snow. So was her worst one.

Kate redirected her course and headed toward one of the last parks in Toronto still populated with trees. She clutched her arms to herself and broke into a jog when her teeth began to chatter. It still took another ten minutes to reach Grandma Lewis's house.

The familiar smells of baking and herbal tea drifted out of the warm home, flooding her on the porch stairs. Kate knocked, hiding her smile before her grandmother would answer the door and see it.

"Come in!" the old woman called from the kitchen.

Kate pushed through the door with a relieved sigh as the soothing heat of the house encompassed her. She slid off her coat and hung it up, shaking off snow and chills. Grandma Lewis was already holding two mugs of freshly steeped tea in the kitchen, and Kate laughed.

"How did you know I was coming?" she asked.

Her grandmother blinked. "I didn't."

The front door squeaked, and Kate turned toward the foyer as a deep, masculine voice filled the house that made Kate forget where she was.

"Grandma Lewis," he said as he nudged the door shut behind him. Two full grocery bags hung from his grip. "They didn't have any brown sugar, so I got…"

His words halted when he noticed Kate standing there. One of the bags almost slipped from his fingers.

He stared at Kate. Kate stared at him.

"Katherine," Grandma Lewis said, carrying the tea past her, "this is Cress."

CHAPTER

27

Kate Kole and The Fae Prince

"Where are my glasses...?" Grandma Lewis searched with a full spin before releasing an exasperated sound. "Oh, for heaven's sake. I left them out on the bench!"

The silence was torturous. The air was thin. Neither Kate nor Cress moved a muscle as the old woman hobbled to the front entrance of her home, pulled on her coat with shaky hands, opened the front door with a squeak, carefully stepped out, and shut the door again.

Then they both moved.

Kate grabbed the nearest picture off the windowsill and held the frame up with its pointed corner aimed toward Cress. But he wrapped an arm around her to trap her, and used the other to tear the picture frame away before she could swing it.

"I'll kill you if you touch her!" Kate shouted at him.

Cress tossed the picture back on the sill and slapped a hand over her mouth. "Quiet, Human! She'll hear you!"

Kate tried to squirm from his grip. Her arm broke free and she snatched the mug of tea off the kitchen table. Cress barely grabbed her wrist in time to stop her from drenching his face with freshly boiled water.

"Queensbane!" he cursed when he yanked the mug away and droplets splattered his hand.

The front door squeaked open and the two split apart—Cress shoved her away, and Kate caught herself on the table, resting against it and wiping the hair from her face. She forced a smile as Grandma Lewis came in, glasses in hand.

Cress leaned back against the wall. He brought the mug to his lips and took a long, careful, slow sip of tea.

"I was just about to teach Cress how to make cookies. If you want to stay a while, Katherine, you can try them when we're finished," Grandma Lewis said.

"Of course, Grandma." Her pointed stare flickered to Cress. "I won't be going anywhere."

"What about the café? Isn't today your big launch?" Grandma Lewis opened the fridge and pulled out the milk.

Kate spoke through thin lips. "It's well taken care of by three *exceptional* workers."

Cress's turquoise eyes flickered up to her, and he glared.

Grandma Lewis set an armful of cutlery that looked freshly washed on the kitchen table. The moment the old woman turned back around and headed toward the towel hanging on the stove, Kate slid a dull knife over from the pile and shoved it up her sleeve.

Cress watched from where he leaned on the wall. His mouth curled into a devilish smile like an invitation.

"Come here, Cress. I'll get you to pour the flour." Grandma Lewis waved him over and Kate watched in dismay as the fae Prince glided across the room and took the measuring cups from her grandmother.

"Oh, and I forgot to mention, Katherine," Grandma Lewis turned around, "Cress has taken over your room. Not that you need it, but I just wanted you to know in case you go in there and see… well. Boyish belongings. You know."

Kate's heart thuds doubled. "What? He's been sleeping here?"

"Oh, relax, Katherine." Grandma Lewis rolled her eyes. "I'm a good judge of character. You know that—"

"After what happened?" Kate interrupted with a shrill voice.

Cress glanced up from the measuring cups. He looked between Kate and Grandma Lewis.

"Are you fussing about that again? That was a long time ago, Katherine. You need to let it go—"

"That man could have killed you, Grandma!" Kate shouted. "How could I let it go?!"

Cress stole a look at the living room. His face hardened ever so slightly, but he pulled his attention back to the measuring cups.

Kate swept over to Grandma Lewis and whispered, "You're too trusting. Not everyone is as good as they seem."

"Oh heavens, Katherine!" Grandma Lewis huffed. "Even after all the therapy, changing your name, and turning your hair purple—"

"It's *not* purple, it's red!"

"—you still can't seem to move on from those troubles of the past. Stop letting the few bad days ruin all your good ones!"

Quietness dragged through the kitchen as Kate stared into her grandmother's eyes. She didn't have the will to clear her throat—it felt like it would take up too much of the room's space. Her voice came out cracked when she spoke again. "I'm cleaning out that stranger's stuff from my room, and you're going to send him away right now," she decided, pointing at Cress.

Kate marched up the stairs, listening to Grandma Lewis's loud sigh in the kitchen. When she reached the top, she shoved the bedroom door of her teen years open.

She slowed her march as she scanned her room, finding everything exactly the way she'd left it. Not a single belonging was out of order; the bed was made, the books were straight, and there weren't any traces of that fae Prince downstairs.

"How long has he even been staying here?" she mumbled to herself.

The door slammed shut behind her and she whirled to find Cress leaning back against it. "Over a week," he answered.

Her hands tightened to fists. "I'll kill you. I don't care if you're a fae or a prince or an assassin or whatever!" Kate promised. "You should *not* have come here."

"You think you can kill me?" The corners of Cress's mouth twitched up.

"I can do anything I put my mind to," Kate assured.

"Yes, I know," he said.

Kate's mouth closed again.

Cress peeled himself off the door and stood tall. He folded his arms. "I know all about the lengths you'll go to for your grandmother, and what you'll do for a measly female neighbour you don't even know, and the sympathy you'll show an old woman crossing the street with her paper bags of human food, and the other things you do for others when you think no one will notice. I know everything about you, Katherine Lewis. I know all about Lily Baker, too. I know your grandmother's real name, and your brother's. And yours."

Heat trickled into Kate's chest. She stepped back, her shoes sliding over her bedroom carpet.

"I know why you're afraid of the sky's anger. I know why you changed your name. I know what you've lost, what you cherish, and each of your little habits. I know you enjoy the colour yellow, and that you scribble painfully adorable little notes in your books. I know that your favourite soap contains sweet, fragrant powders. Like I said, I know everything about you." Cress stepped forward, and Kate's back hit her bedpost.

"Why are you telling me this if you're just going to kill me?" she scratched out.

Cress's mouth twisted to the side. He glanced at her neck tattoo like he had the first day she met him. The butterknife warmed in Kate's sleeve.

She held the fae's gaze as she let the utensil fall into her fingers. Before he could say anything else, she thrust the butterknife at him.

His hand flashed up and wrapped hers, stopping the knife inches from his shoulder. Kate's eyes widened as his fingers turned rough and white like pale stone, locking her hand to the dull blade.

"I'm not going to kill you, Human. I'm not going to kill your grandmother, either, or speak your real names in the way required to enslave you," Cress said. "There's no point now. Killing you will only prolong my suffering anyway with how preposterously wrong everything has gone since we met." His hand softened back to flesh, and he shook her wrist until the butterknife fell onto the carpet. "So, stop trying to stab me with everything."

Kate's gaze followed the knife where it rolled beneath her bed, out of reach. "Why should I believe you? I know fairies love to play tricks," she said.

"Yes, we do. We love to play tricks, and meddle in human affairs, and hand out enchanted kisses. Unfortunately, our tricks don't always bring the results we want." He glared at her mouth. "But what's done is done. I have larger troubles to deal with than hunting a pesky, repulsive human. You should stay away from the fairies from now on if you don't want to get dragged into it."

"I can't just stay out of fairy problems while three of them are living in my apartment. And what about my grandmother?" Kate asked. "Won't she get dragged into your troubles if you're *living* here?"

Cress's jaw slid to the side.

"Cress? Katherine? I thought you two were going to help me with the cookies!" Grandma Lewis's voice boomed up the stairs. "You might be adults, but this is still my house. No boys in your bedroom with you, Katherine! Don't you dare get into any handsy business up there!" she added.

Kate fought a blush, but Cress smiled. "You'll never be so lucky," he promised. He reached back, swung open the door, and stood aside to let her exit first.

Kate took one last sidelong glance at where the butterknife had disappeared below her bed. Then she strode out the door on heavy feet. "You have to leave this house," she said as she passed him. "I won't let you stay here."

Cress sighed. "I agree. And since you refuse to *stay out of fairy problems*, I suppose I should just move in with my brothers."

Kate whirled back to find a smirk on the Prince's face.

"Thank you for the invitation," he added.

"That was *not* an invitation—"

"Ah. Unlike my brothers, you haven't enslaved me, Human. I don't have to obey you. I do, however, have all the means necessary to enslave *you* if I wish it." His gaze cut over to Kate as he reached the stairs. "So be very careful."

The snow picked up as they left, and Kate stole a look at Cress's t-shirt every few moments, visible beneath her late grandfather's unzipped hunting coat. Tiny flakes tumbled down the thin fabric, melting at Cress's collar where they touched his flesh. Finally, Kate huffed and passed the paper bag of cookies to her other hand. They walked through a quieter part of the city.

"You should zip your coat. Don't you have a sweater or something?" she asked.

"Not anymore." Cress stole a glance at the bag of cookies. "You're going to share those, right? I helped make them, too."

She released a grunt. "A fae with a sweet tooth. Interesting."

"A human with a resistance to enchantments." He glanced at her, turquoise eyes pointed. "Far more interesting."

Kate stifled a snooty response, not coming up with anything good enough to say aloud. She chewed on her lip as they approached Hanes Street. "Your fae friends might not be at the café when we get there. I told them they could leave if they wanted," she said instead as they rounded the corner.

Kate skidded to a stop in the snow and nearly choked when she saw a new, large wooden sign above the café door that said, FAE CAFÉ, in bold, burgundy letters.

People headed in and out the door, sliding past each other with to-go cups. From where she was, Kate could see notes written across the paper cups in swooping, artistic handwriting.

"My brothers won't leave," Cress assured. "It's an excellent hiding place from…" His voice trailed off, and Kate glanced over at him when he didn't finish.

"Hiding place from what?"

Cress didn't seem to hear. His gaze darted over the street, and he did a slow, full turn. Kate tried to spot what he was looking for, but only the snow-dusted storefronts and nodding neighbours were around.

"Come with me." Cress's hand slid into hers, and Kate found herself being guided to the opposite sidewalk. "Don't glance at your building as we pass it. Just keep walking like you don't know it's there."

"Why?" Kate clutched the bag of cookies, expecting him to run. But he didn't—he walked along casually, his hand in hers, swaying their arms a little. It might have been sweet if he wasn't a cold-blooded fae assassin.

"We're being stalked," he told her.

Kate craned her neck to see behind them, but Cress tugged her arm, turning her back. "Don't look around, Human. We're going to pretend we don't know."

Kate held the cookies tighter against her stomach. "Well… what are we going to do, then?"

"We'll go on a date. Like normal humans do on that *Dating Tonight* show Thelma watches in the evenings. We'll bore the stalkers to death if

225

we must. But we cannot return to your dwelling where my brothers are hiding while we're being followed." Cress glanced into the storefront window of the sweets shop, seeming to eye the candy apples. He shoved his free hand into his pocket.

"Okay…" Kate tried to see the street behind them in the reflection of the window. "Then let's go to the mall."

Cress raised a brow.

"To get you another coat. And a sweater."

"But I have a coat. And you have my sweater," he said.

"This coat is probably forty years old." Kate poked her grandfathers hunting coat with her elbow. "And your assassins are making a lot of money for me today. Just think of it as a thank you gift."

Cress seemed to think about it for a moment. "Fine."

Snow sprinkled the toque barely covering his pointed ears. Kate watched him study stores, nod to people passing by, and cast an only semi-cruel smile at a toddler and mother racing past.

He still held her hand.

They got to the subway station, and Kate pulled out her wallet and paid for them both. The subway cars swished to a stop moments later, filling the tunnel with wind, and the doors slid open. Cress hesitated when Kate stepped into the subway car. She reached back and yanked him in right before the doors closed.

"You can find a seat—"

"I'll stand," Cress announced. He folded his arms and waited for something to happen.

"Suit yourself." Kate stifled a smile as she found an open seat.

The moment the car jolted forward, Cress grabbed the back of Kate's chair to steady himself. Kate's raspy laugh filled the subway car.

The mall smelled of sticky cinnamon buns and potent perfume. Cress eyed the crowds and read aloud the names of each store he saw. "Shayne would have his pockets stuffed full in a place like this," he remarked.

"You should see my apartment. I'm going to have to buy him a shipping container soon to store all of his trinkets," Kate said. She spied

Cress fight a smile before he turned his head away.

"The outerwear store is this way." Kate took his arm and tugged him to the shop of winter coats and accessories. Soft music filled the store, and salespeople snooped from a distance. Kate lifted a coat from a sale rack by the entrance. "How about this one? It's only eighty bucks!"

Cress's face fell. "It's ghastly!" he shouted, and Kate quickly slid it away.

"Wow, take it easy," she muttered. "The salespeople are going to hear you." She tried another one, and Cress looked at her like she was crazy. He slid past and marched to the back of the store where a long, camel-coloured dress coat hung on a mannequin. He pointed at it.

"I want that one," he decided.

Kate sighed and hurried her feet to catch up. "Of course you do."

Six hundred and thirty-four dollars later, Cress paraded out of the outerwear store like he was in a fashion show. Kate's grandfather's coat was rolled into a ball under his arm. Cress had decided he needed the scarf the mannequin wore, too, and the exact pair of sunglasses.

"So much for a profitable day." Kate slid her wallet away.

"Well, you wouldn't let me pay with fairy gold," Cress said. "It's your own fault, Human."

"You can't just pay for something with a handful of rocks! There are rules here, you know."

"You're too kind-hearted," he stated. "It's weak."

"You're still a monster. It's scary."

He glanced at her, but she couldn't see his eyes past his sunglasses. A laugh escaped her as he seemed unable to come up with a response. Cress reached over and took her hand again. "I like your laugh. It's harmless in both an irritating and infatuating way."

He began looking around again—up at the mall chandeliers and the two-story-tall banners. Kate took in his relaxed walk and his almost-smiles to passing people. He didn't seem dangerous. But Freida's words rang through her mind: *"Unfortunately, almost all fairies are tricky, ma-*

nipulative, cruel, and would jump at the opportunity to torment a hu-man..."

So, there was that.

"Why do you keep holding my hand?" Kate asked.

"They're still watching us," Cress said immediately. "And isn't this what humans do on dates?"

"This isn't a real date though," she pointed out. She stole a glance over her shoulder when he wasn't looking, but she still couldn't see any-one following them. It was the first moment she wondered if he was making it all up.

Cress sniffed the air when the mall's coffee shop came into view.

"I know what we should do next." Kate tugged him toward the hole-in-the-wall coffee shop. "You should try your warm milk this way. Your assassin friends can't get enough of it."

Five minutes later they sat at a table in the mall aisle, and Cress sucked the foam off the top of a latte. He stuck his tongue into the liquid first, then smacked the tabletop and growled. "It's *hot!*"

Kate slapped a hand over her mouth to keep back a burst of laughter. "Give it a minute." She dragged the latte over to herself and blew on it lightly. "You're so impatient," she added. When she was satisfied it wouldn't send him tearing through the food court, she slid it back.

Cress finally took off his sunglasses and set them on the table. He eyed the latte for a moment. Then Kate. Then the latte again.

"Try it!" Kate chuckled.

He reluctantly brought the cup to his mouth and took a small, careful sip. His eyes widened. He began to chug. Kate's face changed as he kept drinking and drinking and *drinking*.

"Um… maybe you should take a break—"

Cress slammed the empty paper cup on the table between them and shouted, "That is the *best* warm beast's milk I have ever tasted in my entire faeborn life!"

Kate covered the blush on her face with her hands as people's heads turned. "Seriously, how did you fool an entire police department into thinking you were one of them?" she asked through her fingers.

Cress reached across and pried her fingers away. She realized he was grinning, and her heart performed a strange flip. His mouth curved sweetly over his shapely teeth. It was the first full smile he gave her. "I'm putting on a show, Human," he said. "For the stalkers."

Right.

The 'stalkers'.

Cress leaned back in his chair, his beautiful smile not budging an inch, and Kate could have smacked herself. He was *trying* to embarrass her.

"Wow. You're enjoying this, aren't you?" She pointed to her red cheeks.

"Very much."

"You're seriously evil."

"You don't know the half of it."

"What's your plan? To embarrass me to death?" Kate folded her arms, trying to calm the flush in her face.

Cress tapped the brim of the empty latte cup. "If I make you like me, Human, maybe my next enchanted kiss will stick." He reached for the paper bag of cookies and pulled two out. He passed one to Kate first, then took one for himself.

"Ah. So, you're trying to make me like you by forcing me to buy you a ridiculously overpriced coat and shouting random things in public while people are watching?" Kate asked doubtfully.

His crisp smile returned. Kate couldn't have looked away if she'd tried.

"Well, I don't need you to lose your whole human mind over me. I just need you to become smitten enough to make you want to do as I wish. Smitten enough for me to convince you to leave this city forever if I decide you must."

Kate's smile faded. "I'm not leaving Toronto."

"You might have to, Katherine Lewis."

"I won't. And why don't you just speak my name in the way needed to enslave me since you know it so well now?"

Cress's jaw slid to the side. "It's forbidden and cruel to enslave another living being. You should not have done it to my brothers, and I should not do it to you."

"You were going to before."

"When I thought you were guilty."

"I am guilty. I *killed a fae*."

Cress looked back and forth between her eyes. "You're innocent, Katherine. You wouldn't hurt a moonbug if it landed on your food."

Kate chewed on her lip. "Don't call me that. My name is Kate Kole."

He almost smiled again. "I'm quite positive by now that it's not."

She dropped her eyes. After a second, she broke a piece off the end of her cookie. "You're not a monster at all, are you?" She stared at the cookie chunk for a moment before eating it. "I think I finally understand why your assassins' life stories all include you."

"Not all of them," Cress said. "Mor's, maybe."

"I don't know much of Dranian's story, but it seems like you saved Mor and Shayne from bad lives. I'm starting to get the feeling you may have saved more than just them, too."

Cress pulled his hands below the table. He still hadn't taken a bite of his cookie. "Don't mistake me for a hero like the fairy folk in one of your books, Katherine. I'm the devil in most people's stories. The last, terrible monster they see."

"Kate," she corrected. "And no one wants to tell me Dranian's story. Even you changed the subject when I just brought it up."

Cress tilted his head, seeming to think about that. "Dranian has an illness," he explained. "He seizes up unexpectedly, trembles, and can't breathe properly or think straight. His blood relatives meant to toss him away for it, but instead they tricked a noble family of the North into purchasing him as a childling guard to keep their son out of trouble," he said.

Kate's shoulders dropped. "Do you mean Shayne's family?"

Cress nodded. "Shayne's father should have cast Dranian out the moment he realized Dranian's illness. But Dranian was determined to prove he could do what other fairy guards did so he wouldn't get thrown to the wicked faeborn forests." Cress flicked a crumb off the table. "Shayne gave him a hard time in the beginning. He stole things, started fights, flirted with the wrong High Lords' daughters... Dranian couldn't keep up. But one day Dranian followed Shayne to the childling academy, and the other noble faeborn fools there began beating Dranian when he seized up, forcing his face to the dirt and demanding he kiss their filthy shoes before they would allow him to stand again."

Kate's fingers pressed lightly over her mouth, thinking of the look on Mor's face at the fundraiser when she made Dranian kiss Lily's shoe...

"So, Shayne went back and broke each of those noble fools' ribs," Cress said.

Kate's jaw dropped. "Shayne *broke* their bones...?"

Cress lifted his shoulder into a shrug. "The healers snapped everything back and the bones melded. But Shayne's father was so angry, he put cold iron in the bottom of Shayne's boots and strapped them on with locks so Shayne couldn't get them off. His feet were bound in them for three days. It's why Shayne hates shoes now." His eyes darted back up. "So, you see, Dranian's story has nothing to do with me."

Kate wasn't sure she was still breathing. She'd made the fae assassins wash mugs and mix fall drinks in the café. Suddenly she was sure the only monster here was her. She rubbed her eyes, promising herself she'd never tell the fae to do anything again. "How did Dranian end up with you then?" Her voice was dry.

"He followed Shayne when Shayne's father sent him off to serve the High Court. Dranian didn't know I recruited Shayne to the Brotherhood of Assassins. All he knew was that the male he spent his whole faeborn life protecting was on his way to challenge the dreaded Prince of the North to a deathmatch. That moody fool sprang out of hiding and nearly stabbed me through the neck, thinking I'd slaughtered Shayne." A smile broke across Cress's face. "Fool."

231

"Unreal," Kate whispered, trying to imagine that. She tapped the table with her fingers. "I think what Dranian has is called panic attacks to us humans. But I haven't seen him have one yet."

Cress adjusted himself in his seat. "He hasn't had one since he's been here."

Two men drifted into view across the mall aisle, lingering by the entrance of a clothing store. Their hair was thick enough to cover their ears. There was something slightly off about them; a strange, silent power Kate had seen in only a few guys this last month, including the one sitting across from her.

"Can I confess something super foremost?" she said to Cress in a quiet voice.

"If you want to."

Kate wrung her fingers as the men's unusual silver and brown eyes took her in. They looked away like they were pretending to not be watching.

"I totally thought you were making the whole '*We're being followed*' thing up," she said.

A funny smile touched Cress's mouth. "I try not to utter falsehoods. Also, your use of the term *foremost* is improper and unusual. I know because I write a lot of excellent letters." Cress glanced at her shaking hands. He reached over, lifted one off the table, and swept to stand in the same motion.

"Let's keep walking," he said, grabbing the hunting coat and cookies. "You haven't shown me how to use those mysterious moving stairs yet."

Kate followed numbly as Cress headed toward the escalator. "Who are those guys?" she whispered. "The ones following us."

Cress's grip tightened. "You would needlessly worry if I told you," he said.

Kate stepped onto the escalator, and Cress took her waist to balance as he hopped on after. The ride to the second floor seemed to drag on for hours. Kate fought the impulse to look back and see if the fae were following them up.

"Your hands tremble when you're afraid," Cress said from behind her. "They're trembling now." A pause. "Also, these moving stairs are terrifying."

They reached the top and Kate turned to face him the moment she stepped off. "I want to go back to the café."

Cress looked her over. "Why?"

"Because Mor, Shayne, and Dranian are there."

"You don't think I'll keep you safe?"

"You're not compelled to protect me. They are," she said. "It's just common sense."

People grunted and swerved to walk around them as Kate and Cress crowded the space at the top of the escalator.

Kate expected him to refuse to lead the stalkers to his brothers again, but instead Cress nodded.

"You go back to them. I'll lead the Shadow Fairies off." Cress took her hand again and turned back toward the escalator. Kate's eyes widened as he stepped onto it and began shoving people aside as they rose up.

"Um... hold on..." Kate started mumbling apologies as Cress pulled her *down* the ascending escalator. He nudged and shoved to make a path. It took way longer than the ride up.

"The magic stairs want to trap us here," he muttered when they finally leapt off. "How outrageous." He slid his sunglasses back on.

"Should we split up?" Kate asked.

"Not yet, Human. I'm planning a large distraction. You'll know when it's best to run." He pulled something out of his back pocket, and Kate recognized the sword handle with the tiny gold and silver wings. She blanched.

"Not here—*Cress!*"

But the blade forged out of nothing, sending a buzzing sound through the mall aisle. He turned himself toward the pair of stalkers by the clothing store.

The two fae looked him over, icy expressions donning their faces.

233

They drew weapons, and soon three long swords were shining beneath the mall lights. Bystanders stopped what they were doing. Some people clapped and cheered like this was part of a theatrical performance. Shoppers pulled out their phones to film it.

"Aren't you worried you'll get hurt?" Kate whispered as she backed away.

Cress grunted. "I'm insulted you'd ask."

"Why?"

"Because there's only two of them. Run now, Katherine." Cress tossed over her grandfather's coat and the bag of cookies.

Kate bumped into someone as she scrambled away. She couldn't take her eyes off where the fae stalkers marched across the mall aisle toward Cress who waited, staring back at them through his expensive, brand-new sunglasses.

The stalkers split up and prowled around the Prince. They leapt from both sides, and Cress spun—his sword sliced the air, catching them both in one swing. Kate shrieked, but the crowd gasped and clapped.

Kate didn't stay to see the rest.

She raced from the mall, bursting into the frigid cold and leaving footprints in the snow. It took her minutes to reach the subway. She was out of breath as she scurried on—a second before the doors swished closed. Nothing followed her in.

Her chest pattered the whole ride.

At her stop, she slipped out of the subway car, jogged up the station stairs, and rushed through the streets to the café with her grandfather's coat in her arms.

She was panting and covered in snowflakes when she got there. She waited, trying to wipe the worry from her face as a few customers came out with drinks nestled between their fingers.

Kate grabbed the door before it closed, and another hand came above hers on the glass, holding it open. She nearly screamed when she looked up and saw Cress there. His sunglasses were broken in his other hand.

"How did—you get here—so fast?" Kate asked through pants.

"What do you mean? What took you so faeborn-cursed long?" he said back.

Bloodstains covered his new, overpriced coat, along with a large cut through the fabric, and Kate glared. "Seriously?!"

"I'm fine, thank you dearly for asking. It was just a regular midday squabble," Cress said with ample sarcasm. But he snatched her fingers and dragged her inside like he had something important to say. The café door slammed shut behind them. A few people filed nearby tables—some of them set their coffees down to stare.

Cress cleared his throat. His nostrils flared as he inhaled to catch his breath.

Kate waited.

He released his heavy lungful of air. He opened his mouth, but he took in another deep breath instead of speaking, and Kate made a face.

"Seriously, just say it," she said.

"All right." Cress cleared his throat and stood tall again. His hand tightened ever so slightly around her fingers.

She sighed and scratched her head as he took an absurd about of time to collect himself. People were still watching.

"I need a new coat," Cress finally said.

Kate gaped.

He held up the hem of his coat where the rip was like he thought she didn't believe him. He waved it a little.

A mug fell to the floor by the counter, smashing into a dozen pieces. Dranian stared with round eyes at Cress's and Kate's hands. Coffee pooled at the fae's shoes.

"Aw, *Cress*!" Shayne ripped off his apron and hurtled it onto the counter. "Why'd you have to do that in front of us?!"

Cress tossed Kate's hand away with a moan-growl. "Oh, for the love of the sky deities!"

Kate huffed in disbelief, still glaring at him for the coat comment. "I'm going to take a shower," she stated, shaking her head as she marched off, leaving them to sort out whatever fae nonsense they were freaking out about. She strode up the stairs, into her apartment, and went straight into the bathroom. The lock of the door clicked behind her, and she rested with her back against the door until she could think straight again.

"What a crazy grand opening day," she muttered as she went to the shower and cranked the lever for hot water.

CHAPTER

28

Prince Cressica and a Royal Beating

Cress released a gritty sound into the alley. "That one was *hard*!" he snapped as Mor shook out his hitting hand. Shayne and Dranian held Cress's shoulders tight, stopping him from racing off.

The alley behind the café was empty, but occasionally a human couple hurried on by or a frail female shrieked and ran away.

"Since we're together again, why don't you tell us why you're covered in fairy blood?" Mor suggested as he wound up for another hit with the wrath of the sky deities.

"Fine." Cress grunted as he took Mor's punch right in his beautiful faeborn cheek. He slid his jaw back and forth to ensure it wasn't broken. "I was being followed by Shadow Fairies. There were only two of them—*Ugh*!" Dranian kicked him in the shin.

"I thought you weren't going to start a war with the Dark until after

237

you had a day to think," Mor said. "Those were *your* words, Cress."

"I provoked them so the human could get away. Now for the love of the sky deities, at least hold your faeborn-cursed punches!" Cress complained.

"Well, that explains it." Mor nodded. "I'm relieved you were just protecting your fairy crush like any weak-minded, irrational, possessive male." Pure and fresh sarcasm. "I was worried you were trying to take on the whole Dark army by yourself like a fool."

Shayne smacked Cress on the back of the head with an open hand. Cress glared at him, and Shayne grinned. "Sorry," the white-haired fairy said with a shrug. "That one was petty. But I enjoyed it."

"I still might," Cress replied to Mor. "But we're best off to hide until Bonswick requests an audience with me. If there's even a small chance he's not here for us, we should avoid provoking him. There's no point in starting a war over nothing."

Shayne tapped his chin and looked between Cress and Mor. "What are you two hiding from us? I know you were whispering fairy secrets the other night when you made Dranian and me leave."

When Cress didn't answer, Shayne smacked the Prince across the back of the head again. "Dranian and I are risking our lives for you, too. You need to tell us what's going on, or I'm going to trot back into that café and kiss our human right in front of you."

Cress's gaze iced over, and Shayne grinned wide enough that his pretty blue eyes shrank. "I'm sure I can enchant her, too. You've been warned," he added.

"Be careful, fool," Cress said through his teeth, but he had no chance to give a royal lecture before Dranian tore the Prince to his feet and shoved him back against the alley wall.

"Apologies, Your Highness," Dranian muttered. "You know I'm not doing this on purpose."

Cress grimaced when Dranian stomped on his toe.

"Fine. I'll tell you every terrible thing Mor and I have kept from you. And then, together, we'll decide what to do," Cress said over Dranian's

WELCOME TO FAE CAFE

shoulder to Shayne.

"What do you mean, *we'll decide what to do*?" Shayne's face fell, his muscles tightening. "You're not still planning to kill Kate, are you? Queensbane, Cress, you can bet your faeborn princeship I'll stop you!" He looked between all the assassins now, backing toward the café. "You three will have to break my bones if you want to lay a finger on her now," Shayne announced.

Cress rolled his eyes. "Shut up, Shayne, this has nothing to do with her anymore."

"Wait, are you saying killing the human is off the table?" Dranian asked with a scowl.

"The High Court will demand evidence of the human's death. They'll sniff the lies on us if we don't go through with it," Mor pressed, though his brown gaze darted warily toward the café.

"I'll tell the High Court I don't have evidence of our success, and I'll pray to the sky deities they believe me," Cress said. "There's no point in killing Kate Kole now. Let's wait Bonswick out."

The assassins' heads bobbed with nods.

Cress hoped they were finished, but Mor wound up and pummelled him in the ribs.

Between hits, Mor told Shayne and Dranian the story of the Queene's crossbeast. It took only a minute, but when he was finished, Shayne didn't seem surprised in the slightest. Though, a fairy grudge burrowed between his brows for not being told earlier. They'd finally stopped hitting Cress.

"Now," Cress said through his teeth. He shoved Dranian back, and the auburn-haired fairy spun into the opposite alley wall. "I'm going to make all of you hurt for a moment before we go back in!"

First, he stomped on Dranian's toe.

Ten minutes later, four North Corner assassins dragged themselves up to Kate Kole's apartment. Mor moaned through punctured lips as he collapsed onto a chair. Cress tumbled to the floor and leaned against a wall, hugging his midsection, and Shayne sat upon the couch, tipping his head back and pinching the bridge of his bleeding nose. Only Dranian seemed able to stay on his feet, though he was limping from his damaged toe.

Cress looked around at the quaint space. He'd only seen the apartment from the window until now, but inside, the rooms felt smaller. Pictures lined the walls of Kate Kole and Officer Lily Baker, smiling. There was one of Thelma Lewis, too, and another male human. Cress stared at the pictures for a long while as he considered who that male was, why he was standing so close to Kate, and why she had pictures of him.

His attention snapped to the human coming from her room, drenched apart from her clothes. She gasped and halted at her bedroom door. "What happened?!" Her raspy voice filled the space.

"You told us to beat him up if he touched you, Human," Mor muttered, nodding to Cress.

From the couch, Shayne snorted a laugh. "I would have come and begged you to stop us, but you commanded us never to disturb you while you were in the shower," he said.

Kate's green-brown eyes flickered from fairy to fairy. When she looked directly at Cress, Cress was certain she was the most fragile, humany-human in the entire realm. Her lips were parted, her hair was damp, her eyes were wide like a forest doe, and she balanced herself on slightly wobbly legs.

How in the cursed Corners had he ever thought she was an assassin?

Cress leaned his head against an end table. He could have fallen asleep that way, but Kate nudged him with her bare foot. So, he grabbed her ankle, and Kate tumbled to the floor before him. He smiled.

"Tell them I can touch you now," he demanded from a dry throat. His eyes slid closed, and he decided to sleep there after all as his mind tumbled into places with uneven floors and tipping walls. "Only if you trust me," he added.

She would be a fool to trust him, even now.

Perhaps Kate Kole ought to keep his brothers bound to stop him from touching her. Perhaps Cress was bad for her. Perhaps... perhaps, in the end, Cress would get her into the exact sort of trouble Mor had warned him about.

As Cress's mind slipped into slumber, he heard her say to the others, "Don't beat him up anymore."

He thought that was the sweet end of it, but then she burst out laughing. Cress's body tensed to react, but every aching part of him objected. So, instead, he peeled one eye open to see Kate falling backward off balance.

"But I have to admit... This is so funny!" She pointed at Cress's swelling face and shrieked some sort of obscure human apology.

Cress grumbled and closed his eyes again, the sound an irritating, lovely poison in his ears as Kate could not seem to stop, hard as she tried. He wanted to curse that infectious, hoarse laugh as it became the lullaby to which he fell asleep.

CHAPTER

29

Kate Kole and the First Week of Business

The café became a warm hug in the middle of the snowstorms, bringing Ontarians in to gather, eat, talk, laugh, and frankly, ogle. Kate listened to their chatter as she ran her fingers along the bookshelf beside the counter. She imagined stories there that would comfort strangers passing through, bring them back for more captivating chapters, and spark conversations among the regulars. She imagined stories about strong fae assassins, burgundy-haired humans, and fairy princes. She imagined making knit book sleeves for the books and mug cozies to keep customers' coffees warm while they read. But there was one problem with that.

"You can *not* go to knitting club, Human. I forbid it."

The words Cress said over and over for the rest of the week.

It was like he thought he was *her* Prince and had the right to make absurd royal fae decrees around the café. Kate either pretended she didn't hear when he gave her instructions, or blatantly disobeyed just to see his reaction. Every second of his tightening skin, thinning lips, and narrowing turquoise eyes was worth it.

It seemed the fae weren't leaving, even after Kate gave them permission to. They never explained why, they just kept working, kept cleaning, kept studying the recipe books and baking odd little pastries they called things like, "Folk Bites" and "Mischief Bombs."

Kate slept on the couch at Lily's place since her apartment had been invaded by assassins. But even though things were beyond busy with the café and Lily's police shifts, it was nice to spend the late nights together sipping steaming nighttime tea and looking out at the stars.

Kate and Lily arrived at the café together in the mornings. The only one who wouldn't smile was Dranian, but even so, the assassin had the entire menu memorized and could mix a drink faster than any human. Shayne invited customers in with warm, dazzling fae smiles that probably left the ladies weak at the knees and the men slightly terrified. Mor kept to himself as he tidied up tables and swept the floors, stifling closed-mouthed smiles whenever Cress tired out the fastest and took afternoon "royal naps" on one of the chairs by the fireplace. Shayne usually snuck over to join him, creating a calendar-worthy picture by a toasty, crackling fire.

At ten p.m. each night, the fae locked the door, poured fresh lattes, and relit the fireplace. Everyone sat around the bistro tables to talk about whatever obscure things popped into the fae's heads. Lily asked peculiar questions, and the fae answered what they could, though, sometimes it seemed like their tongues were stuck when she got snoopy about certain parts of where they came from.

Kate constantly felt the warm touches of Cress's stare on her back. Throughout the days, he asked Kate small, quiet questions like, "What is the purpose of dish soap when water cleans the human goblets just fine?" and "Why do you read such boring literature?" and "Which of my assassins is your least favourite? I want to see if we picked the same one."

The snow roared in like a beast, coming all at once and covering Toronto with a blanket of white. University classes were cancelled for most of the week, but somehow coffee drinkers kept showing up. Parking along the street got overcrowded, and Lily was forced to go apologize to the neighbouring stores about it.

On Tuesday evening, Kate sat down by the crackling fireplace with her laptop and a steaming Ca-FAE Mocha. She rubbed her tired eyes as Cress took the seat across from her.

"What are you doing?" He studied her laptop suspiciously.

"Taxes," Kate said.

Cress tugged the computer over to himself and made a face as he looked it over. "You must pay all of this coin?"

Kate nodded and laid her head down on the table. "I can't stare at that screen anymore."

"Wait a faeborn minute." Cress's fist dropped to the tabletop, and Kate jumped. "You must pay taxes on the coin you earn, and then you must pay taxes again when you *spend* the coin you earn, and then you must pay taxes on—"

"It doesn't make sense. Don't try to understand it," Kate advised, sitting back.

"This is preposterous."

"Yes." Kate dragged her latte over and took a sip.

Cress thought for a moment, his jaw sliding back and forth. He jabbed a few buttons on the keyboard and Kate leaned to try and see what he was doing to her carefully laid out spreadsheet.

"Here." Cress turned the computer back around with a new screen up.

"What is this?" Kate looked over the document. "Wait… is this my novel?!" She grabbed the computer and dragged it closer. "What did you do?"

"I fixed it." Cress pulled his shoulder into a shrug. "Your writing is ghastly."

"My writing is awesome!" Kate objected.

"Says who?"

"Well… some people."

A wide, doubtful smile spread across Cress's face. "Some of the words you use don't mean what you think they mean. Read what I wrote." He tapped the computer screen.

Kate's jaw jutted out as she scanned over her story. Her eyes caught on certain words. Eloquent words. Mystifying words. Her face relaxed when she got to the next paragraph. She read until the end of the first chapter before she looked back up at the fae Prince.

"Fine. This is good," she admitted. "I mean it's still mostly my writing, you basically just softened it up around the edges."

There was a knock on the café door, and a postman set a box outside. The post vehicle drove off.

"Did we order something?" Kate called to Lily sorting receipts at the counter.

"My mugs!" Shayne burst from the kitchen and sprinted to the door, flinging it open. He dragged the damp, snow-dusted box inside, and when the tape seemed too tricky to rip with his fingers, he bit the edge of the box and tore half the lid right off with his teeth.

"Unreal," Lily murmured from the counter.

Shayne drew the first mug out and flicked off the packaging as Kate came over. "Look, Humans!" he shouted, handing it to Kate. The heavy mug had a matte-like stone texture. Across it were words in bold burgundy text: FAE CAFÉ.

"Aren't they delightful?" Shayne took another one out. He gazed at it for a moment, then he kissed it.

"I guess the name is official." Kate smirked over at Lily, who smirked back.

Shayne carried the box to the counter and began unpacking each mug. He even grabbed the scrubby from the back counter to wash them. It was the first time Kate had seen him wash something well. "I picked this colour to match your hair," he told Kate with pride.

Cress stole Kate's computer again before she could stop him. He squinted as he looked from the keyboard to the screen. He pecked at the keys with his pointer fingers, and Kate cringed.

"Did you edit the entire story like that?" she asked.

Cress looked up from the computer. "Of course. It took me all week. I've only fixed it up to the third chapter." He went back to his pecking.

"It didn't need to be fixed," she mumbled, but he ignored her.

Kate spotted a girl with orange-red hair moving into the alley across the street. The girl didn't have a hat, or a scarf, or mitts. She disappeared in the shadow of the buildings where gusts of wind blew snow into small heaps.

"I'll be right back," Kate said, heading for the door.

"Take your coat! It's freezing outside!" Lily's voice faded as Kate pushed out of the café and crossed the road into the alley. She clutched her arms to herself and shivered as she followed the redhead up the stairs to the apartment door.

"Hey!" Kate stopped her.

The redhead turned. She looked Kate over without smiling. "You're the girl who almost got my boyfriend in trouble," she said, but then paused. "Well. Ex-boyfriend." She pulled out a set of keys.

"I came to apologize for all that," Kate said, rubbing the back of her neck.

The redhead stepped inside but left the door open behind her, so Kate stepped in, clasping her cold, bare hands.

"I actually own the café across the street. The guys I work with could probably keep an eye on you if you wanted to shake off a few... you know... bad ex-boyfriends or whatever." Kate chewed on her lip, sure it sounded odd. "I'm just trying to say that if you're ever in trouble, you can come over and we'll have your back."

"Do I seem that helpless to you?" the girl asked.

Kate's mouth moved but no answer came out.

A large, strong body appeared out of thin air in the girl's apartment. The redhead screamed.

"Mor!" Kate shouted. "What are you doing?!" Kate tried to intervene as the girl grabbed a frying pan and swung it.

The pan struck Mor's forehead. He reeled back with a growl, threw a coat at Kate, then vanished again.

The redhead stood frozen, gripping the pan above her head and staring at the spot where Mor had just been. Kate rubbed her temples as she walked over and picked up her coat. "Sorry about that, too."

The redhead spun. Annoyance coated her eyes. "Apology accepted. But I won't be coming anywhere near your café. You people are seriously messed up."

Kate sighed. "Yeah, I know," she said. She paused on her way out. "Listen, if you ever change your mind, Fae Café has warm coffee and a place to talk."

She pulled the girl's apartment door closed behind her when she left, sealing herself out with the cold.

On a humid night, Katherine Lewis had been listening to music with her headphones on while sleeping in the backseat of her parents' car. The weather was an odd mush of melting snow on the roadsides, along with a late fall thunderstorm lighting up the sky in unpredictable flashes. There was so much rain, so much thunder, and so much noise. Only Kate's music was enough to drown it out.

But the car smashing was the loudest sound of all.

There were things about that day Kate didn't remember. Parts of the accident happened too fast. Other parts became frozen in time like a museum of dark pictures trapped in ice lining the walls of Kate's memories.

She didn't remember seeing the headlights of the oncoming car. She didn't remember being dragged out of the car or being taken to the hospital. She didn't remember most of what happened in the numb, cold days that followed.

But she remembered the girl with orange-red hair being pulled from the backseat of the other car.

Kate trudged back through the snow to the café. She found Mor sitting on the counter inside, scowling with ice pressed against his forehead. "She slugged me with a human oven pan," he accused Kate when she came in.

Cress hovered by the door with his arms folded. As Lily babied Mor and passed him a bandage with a slightly sarcastic look of sympathy, Cress leaned forward to whisper in Kate's ear.

"Don't go outside alone again, Human." His tone was dark. "Don't go anywhere I can't see you if you're alone."

Kate sighed. "You're bossy."

His hands found Kate's waist. Cress pulled her into the narrow hallway and placed her against the wall, taking her shoulders and pinning them there. He looked angry.

"What? You have to admit that you *are* bossy—"

"This isn't a jest," he said. "Shadow Fairies aren't to be underestimated, Human."

"You said I don't need to concern myself with those fairies. And you said the two that followed us at the mall would *no longer be a problem*." Kate tilted her head. "What's really bothering you? You're not actually my boyfriend, Cress. We were only pretending."

"Of course I know that. What are you suggesting?" He forced a revulsed face, but his eye twitched.

"So, then why are you so upset that I went outside for like three seconds by myself?" Kate asked.

Cress's throat bobbed. His bright eyes flickered down to her mouth for just a second, and his hands suddenly felt warm on her shoulders.

Kate's heart did a strange twist at the look on his face. "Wait…" she rasped and lifted a finger between them. Time seemed to stand still. "Don't do that."

Cress's eyes flickered between hers. He didn't deny anything.

"The last time you kissed me, it was for a trick."

"Yes," he admitted in a low, detached voice. His hands slid off her shoulders and into his pockets. "That was purely the reason. I have nothing to gain by doing it again. I'm at this café for other reasons."

Kate released an uneven chuckle. "Wait a minute, you're not actually starting to fall in love with—"

Cress's hand slapped over her mouth, halting her words. His eyes were wide.

They stood there like that, frozen in place, until Kate reached up and peeled his fingers away. "—the café," she finished. "I was asking if you were starting to fall in love with *the café*."

The Prince blinked a few times. "Yes, of course. That was totally obvious," he said. His breathing seemed heavier.

Kate hoped his super hearing couldn't pick up her pounding heart. "Right..." Without another word about it, she turned and headed back to the others, not really seeing where she was going. She slumped onto a stool at the counter. She was very aware of Cress existing somewhere behind her. Every movement she made felt like too much.

After minutes of numbly listening to Lily and Mor bicker, Kate glanced back to the hallway. It looked empty. "Where'd Cress go?" she asked.

Lily and Mor stopped talking. Shayne and Dranian looked up from where they fought for foot space on the single foot stool between the fireplace chairs.

Mor's brows pulled together as he sniffed. "He's gone," he seemed to realize. He moved around the counter and went to the door to peer out at the descending blizzard filling the streets. The wind had picked up since Kate was out; it nearly roared now.

Mor gave Kate an odd look as he came back in and stood over her on the barstool. "You smell of worry, Human," he said. "Your rhythm is racing." It sounded like an accusation.

Instead of asking what in the world he meant, Kate turned away and reached for an indistinguishable coffee beverage on the counter that seemed to have no owner. She sipped it, then coughed it back out when she realized it was cold.

Mor hovered for a moment, saying nothing. Finally, he gave up his interrogation and joined the others at the fireplace. They spoke in hushed tones.

Lily slid over a fresh, steaming mug toward Kate to replace the cold one. But she held the drink in place when Kate tried to accept it. "What's he talking about?" she asked.

Kate's gaze flickered up to her friend. "I don't know," she admitted. "I'm not sure what I feel right now."

Lily folded her arms. Her tattoos seemed a little tighter than normal.

"Un-*real*, Kate," she whispered. "You've got eyes for that pushy, en-titled, fairy-tale Prince."

The pulse in Kate's chest tumbled off beat, and she dropped her eyes to the beverage before her. After a moment of cowering beneath Lily's expression, Kate took a long, uncomfortable sip. It felt like ages before Lily finally went back to sorting receipts.

CHAPTER

30

Prince Cressica and A Healthy Breakfast

The morning was filled with a collection of scents: human bird eggs, herbal teas, and beast milk. Cress tapped a finger on the tabletop as he watched Thelma bring over two plates of it. His brows were tipped in, his forehead was creased, and for the faeborn life of him, he couldn't seem to shake his scowl. But Thelma didn't ask about it.

He'd had a miserable sleep in Kate Kole's bed upstairs.

The old woman said a short prayer, then scooped half her eggs into her mouth in one bite.

"Eat, Cress!" She pointed at his eggs with her spoon. "It'll get cold. Then you'll wish you ate fast like me."

She glugged down a tall glass of beast milk, too. When she was finished, she set it on the table with a light thud. Through his stern face, Cress cracked an ever-so-small smile at the line of white milk left on her upper lip.

"Are you worried about me?" Thelma asked through it. "Is that why you're here for breakfast again?"

"I suppose that's part of the reason," Cress admitted, stealing a glance out the window at the crisp, early morning where light snow drifted from the heavens. He wasn't hungry, but he scooped a heap of bird eggs into his mouth. "Mmm," he said dully, so that Thelma wouldn't demand to know if he liked them.

"There's orange juice in the fridge—"

"I'm fine," Cress assured, setting down his utensil. He scrubbed his hair and rubbed his face, then leaned with his elbows on the table like any bad-mannered human, folding his hands with his mouth pressed against them. "What do you do if you like someone, Grandma Lewis?" he asked.

Thelma snorted a laugh. "Any girl would be an idiot not to like back someone as handsome as you." She shovelled in another mouthful of eggs, and Cress nodded, dropping his hands onto the table.

"Thank you. Queensbane, I'm glad there's at least one human here who sees it." He slouched back against his chair and folded his arms. "I *am* handsome," he mumbled to himself.

Thelma kept eating, and when she was finished, she dabbed her mouth with a cloth, erasing the milk stain.

"But what do you do if you like someone you can't have?" Cress asked, leaning forward again. He twiddled his thumbs and waited.

Thelma burped.

"Well, who in the world do you like? The Queen of England?" she asked, and Cress's brows furrowed again. He couldn't tell if she was making a jest. Truly, he didn't even know the human realm had queenes.

"No," he said. "It's someone else." He scratched his chin as he thought of a better way to put it. "What if you liking someone may cause them pain and trouble? What do you do then?" he rephrased.

Thelma folded her ever-shaking hands and looked at Cress more seriously now. "You leave them alone, son. If you being with them will

252

hurt them, then you let them be in their happy life—assuming it *is* happy—and you leave so you're not temped to do something stupid and take that happy life away from them."

Cress tapped his finger on the table again. He slung an arm over the back of his chair. "I don't like that answer."

Thelma shrugged. "Then go ask someone else." She went to stand but halted halfway up. Her lashes fluttered and her hand flew against her chest.

Cress's eyes narrowed as he heard the slight change in her rhythms. The scent of fear filled the air, and a wave of panic followed. The Prince sprang from his seat and caught Thelma Lewis before she could tumble to the floor of her kitchen.

"Queensbane," he said to her. "Are you ill?"

Thelma held tightly to his arm. She stayed that way until the rapid beating of her human heart slowed back to normal. Finally, she looked up at Cress and said, "You know I am."

There was no banter in the woman's tone anymore. It was a tone that told Cress a detailed story her mouth didn't.

Thelma slid off him and shambled to the kitchen counter. Cress watched her with fresh eyes. He said nothing as she moved from the sink to the cupboard, to the table, then back to the counter.

"Do you have a car?" she asked with her back turned.

Cress was about to tell her no, but he thought of Shayne's chariot on wheels back at the café. "I know of one," he said.

Thelma nodded slowly. "Maybe we should go for a drive. I want to see the lake."

Cress thought long and hard about that. After moments of staring at the old woman's back, he grabbed the hunting jacket off the hooks, and he strutted out into the snow.

Cress crept around the café, certain his brothers would catch a whiff of him if he got too close. He headed out back where the ugly red human chariot on wheels was half covered in snow.

He used his sleeve to clean it off. When he opened the door and slid in, it was bitter cold. Thankfully, Shayne was foolish enough to leave the keys inside.

Cress had never commanded a human chariot, but on his first day with the officers, he rode in one briefly with Officer Larrens, and he'd studied the machine. Cress turned the key as he had seen Officer Larrens do.

The chariot squeaked to life. "That's right, wake up," Cress instructed, and he patted it on the wheel so it would know he was a friendly rider, not a cruel one. "Take me to Thelma Lewis's dwelling place," he commanded.

The chariot didn't move.

Cress looked around, wondering if he was meant to use a whip. There were no reins.

A second later, the other door opened, and Shayne slid into the vessel. "Are we going for a drive, Cress?" the white-haired fairy asked.

"I need this chariot. Tell me how to use it. That's a command."

Thirty minutes later, Cress rolled the chariot up to Thelma Lewis's house. She came out the front door immediately with a bag on her shoulder, and her coat zipped up. Her face was bright with a smile as she rushed to the opposite door and got in.

"Yes, this is perfect!" the old woman said.

"I don't know the way to your lake," Cress admitted. "And this is my first time riding a human chariot."

Thelma released a raspy laugh. "You're full of surprises, Cress. I'll show you the way."

Cress nodded. "First, I'll need you to explain how to back the chariot up. I've only gone forward thus far."

Thelma chatted the whole drive, which she claimed took hours longer than it should have since Cress's vessel *"was barely creeping along"* because he *"drove like an old lady."* Human drivers made loud noises with their own chariots as they passed. Some offered rude human gestures, but Cress glanced over at them, releasing rumbling power from his veins and the threat of death in his eyes. Most of them backed off with startled faces.

The snow was nearly melted, but a chill clung to the air as Cress helped Thelma out of the vessel. Wind rippled off the water, sliding up a sandy ledge and tossing the old woman's white and gray hair.

Thelma smiled when she saw the lake. They walked down to the water's edge arm-in-arm. "Oh, to be able to swim one last time," she said with a long-drawn sigh.

Cress raised a brow. "Shall I toss you in?" he offered.

Thelma's cackle echoed down the beach, and he grinned.

The sun was high in the sky, partially blotted out by misty clouds. Thelma seemed to take it in—the heavens, the sand, the glowing patches on the water. After a while, she whispered, "Son, you have made my last moments legendary."

Cress's face changed, but he hid his surprise as he turned to face her, his arm sliding out of hers. He took her shoulders instead. "Grandma Lewis, when are we heading back?"

"We just got here."

"Yes, but..." He dropped his hands to his sides as it dawned on him. "Thelma," he tried her real name. "I had a mother once, and I didn't get to be there when she passed." He shook his head. "Don't do this to her."

"To whom?"

"To... Katherine."

Thelma only sighed. "Oh, Cress. You don't understand. Katherine had to watch her parents die in front of her. I won't be another loved one she has to watch. I'll be a soft passing memory for her. A recollection of good times, not bad ones. That's what I'll be for Katherine, and Lily, and Greyson, too." Her hand came out of her coat pocket around three letters.

Cress closed his eyes. He knew those letters.

Thelma put the letters against his chest and held them there until he took them.

"If this is what you want," he said.

"It is. Now quit being such a whiny baby, and let's go sit on that bench." Thelma smiled as she limped off to a bench by the sidewalk. She brushed aside sand and watery snow before taking a seat.

After a moment, Cress marched up the beach and sat down beside her.

Thelma rested her head on his shoulder. "Now, tell me what it was like to grow up in a place where everyone always wanted to trick you," she said.

Cress folded his arms with the letters peeking out from his elbow. "It was terrible. I had a vicious queene for a mother who wanted to both destroy me and keep me around at the same time. She pitted others against me, hired assassins to kill me, and played mind games to see if I would survive."

"What a life that must have been. Obviously it wasn't the life you wanted?"

"No."

"What life did you want then?" Thelma's voice was quiet, barely a whisper.

Cress studied the peaceful lake as he thought about it. The quietness reminded him of violet grass fields, jade-leafed trees with unusual personalities in their trunks, and warm weather in a gold-spun straw hut. "I wanted a life with my real mother." His throat bobbed. "I just wanted a faeborn life that was simple."

At first, he thought Thelma was thinking about all he'd said. He waited for a response, but as the minutes ticked by and he didn't get one, he turned his ear to catch her rhythm. His heart slid a little deeper into his chest.

Thelma Lewis's rhythm was no more.

Cress remained there, arms folded. A tear slid down his cheek. After a moment, he reached over and took the old woman's hand, even though she didn't hold it back. A low, quiet sob lifted in his throat, a sign of utter weakness he didn't shew away.

There on the beach, he cried for the old woman. He cried for the loss he knew Kate Kole would feel. He cried for the mother who was taken away from him. And he cried for the simple life he'd never been allowed to have.

CHAPTER

31

Kate Kole and All the Burnt Cookies

Short increments of late-morning sunshine chased the snow away. Loud chatter filled the café, along with the smell of fresh-pressed coffee beans and warm community. Chairs squeaked, cutlery clapped together, people sipped, and occasionally a chorus of laughter erupted from one of the groups. Shayne's new mugs decorated the bistro tables, along with Christmas garland and pinecone centrepieces Lily had made. Kate snapped a photo of it all for Fae Café's social media page.

"Taste this," Dranian said in his deep, drone voice. He held a mug filled with cinnamon-smelling milk toward Kate's mouth. "It's meant to mimic Yule gingerbread."

"Why can't you try it yourself?" Kate asked as she took it and sipped.

"Fairies don't eat bread."

Kate nearly hissed out the drink as she laughed. "Gingerbread isn't real bread," she said, handing it back to him. "And I love this. Add it to the menu."

Dranian looked into the mug for a few moments. Then he slowly, hesitantly, brought it to his lips to try it.

"Seriously, where in the faeborn-cursed Corners is Cress?" Mor marched out of the kitchen. "The fool instructed me not to leave, so I can't go out and look for him without being punished..." His voice drifted off as the café bell clinked and the door swished open.

A gust of chilly air rushed in. Cress followed it.

Shanye stopped what he was doing and eyed the fae Prince. "What's gotten into him?"

"Has something happened?" Mor asked Cress. It was more of a demand than a question.

Cress lifted his head to look at Kate. Envelopes were in his fist. After several seconds of staring in silence, he took one out and held it toward her. "I promise, I didn't try and take her from you," he said.

Kate set her phone on the counter and took the envelope. Her name was on the back in handwriting she didn't recognize. She ripped it open to find a letter inside, signed at the bottom with Grandma Lewis's messy, uneven signature.

She only read the first few lines before she walked out the door.

Kate didn't recall the hike to Grandma Lewis's house, but when she got there, she found the lights were out. There was no tea or baking smells seeping from the kitchen when she walked in, there were no dishes left out, nothing even to clean. Her grandmother had put everything away.

Her lip quivered as she took in the evidence, or lack of evidence, of her grandmother.

"Why didn't you tell me?" she asked the silence in the kitchen. A tear slipped from her eyes and burned down her cheek. "I would have been there. I don't care how hard it would have been."

Kate's knees gave out; she crumpled and sobbed into Grandma Lewis's entry rug, the letter slipping from her fingers. She sobbed until her throat and body hurt from it, until her tears soaked the ends of her hair. Until her fingers lost their feeling along with her heart.

A rush of cold flittered through the kitchen. Kate heard the door close, but she knew it wasn't Grandma Lewis. She was lifted from the floor. Kate slapped a hand over her eyes as she shook, trying to hold her breath so she wouldn't cry out loud.

She came against a warm body with a slow-beating heart, and his arms wrapped around her. He held her up as her knees wobbled.

"Cry however you want to." Cress's low voice filled the kitchen. "There's no need to hold it in because you're worried what I'll think, Human."

The strings holding her together snapped.

There was only one other time Kate had ever cried so hard, and she swore afterward she would never do it again. But her unrhythmic, melodic sobs echoed through the house; a soloist telling the story of a lifetime of warmth and wisdom that had reached its conclusion.

Moments later, she was swept off her feet and carried up the stairs. She was set down on the bed she'd spent many of her teen years sleeping in. Her bedroom door closed, and she was left to fall asleep that way with all her memories of Grandma Lewis close by.

Kate awoke in the morning to a crumbly, chocolatey, sweet smell. She rubbed her eyes, trying to remember where she was. Her feet were tucked into a yellow comforter, and a novel she knew well rested on the bedside table. Her stomach growled, reminding her she hadn't eaten in a while. Reminding her where she was. Reminding her of other things, too.

She sat up and inhaled the aroma of baking. It was a smell she'd known on many mornings throughout her teen years. She blinked away the dizziness, trying to sort out why evidence of her grandmother's baking was leaking into her room.

The bedroom door squeaked when she opened it. She drifted down the stairs and tiptoed to the kitchen where the lights were on. The house wasn't cold anymore—the floor was warm beneath her toes as though someone had gotten the living room fireplace going.

Cress's back was turned when she peeked around the corner. He sild off the oven mitts and tossed them on the counter.

Kate was sure he knew she was there, but she cleared her throat just in case. "What are you doing?" she rasped.

"I'm making *freshly baked chocolate chip cookies*." He finally turned and leaned back against the counter with his arms folded. He said 'freshly-baked-chocolate-chip-cookies' like it was all one word.

"Why?"

"You know why." Cress's gaze was heavy, and he didn't blink.

This time, Kate didn't feel like cowering or shifting her weight. She stared back as her mind filled with that moment in the narrow hallway of the café when Cress had put a hand over her mouth to keep her from saying something.

"You like me," she said. It wasn't really a question, but she wanted to hear him say it either way.

"Yes."

"But I'm a *repulsive* human," she quoted.

"Yes."

"But you want me anyway?"

"Yes."

Cress lifted off the counter and crossed the kitchen to where she was. "And I know what I have to do about it now," he said. He chewed on the inside of his cheek. "I need to end my feud with the Dark and leave."

Kate blinked. Of all the things she'd expected him to say, that wasn't one of them. "Leave, *forever*?"

"Yes, forever. So that you can keep your happy life, Kate Kole."

A weak thudding appeared in her chest. "Are you crazy?"

The timer on the oven beeped, sliding through the tension she felt and stealing Cress's concentration. Cress moved for his oven mitts, but Kate grabbed a handful of his shirt, and he halted.

He turned back, his gaze slowly dragging around with him. He seemed to read a story in her eyes. "What do you think you're doing, Human?" his voice was low and quiet.

When she didn't answer, Cress carefully unpeeled her fingers from his shirt. He stepped toward her, forcing her to move back, and he planted his hands flat along the wall on either side of her head, leaning in. Kate's lips parted, but before she could speak, he gently brought his lips against her mouth.

Time stood still and sped too fast all at once. Kate felt lost in a dream, like she was both sinking to the floor of the sea and shooting up to the stars. She inhaled when his hand drifted into her hair, his thumb pushed her chin up, and he kissed her deeper.

That same twisting in her chest turned into a thousand butterflies. She wanted to speak, but she couldn't find words. She wanted to think but couldn't find clear thoughts.

Cress pulled his mouth off gradually. They stayed still for a moment, Kate feeling his chest thudding against hers. After, he leaned around and whispered in her ear, "Wicked human."

He dropped his hold on her like she'd burned his hands, and he pulled away all at once.

"W…" Kate blinked. "Wicked?" She pressed her palm against the racing pulse in her neck.

"You might as well be a siren-song fairy luring men to their deaths," he said, heading to the counter. He slid on the hot-pad mitts and opened the oven, letting coils of smoke roll out.

"Seriously?" Kate said as her senses snapped back into place. "*You* just kissed *me*."

Cress smiled devilishly and looked back at her like he wanted to do it again. He lifted the pan of cookies onto the stovetop and scowled at the burnt tops. Then he tossed the oven mitts on the counter and put his hands on his hips. "You're to blame for this." He nodded to the cookies. Then he said, "And you're also to blame for *that*." He gestured to her mouth with his eyes.

"Of course." Kate shook her head. "I'm always to blame for everything, right? A prince couldn't possibly make a mistake."

He frowned. "Was it a mistake?"

Kate swallowed her words, the pulse returning to her neck. She brushed her hair out of her face and glanced out the window instead of answering.

Cress pulled a plate from the cupboard. It was frightening that he knew exactly where everything was. "It was a mistake," he agreed. "I'm leaving. Before I spoil your happy life." It was like he had to remind himself.

Kate clasped her hands as she watched him get a lifter and place each cookie onto the plate.

"Stay until Christmas. It's two weeks away. Then you can leave," she said.

Cress slowed his cookie passing. "It's a bad idea."

"Because you're worried about those Shadow Fairies in the city?" Kate asked, and Cress put down the lifter. He cast her a look.

"Because I won't want to leave anymore by then."

"I don't think you want to leave now."

A faint growl emerged when he went back to his cookies. "It's a bad idea, Human," he repeated. He reached a teaspoon into the bag of icing sugar and sprinkled the spoonful over the plate. He eyed the last few cookies with the worst burns before reluctantly going for them with the lifter again. They were crisped right to the pan. After he chiselled at one and broke it in half, Kate went over and yanked the lifter away. Cress's gaze followed her as she put the last few cookies on the plate.

"I'll make you a bargain," Kate decided.

"You should never make a bargain with a fairy." His reply was instant.

"Here's our deal: You'll stay until Christmas, and you'll take all the kisses you want from me in that time," she offered with a weird, bashful grin.

"I don't accept," he said right away again, and Kate turned to find him glaring.

"Why?"

"Because you'd be driven to your death if I had to do that to you. You'd never catch your breath if I took *all the kisses I wanted*. I don't think I'd ever *want* to stop. It's a dangerous bargain, and you should know better, Kate Kole. Never make a bargain with a fairy."

Kate was sure she was blushing cherry-red at best, near purple at worst. "Oh," she rasped out.

Cress reached around her for the plate and took it to the table. "You're still a fool when it comes to the fairy laws," he said. "It's a miracle you managed to enslave my brothers. And now your rhythms are so loud, they're impossible to ignore. Don't you know what that does to someone with a fairy crush?" He mumbled the last part.

Kate put a hand over the pulse in her neck again like that might somehow silence it. She made a face at his back as she followed him to the table and sat. But she almost jumped when something thudded against the kitchen window.

Cress stepped over and pushed aside the thick curtains. A wild blizzard raged outside. He scowled at it and dropped the curtains to come sit.

All the lights in the house flickered, and a second later, everything went dark.

Neither of them moved to find a light or open the curtains. Kate could see a vague silhouette of Cress's side, but that was all.

"This weather is crazy," she said through the dark.

"That may be my fault," he mumbled.

Cress's fingers slid over hers on the table. He turned her hand so her palm was up, and a second later, a warm cookie was set on top. "If Thelma was here, she'd bite at you for not eating before the food got cold," he said.

A smile spread across Kate's face. She was glad it was too dark for him to see the tears that filled her eyes, or her stupid grin. "Yeah, she would have." But she went still when a dishtowel dabbed her cheek, catching the tears. She felt the light heat of being watched by him.

"Can you see me?" she asked quietly.

"Yes. Perfectly."

She took the towel and brushed the tears away herself. A moment of silence passed before either one of them spoke again.

"If I stay until the human Yule celebrations, you may have to flee this city and hide somewhere far away from the gate after I leave," Cress said.

"I'm not leaving my city."

"You might have to, Katherine."

Katherine.

Kate broke her cookie into pieces without eating it. "Why?"

"Because Shadow Fairies love to torment humans. And they'll come for you once I'm gone if they detect... Well, it won't be safe for *you*, especially," he said. "The Dark and I have a bad faeborn-cursed history. I'm the hated, young North Prince whose armies drove them back into their Corner. Ordinarily, they wouldn't touch me without the consent of my Queene, but..."

"But what?" Kate squinted, trying to see his face through the darkness.

"I believe my Queene has given them permission to kill me. Possibly even hired them to. My brothers and I are waiting to see if they strike first."

Kate dropped her cookie puzzle to the table. "What? Is this a joke? Those fae who were following us the other day..."

"They may have reasons for being here. Which is why I have a good reason to leave."

"Didn't you say your High Court might *kill* you for going back home without completing your task?" Kate asked. "Isn't it crazy to return to those people, Cress?"

"Perhaps."

265

"Then stay!" She shouted it at him. "Why would any of you run back to a life like that?!" Kate felt hot tears resurface. "I can't let Shayne, Mor, or Dranian go back to that terrible place. They're happy here, can't you see it?"

She heard him release a heavy breath in the darkness. "That's why they'll stay with you, and I'll go. I haven't told them yet," he said. "I didn't want to say anything until you'd mourned your human grandmother."

Kate tossed her cookie toward his voice. She had no idea if it hit him.

"I'll tell the High Court I killed all of you—them for insubordination, and you for committing a crime against the North Corner," he went on. "I'll take whatever punishment is necessary for returning without evidence, but it'll keep the fairies from coming back here to search for you and my brothers in the future."

"Do you really think Mor is going to stay here if you go back?" Kate asked. "Do you really think Dranian will just sit back and watch you leave? They're going to follow you, Cress!"

"I'll leave in the night. They won't know until I'm gone."

"Cress!" Kate stood so fast, her chair tipped backward and clamoured over the floor. Her knuckles banged over the table as she tried to feel her way around. He caught her arm when she reached him, and she realized he was standing.

"You leaving is a bad idea," she said.

"Me staying is a worse idea."

"Stay until Christmas," she tried again. "Just until then, *please*. You can leave on Christmas day, and I won't argue after that."

Cress's grip loosened, and eventually, he dropped her arm.

"Fine. I'll stay for the human Yule celebrations, Katherine Lewis. But I'll be gone before Christmas morning, and you must prepare yourself to move far away from this city after I leave," he said. "That's the only trade I'll make with you."

32

Kate Kole and the Fae on the Naughty List

The snowstorm finally ceased at noon, paving the way for sunlight to make the sidewalks glow. Kate found herself searching the alleys and rooftops for stalking fae with silvery brown eyes. Nothing showed itself during their walk back to the café, and she assumed Cress was the reason. His command for her to not go outside alone didn't seem so crazy now.

A new garland wreath hung on the café door, and a string of golden Christmas lights surrounded the wooden Fae Café sign. There was even new, decorative writing on the window about the butter tarts. But the one thing the café was missing was customers.

"Wait…" Cress took Kate's arm before she opened the door. "Something is happening inside. I can hear human fury."

Kate leaned to squint through the sun's reflection on the window. She shrieked when she saw Ben—the loan shark—tied to a chair with a pastry clogging his mouth.

She flung the door open. The bell rang as she raced in.

"We're closed!" Dranian growled, but he shut his mouth when he saw Kate and Cress.

Ben glared at Kate from his chair. He couldn't move his mouth to shout at her, at least. It didn't make his facial expression any less quiet.

Mor rested in one of the chairs by the fireplace, reading a newspaper with his feet up and stuffed into Kate's favourite pair of slippers. Kate yelled at him, "You let them do this?"

Mor flipped down the page corner to peer over it. "He came in demanding money, and those faeborn fools didn't like it. This has nothing to do with me." He nodded toward Shayne and Dranian and went back to his paper. "What is *Desmount Tech Industries*? Every scroll column is babbling on about them," he added, and then with a mutter, "This text is simple, yet astoundingly informative. I could create a news scroll like this. I'm a faeborn vessel of information."

Shayne had one hand in his pocket and the other around a coffee-filled mug. He leaned with his shoulder against the wall. "Perhaps you should. You could call it the Fairy Post and warn the humans of all the fairy action among them," he said as though they were just having a normal conversation on a normal day and there wasn't a living person tied to a chair five feet away.

Mor snorted. "Then I should warn them of the enchantments you put in the baking," he said.

Kate looked from Mor to the glass display of tarts and cakes, then back to Mor. "Did you just say there are enchantments in the baking?"

"Yes. Those two mixed the batter with magic to ensure that every human who tries it is compelled to come back. The coffee is enchanted, too," he said. "The bad news is that no one really came back here because they liked your coffee, Human. The good news is you have hundreds of lifetime customers," Mor said, and Kate's jaw dropped. Her gaze darted to Shayne's writing in the window that said, COME TRY THE BUTTER TARTS. WE GUARANTEE YOU'LL COME BACK FOR MORE IF YOU DO.

"Are you kidding me?!" she shrieked.

"You're always such a tattletale, Mor," Shayne said as he rolled his eyes.

"We all have roles here. That's mine." Mor shook his newspaper to straighten it again.

Kate slapped a hand over her forehead. "I can't *believe...*" She shook her head and jutted a thumb toward Ben in the hostage chair. "Can we deal with this first, please?"

On cue, Cress sauntered over to Ben. "Are you the fool who's forcing our human to pay so many taxes?" he asked him.

"He's not a tax collector, I just owe him money," Kate said. "Seriously, you guys can't freak out like this every time someone you don't like comes in here."

Shayne sipped a coffee. "This human insect called you names," he said, kicking a leg of Ben's chair. "So Dranian picked him up by his ugly human throat and tied him to that seat."

Kate almost objected, but she looked at Dranian in surprise. "Really? I could have sworn you didn't like me."

Dranian lifted one shoulder into a shrug. Kate bit back a small, flattered smile.

"Let's throw him to the road in front of a speeding human chariot," Cress suggested.

"No way!" Kate yanked the ropes holding Ben, but she stopped when she realized they were torn strips of pink fabric. A big, loud moan lifted through the café. "Please tell me these aren't my bed sheets?" she asked the assassins.

"You keep no ropes here, Human," Dranian grumbled.

Kate removed the pastry from Ben's mouth, and he spat a wad of it to the floor. "*You—*" he started, so Kate stuck the pastry back in. Her cheeks warmed as she wondered how much Ben had already told these fae about how she'd grovelled to get him to lend her money in the first place.

"You can keep this, on the house." She flicked the pastry in Ben's

269

mouth, then swallowed and shifted her footing when his eyes sharpened. "Let me go get you your money. I don't have all of it yet but—"

"That is *preposterous*! She'll be giving you no money," Cress announced.

Ben released a guttural noise of objection.

Shayne peeled himself off the wall. The assassin drank the last drops of his coffee then turned the precious Fae Café mug over in his fingers. "Shall I go fetch my crossbow to finish this human off?" he asked then held the mug before Ben's face. "Or should I just beat the human snot out of him with this?"

Kate's jaw dropped, and Ben's face paled. Ben shook his head quickly.

"Do we have an understanding then, Human?" Shayne asked, wiggling the mug a little.

White-faced Ben nodded, but Shayne pressed on, "Do you understand what kinds of terrible, tricky, mind-bending, body harming things will happen if you ever come back here?"

"Nothing," Kate objected. "*Nothing* will happen—" Cress wrapped an arm around Kate with his hand smothering her mouth.

"Excellent." Shayne took a hold of the bedsheet ropes and ripped them all off at once. "See you never, then." He yanked Ben to his feet by his shirt and half-carried him to the door.

The bell jingled.

Ben was tossed out.

Kate was sure she would faint. Ben wasn't the sort to let things go, and apparently Lily hadn't been around to inform the fae of that important little fact. "Where's Lily?" she asked.

"She read her letter from Thelma Lewis, then she said she had to work. She told us all to leave her alone for a while," Mor said from behind the newspaper.

"Oh."

Kate imagined Lily reading the letter from their grandmother in front of the fae, without Kate there. Lily must have felt the same heavy dread

Kate had, the same surprise, the same numbness. Kate felt a pinch of guilt for not being here when the letter was delivered. She thought about calling Lily at work, to tell her to come home, but she wasn't sure if Lily's request to be left alone included her.

She spotted her phone resting on a bistro table. The Fae Café social media pages were open. Twelve new posts had been published since yesterday—posts Kate hadn't done herself. She picked up her phone and scrolled through the photos. One was of Mor staring at the camera with a death glare like he didn't want his photo taken. The caption below said:

AN INTRODUCTION TO
THE HIGH COURT OF THE COFFEE BEAN

MEET MOR: A HANDSOME, COLD-BLOODED FAE ASSASSIN IN A CUTE BURGUNDY APRON, READY TO STAB YOUR ENEMIES AND POUR YOU A TASTY LATTE AT YOUR BECKONING.

Kate squeaked a laugh and scrolled to the next photo of Shayne modelling beside a whipped drink. She read the caption aloud, "Come to Fae Café where the coffee is hot, and the fairies are even hotter."

Mor grunted from the corner, and Shayne bit his lip over a grin.

Kate kept reading, "This official announcement has been approved by High King Shayne, ruler of the Coffee Bean High Court." She sighed through a smile and shook her phone in the air. "I'm totally not over that act you just pulled with Ben, but thank you for this. I needed a laugh today." Her thumb hovered over the call button as she thought about Lily again.

A police car rolled up outside. Kate lunged to pick up the pink ropes off the floor and stuff them into the garbage can. "Everyone act normal!" she shouted as Lily climbed out of the passenger side. Connor got out, too. "Lily can *not* find out what happened here this morning or she'll flip."

"What is *he* doing here?" Cress pointed at Connor through the window as the officers walked up.

The café door swung open, and Lily halted. She looked around at the abandoned tables, the empty counter, and the four fae looking off at the walls avoiding eye contact.

"Where is everyone?" she asked. "I was just telling Connor that this place was buzzing with customers."

Connor rolled his eyes. "I knew you were lying." But his face changed when he noticed Cress there. "You," he said.

Lily glanced at Kate, and their eyes locked for a moment.

"Are you okay?" Kate asked first.

"Are *you* okay?" Lily folded her arms, hugging them to herself.

"You shouldn't be working today. You should take a few days off until the funeral. Or at least work here with us," Kate said.

"I've been searching everywhere for you," Connor interrupted to say to Cress. "Just so you know, I informed the department about that stunt you pulled on the docks. You're in big trouble."

Cress tilted his head. "Shall I inform the department of what you were trying to do to Kate that night?" he asked, and Lily's eyes widened. She pushed Connor—his back slammed against the door.

"I'm going to beat the idiocy out of you, Connor! You can report me for threatening you, I don't care!" she shouted at him. "I've warned you to stay away from Kate too many times!"

Connor pointed at Cress. "He threw me off a dock!"

A wicked smile found Cress's face. "I did."

"What is your deal, anyway?" Connor shoved off the door and took a hostile step toward Cress. "You don't show up for work, and then you mess around in my personal life? Who do you think you are?"

Cress blinked down at the policeman. He took Kate's hand. "I'm Kate's boyfriend," he announced. "We go on dates."

Kate tried to tug her hand away, but Cress's grip turned to stone around hers. "Cress… You're not—"

The bell rang through the café again. A sunburnt, hazel-eyed teenager in a hoodie came in, and everything Kate had just been thinking evaporated. "Wow!" he said, looking around.

"Greyson!" she said.

Cress dropped her hand when she rushed for her brother.

Greyson caught Kate into a hug. He patted her back and rubbed back and forth across her shoulders. It said enough about the loss they both felt. "The police called yesterday. I took the first redeye flight home," he said. "I didn't even know I was Grandma's emergency contact. It makes no sense when Lil is a cop, but whatever. I tried calling you."

"Watch your human hands," Cress mumbled as he eyed Greyson's gestures on Kate's back.

Lily rolled her eyes. "This is Kate's *brother*, Greyson," she explained, still glaring at Connor as she marched to the counter and dragged over the coffee maker.

The coldness dropped from Cress's stare. He still looked Greyson over as though recognizing him from somewhere.

Greyson let Kate go and smirked. "Who the heck is this whack job?" He jutted his thumb at Cress.

Kate opened her mouth to explain but, *"He's an assassin who came to kill me,"* didn't quite have a nice ring to it. She sighed and took Cress's hand against every warning in her body. She patted his knuckles. "This is my boyfriend," she said.

Cress's smile widened. He looked right at Connor.

Without missing a beat, Greyson nodded. "Oh, that makes sense then," he said. He grabbed Cress's free hand, shook it, then headed over to the counter where Lily was. "One Americano, please. And one Canadian police officer bestie to go with it." He winked, and Lily shot Kate an odd smirk.

"We're not finished," Connor promised Cress. His hand rested on the hilt of his gun. "I'm friends with all the captains on the force. You don't want to mess with someone like me."

Mor's chuckle lifted from behind the newspaper, and cold malice filled Cress's smile. "I can't wait to mess with someone like you," Cress assured.

Lily reached for a paper to-go cup, seeming determined to ignore the tension in the air. She shook her head as she poured a coffee, slid it over to Greyson, and said, "Welcome to Fae Café."

It wasn't easy to sneak out without Lily noticing. Thankfully, Lily was so tired from being overworked and emotionally spent that she was sleeping like a log by midnight.

Kate waited until she was outside breathing in the cool night air to zip her coat, not risking the noise. She trudged through the crunchy snow, shivering as flakes left the black sky and turned to glittering confetti beneath the streetlamps. Her last conversation with Lily rang through her mind:

"I've fallen in love with them, Lil. I've gotten too attached to four fairy-beings who came here to kill me. I'm crazy, right?"

"Maybe a little. But I think I've fallen for them, too. And crazy doesn't even begin to cover it." Lily had been brushing her teeth, but she stuck her head out of the bathroom to say it.

"So how do I keep him here?"

"Cress?" Lily's spitting had been loud enough to wake the neighbourhood, but she came out of the bathroom wiping her mouth and said, *"I guess we have to figure out what's forcing him to go back and get rid of the problem."*

Even several blocks away, it was still Lily's voice ruling Kate's conscience as she kicked through the snow on the sidewalk.

The parking lots at the university were empty of cars, and the buildings seemed like haunted castles at night. Only the student housing across the campus had a few lamps on inside.

Kate wandered into her literature class building, relieved to see the hall lit up with murky yellow bulbs. All the doors were closed, the class-rooms left in darkness. Her footsteps echoed as she made her way through.

The crime scene tape remained across the library doors. Kate ducked beneath it and pushed her way in, instantly met with the smells of drywall and fresh paint. The floor was cleared of damaged books, but dust and a few torn page corners weren't swept up yet. The desks were pushed to the middle, leaving two large aisles down each side where it looked like construction had begun to patch up the holes and fix all the broken shelves.

Kate wandered around the mess and made her way to the back. The map of pink yarn was gone, but she followed her memory to the shelf where the *Fairy Book of Rules and Masteries* was hidden.

She spotted it on a higher shelf than before. It was almost like some-one had tried to make it difficult for her to get it again. Kate grunted and started climbing. She reached for the book, her fingers barely brushing the spine, and she flicked it out inch by inch until the tome tipped off and landed on the floor with a *bang*.

Dust trickled down, and Kate coughed as she knelt and flipped the book open. She got to the page about enslaving a fae, and she ran her finger down the list of names, ignoring the written cautions and warn-ings. She slid her phone out of her pocket and snapped a picture.

One picture was all she would need when she approached the Shadow Fairies and spoke their names to enslave them. One chance was all she would have to keep Cress from having to go back.

CHAPTER

33

Prince Cressica and the Memories He Couldn't Find

Humans flocked the cathedral in pairs and small family herds. It seemed Thelma Lewis had left quite the impression on many in the realm. From his seat at the back, Cress watched the wooden benches fill with well-aged human females in odd hats and black garments. A few hobbled to where Kate, Lily, and Kate's-brother-Greyson stood at the side, dressed just as dully as everyone else. Though, Kate's burgundy hair was down and lovely. A pair of Thelma's earrings hung from her earlobes.

Cress wore black according to the human custom, but nothing fit quite right. Half his garments belonged to Kate's-brother-Greyson, and the other half were stolen by Shayne from a "donation bin." Cress's sweater was so tight, he was sure he would burst out of it in front of all the mourners.

He'd ordered the rest of his assassins to stay at the café. Cress only came himself to keep an eye on their humans. And perhaps he wished to say one more farewell to Thelma Lewis, too.

Ghastly music filled the space when a human male went to the front and sat at a wooden machine with ivory buttons. A dozen pipes came out the back, riding up the wall into the intricately painted ceiling.

Those standing began to sit. Cress's nose wrinkled from a prickling sensation as someone passed by in the aisle. His attention was on Kate taking her seat until a male with a head of dark hair slid down the row and took the seat directly behind her. The male turned and looked back, right at Cress.

The wind and sky and earth crashed into Cress all at once.

Bonswick's glower was glassy and silver. The High Lord of the East cast a wicked, cruel smile toward the back of the cathedral. He placed a casual hand on Kate's shoulder and leaned forward to whisper in her ear. Kate turned and gave him a faint smile without really looking back.

"Look at him," Cress whispered. His blood was ice cold. "Look, you foolish human," he begged her, but Kate stared at the front where a human in long white robes glided across the stage.

Cress clasped his hands. His fairsaber was warm against his back; his fingers itched to grab it.

The human *celebration of life* service dragged on. Kate gave a short, teary speech during which Bonswick glanced back again and pouted in mock sympathy. There was nothing Cress wanted more than to spring over the wooden seats and stab Bonswick where he sat.

Lily and Kate's-brother-Greyson gave speeches, too. Songs were sung, and memories of Thelma were shared that warmed the space, apart from the second bench to the front.

The moment it ended, Cress leapt up and moved around the pews. Humans shuffled his way, and he stopped when he realized he'd stood out of turn. Those at the front came toward the back, so Cress swept to the side to let them pass. He trained his icy turquoise gaze on Bonswick who followed so close to Kate Kole's back, it was a wonder she didn't feel his faeborn breath.

Cress let the humans pass.

He let Kate pass.

He slid into the exodus beside Bonswick, his hand beneath the back of his sweater on his fairsaber.

"Prince," Bonswick said quietly when Cress was close enough to hear. "What's worse? To be hated, or to be betrayed?" A slow, mean smile spread over the High Lord face. "Or both?"

Cress said nothing as they marched outside.

Bonswick's eyes sparkled as he lifted his hand toward the zipper that held the back of Kate's dress together. Cress shoved him off the side of the cathedral stairs before the fairy's fingers made contact.

Bonswick didn't fight as Cress followed and dragged him around the side of the building. The fairy howled in laughter when Cress drew his fairsaber and pointed it at his chest. The tip pressed delicately over the High Lord's heart.

"Let's settle this now," Cress said in a deep voice. As the words left his lips, creatures of the inhuman sort emerged from behind trees, around the side of the building, and out of the snowy shadows. They stared at Cress with silver-brown eyes, a long past of hatred, and a hunger for blood.

Bonswick drew his own fairsaber. "I volunteered my services to the North. I'm here to ensure you're slayed, Prince Cressica. You've been black marked for betraying the High Queene."

Cress found his cold blood slink back to its slow, warm river of red.

Levress knew.

Cress stood taller, his boots digging into the snow and bracing for impact. "Try to slay me then," he invited the High Lord.

Bonswick angled his head. "It's not just you I'll kill, Prince. It's your brothers, too, including that leech you love so much."

Cress's grip tightened on his saber, his gaze flickering to the Shadow Fairies around the cathedral yard drawing weapons. "Funny, I thought you hated Mor for being a Shadow. How strange when you're a Shadow Fairy yourself."

"No, you fool. I hate that leech for *betraying* the Shadows." Bonswick's face grew repulsed. "But hearing him cry for mercy will only be a bonus. You're the real prize. I'm to save you for last and bring you back to the North with me, alive. You cannot imagine the terrible death that awaits you there."

Cress nodded. "At last, I know why you're here," he said. He repositioned his fairsaber toward the Shadow Fairies inching in. "Shall we?"

"Careful, Cressica," Bonswick said. "They despise you almost as much as I do."

"It's mutual," Cress assured.

Before he took his next breath, ten Shadow Fairies swung at once. Cress stopped six with his fairsaber, and turned his skin to stone to deflect three, but one left a cruel, cold iron slash along his midsection. He released a guttural growl and aimed for Bonswick next, but Bonswick vanished, and Cress's saber sliced through air. The High Lord reappeared at the back of the yard.

The Prince kicked a fairy aside and marched toward the High Lord of the East. An arrow zipped past, the wind of it fluttering Cress's hair, and he halted.

Bonswick leaned to avoid the arrow before it could scathe his fair cheek. The Lord's glassy eyes narrowed on someone behind Cress, and Cress's flesh tightened.

Shayne's scent drifted over the yard.

"Leave," Cress commanded as the white-haired fairy appeared at his side with his crossbow raised.

"Absolutely not, Your Highness," Shayne said.

"That's an order."

A warped grin found Shayne's face. "So then punish me. Put me to death. Do whatever you want, Cress." Shayne dropped his crossbow to the ground and drew out a set of short fairsabers instead. "But let me fight a little first."

There wasn't time to argue before growls tore over the snow and Shadow Fairies lunged. Shayne smashed the first one away as Cress

279

blocked the next, the pain of his cold iron wound sizzling deeper into him. Cress turned his body feather-light, rising into the air and rushing toward Bonswick.

Bonswick redrew his fairsaber as Cress came above him, turned his body to stone, and dropped.

The Prince nearly crushed the High Lord of the East. Bonswick spun out of the way, but Cress's blade caught his chin. The glassy-eyed Lord recoiled, his fairy blood speckling the snow. He looked back with rage.

"You'll be the fairy to die today," Cress promised him.

Bonswick touched the blood on his face. "No, Prince. *He* will be the fairy to die today." He pointed to where the Shadow Fairies drove Shayne against the cathedral wall. Shayne's sabers were torn from his grip. Fairy blood covered the frost where six Shadow Fairy bodies lay in his wake.

"Wait!" Cress shouted when a Shadow Fairy placed his saber at Shayne's throat. "Wait, Bonswick! I'll make you a bargain!"

The Shadow hesitated, looking to Bonswick.

"For that insubordinate fool?" Bonswick chuckled. "I thought you'd save all your bargains for that human you've allowed yourself to bond to as your forever mate. Did you really think I wouldn't pick up the taste of fairy crush in the air?"

"Let them have me, Cress!" Shayne spat blood in the Shadow Fairy's face. "Never make a bargain with a—"

Shayne was struck. He rolled through the snow.

Time seemed to stand still as Bonswick decided what to do next. Cress couldn't take his eyes off the saber above Shayne's back, pointed down, waiting for Bonswick's command to drop.

A fairy pressed Shayne's head down with his boot, forcing Shayne's cheek into the snow. From the ground, Shayne gave Cress a look that resaid what he'd uttered aloud: *Never make a bargain with a fairy.* It was what Thessalie had taught Cress since the day he'd entered the Silver Castle. It was the reason Cress had never made a fairy bargain in his entire faeborn life after the one he had made on behalf of his mother.

"I'll go with you," Cress said to the High Lord. "You can take me back to the North Corner to face the Queene's wrath. I won't kill you, I'll come willingly."

"When?"

"On the humans' day of Yule tidings."

Bonswick listened with a bored face.

"You know I can kill you now, or tomorrow, or the next day if I please. I'll do so if you don't take this bargain," Cress added, cutting his cold gaze over to the High Lord. "But you must leave my brothers and the humans out of it."

Bonswick raised a brow. "I don't make bargains for humans," he said. "And I want Mor."

"You can't have him."

The High Lord of the East glanced at the fairsaber getting danger-ously close to plunging down between Shayne's shoulders. "Shame," he said. "I wanted to kill that one."

Cress's chest deflated with relief, but his gaze slid toward the road past the trees where oblivious humans congregated as they dispersed to their chariots on wheels.

"No humans," Bonswick decided. "But I will accept your bargain for this fool, and the leech, and the last fairy with the ever-scowl, too. On the morning of Yule, you belong to me."

Cress remained as still as stone until the Shadow Fairies released Shayne. Sounds of the human city flooded the cathedral yard, crawling into Cress's ears, drowning his faeborn mind.

Somewhere on these snowy roads, Kate Kole was on her way back to the café. His chest tightened as he thought about Mor's warning—the one Cress had ignored but should have listened to from the start. The one that was meant to remind him what would happen to Kate if the Shadow Fairies sensed what she was to him.

Kate had no idea what was coming for her.

The skies glowed with lightning blasting through the flurries to create a most uncommon picture of human weather. Cress tore off his coat as he entered the academy library where moist dust and heavy air told him the story of new construction and the intent to return this fairy-meddled space to normal.

Shayne went straight to the back to find the *Fairy Book of Rules and Masteries*. He returned carrying it as Mor dragged a desk over for them to work at.

"Dranian isn't happy about being the only one left with our humans," Shayne said as he flipped open the book and began leafing through pages. "But what else is new about that faeborn grouch?"

"I think leaving him alone there was foolish. Dranian can't take on the whole Dark army if they show up for Kate," Mor said as he pulled out the notebook he stole from the café drawer. He clicked a human ink pen and began scribbling his ideas, both realistic and preposterous. Cress leaned to read them while Mor was looking down.

Shayne slid the book onto the table and sat, but Cress continued to pace.

The Prince pressed light fingers against the cold iron gash in his side. There was no hiding the blood, even on black garments. Kate's eyes had gone round when she saw it.

He'd lied.

He'd lied to Kate Kole.

So had Shayne.

"A few of the Shadow Fairies followed us, so we fought them off. That's all there is to it," Shayne had said when they returned to the café and she'd asked what happened.

Cress rubbed his temple where a fresh headache beat like a cruel war drum behind his eyes. It was better that Kate had no idea she was a target, that Cress had bound his death to his brothers' survival, or that she was his forever mate. His tongue still felt hot from the falsehood. He knew the fairy curse would grow more painful the longer he didn't tell the truth.

Faeborn-cursed fairy magic.

"Why would you make such a bargain, you fool?" Mor finally dropped the notebook and glared at Cress, and Cress was sure the fairy had been itching to shout that question since the moment they left the café.

"I was already planning to go back to the North, so this bargain makes no difference," Cress told him. He sniffed, picking up an odd scent of powder that reminded him of Kate's hair soap. He wrinkled his nose as he turned toward the back shelves. Tables creaked and notepapers ruffled as his power slipped over the floor and sought out a story of the past. He was sure he could smell her here recently, though, that didn't seem possible—

"But now you've lost the choice!" Mor cut into his thoughts, and the wind in the shelves ceased.

Cress turned back to the curly-haired assassin with the largest faeborn scowl in existence. "The only difference to my plan now is that when I leave, you three won't be hunted by the Dark," he said.

Shayne folded his arms, his usual smile gone. "That's not the only difference. Now you know that when you return, you'll die at Levress's hands. You didn't know that before."

Cress nodded to the *Fairy Book of Rules and Masteries*. "We only have fourteen days to find a way for *all* of us to faeborn live, including our humans. If we fail to find a way around this bargain, I will go with Bonswick. And you *will* stay here. That is my final order to you, as the Prince of the North."

Shayne growled and stood, pressing his fists on the table. "We will return with you and share the same fate—"

"Then I've made this bargain for nothing! You did not obey me in the yard, Shayne, so at least obey me with this!"

Mor and Shayne looked the same—tight fairy skin, furrowed brows, large frowns.

"Don't make my death meaningless. It's insulting," Cress muttered as he followed his nose to the back shelf where the *Fairy Book of Rules and Masteries* came from. He touched the ledge, finding dust missing. Finding that things had in fact been meddled with.

He rubbed the dust between his fingers as he went to the opposite back corner of the library where he sniffed out a different sort of feeling; one with invisible, bubbling anger, and paper-thin traces of an ancient fairy beast. He stared at a particular panel in the wall siding. His senses picked up a low, beastly growl seeping out from many months ago, hidden inside a memory that *should* have been his. He shoved the panel, and it popped open like a door, revealing a dark spiral staircase. Cress had a feeling the staircase would lead him to all the High Queene's darkest secrets, hidden away with the humans so no fairy might stumble upon them—as he was doing now.

Pea-sized flames spurted to life in the staircase when he stepped in.

"Careful," Mor's voice said from behind him. The fairy's dark silhouette filled the staircase entrance. "You may not want to remember what happened down there, Cress."

"I want to remember slaying Levress's prized creature. I want to remember the pain and illness it caused her when I got my revenge for her betrayal against me and my mother."

Mor didn't stop him from following the stairs down to a cold, dim room where scrolls and books lined gilded shelves, and all sorts of fairy gold spilled from pots marked with ancient fae symbols. Cress laughed at the trouble he might cause with all of this.

"Perhaps we should just buy Bonswick off," he suggested when Mor's scent flitted in behind him.

"It's all cursed. It's why it's here. The High Court of the North didn't want this treasure in the Ever Corners," Mor said.

Cress's gaze danced over the room, taking in faded bloodstains and spilled bowls of gold. Paintings were torn to shreds, and a barrel was split in two. Splinters coated the stones. "It must have been quite a fight."

"Well, you were quite angry."

Cress nodded. "I'm angry now, Mor," he admitted. "I want to finish what I started and take her down."

Mor took a hold of Cress's shoulder. The assassin's brown-silver eyes were filled with remorse. "I don't think it's your job anymore, Cress. Let the next generation of fairy rebels deal with her."

"Are you suggesting I let her get away with the horrors she's committed? Her lies? Her stealing childlings from their homes? Her murdering innocents? Look at all she's done to me, Mor!"

"You already tried to take her down. You'll die now because of it. Because I stole your memories before you were able to destroy her," Mor said. His throat bobbed.

Cress looked at the floor. After a moment, he turned away, pulled his fairsaber out, and studied the silver wing details that represented his allegiance to the High Queene. "The entire North Corner would have already killed me if you hadn't intervened. You spared my life."

"For now." There was an unusual edge to Mor's voice that left a remnant chill on Cress's skin. "Unless I can convince Bonswick to spare you. Only he could lie on your behalf to the North Court." Mor's tone was one Cress had only heard a few times in their faeborn lives together. "He wants me, doesn't he?" he asked flat out.

Cress rolled his saber handle in his grip as he thought about how to answer. "Mor..." he started, but he bit down on his tongue. Finally, he slid his fairsaber away and turned back with the chosen words, *"Bonswick will never have you as long as I'm alive,"* but phantom moonbugs burst into flutters in his chest when he realized Mor had already vanished.

CHAPTER

34

Kate Kole and One of Life's Great Mysteries: Hot Dogs.

The café bell almost broke off when Cress barged in. Kate dropped the chalkboard she was hanging on the wall. The chalk rolled across the floor and bumped into Cress's boot and the board hit the floor with a *clang*.

"Where is he? Did he come back here?!" Cress asked through a strained growl that reminded Kate of a struck puppy. She abandoned the chalkboard.

"Who?"

"Mor!" Cress shouted his name. It echoed through the café.

"He hasn't come back yet. I thought you were with him." Kate picked up the chalk at his feet and stood.

A body materialized beside her.

Her throat was grabbed, and everything after that happened too fast.

Kate gasped as she was rushed backward across the room and slammed against the kitchen wall, rattling the artwork above. A dark-haired fae stood over her with glossy, silvery eyes. His pale fingers tightened around her neck.

"Human," he whispered in a soft voice. "You will be the price he pays."

"Bonswick!" Cress shouted by the door.

The fae vanished. He reappeared behind Kate with his fingers still holding her throat, bringing Cress to a halt. A sharp pain touched Kate's side, and her wide eyes fell to a blade pointed at her waist.

"I think we need to lay down some rules in regard to our bargain," the dark-haired fae said.

Cress's turquoise eyes were pinned on the spot where the fae's blade was ready to drive through Kate's side. "I did not send Mor to you," Cress swore. "Let her go."

"Yet, he came." The fae tilted his head so it brushed against Kate's hair. "You for them, Prince. That was the bargain. But they cannot *attack* me, or *approach* me, or even *speak* to me anymore. Or she will be the price."

Cress swallowed. His hand wrapped his sword handle, but the blade didn't form. "I agree to your terms. Just let her—"

"What bargain?" Kate asked from a dry throat.

Cress looked at her face for the first time.

The fae chuckled in her ear. "You'll be left without a mate soon, Human. How agonizing that will be for you, now that you've bonded," he said, and Cress paled. "He's always been a cruel, heartless prince in the North, but I never expected him to hurt a weak human like this. To leave you in eternal pain. That is possibly the most heartless thing he's ever done in his cursed life."

"That will *not* happen. Her feelings aren't fierce enough for that." Cress's sword appeared from its handle. "You should have sensed as much with your *astute* intuition."

From the corner of her eye, Kate saw a body drift from the kitchen.

"Wait, Dranian!" Cress held up a hand, and the fae behind Kate flinched.

287

She dared a glance over at Dranian. He held a silver blade against the fae's jaw.

"Careful, Prince," the fae said with a diabolical smile. "You can't protect her, remember? And what's worse? To watch your forever mate die, or to walk to your own dreadful death? Or both?"

"Leave before I drown our bargain in your fairy blood." Cress sounded like he was half threatening, half begging.

A deep laugh boomed in Kate's ears. The fae released her neck, and suddenly the warm body disappeared from her back.

Cress strode over and took Kate's chin. He tilted her head, looking over her neck everywhere the fae's hand had been. "There's no death touch anywhere," he seemed to be telling Dranian. "She'll live for now."

Dranian marched to the windows and peered both ways down the street. Neither of them explained what had just happened—*why* it had happened.

"Cress," Kate pulled his hand off her face, "what bargain?"

Cress avoided her gaze. She waited for an answer, but all he said was, "This isn't something that concerns humans."

Kate drew back. She was about to point out how wrong he was—that she'd just had a knife aimed at her side—when two bodies materialized in the middle of the café, knocking over a chair, and Kate's stomach dropped.

The dark-haired fae was back. He tossed Mor forward. Mor's hands were bound, his face was bruised, and a muzzle of fabric was tight in his mouth.

The dark-haired fae said, "I will walk out of this realm unscathed, with you, or they're *all* dead. This is your only warning."

Kate bit back a whimper as Mor looked up through a swollen eye.

The dark-haired fae vanished again.

Dranian tore Mor's muzzle off, and Mor spat a flat metal medallion to the floor. He gasped, his breathing moist and strained as Cress kicked the medallion away like it was poisonous. It skidded over to where Kate was paralyzed by the wall.

"What in the name of the sky deities happened?" Dranian demanded.

"Don't ask him questions. He can't speak," Cress said. He stared at Mor with a mix of expressions as Mor's raspy breathing filled the café.

Kate carefully picked up the medallion from the floor. A set of wings were carved into it, similar to the picture on Cress's sword, and a pin was on the back like it was supposed to be fastened to a jacket.

Dranian strode to the kitchen, and the freezer door slammed. He returned with a bag of ice and handed it to Cress who took hold of Mor's chin. "Show me," Cress commanded.

Mor slowly let his tongue out, revealing dark burns and blisters. Cress carefully touched the ice to it. Mor seemed to fight a reaction, but he made no noise.

Shayne burst into the café gripping his crossbow. He took one look at Mor, snarled, and stormed back out to the street. His white hair disappeared past the windows.

Cress instructed in a quiet voice, "Stop him."

Dranian left.

Even though Mor's curls were a mess, his eyes watery, and his tongue destroyed, he glared.

Finally, Cress glared back.

"If you ever try to trade yourself for me again, I will kill you on my own, you fool," he promised. He grabbed Mor's hand and dropped the ice into it.

Mor lifted the ice to his mouth in silence.

Cress picked up his sword handle as he stood. He marched past Kate to the apartment stairs without so much as a glance, and he disappeared into the stairwell.

Kate slid the medallion into her pocket and moved for the sink. She filled a glass with water. When she carried it over to Mor, he was staring off through the window.

"I don't know what happened," Kate said, her eyes glossy, her mouth pinching together. "But please don't ever do that again."

Mor accepted the water. He brought it carefully to his parched, cracked lips, and he sipped, wincing as it drained into his mouth.

Kate looked back at the stairs where Cress had left.

A bargain.

"You for them, Prince. That was the bargain."

Cress was unapproachable for days. He and Mor cast each other glances when they thought no one was looking. Mor remained silent, but his sweep strokes turned into long, rigid movements that flung dirt against the walls when he wasn't paying attention. For the first time, Dranian appeared to be the happiest fae at Fae Café, which was saying something.

Kate caught the fae gathering around the bistro tables late at night, pulling out notes and pages torn from books. They argued, they got angry, they broke chairs—only to have them fixed again before morning—and they planned. But they never told her why.

They all went quiet when she drew close, so she started leaving the café as soon as it closed each night, and she stayed up in her apartment where Shayne had strictly instructed her to live again from now on.

The tension seemed to drain a little after a few days. Mor started rasping out short answers to questions and Shayne was becoming himself, blowing kisses to customers and drawing clever pictures on the chalk board. Usually he drew coffee, cookies, or cake, but sometimes his drawings were unfathomably inappropriate, and Kate had to scrub them off in the morning before customers came in.

Kate caught the assassins chuckling about something in her apartment on Sunday afternoon when the café was closed. It was the first bout of laughter she'd heard in days. She listened through the door for a few minutes before pushing her way in.

Greyson was there. Her brother slid a heaping plate of hot dogs over the counter toward Cress, Mor, Shayne, and Dranian sitting at the island chairs.

Cress picked one up and jiggled it. "What is in this meat tube, exactly?" he asked with a peculiar face.

Greyson chuckled. "You don't wanna know." He stuffed half of his own hot dog into his mouth. "Are you sure you don't want a bun?" he asked through the mouthful. His hotdogs were the only ones with buns.

"We don't eat that poison." Cress nodded toward the open bag of hotdog buns on the counter, and Greyson nodded.

"Ahh, you're doing the gluten-free thing. Cool."

The rest of the fae lifted their naked hot dogs and began taking cautious bites; Shayne dragged his through ketchup first.

"Mmm." Shayne nodded. "This is good. I like human food," he said.

Greyson laughed like Shayne was making a joke. He shoved the rest of the hot dog into his mouth and reached for another, and Kate wondered if she should tell Greyson that Shayne hadn't been making a joke.

She came to the counter. Cress's gaze darted to her without the coldness that had kept her on edge all week.

A second later, the Prince went back to eating and reached for the ketchup. After heaping a puddle onto his plate, he tipped the bottle over and squeezed some onto Dranian's plate, too. A lob fell on Dranian's leg, and the auburn-haired fae scowled. Cress cracked a smile that warmed the layer of frost in Kate's chest.

The apartment door swung open and banged against the wall.

"I got sweaters for the party!" Lily hauled a thrift store bag into the room. She carried it to the kitchenette and dropped it on the counter, knocking over the mustard. The first sweater she pulled out was a forest green knit with a reindeer and a red button for a nose. She threw it at Greyson, who lit up and held the oversized garment up to his shoulders.

Lily tossed sweaters at each of the fae, then tossed one to Kate. Kate ran her fingers over the yarn. She hadn't told Lily yet about anything that had happened since Grandma Lewis's funeral. She was too worried about what Lily might do if she found out about the Shadow Fairies and what they did to Mor. Lily was under the impression Mor had just burned his mouth on coffee.

"Mine isn't ugly at all," Kate said when she held hers up.

"Then trade me, Human," Cress said. He turned his around to reveal an oversized brown thing with wood toggles and a patch over the chest pocket that said: SANTA'S HELPER. "Mine is hideous."

"It's supposed to be ugly. It's an *Ugly Christmas Sweater Party*," Lily said.

Cress eyed Lily doubtfully. "Who's Santa? And why must I help him?" he asked.

"I am *not* an elf!" Dranian stood from his seat, red cheeked. His sweater dangled from his fist, and he shoved it back toward Lily.

"What's the problem?" Lily opened it to see, and Cress, Shayne, and Mor burst out laughing. Shayne even threw his head back and roared.

"It's insulting!" Dranian growled.

Lily made a face. "It just says 'Christmas Elf'. What's so bad about that?"

"I'm not wearing it."

"Fine." Lily put her hands on her hips. "You can show up wearing nothing then."

"Careful, Human. He might do that," Cress warned.

"Mine is awesome," Greyson said, pulling his on over his hoodie. "I'm wearing this sledding tomorrow."

"Sledding? What is that?" Dranian mumbled in what seemed like a pathetic attempt to change the subject.

"It's where crazy humans hop on speeding boards and plummet down a hill," Kate said. "It's actually fun." She didn't add that it would also be the perfect distraction from all that had happened.

"You guys can come. I'm going with Lincoln and Tegan in the morning," Greyson said before taking another bite of his hotdog.

"We try not to leave here if we don't have to." Shayne folded his arms and stole an odd look at Cress across the counter. But then he added with a grin, "Our human bosses are mean."

Lily rolled her eyes. "I'm taking your sweater back," she threatened, almost smiling.

"I'll go with you," Kate told Greyson.

Cress's gaze darted over to her, landing heavy and warm. It looked like he was about to object, but he said, "I'll come, too."

"Cool." Greyson launched into a story about how he and Lincoln had built the world's biggest sandcastle in Florida and how they planned to build an even bigger castle out of snow. But the voices in Kate's apartment seemed to fade when seconds passed, and Cress didn't look away.

Kate didn't look away, either.

After she'd found out about the bargain, Kate had tried to convince herself she'd be fine with her life once Cress was gone. But deep down she knew she would never be fine with letting him go back to that place to meet such a terrible fate.

She dropped her stare first and studied her socks as it dawned on her all over again.

Her pretend boyfriend. Maybe not so pretend after all.

Silver bells threaded along the *Yarn & Stitch* door, and piles of snow littered the windowsills. The light melody of a Christmas carol drifted through the street from a shop down the road, and cars rumbled by with drivers entirely unaware of the mythical creatures huddled together knitting inside the yarn store.

Kate adjusted her pink sweater beneath her coat as she went in. Tea and tarts filled the table between the couches, steam coiling from the pot in waves. Kate kicked the snow off her boots, and all the knitting fae women lifted their heads.

"Ah." Freida set her porcelain teacup on her lap. Her makeup and dazzling earrings were gone again. "My fairy goddaughter. It's been a while, Kate Kole."

"I haven't been avoiding you on purpose," Kate said as she shucked her coat and hung it on one of the hooks. She sat down beside Hazel and was about to explain when Hazel made a horrified face and scooted away.

"She smells of male fairy assassins!"

There were a few gasps, and some of the other women inched away, too.

"Yeah… well… that's why I didn't come back until now," Kate admitted.

"Yuck!" Hazel plugged her nose. Then, with a nasally voice, she added, "And her tone is giving off… heartache. She feels strong heartache, too." Hazel glanced over at Freida, who watched and listened to it all.

Gretchen stabbed her needles into her yarn ball. "Did you forget that Prince attacked us, Human? That he would have killed us all if he could have? And you've gotten cozy with that heartless blood spiller," she said in her high voice.

"Did you forget that *you* led him here?!" Hazel added, and Freida lifted a hand.

"The human did not lead him here. Our own fairy yarn did. Let's not blame Kate Kole for a thing she didn't do," the old woman said.

Kate cleared her throat and settled deeper into the couch. "He hasn't attacked you since, though. There's a reason for that."

"We already know," Freida said. She picked up her yarn and began to knit again. "I sensed the fairy crush weeks ago, remember? I can hear it in your tone now, too. That's a dangerous game to play, Kate Kole. You should never fall for a fairy. And you should never allow a fairy to fall for you."

Kate folded her hands. "I need your help," she said.

"Yes, that's obvious," Freida said. She slid her needles from the yarn, tied the ends of her work, then held up her masterpiece: a long red scarf. "But don't ask for help from us, fairy goddaughter. You won't get it. Not for *them*."

"Why?" Kate hugged her arms to herself. "What's your problem with them?"

"*Our* problem with *them*?" Freida almost smiled, and Gretchen grunted. "We're a black-marked bunch. We were once the Brotherhood's counterpart, sent into all the Four Corners of Ever to hunt down enemies of the North by their side. But we abandoned our Queene and fought our way out of the North. The Brotherhood killed many of us that day. And after, they hunted us across the Corners until we slipped across the gate. We've been hiding here in blissful peace ever since." Freida nodded toward the women around the couches. "Those assassins you smell of have instructions to kill us the moment they see us. They're still loyal to that heartless creature they call a queene."

"They're not!" Kate shook her head. "Mor, Shayne, and Dranian are going to stay here, like you. Only Cress is going back to where he came from, and that's why I need your help."

Gretchen's knitting needle snapped in half. She gripped both pieces tightly in her fist, shaking a little. Hazel slapped a hand over Gretchen's knee to keep her still. Even Freida's face was dark when she looked up.

"I will never trust them in my faeborn life after the blood they shed of my sisters. We will not share the human realm with them, Kate Kole. If they stay, we will kill them," she promised.

Kate's mouth parted. "But they're not coming after you anymore! Can't you help them just once? Cress is going to die if he goes back!"

Freida stood and rounded the table. She crouched before Kate, unrolling the red scarf, then she wrapped it around Kate's neck in a loose knot, tucking it in nicely at the edges. "I'll protect you if I can, fairy goddaughter. But I will not extend that generosity to them. We hope to see you at knitting club again if you survive whatever's coming for those faeborn fools you're keeping company with."

With that, the old woman went back to her place on the couch and started unravelling a new ball of yarn. It seemed like the chat was finished.

"Then what should I do about the Shadow Fairies who've been following us?" Kate asked. The entire knitting club ignored her. So she stood. "Fine. I'll enslave them like I did with the others. Any objections?" she asked. And then, when no one still spoke up, she said, "Is anyone here concerned that I might die when I go try to do this?"

Freida sighed but said nothing.

Kate looked from one woman to the next. She shook her head as she went to get her coat without a word. The club knitted in silence as she pulled it on and opened the door of the *Yarn & Stitch*.

Freida's voice was faint when she finally broke the quiet. "The names you plan to use won't work on them, Kate Kole. And you'd be a fool to try and learn their real names. The moment you attempt to enslave a Shadow Fairy, it'll show up behind you and run you through with a fairsaber before you can take your next breath."

Kate stood in the doorway until Freida finished her warning.

She pushed out into the street without another word.

CHAPTER

35

*Prince Cressica and the Greatest Faeborn Snowball Fight
in All of History*

The Prince stood at the top of the hill with his arms folded watching Shayne and Dranian bound down on a human sled, their pompom hats bouncing along with them. Kate's raspy laugh flooded the hill as she reached the top after a painfully slow climb. She was out of breath, her fair cheeks were flushed, and she was smiling wide enough to bloom fresh flowers right here in the human realm snow.

And only the sky deities knew how adorable she looked in that wretched hat.

Cress cleared his throat and looked back at Shayne whipping a ball of snow into Dranian's face below.

"Aren't you going to try it, Cress?" Kate asked, panting. She wobbled on her feet over the uneven snow as she tried to reach him. It was all Cress could do to keep himself from grabbing her to carry her around for the rest of the day before she lost her footing and broke all her little frag-ile human bones.

"Absolutely not," he announced. "This is a game for immature child-lings."

Kate licked damp snow from her lips as she smiled.

Oh, sky deities, have mercy. Cress could not look away.

She tugged him toward her sled. "Just try it once," she begged. "Please? You won't regret it."

Cress yanked his arm back. "Absolutely not."

"*Cress.*"

Why did she have to say his name like that?

A foot came against his back, and Cress was shoved forward. He whipped around to glare at Mor. The curly-haired fairy winked.

"How insufferable," Cress muttered as he marched toward the sled after all. "I'll try it only one time."

He sat down on the wooden board and was about to inch forward when Kate climbed on in front of him, shoving his legs out of the way. His faeborn heart punched against her back, though he doubted she could feel it.

Mor appeared like a cursed nightmare that wouldn't rest. He pushed against Cress's shoulders, and the sled tipped forward. Cress's royal eyes widened as the wooden board picked up speed.

He screamed a little.

They slammed into the snow at the bottom and tumbled off. The sled spun away, and Cress sprang to his elbows so he wouldn't crush Kate when he landed on her. Kate was laughing too hard to realize. He blinked down at her smiling mouth. He wanted to kiss her when she laughed this way. He wanted to so severely, he almost did it.

He released the breath he was holding and moved to climb off.

Sledding had been a bad idea. Him being anywhere near her for the next week until the human Yule celebration was a terribly bad, faeborn-cursed idea.

He stilled when Kate grabbed the sides of his face and planted her lips on his in a light kiss. It was just one, brief, dreadful second. But it sent the human realm spinning.

"Stop that," he whispered, turning his gaze cold so she would see how serious he was.

Kate's smile widened. "I don't want to."

"You're making this difficult for both of us, Human."

"That's the idea."

There was a mark of seriousness in her tone.

"Gross!" Kate's-brother-Greyson shouted from a few feet away. "Save it for when I'm not around, you two." A snowball smacked Cress's back, and Cress looked over to find Kate's-brother-Greyson and the two humans with him snorting laughs.

Kate reached for a handful of snow and packed it into a ball. "You're my boyfriend; call it official or don't. But I'm going to make it difficult for you right until the end," she promised.

"Why?" he asked.

"It's the only chance I have left to make you change your mind about giving yourself to that black-haired creep. Now move aside so I can pelt my brother with snow."

Cress rolled off, releasing Kate to hurtle the snow pocket at the humans. He watched her as he stood, only partially aware of the humans shouting something back.

Kate scrambled over and ducked behind him as three snowballs splashed against his chest. She peeked around his arm. "What are you doing?!" she shouted at him. "Fight back!"

Cress settled his turquoise gaze on the humans. He dropped to scoop a measurable amount of snow and clenched it tight in his fist until it was as solid as rock.

The battle raged for over an hour. After being washed with snow and delivering wrathful catapults of ice pellets to his enemies, Cress marched up the hill, allowing Kate to ride down with Lily. Shayne and Dranian— who had ducked behind a drift for cover when the fight began—held the fairy side of the war on their own.

Cress reached the hilltop and paused to rest. A minute later, he walked up behind Mor, planted his foot against the assassin's back, and shoved him forward. Cress flashed a delicious smile when a powdered-faced Mor stopped rolling at the bottom of the hill and looked up at him with a snarl.

The crackling in the café's fireplace at night reminded Cress of the Hall of Silver. He watched the dull flames lick up the logs from where he sat in a plush chair. They were just flames. It was just fire. There was nothing hidden within it, no lure or whispers left by noble fairies playing mad games.

When he was just ten years old, Cress had listened to the call of a fire for the first time. He'd wandered over with pure childling curiosity and found himself sticking his hand into the flames.

Nobles in the castle had erupted with laughter when he realized and tore his hand back out. It was the last party he ever went to by choice. Every gathering Cress had attended since then, he'd been forced to go to at Queene Levress's command.

Cress was curious of the savage death the Queene would deal him when he returned to the North. She had done merciless things to fairies who'd betrayed her far less than Cress had.

"Mor," Cress said, and Mor glanced up from where he read his recipe book by firelight in the opposite chair. "I need you to do something important for me."

Mor pressed down a page corner and closed the book. "What do you have in mind?"

"On midnight of the human Christmas Eve, I want you to steal my memories of this place. And I want you to deliver me to Bonswick," Cress said. "I'll write myself a letter before then and sign it with my own fairy blood. Give me the letter once you wipe my memory clean, and don't follow me back across the gate."

Mor thought about it. "No," he said.

"I'm asking as your Prince. And your friend."

The curly-haired fairy folded his arms.

"I trust you more than anyone," Cress said. "I know I'll do whatever you tell me to, even if I can't remember why."

Mor's brown-silver eyes flickered. "You're assuming I'll let you go back to the North High Court."

"Yes." Cress glanced back at the rippling flames. "I am."

Mor worked his jaw. "You fool," he whispered. "I can't honour that bargain you made with him."

"Careful," Cress warned. "I'm still a prince even if I'm to die, so do not call me names. And promise me you'll do as I ask." When Mor said nothing in return, Cress added, "I went after the Queene alone, so I'll face the punishment alone. Promise me, Mor."

Mor adjusted himself on his seat. After a moment, his broad shoulders dropped, and he twisted the recipe book back and forth so the paperback spine cracked.

"If I go back with my memories, Levress will use a Shadow Fairy to look into my head and she'll know I'm lying about you all being dead. Promise me, in return for you stealing my memories before. This is how you can make it right with me."

The crackling fire logs seemed to grow louder in the quiet café. But finally, Mor dropped his silver-laced gaze to the floor. "I promise, Your Highness," he said, almost too quiet to hear.

Without another word, he got up and left for the stairs.

A minute or two sailed by before Cress spoke again. "I know you're listening," he said into the café's shadows.

Shayne sauntered from the hallway and plunked down in the open seat Mor had left behind. "Well, that wasn't dramatic," he remarked. "I expected him to at least throw a faeborn punch."

"Mor is simply accepting my fate. Going quiet is his way." Cress leaned his head against the backrest of the chair and closed his eyes.

"I've been thinking," Shayne said.

"How horrifying."

"We've been trying for days to come up with a way to undo that bargain with no luck. Accepting our failure to save you is one thing, Cress, but the Dark will come back for Kate once you leave. I'll do my best to protect her, but you saw how fast things turned around in the cathedral yard."

Cress sighed. "I have one last option with Kate Kole. I'll send her far away from here where no fairy can find her. You must all leave with her. Establish a coffee tavern like this one," he twirled his finger around in the air, "somewhere else."

"How will you get her to do that, Cress? Are you going to utter her real name?" Shayne guessed. "It seems rather cruel of you to enslave her now, but maybe it's best."

"I told her I wouldn't enslave her. Which is why I'll try one last time to enchant her with a kiss before the day of Yule celebration comes. And then I'll kindly ask her to leave this human city."

Shayne was leaning forward with his elbows on his knees when Cress opened his eyes. The fairy dragged a hand through his silken white hair. "Why enchant her instead of simply enslaving her? Only enslaving her will guarantee she obeys," he said.

"She'll forgive me if she's enchanted. She won't if she's enslaved," Cress said. "By the time her enchantment wears off, she'll be long gone and can continue her happy life somewhere else."

Shayne tapped a finger against his knee as he thought about that. "Make sure the kiss lands right this time, Cress. Make sure she can't pull away when you roll the enchantment off your lips. She likes you now, so it might actually work."

Cress swallowed and glanced at the fire one last time. "Yes. I think it will," he said.

CHAPTER

36

Kate Kole and The Other Enchanted Kiss

The café was gold with early light and glistening with fresh, powdery snow clinging to every shallow ledge when Kate came in. She glanced at Freida's red scarf hanging on the coat hooks, unused since the day Kate had visited the knitting club. She walked over and covered it up with her coat, then headed for the counter.

Cress stepped in to cut her off. Two steaming, full-to-the-brim mugs of coffee were in his hands. He handed them to her.

"Would you hold these for a moment, Human?" he asked with an odd smile.

Kate took them carefully, her eyes darting back and forth between the mugs while she tried not to spill any. "Why'd you make them so full?"

Cress's fingers drifted from the mugs to her wrists. Kate's eyes fired up to his when his light touch moved up her arms, over her shoulders to her neck, and then slid gently back into her hair. The coffee sloshed over the mugs' brims when she took a small step back, and she froze again before they spilled.

Kate's eyes were wide as Cress brought his mouth in and kissed her softly. It was sweet, and careful, and deep, and *not* casual at all. He held her head still, keeping his lips firmly on hers as the seconds sped by. Kate's mouth was left parted when he pulled back. She was sure she hadn't blinked since the second he handed her the coffees.

Cress studied her. Like he was waiting for her to say something. But she had no idea what to say after that.

"What are you doing?" Kate demanded. Coffee rolled over the mugs' edges and dripped to the floor as she failed to hold still. "And don't lie and say you did that just because you think I'm pretty or something stupid like that."

Cress tilted his head, seeming more frustrated than anything. "You're not *that* pretty. You're just adequate," he said. Kate's jaw dropped a little, and he raised his hands as if she'd misinterpreted. "I mean, you're quite pretty for a human, of course. But you're nothing compared to a fairy female. My betrothed is far more beautiful." Then he muttered, "Even if she has the ugly soul of a hungry hogbeast."

Kate blinked.

Two full cups of coffee were splashed into Cress's face. He grimaced as the liquid rolled down his neck and soaked his shirt.

Kate walked over and slammed the mugs down on the counter before storming up the stairs to her apartment. She tapped a fist against her heart to make sure it was still working. She felt hot.

Mor stood before the full-length mirror in her room, tying his apron.

"Cress is engaged?!" Kate shouted at him when she barged in.

Mor raised an eyebrow. "Yes. To the High Princess of the North." He went back to smoothing his apron.

Kate gaped. She tried to smack his arm.

Mor buckled and raised his hands as a shield, so Kate grabbed a novel off her bookshelf and tried to smack him with that, too, but he darted out of the way too fast.

"You don't see a problem with keeping that from me?!" she barked.

"Queensbane, what's wrong with you, crazy Human?!" he shouted back at her, using his height to reach over her and pluck the novel from her fingers.

Kate marched back out of her apartment, banging the door behind her. She thudded down the stairs to find Cress leaning against the counter on his palms—no, *gripping* the edge of the counter so tightly that his knuckles were white.

Shayne was a basket case of laughter on the floor behind the counter. "How?!" he wailed. "How could you let it happen again?! How—" He slapped a hand over his eyes when tears gushed out. "How did you manage to get enchanted *twice*?!"

"Stop. Laughing. Or I'll *Cut. Out. Your. Tongue.*"

Kate didn't wait around to hear more. She went back to the coat rack, grabbed her coat—and her red scarf—and swung the door open. Cress appeared and yanked the door shut before she could leave, creating a robust fae barrier between her and escape.

"Let me explain," he said, but Kate pushed against him. "Katherine!" he tried. "Human, I didn't mean for this to... I mean I..." He put a hand over his forehead like he had a headache, and Kate slipped under his arm while his eyes were closed. "You can't go out alone!" he growled after her.

Kate met the cold while she was still buttoning her coat. She moved to avoid pedestrians, refusing to look any of her friendly neighbours in the eyes so she wouldn't be forced to greet them. She heard the café's bell behind her, and she knew Cress was following her.

She walked down to the harbour and all around the cold city on the longest walk of her life.

Cress never caught up or tried calling out. He never showed himself.

But his warm gaze was on her back.

It was three days before she saw him again. Kate returned to the café the following morning to find out that Shayne had locked Cress in her upstairs closet. *"It's for his own good. He would kill me later for letting him humiliate himself by tearing apart the city to get to you at all hours. It's for your own good, too,"* was what Shayne said.

Kate counted down the days and hours as they passed. She stared at the calendar on the wall, dreading the arrival of Christmas.

She started washing dishes with vigour on the third day. A mug splashed back into the soapy water when Cress emerged from the stairs of her apartment. He looked angry and exhausted. Shayne had a shiny, new black eye on his handsome face.

Cress stopped walking when he saw Kate.

She dried her hands on a towel and went to meet him, but he grabbed her wet hands around the towel. "I want to make you laugh, Human. Hearing your laugh is my highest obsession. And your smile, too. And for some faeborn-cursed reason, I'm fascinated by your lack of evil—"

"Aaaaaand back into the closet you go," Shayne said, yanking Cress back by his shoulder. "I guess it's not worn off yet."

Cress growled but didn't object. "I thought I was okay to see her, but I'm not," he muttered to Shayne. He glared at Kate this time. "You did this." He pointed to his own head.

"No, *you* did this," Kate assured, refusing to take the blame this time.

Cress snarled as he headed back up the stairs, followed by Shayne.

Kate went back to washing the mugs, shaking her head.

A snowstorm picked up outside. A few teenagers pushed in and patted snowflakes off their hats and mitts.

"Three more days," Kate whispered below the howling of the wind against the windows. Her gaze flickered back up to the calendar where Christmas Day was highlighted in red with a small drawing of holly berries.

"Three more days until I lose you, Cress," she said to all those in the café who weren't listening.

"I have a question." Lily untangled Christmas lights by the window. The tree sat in the café's corner, covered in tinsel that sparkled in the early morning light. The sweet scents of pine and sap filled the café.

From her seat by the fireplace, Kate flicked aside the Fae Café social media page on her phone. A different photo filled the screen, one with a list of obscure fae names. She quickly pushed that screen away, too, and stuffed her phone into her pocket.

"What's your question?" she asked Lily.

Lily rested her elbow on her knee where she squatted. "What happened to the real Officer Riley?"

Strange, terrible thoughts came to Kate's mind as she made her guesses. She'd never found the nerve to ask the fae.

"He's wandering around the human realm with his pockets full of fairy gold," Cress announced as he strutted over. He stopped, standing over Kate's chair. Though it seemed like most of his anger had passed over, his brows were furrowed. He extended a hand toward Kate like he wanted to help her up.

"Are you feeling better?" Kate asked warily. She gave him her hand, and he tugged her to her feet.

"Yes." He mumbled it. "But I curse the day I met you, Kate Kole."

That brought a smile to her face. "How sweet."

He grunted and tugged Kate to the coat rack. "Human—"

Kate cut him off. "Your *fiancée* seems like a real gem with that 'hungry hogbeast personality'. I can't imagine why you left her to come here for even a moment."

Cress's turquoise eyes darkened a little.

"She must be happy you're going back. That is, if you're still planning to go back," Kate remarked, hugging her arms to herself. Cress didn't contradict her, and Kate released the breath she was holding. "I was sort of hoping that kiss thing had changed your mind. But I guess we're still at square one. Lucky her."

Cress's jaw slid to the side. "I cannot articulate the joy and merriment it will bring me if you're jealous," he said. And there it was—the first hint of a smile. He smothered it away though and hardened his face.

"Don't flatter yourself," Kate said.

"I don't need to do such a thing, Human. You're doing it for me."

Kate shook her head in disbelief. "You're the worst."

"You're irritatingly immune to tricks."

"You're astoundingly self-absorbed," she stated.

"Yes, well, I'm a prince. It's only natural. Now, for the next two days until the human Christmas, you're mine, Katherine Lewis." Cress reached for her coat and handed it to her.

After blinking at it, Kate reluctantly took her coat and slid it on. "Where are we going?"

"On a human date. And I'm going to buy you something that will make sure you remember me long after I'm gone."

Kate made a face. "You mean *I'm* going to buy something—"

"Call it whatever you like. Let's go."

The air was cold but even so, the walk to the subway felt short. As did the ride to the mall.

When they came in, Christmas carols hummed through the aisles and the smell of cinnamon buns wafted from a baked treat kiosk. Stores were filled with sale signs, frantic retail workers, and rushing shoppers.

Cress took his time. He slid his fingers between Kate's as they walked hand-in-hand like their last date.

Kate thought of the calendar back at the café that was haunting her days and nights. Her grip tightened around his knuckles. "What did you want to buy?"

"Something that will distract you once you meet a human male in your happy life. Something that will catch your eye every time you walk past it and remind you that you liked me before you liked him. Something *big*."

"What makes you think I like you?" Kate chuckled.

"Oh, come on, Human." Cress's wide grin said it all. "I'm handsome and powerful and you're a weak human who can't help herself."

"Tell that to the last two enchanted kisses you tried to give me—"

"I don't want to talk about that." His smile fell. "I'm bad at fairy tricks because I avoided them as a childling. That's the only reason," he assured, veering Kate into a store of framed prints and paintings.

Artwork hung on the walls like a miniature museum. Cress scanned the pictures one by one.

"Human art is horrendous," he remarked, and pointed. "Look at that one."

Kate pushed his hand down and fought a blush as a sales worker walked by and heard everything. "Well, you don't have to buy me art. Why don't you just get something small? Like a pair of earrings?"

Cress's nose wrinkled. "No. It'll be something big. Something you must put right in the middle of your new house."

"My new house?" Kate raised a brow.

"The one you move into when you leave this city."

Kate slid her hand out of his with a sigh. She pulled off her hat and raked her fingers through her hair. "Is that what this is about? You're going to try to convince me to move from Toronto again?"

Cress turned to face her, his expression serious now. "It's the only way, Katherine."

"I outwitted *your* assassins. I'm sure I can survive any other fae that show up after you leave." She thought of her phone in her pocket. "You're being ridiculous."

Cress stared at her until she put her hat back on. Then his eyes lifted to something behind her, and his face lit up. "That one!" he said, pointing to a painting by the entrance. "Give me your wallet, Human," he said. "I'll buy that one for you."

Kate turned to find a watercolour painting of a sunny countertop. Atop the counter was a detailed painting of a basket full of chocolate chip cookies.

CHAPTER

37

Kate Kole and All the Things She Couldn't Say

The painting fit better with the café vibe than Kate had expected. It brought a new warmth to the space and seemed to bring the scents of fresh baking to life whenever someone made a cake or tart in the kitchen.

Cress took on the role of Santa Claus. He came into the café with new presents every hour, and Kate continued to find the cash in her wallet gone. He left his mark on everything: small presents under the tree, a handsome "selfie" he took on her phone and got Shayne to turn into her wallpaper, a failed cake baking experiment he turned into a trifle and put in the freezer "for later, when we all missed him." Kate didn't tell him that a whipped cream trifle wouldn't freeze well, and it would likely end up in the garbage.

When the Bonswick guy first let Kate in on the bargain Cress had made, Kate thought Cress was trying to find a way out of it. But as she watched the Prince make up for the time he lost while locked away letting the enchantment wear off, she realized a shift had taken place at some point. It seemed like Cress had accepted he was leaving.

Mor bristled every time Cress mentioned "for when he was gone." Dranian mumbled things under his breath like, "Foolish Prince," and "…walking to your death," and "Someone needs to get you a sweater that isn't so faeborn tight."

Snow speckled the evening before Christmas Eve. Everyone went to bed early so they wouldn't be tired for the ugly sweaters party Lily had planned the next day, but Kate remained at a bistro table working on her novel. Cress carried over two teas and slid one over, warming the air with steam and the spicy scent of chai.

"You seem rather invested in that story," he said. "But you know the ending is cursed."

Kate slowed her typing. "I'm going to fill this bookshelf with copies of this book." She nodded toward the ledge behind the counter. "We're going to sell it here as a *Read and Sip combo* where people can buy a book, get a free coffee, and stay as long as they like to read by our fire. And everyone is going to get to learn what a fae is really like."

"Aren't you worried the humans will grow suspicious that the story is true?" Cress sipped his tea.

Kate laughed. "No one will think this is a true story. People don't believe in fairies, Cress."

Cress chewed on the inside of his cheek. "Let me finish it." He took the computer and slid it to himself before Kate could say yes or no.

"What are you going to write?" she asked warily. She leaned to try and spy as he began pecking at the keys, but he tilted the screen down so she couldn't watch. Kate slumped back into her seat.

"You can read it when I'm finished," he said. But a second later, he glanced up and seemed to take in her unbrushed hair, the bags under her eyes, and her stretched collar. "Go to bed, Katherine. You're tired."

"I'm fine. It's just stress."

"Why are you stressed?"

"Because of you."

Cress's turquoise eyes turned doubtful. "Your feelings about me leaving are your own fault. I never successfully enchanted you."

Kate snorted a laugh. "Right, it's always my fault."

Cress grinned. "Now you seem to be getting it, Human."

He went back to reading the novel, and Kate's smile faded. "You can't go, Cress," she rasped. "All I think about is running off and doing something crazy to make you stay." Her phone felt heavy in her pocket.

Cress pursed his lips, his brows bunching together. "Yes, I know. It's been written all over your faeborn-cursed face all week." And then he added, "Do you know how difficult it is to have a girlfriend who speaks with a tone like that all the time?"

"What does my tone tell you?" she asked.

"It tells me you've more than *thought* about doing something crazy. It tells me you have plans to do something if I can't figure out a way to change the bargain. It tells me you perhaps care more than I thought. And that's dangerous."

Kate became aware of the popping logs in the fireplace.

"We should enjoy our last day together. Your brother's loud human friends tell me it's supposed to be *the most wonderful time of the year*." Cress closed the computer. He inhaled like he was about to say something else but singing erupted outside, lifting through the café with muted harmonies.

A small crowd was gathered past the café door with open songbooks. Shayne came bounding down the apartment stairs and flung the front door open, letting the music of a dozen carollers fill the space. Kate jogged over to watch, too.

Shayne grinned as the carollers broke out into slightly pitchy harmonies. He tried to snap along, missing a few beats.

Cress didn't hide his repulsed face as he joined them at the door. "Must we stand here and listen to this?" he whispered to Kate.

"It's kind of a common courtesy to stay and listen until they're finished," she said back.

"How horrifying," he mumbled, eyeing a man at the back singing louder than the rest. "That human should lose his tongue."

"Shh." Kate closed her eyes and leaned against his shoulder to listen. A moment later, his arm wrapped around her, blocking out the cold night air. "This brings back good memories," she said. "I used to sing in a choir when I was young. I bet you didn't know I can sing."

Cress released a soft grunt. "Your singing has haunted me since I came here, pesky Human. I bet you didn't know *that*."

The carollers finished their song, and Kate felt Cress breathe a sigh of relief. He barely turned away before one of the carollers started a new song and the rest burst into harmony again.

Cress's jaw tightened, and he glanced at the sky like he was trying to keep from rolling his eyes. "What in the faeborn-cursed human world is wrong with these people?" he said loudly.

"I like it," Shayne said with a shrug.

Cress grunted. "Of course you would, you tone-deaf fool."

Christmas Eve morning came too fast, chasing away a humid mist that rolled in through the night. The temperature dropped with the sunrise, and everything froze to ice, blanketing Kate's bedroom window in frost. Fresh white flurries skated past.

Cress was standing by Kate's bed when she awoke. She rubbed her eyes and sat up, realizing she was in her own apartment. She'd planned to spend the night at Lily's.

"Did I fall asleep downstairs?" she guessed.

"You've been sleeping terribly," he said, "so I ensured you'd have a restful slumber. Lily Baker unleashed dull human insults when I told her I was sneaking sleep remedies into your tea and keeping you here with me through the night. She called me a *'creep'* and warned me to *'keep my hands to myself'* before she left."

Kate raised an eyebrow. "Yeah, waking up to find you watching me isn't creepy at all." She wasn't sure if he picked up on her sarcasm. She hid a smirk and rolled back over.

"My presence helps you sleep. It's a forever mate thing." He mumbled the last part.

Cress walked around the bed and crouched to put his face before hers. "This is our last day together, Katherine," he said. "I plan to make today the most fun of your boring human life."

Kate's fingers tightened around her bedsheets.

The last day.

"Cress—"

"Don't do anything foolish," he added, and Kate's eyes widened when he pulled her phone out of his pocket. The photo of the fae names from the *Fairy Book of Rules and Masteries* filled the screen. "I'm holding onto your magic mirror so you don't use it. Human fool," he said with a slight growl. "Don't you know that the Dark don't have the same real names as those from the North? These won't work."

Kate watched the phone until he slid it away.

Cress glided his arms beneath her and lifted her out of bed. "Coffee first," he said, carrying her from the bedroom to the kitchenette. None of the other assassins were around, but Kate's laptop sat open on the counter with her novel filling the screen. Cress plunked her onto one of the barstools.

As he puttered around to brew the coffee, Kate pulled her computer over to read.

"How late were you up working on this?" she asked, scrolling to the bottom of the file.

"I finished it," he said. The coffee maker began to chug.

New paragraphs filled the novel's final pages. A small smile formed as Kate scanned them. She was still reading when Cress carried a piping hot mug of coffee to the counter. The more she read, the harder it was to keep reading.

Finally, Kate pulled her eyes away and took a sip of her coffee. He put in way too much sugar, and she fought a gag.

"This ends with me belonging to you, Cress," she said, meeting his gaze. "The fae Prince and the human end up together."

"You wanted it to end darkly?" he asked, drinking his own coffee. "You want it to end with me being tortured to death?"

Heat struck her at the thought. She'd imagined him being killed, but never being... *tortured*. A tremor started in her hands, and she sat on them. "I was waiting to see how things play out and end it with how it all really happens," she said.

"Hmm." Cress's mouth twisted to the side. He set his mug down, walked around the counter, and turned her seat to face him. "I want you to be mine. That's how I want the story to end," he said. "With us living a simple life, and you being happy." He glanced at her neck tattoo when she swallowed.

"Don't give me false hope," she warned, pushing the laptop away. "Is there any chance you think things could end differently in real life?"

"No." He leaned in and planted a soft kiss on her mouth. "But if I can't be happy in this faeborn life, then I want it to at least end this way in the story humans will read."

Her vision glossed over. "Are you trying to enchant me again?" she tried to joke, but a hot tear rolled off the ledge of her eye and painted a clear streak down her face.

Cress cast her a smile and swiped the tear away with his thumb. "I know by now, Human, that enchanting you is not possible." He tugged her to her feet. "Forget the novel. Let's get ready for the *ugly human Christmas sweaters* party. Lily insisted we have a full day of festivities in our hideous garments. I think she believes that throwing a celebration will make it easier to let me leave at dawn. But I've made sure you'll all suffer in my absence by finding little traces of me in every corner and cranny. I expect you all to miss me terribly."

CHAPTER

38

Prince Cressica and the Merry Christmas of Faeborn Madness

Dranian arrived at the party with no shirt or hideous sweater. Nothing but garland "suspenders" covered his broad assassins' chest. He also wore a pointed red hat with a fluffy fur ball on the end, but his cheery garments didn't make him seem any happier. The fairy frowned and grumbled while he got the fire going and carried mugs of warm beast milk out from the back.

Cress scratched his neck beneath his uncomfortable human sweater and approached the counter where a platter of *freshly baked chocolate chip cookies* called to him with the sweet voice of crispy crust and sugar. But his eyes were on Kate, even when she was out of earshot. He kept his face composed to seal away the anger threatening to erupt as he watched her be. It was the same anger he had hardly been able to contain these past days. The same anger that boiled just below the surface of his princely scent and ice-toned eyes.

Today, he hated that he was a faeborn prince, from a faeborn realm, born of a fairy kind. He tore his eyes off the human girl across the room for just a moment to choose his cookie. After a quick count, he selected the one with the most chocolate chips, as only such a dessert was worthy of a prince.

When he bit into it, he spat it back out.

"What is this?" he demanded, turning the dessert over in his hands.

"Lily brought those," Mor said.

"And what in the name of the sky deities are *these*?" Cress plucked out one of the chocolate chips to find it squishy. He made a horrified face. "What is it, Mor?! Why does it squeeze like a bug?"

"It's a raisin." Kate appeared and took a cookie for herself. She bit into it. "They're not everyone's cup of tea, but I don't mind them."

Cress stared as she consumed the bite instead of spitting it as he had done. He held his cookie toward her and pointed at the raisins. "This is human trickery of the highest sort!"

Her raspy laugh filled the café when Cress tossed the rest of the cookie back onto the plate.

"Kate." Lily approached, and Cress glared at her for her raisin cookie trap. But the fair featured human was looking down at her phone. "I can't believe this is happening but work just called. There's an emergency downtown and they're calling everyone in."

The disappointment that came over Kate's face turned something in Cress's chest.

"But it's Christmas Eve," she said with a tone that told stories.

Mor sighed and sipped his beast milk. Then he winced at Dranian's bare fae chest as Dranian appeared. "Put on a cloak, Dranian," Mor said. "These aren't the Brotherhood training quarters. You'll catch a cold."

Lily looked up at Cress. The human police officer didn't need to point out that if she left now, she may not see Cress again. But there was enough goodbye in her eyes without speaking it into the air.

"Best of luck tomorrow, Cress," was all she said.

The sound of Mor's mug echoed through the café when he dropped it too hard on the counter. "Yes. Best wishes of luck. That ought to save him," he mumbled.

Cress shot Mor a look. He shoved the plate of not *freshly baked chocolate chip cookies* toward him. "Try one." He invited his friend to experience the horror.

"It's fine, Lil. Go." Kate flashed a smile.

Lily said a few more apologies. Minutes later, she jogged out the door and disappeared into the snowy afternoon.

Human Yule music flitted through the space, the sort Cress was growing to adore simply for the nonexistence of ulterior motives even though it was clickety-clangy and there were far too many smashing cymbals.

Cress took Kate's hand and tugged her toward the fireplace. He'd only ever danced with fairy females before, and rarely by choice. He wanted to know what it would be like to dance with a human, one such as Kate Kole/Katherine Lewis/his mate who still didn't seem to know it.

Finally, Kate's smile returned; a real one this time. Cress relaxed and felt the clouds part in the sky outside. A beam of afternoon sunlight glittered over the street as Kate swayed in his grip.

"You dance like a wild childling goat from the haunted woods," Cress told her. "But I dance well enough for the both of us, so don't worry your little human mind over it." He shoved her into a twirl, but she came back rolling her eyes.

"Why am I not surprised? You hate everything about humans, don't you?"

He caught her and trapped her body to his with his arms. "That's preposterous, Human. I like many things about *you*."

A catchy tune rang through the café next. It didn't seem fitting for a slow dance anymore, and Cress realized he didn't know how to move to a song with quick rhythms.

Kate grinned as though she realized. "We don't have to dance anymore. I'd hate for you to turn into the wild childing goat here. And do you really like *many things* about me, Cress?"

"Of course. Most fairies would call it shameful to fall in love with a human, but that didn't stop me."

Kate stopped swaying.

A cold wind brushed through the café when someone opened the door. Kate's-brother-Greyson came in wearing his hideous human Christmas sweater and called across the room to Mor at the counter, "Where's Lily?"

But Cress only looked at his human mate, who looked back at him with a troubled brow.

"Then stay," she said.

Stay.

How he hated that word. A word that might have had the power to change the order of the stars in the sky. A word that could break hearts and crumple fairy empires if uttered in the wrong setting.

"You don't understand what you're asking of me," he said. "I will not stay." It was best she accepted it. He brushed her hair from her face. "Now give me all those kisses you were so willing to bargain away before."

Kate's-brother-Greyson turned on the new rectangular mirror device on the café wall to the nightly news. The boy's face drained of colour, his rhythms elevated, and Cress knew something was wrong even before the rest of the souls in the café came around the tables to watch the moving picture. Humans in the mirror talked of something happening in a vaguely familiar part of the city. Mor turned down the human Yule music to hear.

Images flashed over the mirror to two human police officers on their knees with messy hair and bruises, being held in place by other humans in black masks. The dark room they were in made it difficult to see, but not enough to hide their identities. One of the captured officers was Officer Connor Backs whom Cress detested.

The other was Lily Baker.

Cress's eyes slid closed. He set down his warm beast milk.

This would steal away precious moments from a day he could hardly let go of. But Kate's gasp lifted beside him, and her hand squeezed his arm. He knew what he would do even before she asked.

"Save her! Please!" she begged the assassins.

Cress swallowed.

"I can't lose Lily!"

"Mor." Cress's eyes opened, taking in the sky view of the street in the mirror that told him exactly where Lily Baker was at this moment. "Do something about those human cameras so we don't end up all over the human news like that incident when I fought the Shadow Fairies at the mall."

The air turned crisp as four fairy assassins marched past human cameras and congested crowds. Officer Riley's uniform hugged tight to Cress's body. Shayne slipped three vests from the back seat of a police chariot on wheels and handed one to Mor and Dranian.

The human officers were positioned far back from the building with their measly human weapons drawn, hiding behind chariot doors and shields. They shouted things and strategized. Not one of their weapons looked as menacing as the crossbow Shayne carried in as he fastened his officer vest on.

Cress nodded at Mor, and Mor vanished.

Human cameras fell off their legs one by one and tumbled to the road around the scene.

A male officer glanced over at Shayne's crossbow as the fairies approached. He nodded. "Nice," was all he said.

Cress studied the building's entrance. "Is that where the human hostages are?" he asked the same male officer.

The officer looked at Cress oddly, but he nodded again. "I hope they're still alive. There hasn't been a livestream video in over twenty minutes."

Cress sniffed. "They're alive." He turned to Mor just as the fairy returned. "Get us inside."

And just like that, the four fairy assassins vanished into thin air.

In the same second, they appeared in a dark room. Humans in masks jumped in surprise; one of them shrieked.

Lily's face was tear-stained. "Thank goodness!" she said, crumpling forward. Her hands were bound behind her back.

Human weapons were raised. Dranian slid left to stab, and Shayne fired an arrow at the human on the right. The human weapon stones meant to pierce Cress's princely flesh fired off at obscure angles and went into the walls. Cress waited until his assassins finished. Then he let his dark, cold turquoise gaze settle on the masked humans who had ruined his hideous human sweaters Christmas Eve party.

"Who are you...?" one of them dared to ask.

"Cressica Alabastian, High Prince of the North Corner," Cress answered. "You might as well start bowing."

Human shrieks erupted when the fairies swept through, kicking and snapping knees.

"That's what you get, thugs!" Lily shouted at them as justice was served. Her black eyelash ink ran down her cheeks in streams.

Soon every human in the room apart from Lily Baker and Officer Connor Backs was wailing and kneeling.

"Officer Riley?" Connor Backs blinked like a fool as though he'd just woken from a deep sleep. He was a full twenty seconds too late in registering what was happening.

Lily's hands shook when Cress tore the binds from her wrists. She failed to stand on her wobbly legs, so he lifted her to carry her out. Shayne, on the other hand, picked up Connor Backs and flung him over his shoulder with the officer's wrists still bound and his human rear up. The fairy carried him out that way.

"I totally thought I was going to get my fingers chopped off or something," Lily said through heavy breaths. "Don't tell Kate about this," she begged.

"I'm afraid she already knows, Human," Cress said as he carried her out the front of the building. The crowds exploded with surprise and cheers. Police officers all down the road lowered their weapons.

Two fixed cameras took it all in.

"So much for being faeborn subtle," Mor said.

Shayne laughed. "Did you actually think we'd get away with no one noticing we were here?" he asked, patting Connor Backs on the buttocks.

"I'll deliver you to the human medical building," Cress told Lily. "But make no mistake, Lily Baker, if you ever trick a fairy into eating a raisin cookie again, the sky deities will show no mercy. I hope you realize that what happened here today was punishment for that wretched cookie I ate this morning."

"I saw him," Connor mumbled from where he hung over Shayne's back. Shayne turned so Connor could see the others. "The guy who was telling all the bad guys what to do…"

It seemed Connor Backs was muttering nonsense after his little fright with the humans. Cress sighed and trotted the rest of the way down the stairs.

"Who?" Lily called back to ask. She still looked as though she might faint. "What guy? I never saw a guy. And what do you mean 'bad guys', Connor? Call them *culprits* like a real cop."

"He had weird silver eyes. And I swear he disappeared into thin air." Connor's voice slipped through the wind, running along the back of Cress's neck and inching into his faeborn heart.

At Cress's side, Mor stopped walking.

Dranian cursed.

Cress felt the reddest anger and darkest fear in existence burn through his veins.

Cress pushed into the café, snapping the bell right off its perch. His faeborn heart quickened as he spotted Kate's-brother-Greyson sitting on the floor in a trance, shuddering and hugging his knees to himself. The human's two loud friends were stricken beside him, shouting into their magic mirrors at other humans asking all sorts of questions from their side. The rest of the café was empty.

Cress's jaw turned as hard as stone.

"Where is she?" he asked the humans, his brothers, the air of the realm, the sky deities themselves, anyone or anything that would listen.

His faeborn chest pounded. His hands became fists.

Bonswick would die by a thousand slashes if Kate Kole was dead.

CHAPTER

39

Kate Kole and the Old Woman in the Pink Scarf

30 Minutes Ago

The camera feeds cut out one at a time, the talking reporters disappearing from the screen. The main feed returned to the news anchor who claimed they were having technical difficulties. The newsroom tried to contact someone on the scene to tell them why all the feeds cut out.

Kate fiddled with the sleeve of her sweater as she and Greyson watched from the café bistro chairs. She hadn't been able to form a clear thought since the assassins left. There was no cell in her body that would survive if something happened to Lily.

"You think…" Greyson released a nervous hiccup. "You think your boyfriend can really save her, Kate?" he asked.

"I know it seems crazy to have sent the baristas, but they're good at… certain things," Kate said.

Neither of them looked away from the TV, even when the broadcast went to a commercial break.

"That doesn't sound crazy," Greyson said after a few moments. "I know there's something off about them—it's super obvious. You don't have to tell me what it is. I'm just glad they're here for this."

Kate didn't object to his observations, but she didn't explain, either. "Yeah," was all she said.

Lincoln and Tegan shuffled in through the café door and hung up their coats. "Sorry we're late, we were watching the news! Grey, Lily is totally on the..." Lincoln stopped when he realized the news was on the TV. He slid into a bistro chair without another word. Tegan snatched a cookie and slid into the opposite seat; eyes glued to the screen as the feed flipped back to the 'live on the scene' reporters.

The restored news feed showed police officers emerging from the surrounded building. Kate breathed a sigh of relief when she recognized Cress in Officer Riley's uniform. Lily was in his arms, and Kate could have cried.

"See?" she said to Greyson. "I told you they'd..."

Coldness crawled up Kate's back. A faint shadow appeared of someone standing beside her.

"Wow!" Tegan said through a mouthful of cookie. "Where did that guy just come from—"

A cold hand grabbed Kate's arm, and she was yanked backward against a hard chest.

"Hey! *Not* cool!" Greyson shouted and leapt from his chair.

Kate tried to pry the cold fingers off as a chilling voice whispered in her ear, "I've enjoyed watching the North Prince follow you around, Human. That's what us fairies do. We watch. We wait. And then, when no one is looking, we grab what we want."

The last thing Kate saw before she vanished was Tegan and Lincoln springing from their chairs and the look of horror on Greyson's face.

Light and colour burst into being around Kate, sharpening into the lines of a new place. She gasped as she was dropped onto clean white tiles.

The air felt cooler.

The late afternoon light was replaced by artificial light.

The smell was different.

She looked up in dismay at a wide, curved staircase she didn't recognize. Tall crystal windows with red silk curtains lined an enormous lobby, a giant chandelier hung overhead, and silver-and-brown-eyed fae stood around the room. They sneered as Kate stood and turned, taking them all in. She was in someone's home. It looked like the mansion of a wealthy family. She didn't want to imagine where that family was now.

Her mouth was too dry to speak. She watched the fae with black hair walk to a row of chairs at the side of the room. He grabbed one and dragged it back, filling the space with screeching echoes. It left marks on the tiles.

He tossed the chair toward Kate. "Sit, Human."

Kate sank into the chair. She pictured her baristas trying to enter this place, certain they'd be driven into the ground with this many Shadow Fairies. She clasped her trembling hands, trying to sort through her foggy memories.

"Bonswick," she whispered. "That's your name, isn't it?"

Instead of answering her question, the fae looked her over with shameless interest. "I'll never get it," he said. "A prince who had everything he wanted falls for a helpless human insect. What a tale for the legend books."

The fae—Bonswick—grabbed the armrests of Kate's chair. His mouth came provocatively close to hers and curled into a wicked smile. "What's worse, Human? To be able to do nothing to save yourself, or to be viewed as an insect on the shoes of the fairy gods?" he asked. "Or both?"

"You think I'm an insect?"

"Yes. You are unworthy to exist."

Kate held his gaze as she slid a hand into her pocket. "That's sweet of you."

His smile widened as he dragged his thumb across her bottom lip. "You speak like a sarcastic fairy female. Perhaps that's why he doesn't think of you as a human."

"Maybe."

Kate tore the medallion from her pocket and smacked it against his cheek.

Bonswick ripped himself back, kicking her chair over as a sizzling sound filled the room. The medallion clattered to the floor, and his hand slapped over his pale cheek.

Kate crashed to the tiles and rolled from the chair. She winced and licked her lip, tasting blood. Through her fluttering lashes, she eyed the closest window, half-hidden behind a fae body. It was cracked open an inch; icy air slid through.

Her hair was grabbed, and she was yanked to her feet. The fae bent her head backward to expose her throat, his silvery eyes grazing over it like a hot string running along her neck.

"That was for Mor," she rasped, throat bobbing.

His warm breath rushed over her when he laughed. "Queensbane," he whispered. "Maybe I can understand after all, Human." He tossed her back toward the chair, and Kate landed in it with a thud that echoed into the tall ceiling.

A poorly timed laugh tumbled from Kate's mouth. She tried to stop, but it bubbled out faster than she could control it, her nerves turning her self-control to mush.

The fae grabbed her hands. His nails dug into the flesh above her knuckles and turned her last chuckle into a shriek. He pinned her like that until Shadow Fairies brought rope and wound it around her chest, tying her arms down to the chair.

"Laugh all your wishes away, Human. I can make you miserable while I wait for the illegitimate Prince to come hold up his end of our bargain," Bonswick said. "And I assure you, you'll wish you'd never met me after he's gone." He tore his nails out, and Kate gripped the armrests, fighting to not release a sound.

Greyson's face had been horrified before Kate vanished. Lily had just been a hostage on the job. Neither of them would be okay if Kate didn't make it back. It was the first pulse of fear that paralyzed her into the chair.

Yet, still, she hoped he wouldn't come.

As the hour trickled by, Kate watched the large wooden entrance doors, willing them to stay closed. The fae spat on her as they passed and whispered lullaby-like songs that made her want to get up and dance. Her feet moved, and she tried to stand, but she only lifted the chair along with her, and they all burst out laughing.

Shadow Fairies blew her kisses, and icy wind flitted over her skin. She shivered as a prickling sensation pulled her flesh tight. She'd never felt a menacing cold that struck so deeply into her bones. Her knees shook as she tried to catch her breath.

Lily's voice entered her subconscious through the haze. She imagined her friend telling her to try and figure out where she was, to gather clues and find an escape route. Kate glanced back at the cracked-open window. Her head was growing heavy, and her thoughts spun. If she'd been brought here by normal humans, she might have stood a chance at outrunning them in a sprint. But there was no way she was going to escape a pack of fae, especially ones that could disappear and reappear in front of her.

She squeezed her eyes shut when one of them sang again. A tear escaped, running down her dry cheek as she tried to block out the sound. The sweet, horrifying tune trickled over her flesh and into her ears like a hot ribbon. She'd never heard anything like it. She never wanted to again.

The singing ceased, and whispers filled the room. A familiar touch of warmth pressed her cold skin. Kate's eyelids were sticky when she peeled them open, and through her dizziness she saw a blurry silhouette of someone walking toward her in a police uniform.

She shook her head. She wanted to tell him to stop.

Bonswick sliced through her ropes with a dagger. He grabbed a handful of Kate's shirt, wrenched her from her seat, and threw her forward.

Cress caught her. He wrapped a warm arm around her frozen body, and he pressed his mouth to her ear. She could feel his heart through her numbness.

"Katherine Lewis," he said so quietly, Kate almost didn't hear the words, but her body went rigid involuntarily, "I want you to walk out of here without looking back. And I want you to go live a happy life."

Just like that, Cress released her.

Kate found her feet moving—one in front of the other. A sound escaped as she realized she couldn't stop, nor could she turn her head right or left to see if he was okay.

Mor, Shayne, and Dranian stood in the lobby, doing nothing but watching the things Kate couldn't see with dismal faces. Dranian shook. His sharp breathing turned desperate. His lashes fluttered as he crumpled, trembling—Shayne caught him before his knees smashed to the floor.

Kate couldn't stop. She passed them and walked toward the grand entrance with a sob, eyes ahead to where a well-aged woman with a pink scarf and a fancy coat waited outside the open doors with a long, serrated sword in her grip. Her opal earrings reflected the glorious entryway lights.

"Come, fairy goddaughter. I'm only here for you." Freida extended her hand, and Kate found herself taking it.

"Don't let them take him, Freida, *please*," she begged. "Please, I'll do anything. I don't want them to take him."

"What's done is done. The rest of your Brotherhood allies are only here to see the Prince of the North Corner off. They will leave this place as soon as he's gone." Freida marched down a wide set of snow dusted stairs. She pulled the scarf off her neck and wrapped it around Kate, even though it did nothing to stop Kate's shivers. "You'll stay at the *Yarn & Stitch* overnight with us until the Shadow Fairies are gone. After that, you can do what you like, Kate Kole."

"I don't want to go to the *Yarn & Stitch*—"

"Too bad. The Prince has made us a bargain, and we'd like him to keep his end of it," Freida said. "We must keep you with us until he's gone if we wish for him to stay silent about our hiding place."

"But..."

"Just come. It'll all be over soon," Freida said.

Kate swallowed.

This was it. There was no going back.

This was goodbye.

40

Just Kate Kole

The morning air felt cold when Kate was released from the *Yarn & Stitch* the next day. She dragged her feet back to the café to find it quiet. The closed sign rattled on the door when she came in, but the broken bell made no sound. None of the three fae assassins inside looked up from where they sat in different places, staring off at nothing. Lily washed dishes in the kitchen, gazing ahead with unshed tears brimming red eyes and a blank look on her face.

The quiet café screamed of Cress's absence.

The painting of chocolate chip cookies sat high above the counter, and Kate sank against the wall, sliding down to sit on the floor. She stared at it.

No one moved for hours.

CHAPTER

41

Prince Cressica and The Cruel Tortures of Fairies

Cress had remained silent since the moment the Shadow Fairies bound his hands to lead him home. He stayed that way as he passed through the gate back into the polluted magic air of the Four Corners of Ever and was led into the forest, through the villages, past the quarry, and brought to the Silver Castle. No one tried to stop the group of Shadow Fairies, though Northern fairies in the cities drew back and hid away at the sight of the silvery brown eyes in their midst.

The Prince was led through the castle's front entrance where every noble eye could witness. He was taken down the crystal halls to the High Court meeting room. There he stood trial, in the same silence.

"You will die by strokes of cold iron, performed by the Brotherhood of Assassins," the newest member of the High Court decided—a fairy whose shadow seeped across the castle floor and brushed Cress's boots. A fairy who smelled of trouble. A fairy whose silvery ribbons could not be hidden in his brown eyes, even in the room's darkness.

Cress grunted a laugh of disbelief. So, the Queene had invited the devils of the Corners into her home with open arms, after all. She'd been more frightened of Cress than them.

Cress lifted his turquoise eyes to the shadows where Queene Levress sat on her throne and said nothing. She did not show herself to Cress, she did not intervene to save him from the court's judgement. She did not speak at all. But she glared with all the coldness of the North ice fields.

Death by his own assassins. How fitting, and how terribly cruel.

The prison cells in the Silver Castle were gilded, but Cress suspected an illusion. He didn't dare inch too close to the walls or the bars.

Some heartless fool heaped logs onto the fire at the end of the hall, turning the dungeon oven hot. Sweat dripped down Cress's face, and he tore off his preposterous human officer uniform when he couldn't sleep through the night.

The next night was worse. Glowing bugs crawled along the cell walls, giving off a putrid scent.

On the third morning, a sliver of light broke into the dark basement as though a door had opened at the end of the hall. A fairy added more logs to the fire. Cress paced back and forth seventeen times, inhaling the heat.

Ice cold water splashed over him.

He gasped and whirled, choking for breath as his gaze settled on a female with long, white hair and deadly eyes. He nearly cursed the name of Levress before he realized it wasn't the High Queene. He blinked and brushed the water away, getting a good look at Haven for the first time in a while.

"That was refreshing," he growled through his teeth.

"You needed a bath." Haven's song-like voice filled the cell, and Cress braced himself against her lure. The air in the prison turned heavy.

A servant stood on either side of the Princess. One stepped forward and carefully passed something through the gilded bars.

"A wedding gift?" Cress guessed with potent sarcasm. "Did you forget we're not getting married anymore, you foolish female?"

"It's your garments for this evening," the Princess said.

Cress reluctantly took the bundle from the servant and unrolled it to find his leather Brotherhood of Assassins uniform, complete with black garments, navy shell plates, and lightweight pauldrons.

Of course Levress would want him to die in this.

"Leave so I can change," Cress said, coming right to the bars and standing over Haven. She was a twig-tree in comparison to his size. Perhaps he wanted her to notice.

"I'm currently negotiating a bargain that I thought you might be interested in, Cressica," she said.

"I don't care," Cress promised, and when it seemed Haven would not leave, he decided to change in front of her. She closed her mouth when he slid off his pants. She even glanced away, and Cress smiled cruelly. "I gave you a chance to leave," he said, pulling on his assassins' uniform. "And don't act all innocent. We both know you hand out curses like childling sweets."

Haven's eyes rolled ever so slightly. "I'm relieved we're not getting married, you fool," she said.

"That makes two of us." Cress flashed another smile.

"But not for the reasons you think."

"Enlighten me, then. Allow me to die of boredom before I meet my real fate."

Haven's soft mouth twisted to the side; her pale lashes fluttered. "I've always seen you as a brother, even though we're not related by blood," she said. "I did not agree to our marriage, either. It's our mother who—"

"*Your* mother," he cut in. "*My* mother is dead."

Haven sighed. "It's *my* mother who wanted to force this upon me. I despise you, you faeborn monster. It's true that I've never liked you, but that's only because my mother was more impressed by every faeborn thing you did than anything I ever did. If I had wedded you, Prince, you would have tried to rule over me like she does."

"Yes. That is what I would have done," Cress agreed, dragging on his shoulder plates.

"So, I understand the tortures of being raised by Levress," she articulated, and Cress slowed the clasping of his shoulder buckle. "We have that in common," she added.

Cress's gaze flicked up to her sharp, malicious one. "Are you trying to tell me you'll miss me?" he asked doubtfully.

"I wouldn't miss you if you were gone, Cressica. But that doesn't mean I want to watch you die after I watched you suffer alongside me all these years," she said. "That's why I've invited someone else to this discussion."

Cress folded his arms. He yanked them free again when Bonswick sauntered down the aisle.

"I will never make a faeborn-cursed bargain with him again!" Cress swore. "Get him away from me before I break these cell bars and destroy you both," he threatened Haven.

"You're not making any bargains, Prince." Bonswick's silvery eyes darted to Haven. "She is."

"I'll marry Bonswick once you're gone," Haven told Cress. "I'll announce the betrothal at dawn. But in return, I've asked him to go back to the human realm—" Cress flinched at her words, "—and convince his Shadow Fairy allies that there's no more reason for them to be there. Perhaps he will steal their memories, or worse." She glanced over at the silver-eyed fairy. "And then, when he comes back, he will tell our High Court he killed you. We've meddled in human affairs long enough. There must be hundreds of broken fairy laws in the air by now. It's going to start bringing curses upon the Ever Corners if we don't stop."

Cress grabbed a gilded bar. He growled and tore back when the disguised cold iron burned his palm. He shook his hand out as he glared at Bonswick. "How can he claim to have killed me himself if I'll already be dead by tonight? And he'll do no such thing in the human realm, Haven. You cannot trust him! He wants revenge on me, that is all."

"He will do what I ask if he wants to be Low King of the North," Haven said. She turned to Bonswick. "Shall we make a bargain, Lord Bonswick?"

A crooked smile found the fairy. "I don't think a bargain is needed," he said, his gaze still on Cress. "I will do this as a gift to my future wife. Consider it done."

Cress shook his head. "No, do not let him out of your sight—"

Bonswick vanished, and Cress punched the cage bar. "Haven!" he growled. "You cannot trust that fool of the East! Why do you think he refused the bargain?! He will try to outsmart you!"

Haven's mouth curled into a smile. "Yes. He will try."

"How can you marry such a faeborn fool?" Cress asked. He paced in his cell. He could hardly keep himself from trying to kick through the iron bars.

"Because this is how I ensure that the North stays mine," she said, folding her delicate, pale arms and pinching the ends of her white hair. "You would have ruled over me, remember? Bonswick is someone I can keep under my thumb if I wish. I will rule the North Corner, directly below my mother. Bonswick will simply fill the space as my faeborn husband."

Cress shook his head. "He won't just do that. He won't do what you asked, either. He's probably in the human realm..." He released an anguished sound. "Sky deities have mercy, he's probably..."

"Prepare yourself, Cressica," Haven said, then bit down on her finger until a bead of her fairy blood rolled down it. She touched the bloodlock put in place by Levress, and the lock snapped open. "Your entire Brotherhood will try to kill you the moment you step out of here. I will give you twenty seconds before I scream the alarm that you've escaped."

The gilded cell bars slid to the side, revealing a wide-open door, and Cress blinked, certain he was imagining it.

He slowly stepped out of the cell, and the servants shuffled away, cowering. When no one rushed to stop him, he looked down at Haven with hard eyes. "I thought I grew up without a family. I suppose I was wrong," he said.

"Ten seconds," Haven said, and Cress's face changed. She slapped his fairsaber handle into his palm.

Cress whirled and raced down the dungeon aisle, past the blazing fire, and up the glass stairs. He barely made it to the top when Haven's shrill scream tore through the air like a winged leafbird, flapping its way into every hall and room of the Silver Castle, alerting every powerful and wicked fairy that he had escaped.

Cress grunted, drawing his fairsaber blade. "That was *not* ten seconds," he muttered. He took three more steps before a fairy wearing the replica of his uniform drifted around the corner. The assassin was familiar—all of the Brotherhood would be. Cress's jaw hardened, and he forced himself to forget the fairy's name, and where the fairy came from, and to simply fight.

Their fairsabers collided, and Cress kicked the fairy backward into the crystal wall, then turned light and leapt into the air. The assassin hurled a pin dagger at Cress flying over him. Cress batted it away as he landed on the other side.

A shuffle sounded around the crystal corner. Three more of Cress's assassins filled the hallway. Cress looked at his brothers to his left, then at the one remaining on his right.

It was a flash of silver as they all struck at once.

Cress took a slice in his abdomen.

He took another in his thigh.

He was dripping fairy blood from his shoulder when he staggered off, leaving the four assassins as weak fairy bodies on the floor, his only consolation that they would meld their bones back together and heal over time.

Assassins lined the hallways all the way out of the Silver Palace. It was a battle of strong iron blades and stronger iron wills.

When Cress emerged into the courtyard a mess of swollen eyes, a battered lip, and too many stinging cuts to count, he found the yard filled with dozens of his brothers in the black garments of the North Brotherhood.

Too many.

Far too many.

Cress twisted his fairsaber in his grip and dug in his heels.

Ash and wind rumbled over the grass as he charged. He knew their every move. He had learned alongside these fairies and taught some of them himself. But when he tripped on a starbud bush, landing on its midnight-blue petals, he squeezed shut his eyes and braced for the death stab that was coming.

A second passed. Cress heard heavy breathing around him.

"Get up, Cressica," a low faeborn voice commanded.

Cress peeled one eye open to see the blade of Thorne—fellow assassin teacher—at his throat. The assassin was not tilting it to run Cress through.

"Kill me," Cress invited, looking from assassin to assassin. "End this misery I've found."

Still, they waited.

Cress climbed to his feet and held out his fairsaber toward them. They remained still while he found his balance. And his bloody lips pulled into a smile.

"You fools," he said. "*She* will figure out you're letting me go. She will punish you for it."

Thorne swung at him, and Cress dodged it easily. "So be it." Thorne's voice was a deep rumble of sound. "Half of your brothers do not wish to betray you today." The assassin nodded toward the garden path that would take Cress back to the villages and through the forest, past which was the gate to the human realm.

"Well, let's make a show of it, then. I'm sure the Queene is watching." Cress smashed Thorne's blade from his hand. He cut a few fairy shoulders on his way to the garden path and even dug his saber right through a faeborn calf, praying to the sky deities the assassin would forgive him for it.

Cress wasn't fast as he raced below plump purple fruits dangling from crisp branches in the garden. He staggered past the golden trees whose bark turned orange in the wild morning sky, leaving a trail of fairy blood his assassins would be forced to follow. If only half his Brotherhood was showing mercy, the other half would catch up once they realized.

Cress reached the villages out of breath, clutching his chest and spitting crimson onto the green soil. Fairies emerged from leaf houses and branch huts, the most powerful ones touching buds to see them sprout. Cress took it all in as he passed, tucking the images away for later when he wanted to remember what the Ever Corners were like.

He raced against his burning cuts, his assassins, and most importantly, Bonswick.

Two dozen minutes later, Cress staggered to the gate; a rippling hold of power, built with an arch of seamless stone and whispering with the magic of the ancients. It seemed the fairy guards had taken the day off, and Cress imagined Haven had something to do with it.

Cress looked back one last time at the Four Corners of Ever when he reached the arch.

Then he went back to where he belonged.

Humans watched the Prince with odd faces as he limped over the sidewalk, clutching his shoulder where blood and power leaked out. His assassins' armour was coated in the purplish fairy blood of his brothers, his hair was stuck to his forehead, and his eyes stung from blinking so much as he grew faint.

Cress smelled the coffee when he got close, and the potent scent of sour fruit. It filled his faeborn chest with a flutter of hope as he rounded the corner...

Mor.

That was who he saw first.

Cress was sure he wasn't seeing correctly. He blinked his blurry eyes.

Mor's body lay in the street, half on the sidewalk, half on the road. His curly hair was unbound and covering his face. Human healer chariots rumbled up with red flashing lights, and humans sprang out with boxes of supplies.

Cress's gaze went in and out of focus as it wandered to Dranian's cooling body. Cress staggered forward a step, loosing feeling in his hands and feet. Shayne lay beside Dranian, his white hair stained with dark blood, his blue eyes open and staring toward the heavens at the cruel sky deities who had not saved him.

Females Cress knew as the Sisterhood of Assassins lay sprawled across the ground, torn up yarn and broken knitting needles scattered between them, killed like animals. Kate's fairy godmother was among them. One of her bright earrings had been torn right off.

But there were other bodies.

Human bodies...

Cress swallowed as he stepped in, catching whiffs of fear and distant shouts that had taken place in the very recent past, perhaps only hours ago. He was sure the bodies were still warm. Kate's-brother-Greyson lay just outside the café door, the hood of his human sweater drenched in snowy slush and sour human blood. Past him, Lily Baker lay in her officer uniform, lifeless with her weapon tossed to the snow just past her reach.

And... Cress croaked when he saw her.

Kate Kole's unmistakeable burgundy hair was half torn out of its tie. One arm was flung over her stomach, the other reaching as though she'd been trying to find help. The faint scents of her powder soap laced the air, and Cress slapped a hand over his eyes, refusing to see it any longer.

His brothers.

His humans.

His reasons for living.

"They're all gone, Cress. You're too late." A cruel voice lifted from behind him.

Cress ground his teeth and spun, aiming his fairsaber at Bonswick's throat. But Bonswick was faster.

Cress felt the fairy's cold iron blade pierce through his body and come out his back. He tasted fairy blood on his tongue. His numb fingers dropped the handle of his fairsaber, and he fell to a knee, held up only by Bonswick's silver blade impaling him.

Cress's power recoiled as he shuddered, choosing to accept this finish. He'd failed to protect Mor after all. Shayne, Dranian, the humans. Her.

His mate. She was innocent. She always had been.

This was right. This was the proper end, the one the Prince of the North deserved. Cress's turquoise eyes slid over to find her one last time.

He had written an ending to this story; a false one. But even so, this was not how he saw their real story ending.

Bonswick tore his blade back out, and Cress collapsed in a lake of his own deep red. Dozens of Shadow Fairies at Bonswick's side watched as the Prince of the North took his last breath and let his eyes fall closed.

"Time to leave. Great things await us in the Corners now," he heard Bonswick say. Then he heard the soft *pops* of vanishing Shadow Fairies.

Once upon a time, a fairy prince waged a war on a powerful queene. But he lost. And all those he loved paid the price.

Cress's fairy life leaked away. All his memories floated off with him. He relaxed to let himself go, until a raspy voice broke through the darkness.

"Cress?" she said. "Cress!"

Queensbane...
Kate Kole was alive.

CHAPTER

42

*Kate Kole and the Thing That Happened
Two Hours Ago*

It was a quiet morning, the day after Boxing Day. Kate kept to herself, editing her novel at the table in the corner while Lily mindlessly puttered around in her police uniform to get things cleaned up before she had to leave. They'd spent Christmas night together with the fae baristas drinking apple cider and sharing childhood stories—which turned out to be far more of a sinister event than Kate or Lily expected. Kate hadn't spoken a word all day. Neither had Mor or Dranian, so it was really just Shayne who told everyone's stories, and Lily who told hers and Kate's.

"I don't understand why you have to go in, Human," Mor said as Lily packed the garland and pinecones from the bistro tables into boxes. "You said officers don't have to work after they've been held hostage and such."

"I have to do two months of therapy and get the department's therapist to sign off before they'll let me go back on patrol." Lily rolled her eyes. "Trust me, it's not like I want to go."

"And you still have to wear your uniform?" Kate made a face from the corner. Her voice had cracked when she spoke up. She went quiet again.

At least everyone was talking.

Her fingers traced over the keys of her laptop, imagining a fae prince pecking at them. She'd read the entire novel twice in the last twenty-four hours. She'd just started back at the beginning.

Greyson pushed through the café door with an uneasy expression. He held up a box of takeout from the street meat truck. "Hotdogs?" he said to Mor.

Shayne appeared from the kitchen. "Hotdogs?" His grin appeared, and with the combination of his handsome smile and Greyson's food surprise, it brought a little warmth to Fae Café for the first time in three days. "I'll get the ketchup!" Shayne disappeared back into the kitchen.

Greyson set the box on the counter and took a wary look at Mor. It seemed like he wanted to ask if the fae was all right, but he dragged a hand through his shaggy hair and turned to Kate instead.

"You ever going to let me read that?" he asked.

"When it's published," Kate told him.

"What's the title?"

Kate thought about it. "I'm going to call it *High Court of the Coffee Bean*."

Mor grunted. "That's ridiculous." But the corner of his mouth turned up. "And just because we've established a new High Court here among the humans doesn't mean I'm acknowledging Shayne as my High King," he added.

"You'll submit to my rulership unless you want your pretty, luminous hair to end up in fairy locks," Shayne said as he appeared and plunked the ketchup bottle on the counter. His grip tightened around it when a presence appeared at the door even though the door hadn't opened.

Kate fell out of her chair when she saw the dark-haired fae with glossy silver eyes standing past the tables.

Shayne ripped a short blade from his pocket and sent it spiralling across the café, but Bonswick stepped aside, and Shayne's blade speared the window, releasing a web of cracks. Lily tore her gun out, her hands shaking on the grip, and Greyson took Kate's arm.

"You can't be here, Bonswick," Mor said in a low, dark voice. His sword came to life from its handle. "You made a faeborn bargain."

Bonswick's lashes fluttered like he was stifling an eye roll. "I did make a bargain with that illegitimate Prince. But the nobles are playing fairy games again."

"Keep us out of your games," Shayne said, drawing out another short blade. He held it up and eyed where it seemed he wanted to throw it—at Bonswick's head.

"Ah, you'll want to be a part of this one, fool. And please, tell your growling pet over there to lower his bow." Bonswick nodded toward the hall. A second later, Dranian emerged holding Shayne's loaded crossbow. He placed the arrow tip against Bonswick's temple.

"I think," Dranian said, his deep voice rumbling over the café, "I'd like your death to be slow."

"Then you and your humans will meet Levress soon. It seems Cress's leech-ally failed to erase his memories before he went back." Bonswick's glassy gaze cut to Mor.

Mor lowered his sword. "He begged me, but I couldn't," he admitted to the others. "I wanted him to die with his best memories. But Cress would have fallen on his fairsaber before he let Levress see inside his head."

"Well, he's still alive. For now." Bonswick reached up and pushed the arrow's tip away with a finger. "And it seems my future wife would like to show Cressica Albastian some mercy, even though it makes me ill. But I'll forget all about him soon, and he'll be a mere pin sized stain on my long legacy as King of the North."

"What...?" Mor's blade retracted. It looked like he was about to drop the handle to the floor. "Cress is still alive?"

"He's about to try and make the greatest faeborn escape in North Corner history. I'm only here to ensure the Dark believe you're all dead before I go back and viciously rule over the North Corner of Ever for the next century." Bonswick tilted his head in a catlike way. "So, let's get to it. The Shadow Fairies aren't going to believe in your deaths unless I give you true cuts so they can smell your fairy blood." His smile turned diabolical when he looked at Mor again.

The fae assassins exchanged looks. A silent conversation passed through the room as they studied Bonswick, sniffed the air, and deliberated. Kate looked at Greyson, who tightened his grip on her wrist.

"Not the humans," Shayne decided. "Give us true lashes, but don't touch the humans. They won't heal like us."

Greyson dropped Kate's arm and grabbed the ketchup from the counter where Shayne had put it.

"Shadow Fairies aren't daft, fool. They must see blood—"

"We'll use this!" Greyson held up the bottle, and Bonswick's silver stare settled on him and the ketchup. "What is that, precisely?"

"It's human fruit syrup," Shayne said. "It's delicious."

"Wait. I have one more idea." Kate stepped in to take the fae's stare off her brother. "I have a fairy godmother who I owe a favour to. Her biggest fear happens to be the North Corner finding out she's here." Kate glanced over to Mor. "Let's make peace with the Sisterhood."

"I won't help abandoners," Bonswick stated dully.

"I can make this really difficult for you if you don't," Kate warned him. "I can mess up this plan and make your future wife really mad. What'll happen to you if she gets mad?"

"*Kate*," Lily whispered, casting her a *"What are you thinking?"* look.

Bonswick's lip curled into a snarl. It seemed like he was about to object again, but he tapped his pale fingers against his thigh and said nothing. A second later, he released a repulsed grunt and muttered, "Humans."

From across the room, Shayne smiled and winked at Kate.

CHAPTER

43

Prince Cressica and the Ending No One Saw Coming

Faint beeping was the tune that carried Cress out of his deep slumber. Sharp scents filled the air that were not of nature—terrible and stuffy and smelling of a hogbeast's buttocks. In fact, he had to open his eyes to convince himself he was not stuck in a creature's rear. He sniffed and grimaced, then took in an ugly white ceiling made of panels.

Aches burned through his body when he tried to move, but he paused when he realized someone's hand was in his.

A human sat in a chair, leaning her top half forward on his bed with her cheek pressed down to the white bedsheets. Her burgundy hair was pulled back with a tie, but loose strands fell over her sleeping face. Cress's hand tightened around hers.

He could hardly believe the subtle sound of her rhythm, or the fragrance of her soap, or the light sound of her breathing.

The back of his bed was tilted up, turning it into more of an odd, mattress-covered chair. His armour had been replaced with a white shirt, and the waistband of loose black pants peeked from the sheets covering his legs. A short moment of horror washed over him as he wondered if Kate had changed him like one might have changed the garments of a squealing childling.

He noticed a thick stack of papers in her other hand. The top page had slid off and was out of reach on the floor, but Cress tugged the rest from her fingers.

The Prince leaned back, a smile forming over his mouth when he realized what it was.

HIGH COURT OF THE COFFEE BEAN, it read.

Cress scowled at the horrendous title, then smirked, because deep down he liked it more than he would ever admit to his human mate.

The door to the room flung open, and in marched Mor. The inches of his exposed skin glistened with cuts still healing, but he looked otherwise as healthy as a fresh-born crossbeast.

"Cress," Mor said when he saw that Cress was awake.

Shayne and Dranian appeared in the doorway at the same time, both trying to push in first. The ruckus made Kate stir, and Cress lifted a finger to his lips to hush them. But he looked from one fairy to the next, sure there were no words to express his relief to see them—even for a remarkable poet and writer such as himself.

As Mor smiled and tiptoed over to shove Shayne and Dranian back out of the room, Cress leaned against the chair-bed and dragged the manuscript over his lap.

He read until he was insulted by Kate's use of adjectives for the fae Prince. Then he smacked his hand down on the top page to startle her awake so he could give her feedback.

349

44

Kate Kole and Book Release Day

The café kitchen got warm in the summertime. Shayne set up fans on the counter by the oven, but he seemed more interested in posing in front of them with his hair blowing and taking selfies than actually working.

Kate and Mor sprinkled chocolate shavings and gold pearls on the freshly iced red velvet cake Cress had spent the morning baking. They watched as the white-haired fae puckered up for the camera across the kitchen and poked the button a dozen times. His phone would run out of space soon. He'd probably ask Kate to buy him more storage.

"I'm sure he doesn't realize we're watching him," Kate said in a loud whisper.

"I'm sure he does." Mor reached to get the cake lifter from the top shelf.

"Mor," Kate asked, brushing the sprinkles off her hands and turning to face him. The fae raised a brow. "What's a forever mate?"

Mor fumbled the cake lifter, and it clattered over the counter into the sink. "I... um..."

Kate watched with wide eyes. She'd never seen Mor flustered. "You don't have to tell me if it's going to give you a heart attack," she muttered.

"Well... Human... It's a fairy thing." He blushed—*Mor* blushed. "It's when a fairy bonds to someone in a way that can't be undone. It's an unbreakable tether... It essentially means that a fairy's heart has fallen for a person they will chase forever." Mor shifted his footing as he plucked the lifter from the sink. "It's exactly how it sounds. Forevermate."

"Hmm." Kate tapped a finger against the counter as she thought about that. "How does it happen?"

Mor cleared his throat. "Well, it starts with a fairy crush—"

Cress marched into the kitchen, and Mor slammed his mouth shut. He didn't move a muscle as Cress walked around the island. The Prince glared at Shayne taking pictures for a moment. Then he nudged his way into the shot, moving Shayne aside with his hip so they could both fit, and flashed a gorgeous smile for the camera.

"I guess that's all you'll tell me right now." Kate smirked and lifted the platter of cake. "Time to go!" she called to the fae modelling at the fans. "Bring the Fairy Post!"

Mor grabbed the stack of freshly printed newspapers from the counter where articles with magic fairy recipes, warnings of common fairy tricks, and short folktale stories filled the columns, along with a *News for the Fairy Folk* section where he wrote messages to all the fae hiding in the human realm—if there were any others. Mor had even created his own crossword puzzle of fae words that ranged from *deathtouch* to *pixie dust* to *handsome*. "I'll hand these out myself," he said.

Cress and Shayne rushed around the island, meeting Kate at the same time. Shayne's finger came dangerously close to stealing a lob of icing off the cake before Cress slapped it out of the way.

"Touch it, and I'll cut your finger off!" Cress threatened.

Shayne grinned as he grabbed the kitchen door. He swung it open for

Kate to carry the cake through, but Cress stopped her first.

"What is it?" Kate asked, noting his peculiar smile.

"I'm proud of this book we wrote together. I will ensure every human in this realm reads it."

"You mean you're proud of the book I wrote," she corrected for the hundredth time. "You just fixed some things up."

Cress's smile turned slightly snarl-like, but he nodded. He planted a light kiss on her mouth. "I helped though."

Kate headed out of the kitchen with a laugh.

When she emerged, camera flashes filled the café along with an eruption of cheers. Journalists, booktokers, and other book-loving social media gurus who'd received advanced copies of Kate's book filled the bistro tables, sipping on items from the new summer coffee drink collection and becoming unsuspectingly enchanted by fairy spells. At the back window, a firefly-like being fluttered up the glass and sat on a high sill to watch, telling Kate that Freida was still spying on her via Gretchen. Or maybe her fairy godmother just wanted to know if Kate was doing well.

Kate placed the cake on the counter and turned to face the small crowd filling the café to the back corners. Cress slid into a bistro seat off to the side, sipping a mug of warm milk even though the rest of the staff—Lily, Greyson, Shayne, and Dranian—stood along the wall fashioning their new burgundy summer aprons with the Fae Café logo. Mor handed out the Fairy Post papers to the crowd and soon dozens of book lovers were flattening out their newspapers on the tables and learning about fae things.

"The Fairy Post is a newspaper we give out with every purchase at the café. You can also subscribe to get it in digital form, or for a low monthly fee, we'll mail you a newspaper every season," Kate explained. Someone at the front clicked a pen to begin working on the crossword puzzle. "It gets delivered by owl carrier magic," she added with a wink, drawing a few chuckles from the crowd.

"Tell us how you wrote such a fantastic book!" one of the journalists called out, and Kate fought a blush as she pushed her hair behind her ear.

"Well, it's a long story. No pun intended," she said, and the journalists cackled.

"The greatness of the story is in the blossoming, delicious, *irresistible* words. And the Prince, naturally," Cress mumbled from his table, not quietly enough.

One of the girls turned in her seat, seeming to melt at the sight of the dazzling guy giving insight into a book he didn't even write. Kate hid her smirk behind her hand and pretended to brush her nose.

"You must read a lot of books," the girl said, smoothing down her summer dress and looking him up and down. Several journalists leaned to try and see him around the people in their way.

"Well, I do consider myself something of a literary genius in comparison to humans," Cress admitted and flashed his beautiful smile at the room.

Everyone laughed like they thought he was making a fae joke as one of the café's hired actors. But Kate's smile dropped. She knew he wasn't joking at all.

"Who is this other author you have listed at the bottom where it says, *'Written with help from C. Prince?'*" a journalist stood to ask Kate.

Kate yanked her gaze from Cress. "I made that up," she decided, and Cress spat his milk. "I wrote the book by myself."

Accusing turquoise irises turned Kate's skin warm as the social media gurus asked more questions and snapped photos. Kate gave them the smile she'd practiced in the mirror before coming.

Cress stood and wandered over until he was beside where she posed. After a few photobombed pictures, he leaned over and whispered, "Human." Kate felt her body go rigid as she waited for her orders. "Dig your hands into that faeborn cake and eat it. Make it nice and messy."

Kate's smile faded. Her big eyes took in all the cameras, notepads, and cell phones with videos rolling. Only Cress was smiling now.

"Un-real, *Cress!*" Kate mumbled through tight lips as her body turned and her hand went for the red velvet cake. "I'm going to ruin your life!" she promised. The eating part happened as terribly as she'd feared.

A moment later, she stared at an ogling crowd with icing and red velvet cake crumbs covering the bottom half of her face and stuck in all the cracks of her teeth.

Cress watched from the back with his arms folded and a satisfied smile on his face. Snickers escaped from Lily and Greyson suffocating through fits of giggles by the wall.

"I mean, I should intervene, right?" Greyson didn't even whisper it, and Kate glared over at her brother. His cheeks were red. "I should stop Cress… but this so funny!" he said.

Lily was no help, either. She put a hand over her mouth and turned her head away, but it didn't hide her giggle-snorts at all.

"*Lily*," Kate tried, but opening her mouth only made the journalists snap more pictures with her horrid, cake-filled teeth showing.

"I'm worried that once people read her book, they're going to remember how she attacked that cake and realize that everything in the book is true," Greyson whispered to Lily, avoiding Kate's pointed gaze.

Lily sighed when she got a hold of herself, and she shot Kate a smile. Kate did *not* smile back.

"No, they won't," Lily said. "No one would ever believe any of this was real."

Shayne bit his lip over a ridiculously wide grin. He was the only one who cast Kate a somewhat sympathetic look. Moody Dranian sneered like this moment was the revenge he'd been waiting for his whole life.

Kate's hands were clasped tightly when Cress sauntered through the journalists and joined her at the front again as if he just couldn't stay away from the spotlight.

"I'm sure you're all wondering why this scribe made such a mess." He addressed the crowd like he was the natural born ruler of Toronto. "Well, I asked her to, and she can't resist me." He turned to Kate with a wicked smile and flicked a spongy lump of cake off her chin before leaning to plant a kiss on her sugary mouth.

Kate grabbed his collar before he could pull away, holding him there, and Cress's eyes flashed open as their lips fought for a split second.

The Prince tore back, staring at Kate with round, turquoise eyes. His hands were balled into white fists at his sides.

Kate's red-toothed smile was real this time.

"Cress," she said in her sweetest voice, "don't let me have it all. Please—" she shoved the platter of destroyed cake in his direction, "—let's enjoy it together."

"I don't want to," he said through his teeth.

Kate batted her eyelashes. "Please?" She pouted and watched the Prince's face turn anguished with the sort of spellbinding, enchanting love that wouldn't wear off for at least seventy-eight hours.

Mor took Shayne's phone and raised it to take a video. Dranian leaned over to watch the screen.

Cress took in a deep breath, gazing at Kate like she was the glory of the sun itself. His mouth twitched as an internal battle seemed to rage in his mind, but...

He grabbed a large handful of icing off the platter.

Bellowing laughter broke out from the staff—even Dranian cracked a decent smile. Jaws dropped in the crowd; journalists let out horrified gasps. Some of the social media influencer girls got up and left with repulsed faces as Cress joined his lovely forever mate in cake-splattered disgrace before three dozen sets of eyes.

It went on for several glorious minutes. Then Kate heard Shayne sigh by the wall. He swooped in to address the journalists himself, and in a loud announcement, he said,

"Welcome to Fae Café!"

The Faeborn End of It All

355

Thank you for reading *Welcome to Fae Café*!
If you liked this book, please leave a review!

Christmas fantasy books by Jennifer Kropf:

A SOUL AS COLD AS FROST

A HEART AS RED AS PAINT

A CROWN AS SHARP AS PINES

A BEAST AS DARK AS NIGHT

CAROLS AND SPIES

*Join Jennifer Kropf's newsletter at www.JenniferKropf.com for new
book alerts and free eBooks*

ACKNOWLEDGEMENTS

I was the kid who couldn't focus in class because I was daydreaming about fighting off evil pirates in magical fairy lands. I drove some of my teachers crazy, and I got scolded more times than I can remember, even in high school. But I couldn't help it. Every time I tried to focus on math, fairies popped up between the numbers and waved to say hello, and Peter Pan tapped my shoulder and asked if I wanted to visit Neverland. So, before I begin, I need to thank my teachers for dealing with all that.

My biggest thank you goes to the BookTok community for being so enthusiastic about this book idea when I made that TikTok post about fae trying to learn how to do basic things in the real world. This has been the most fun I've had as an author to date. You all deserve an award.

Thank you to my editor, my friend, and my bestie for the restie, Melissa Cole. Siblings rule. Doing life together is a win. Thank you for reading my novels ever since we were twelve and thirteen and I made you read the same story a zillion times over every time I made a change.

Thank you to my content editor Jesse Calder for making me laugh out loud more than once with your comments and critiques. I'm glad to have a blood-related ally in the book publishing business now.

Thanks to my sister Steph Clayton for letting me use your house as my office for five months while you were away doing missions work on the other side of the world. I wrote most of this book in your house.

Thanks to my parents, as always, for being great parents, for letting my imagination run wild, and for letting me run off and explore the forest behind our house where I dreamt I was Lara Croft Tomb Raider hunting down tomb thieves.

I also have a few incredible author friends who have meant more to me than I think they realize these last few years. I want to say a big thanks to my friend and fellow Canadian author Stefanie Lozinski for being so pumped about this book when I told you about it over lunch and coffee. I'm still so relieved we found each other and that we live close enough to meet up!

I also want to thank my earliest book friends that I adore: Alice Ivinya, Lyndsey Hall, and N. D. T. Casale (Nicole.) What fun we've had making books, eh? It's amazing to see how far we've all come since those early days when we were just getting started and learning how to do this author thing.

Thank you to my Patreons Amanda Shafer, Sarah Breed, Danielle, Redlac, Lyndsey Hall, and Kanyon Kiernan. Thank you for helping me pick a cover for this book, for cheering me on, and for being part of the discussion! When I started a Patreon, I had no idea how much I would come to rely on this team.

Thank you to my beta readers Valerie Whitten, Kelly Port, Rae Myer, Laura Robinson, Sarah Breed, B. L. Chabot, and Rugile Lisinskaite who read "Fae Café" back when it was really terrible and super dark and didn't have nearly enough lighthearted moments. Your reactions to key moments in the last half of this book made my day.

And thank you to God, King of all Kings and Lord over all Lords, for giving me all the necessary ingredients to think up, write down, publish, and market books. When I was in college for marketing, I really didn't get it. I wondered what I was doing there, right up until graduation day. Now I get it.

Lastly, thank you to *you*, the reader. If you're reading this, it means you made it to the end and didn't give up at any of the boring parts, so feel free to slap this book and imagine it's me reaching through and giving you a high five. You're amazing.